PAUL COSTOFF

Welcome to Your Life

First published by Keeper Publishing 2020

This book is a work of fiction. References to real people, events, establishments, organizations, or locales are intended only to provide a sense of authenticity and are used fictitiously. All other characters in this novel, and all incidents and dialogue are drawn from the author's imagination and should not be construed as real.

First edition

ISBN: 978-0-578-80603-7

Cover art by Bailey McGinn

This book was professionally typeset on Reedsy.
Find out more at reedsy.com

*For everyone who is making the best
of their unexpected life*

Acknowledgement

I started this project a long time ago and it's a little surreal to finally be completing it. In a general sense, I'd like to thank everyone who knows me, puts up with me, and loves me. I love you, too. There's a few people who merit some more specific mention and gratitude.

Thank you to my girlfriend Kristin Caldwell for the countless hours of reading, listening, editing, proofreading, troubleshooting, for the steadfast encouragement, and for making the last six years of my life the best six years of my life.

Thank you to my dear mother Carol Ciccotosto, always my biggest cheerleader, my first and forever my favorite English teacher. I am so grateful for you. And thank you for being one of my readers even though it contains the word "fuck" 138 times and most of it takes place in a bar.

Thank you to my three children Rianndra, Wyatt, and Mason for enriching my life in a million different ways. I'm enjoying the people you've become.

Thank you to my sister, Julianne Froelich for always believing in me and supporting me.

Thank you to my early readers, Ted Fist, Paula Dockery, and my favorite cousin on my dad's side who has always inspired me with her own incredible creativity and art, Makeal Flammini. All of your feedback helped soothe my anxious, self-doubting mind.

Thank you to the great Reedsy partners I found in Bailey McGinn (baileydesignsbooks.com), who created my awesome cover design, and in Nicole Fegan, for her editing work.

Thank you to Kevin Diaz for taking the photo of me that I've been using as my official author guy photo. I'm going to continue to use this photo long after I cease to resemble it.

Thank you to all of my former students for entertaining me on social media and for sharing your lives. Your energy, creativity, and passion continue to inspire me.

The following people were very important in my life and I wouldn't be the person I am without them: Chris Costoff, Elijah Hanny, and Ron Ono.

I also want to thank Boyd, Sean, Mike, Tim, Jon, Angie, Mark Twain, Alan Watts, George Orwell, Tom Petty, Edward Abbey, Kurt Vonnegut, and the Buddha.

I

Part One

Chapter 1

The yellow glow from a security floodlight filtered in through the bent and grimy venetian blinds. A tangled cord left them stuck open on one side, and in their angling down across the double window, they offered a static, malevolent wink to the figure sprawled across the mattress. The buzzing of an alarm demanded his attention, and from under the faded brown comforter, a hand reached out and found the snooze button. The eyes blinked open and for a moment they stared at the ceiling. Guy rolled to his side and used the dim light to take in the rest of the bedroom. It looked the same as yesterday. And the day before. And the day before that. Clothes, dirty and clean, adorned much of the floor and the chair and hung from the closet and bedroom doorknobs. Interrupting the otherwise bare walls were a couple of posters featuring young bikini models who had long since gained weight and grown up. Holding bottles of beer and frozen in time, they smiled down at him. On a little table next to his bed, the angry red numbers on his alarm clock glared at him: 5:10am.

"Three thousand, one hundred and thirty-two," Guy muttered as he sat up and turned to put his feet on the floor. It was Sunday, October 11, 1998. Sunday mornings marked the beginning of his work week and they were the worst. At five o'clock on a Sunday morning, there was no more hope of sleeping in, no more hope of moving out, and no more hope of moving on. On Sunday mornings, after two more days had passed and Guy had not heard the words that he feared and yet so desperately wanted to hear, the reality of another week at the Gas and Go smacked him awake and forced him out of bed.

Guy rubbed his eyes and face, repeated his number, "three thousand, one hundred and thirty-two," and mentally drew another small black line. He imagined the walls of a jail cell covered with those lines in groups of five marking his time. For twelve years he's been grumbling the day's number and etching another vertical black mark on his depressing mental wallpaper. For twelve years he's been driving to work in the dark, the only car on the road. It's been twelve years of "Gonna be a hot one today" or "Wooo, boy it's cold out there!" Twelve years of being very bored and usually very broke. But most of all, for Guy Bradford, it's been twelve years of waiting. Twelve years of expecting every week to be his last and twelve years of dreaming about the future. Each one of those dark black lines represented another day spent behind the counter at the Gas and Go on the outskirts of the little town of Richmond, Illinois.

Guy stepped around the clothes on the floor and into the small bathroom. After relieving himself, he leaned over the little sink, hands on the sides to support himself, and stared back at his reflection. "Fuck me," he muttered, surveying his reflection. "And fuck you too," he swore at the tired image looking back at him before splashing some cold water on his face. Returning to the bedroom, Guy threw on some jeans and a plain brown t-shirt, grabbed his money and his keys, and headed out the door for work. For the three thousandth, one hundred and thirty-second time.

It's a short walk from Guy's ground floor apartment to the parking lot. Depressed but not bitter, humbled but not yet beaten, he shuffled toward his car. Even though it was early, he could already tell it was going to be a beautiful autumn day. No clouds obscured the three-quarter moon lingering in the south, and as Guy walked to his car, the eastern horizon began to glow with the anticipation of sunrise. The air was cool—not quite cold—and a gentle breeze rustled the drying and dying leaves in the trees over Guy's car. A thin, low fog clung to the remnants of harvested corn stalks in the field adjacent to the parking lot. Two deer looked and froze at the sound of his car door. And then, as Guy turned the key, the screaming whine of his long-neglected alternator belt shattered the morning stillness. The deer bolted, at least three dogs woke up barking, and most of his neighbors silently cursed him as they rolled over trying to salvage their opportunity to sleep in. Guy turned on his radio and drove his beat-up Grand Prix out of the lot and onto Route 12 without even a pretense of stopping at the stop sign. As his sole working headlight scoured the ditch to his right and the sky just over the trees blushed harder at the approaching dawn, one thought occupied Guy's mind: three thousand, one hundred and thirty-two.

On mornings like this, like so many other mornings, the black tally marks on Guy's self-conjured cell walls were so thick that he could not see past them. He didn't see the moon or the deer standing in the morning mist. He did not hear the wind as it tugged the leaves from their branches or the barking of the dogs. Guy did not pause to take in a deep breath of the brisk fall air. All of the promise and potential of a new day was on the other side of the wall. But later, when the coffee was done and caffeine was prying his eyes the rest of the way open and the steady assault of "Good Morning Guy", "How ya doin' Guy?" and "Boy, it oughta be a nice one today" inevitably began, the black marks began to fade. But until then, it was not a beautiful early morning in October. It was only a number: three thousand, one hundred and thirty-two.

Chapter 2

Guy made the five-minute drive through town and turned into the gravel parking lot of the Gas and Go. He pulled in behind the rectangular stucco building and parked alongside the dumpster. There was no reason to lock his car, and so, he did not. Without looking up or around—just staring blankly ahead—Guy walked through the low cloud of settling dust, around the dumpster, past the two brightly-lit soda machines and the battered Eskimo Ice freezer to the front door. There he paused and held his ring of keys up to the dim light leaking out from the store to look for the one that would let him inside. Once he found it, the routine continued. Lock the door behind him. Turn off the alarm. Turn on only the interior light. Turn on the stereo. Start the coffee. Open the safe. Turn on the cash register. Count out $50 for the drawer. Check and stock the coolers. Turn on the pumps. Pour some coffee for himself. Turn on the rest of the lights. Unlock the door and bring in the newspapers. For the three thousandth, one hundred and thirty-second time.

Guy grabbed a cellophane-wrapped package of chocolate snack cakes from the shelf and a big Sunday newspaper. He sat on the tall stool behind the counter, sipping coffee, eating the cakes, reading the paper, and slowly beginning to wake up.

At twenty after six, Jacque barged in. "Wake up, my friend!" he yelled, grinning at Guy, his arms full of large donut boxes.

Guy stood up, stretching as he spoke. "I'm up, man, I'm up. Hey, what happened to the kid? Was he a no show? Did he quit on you?"

"No, he's a good kid. Besides, he knows if he no-showed me on a Sunday

6

morning, I would go to his house and wake him up. And then I would kill him. And then I would make him work anyway!" Jacque cackled at his joke. "He's at the shop now. But his momma needed his car for something, so I get to be the delivery man this morning. It's good once in a while. I get to smile and say good morning and make nice with all my customers. I also get to check out all of the pretty new girls working in all of the different places." He raised his eyebrows a couple of times.

Guy rolled his eyes and came around the counter to take the boxes. There was a case by the coffee with a sign on top from Jacque's bakery that read "When it's *Not Your Average Bakery!* they're *Not Your Average Donuts!*" While he filled the case with the fresh donuts, his friend went to the van to get the rest. He returned and together they finished stocking it, stored the surplus for later that morning, and moved to the counter so Guy could pay Jacque.

As Guy opened the drawer to get the check out, Jacque spied the last quarter of his little chocolate snack cake on the counter. "Oh, man, what are you doing, Guy? Why are you eating that shit?" he scolded, pointing at it and throwing his hands up as his voice rose. "That shit is shit, man. There's so many preservatives and chemicals in those things, it's crazy. Don't put that shit in your body, man! You poison yourself! Why can't you wait? Why? I got six dozen of the best donuts. Ever! Organic flour, all natural shit, my friend. And you can't wait twenty fucking minutes? You gotta be eating that plastic shit that's not even real fucking food?"

"Aw, Jacque," Guy looked and felt guilty. "I'm sorry man. I love your donuts. But I'm not even really awake yet when I get here. Sometimes I just grab 'em out of habit."

"You gotta stop that habit, Guy! You got to take care of yourself. You ain't a kid anymore, you know. I know your birthday motherfucker. You gonna be thirty very soon!" Jacque paused and sighed. "Always the same. I don't know why I care when you don't." Still shaking his head, Jacque took the check from Guy and pocketed it.

"You want some coffee for the road?" Guy offered, trying to make peace.

Jacque laughed. "No thank you, my friend. I do not want any part of your shit coffee that came from some giant, monoculture plantation, carved out of a section of vital and beautiful yet rapidly disappearing rainforest." His voice grew louder again, "I do not want any coffee from a nightmarish dystopia where some multi-national agri-fucking-business sprays chemical toxins that not only kill off the insect part of the food chain and wash into the streams to mutate the fishies and the frogs, but also poisons the lungs and skin of its impoverished workers and, as a special fucking bonus, mutates their goddamn sperm inside their goddamn balls so that even their future children can share in the magical fucking process of bringing you and millions of others in the United States of Apathy a cheap cup of coffee that you will pour into a Styrofoam cup. A cup that will get used for, at most, twenty minutes before finding its way to a landfill where it will biodegrade at about the same time the fucking sun goes supernova." Jacque took a breath to collect himself and finished more calmly, "And besides that, your coffee pot hasn't been cleaned in months."

"I rinse that pot out every morning," Guy countered.

"Rinsing is not cleaning, my friend, and your coffee is shit. I have to go. People are depending on my donuts this morning. See you at The Duke later for the Bears game?"

"Yeah, I'm planning on it."

"Good," Jacque replied. And then he was gone.

Guy threw the rest of his "shit food" in the garbage can, refilled his coffee and grabbed one of Jacque's chocolate donuts. He began to go back to the paper, but instead his mind fixated on Jacque's birthday comment. "Thirty," Guy quietly spoke the number out loud. He didn't like the sound of it. Slouched on the stool, he looked around the little convenience store. *How can I still be here?* he wondered. *I am going to be thirty. Fuck. Fuck, fuck, fuck, fuck, fuck. I fucking hate this. I want a cigarette.*

He went to his car, grabbed the box of smokes off the passenger seat, fished one out and lit it. Forget three thousand, one hundred and thirty-two—thirty was the bitch of a number now. Guy plopped down on an old plastic chair that sat by the Coke machine. He stretched, took off his baseball cap and ran his fingers through his hair. *I'm not supposed to still be here*, he thought and took a deep drag on the cigarette.

8

Chapter 3

As the screeching from the parking lot invaded the apartment and vanquished what was left of Sophie's sleep, she helplessly surrendered to consciousness. Her head throbbed and her eyes stayed closed, begging, along with the rest of her body, for more sleep, but the battle had already been lost. The noise screamed louder at her as if to make certain she was awake before it slowly faded. *Shit*, she thought, *that guy still hasn't fixed his car?* She felt her body tense. *Why won't that guy get his stupid car fixed? One morning a week where I don't get woken up by a bell or moaning or coughing or some other garbage and I get this guy?*

"Bear!" she complained, jabbing her elbow into his ribcage. "You said you were going to take care of that."

Bear grunted but didn't move.

"You told me you'd find out whose car is making that noise and tell him to fix it. I am so tired." She nudged him again, but to no avail. "As soon as you take care of it, he'll stop waking me up and I'll stop waking you up." She threw one last elbow into his lower back.

This time there was a mumbled, drowsy, "Hey! Cut it out."

Reluctantly awake, Sophie rolled over out of Bear's reach. Sitting up, she hung her legs over the side of the bed, stretched, yawned, and rubbed the grit out of her eyes. How nice would it be, she thought, to actually get a decent night's sleep? Oh, to flop down and sprawl completely across a huge bed with no wrists or ankles hanging over the edge. Alone. And a real mattress where she couldn't feel every spring poking her—with crisp, clean, white (not used-to-be-white) sheets that didn't smell like cigarettes,

9

B.O, or drool. How nice would it be to sleep in that magical bed and not get woken up by a bell, moaning, yelling, or someone's loud car?

The thought of it almost made her climb back into the bed, as if with wishful thinking and more sleep she could dream her way there. But the sight of the faded and dull mismatched sheets along with Bear's large frame cratering into the center of the mattress, his mouth open over a small dark spot on his pillow…ugh. Sophie stood up and left the room wondering which was worse: Was it the lumpy twin mattress on the floor of her room at Frannie's where she listened to that decrepit old woman labor to breathe through yet another night? Or was it this perpetually dirty, messy, dump of an apartment/workshop that Bear called home?

Shuffling into the kitchen, Sophie found the coffee pot just as she had left it the previous Sunday: half full of coffee for Bear. She surveyed the kitchen. It looked about a week worse than last weekend. Another pizza box on the table, two more bags from fast food joints, the ashtray twice as full, sink piled higher with dishes, and the empty coffee can still sitting on the counter. Frustrated and disappointed, Sophie swore to herself. She came over one night a week and he was too lazy to even pick up his own garbage?

Even though she had been through it many times, it always amazed her how quickly a guy could begin to take her for granted. In the beginning, they wore clean shirts, brushed their teeth before they went out together, and cleaned their apartments before she came over. She could smell the chemicals as proof. For most of them, it was probably the only time their bathrooms got cleaned. Floors were swept and vacuums were borrowed. But then the cleaning became picking up. Garbage was thrown away and dirty clothes were tossed in a closet. Dishes made it to the sink and counters were still pretty clean, but floors and toilets were untouched. Then it was only kind of picked up, like the frantic, desperate "someone's going to be here in five minutes" type cleaning where garbage and other detritus is just shoved somewhere in a half-hearted attempt to hide it. In the later stages, when she showed up, they would graciously move dirty clothes off their couches so she had a cleared space in which to sit while they half-heartedly apologized and made excuses about being so busy lately.

With Bear, it had only been a couple of months and he was already past that stage. No excuses, no apologies, no effort. Too bad, Sophie thought, he had treated her decently otherwise. And he was a pretty funny guy. But he either didn't give a shit or was legitimately clueless. It didn't make a difference. She swore she wasn't going to try and change anyone or teach anyone at this point in their lives. Besides, did anyone ever really change? Could they?

She walked to the bathroom feeling crumbs from the once-swept floor sticking to the bottoms of her bare feet and took a long look in the mirror. *Am I just getting old?* she wondered. *Are those crow's feet?* Sophie squinted and examined her reflection. *What about the hair? Any gray ones yet? No, still safe there.* She smiled a flirty smile, but her tired, makeup-less face and unkempt hair betrayed her. *Eh, maybe I am,* she mused. No, she caught herself. "That's bullshit." She spoke quietly but firmly and looked herself in the eye. "You are barely into your thirties, Sophie. You are smart. You are beautiful. Be patient. Two and a half more years. You can do this for two and a half more years." But even her confident tone couldn't chase all of her doubts away. As she splashed water on her face, she thought about Frannie and how hard it was to stay positive around her. It wasn't the first time that she wished someone would hurry up and die. She was ready to move on.

Sophie returned to the kitchen. If she was going to stay up, she was going to need some caffeine. She considered reheating the stale coffee still in the pot but dismissed that idea as she remembered it was now a week old. Maybe there was a soda in the fridge. She hated that the sugar made her crash after about an hour, but it would at least keep her awake until she was able to get some real coffee.

Opening the fridge, she stared at a two-liter of Sprite. Damn. No caffeine. On the large main shelf, the bottle of Sprite was keeping company with two jars of pickles, an assortment of mostly expired condiments, a half-gallon of whole milk, a loaf of bread, and a carton of eggs. Sophie already knew the treasures hidden in the two drawers, but she still checked to confirm.

In the drawer on the right were several large red peppers in various stages of freshness. And on the left was a fairly ridiculous assortment of cheeses. She laughed to herself as she let the door close. Long after Bear's name and face were lost to her, she would probably still remember that she went out with a guy who seemingly lived on peppers and cheese.

Turning to look at the mess in the sink, Sophie sighed. She could clean the kitchen and send Bear out for juice and coffee while she made breakfast, but she loathed playing the girlfriend stereotype. Sophie looked over to the couch and considered going back to sleep. No. No way. The couch itself was covered with crap. No blanket around, not even a throw pillow for her head, and a big overfull ashtray on the coffee table for potpourri.

But that wasn't even the biggest problem. Bear's living room was also his workshop and it was populated with wooden bears in various stages of carving and painting. This was Bear's side job for the summer tourist traffic and the living room was his work area in the off-season. When the bears were finished Sophie didn't mind them. But when they were only partially finished, they gave her the creeps. Instead of incomplete, they seemed deformed and sad. As their faces began to emerge out of the wood, their blank eyes stared at her as if pleading for someone to free them. And because Bear painted in stages, some stood blind, mouths agape. Others just had these helpless, blank, pupil-less eyes. There was no way she would be going to sleep on the couch in the creepy bear room.

The clock on the microwave showed 5:32am. Nothing would be open. If she went to get coffee now, she had nowhere to go other than back to Frannie's and she really didn't want to do that. Whenever she returned early, Frannie's kids found some excuse to leave and she would be back to work already. She peered out the small window over the sink. This early in the morning, everything just looked cold. If it were summer, she could go to the park and chill or even nap. She grimaced. An egg, cheese, and pepper omelet did sound good. And free. Free was important. Sophie started cleaning the kitchen.

Chapter 4

Bear first heard it as he weaved his way through the tables back toward the bar. Turning, he saw people talking and laughing. He quickly scanned the floor for where he thought the bottle had landed. Nothing. Doubting himself, he turned back toward the large rectangular bar in the center of The Duke. Crash! More breaking glass. Again he spun around and again nothing. Then another crash behind him, but toward the bar. Was he the only one hearing it? Nobody was reacting. Every time he turned, there were more unseen bottles exploding on the concrete. Bear could feel the adrenaline starting to flow. Turning and looking and looking and turning, he backed toward the wall trying to get the whole scene in front of him. And then, one final loud crash woke him up.

"What the hell is she doing?" Bear asked the empty bedroom. He squinted toward the clock. It wasn't even six yet. He rolled over and buried his face into the bed and pulled a pillow down over his head to cover his ears in a futile effort to block out the racket. Still the banging of the dishes intruded and the idea that this was likely his punishment slowly came into focus. He had promised to figure out whose car was making noise and talk to him. But he hadn't done it. And he hadn't cleaned the kitchen before he left for work. And now three short hours of sleep later, he was paying for it. There was no way Sophie was going to let him go back to sleep now that she was up.

Bear sighed and switched the pillow from over his head to under it, lay on his back, blinked at the ceiling, and wondered if she was worth it.

She could be a little moody. He first hooked up with her on 4th of July weekend. August, September, October, he counted...so it was three months already. It didn't seem like it, but he supposed that was because he only saw her once a week. Her habit was to come into The Duke pretty early on Saturdays—around sixish usually. She'd hang out and drink her vodka grapefruits and flirt with him a little. She hadn't really known anyone in town because she was from Iowa or something and was just here for work. Bear introduced her around and it did seem like she'd made a few bar friends. She played pool with Jacque and was pretty damn good, too. That's how she caught his eye, bending over that pool table to line up her shot. Bear smiled just thinking about it. It was a great view from either the front, with her blouse hanging open just enough to reveal the lace of her bra holding in those wonderfully right-sized tits, or the back, and that firm round ass snug in her blue jeans. That night he had appreciated both.

The noise from the kitchen continued and Bear laughed to himself. Gorgeous blonde, great body, comes over once a week to spend the night with him and then goes away. No needy, clingy drama, no bitching about him spending every Friday and Saturday working at The Duke, no crazy family, no kids, no jealous ex. *What the hell do I have to complain about?* he thought. *She's definitely worth some occasional Sunday morning crabbiness.* Bear climbed out of the bed, grabbed some shorts and headed to the kitchen to make peace.

"Hey, sorry about the guy with the car noise," Bear offered. "I did find out who it is though. I figured I would run into him at The Duke, but he didn't show up this weekend. I'll knock on his door or something this week."

Sophie looked up at him as she finished wiping the kitchen counter. There was no point in fighting about it now. They were both up and she needed some coffee for her breakfast. "Thank you. You know I never get to sleep in at Frannie's." Then she smiled, "What are you doing up? I didn't wake you, did I?"

"Don't give me that shit," Bear laughed. "Do I have any dishes left that aren't broken? Or chipped?"

"Hey, if you had any coffee in this place, I would be chillin' on your couch

14

and you could still be snoring away. At least you have a clean kitchen now."

Bear gave her a hug and pressed her into the corner against the counter. "Thank you for cleaning my kitchen," he said leaning in for a kiss.

"Back off buddy," Sophie replied as she pushed him away. "You are not out of the woods yet. I need some caffeine and you don't have anything other than week-old coffee. Go find me some fresh stuff and I might make you an omelet."

"With peppers and cheese?" he asked enthusiastically.

Sophie laughed out loud. What the hell else would I make it with? she thought. "Yes, Bear. With peppers and cheese. Coffee. Now. Go."

"I'm gone."

Chapter 5

As Guy took a final drag from his cigarette and stood up, Bear Miller's black pickup rolled in and parked on the far side of the building. Guy watched him reach across to the passenger's seat for a hat before opening his door and stepping out. Walking around the back of the truck, he paused to stretch. Bear wore his standard blue jeans, t-shirt, partially-buttoned plaid flannel, untied work boots, and his faded blue baseball cap with The Duke's logo barely still visible.

"Mornin' Guy. Please tell me that you are open and have some coffee made already," Bear greeted him as they both walked toward the door from opposite sides of the building.

"Yes to both," Guy smiled. "I'm not used to seeing you this early in the morning. Are you picking up your bears? Had a few lookers yesterday but didn't sell any." On a patch of grass near the highway, Bear displayed and sold his carved bears. He had a storage trailer with a couple of them standing next to it.

"No. I'll probably pack 'em all up tomorrow. People don't usually buy them on the way home in the rain."

"Rain tomorrow, huh?"

"Yeah, all day."

"So what are you doing up so early on a Sunday? What's the occasion?"

"The occasion is that one of my neighbors has a real loud loose belt on his Grand Prix, works early on Sundays, and my current piece of ass is a light sleeper."

"My car woke you up?" Guy asked.

"Not me, man. I don't hear shit. But this girl hears everything. And once she's up..." Bear shrugged.

"Sorry about that, man," said Guy sheepishly. "I think it just started doing that in the morning. It doesn't do it the rest of the day and I guess I forget about it then."

"Yeah, it's the colder weather," Bear explained as they went inside, "but you're killin' me man. Sunday mornings are supposed to be about sleeping in and a good morning bone. It's the only night this chick can stay over and it's two weeks in a row she wakes up all crabby to the sound of your car."

As Bear headed toward the coffee, Guy walked around the counter to the register. "I didn't realize it was that loud. So, what makes the noise? And how much is it going to cost me?" Guy asked. It was always something. Just when it seemed like he gained a little ground financially, something came up to drag him back down.

Bear answered as he poured coffee into two large Styrofoam cups, "It sounds like it's just a loose belt. Take it over to Tony's and ask him to look at it. It probably only needs to be tightened. It should be cheap."

"Tony's?" Guy laughed. "You really trust that guy with your truck?"

"Hey, when he's sober, he's a good mechanic. And he's honest and he's cheap," Bear countered. "But I don't care where you take it. Just get the fucking thing fixed so I can sleep in and get laid next Sunday."

Bear paid for the coffee and changed the subject. "Hey, did you hear about Dean?" he asked.

"No," Guy lied. "How's he doing?" Dean was Bear's younger brother and Guy knew all about him. They had graduated high school together, just a couple of years after Bear. Great friends when they were little, then slowly drifted apart in high school. They were still friendly but ended up hanging out with different people. After graduation, Dean went away to college in Missouri and, other than the occasional visit, had not returned. Every time Guy heard about Dean, it seemed like there was another milestone. Hey, Dean graduated college. Dean got accepted to law school. Dean went to Europe. Dean just graduated law school. Dean got hired by a big firm downtown. Dean bought a condo. Dean's engaged. Dean's wedding is this weekend. Dean's wife is pregnant. Dean bought a house. Dean and his wife just had a baby. Each piece of news stung Guy. *Now what?* he wondered.

"He made partner! You know he's gotta be making some serious cash now. And he and Gina are going to have another kid," Bear said proudly.

"Wow, that's great," Guy said with false enthusiasm. "He is really doing well, man."

"He's livin' the dream, baby," Bear laughed. "Hey, I gotta run. Get your belt fixed!"

"All right," Guy agreed. "See ya."

The bell on the door jangled as Bear left the Gas and Go leaving Guy alone again. Tony, huh? The auto mechanic who doesn't drive. As far as Guy knew, Tony hadn't driven in years. Not legally anyway. He was the kind of guy you would see riding his bicycle somewhere and you'd immediately think, "DUI. That dude has no driver's license." There was no way he could be mistaken for someone riding for exercise or for pleasure. He typically had his mechanic's jumpsuit on and was headed down the side of the highway toward The Duke. And that's where he would spend his evenings. Watching a game, bullshitting with whomever, and becoming louder and dumber with each passing hour and with each passing drink. But Bear trusted him. And Guy trusted Bear. *What the hell,* thought Guy, *it's got to be better than taking it to the dealer. I never get out of that place without spending a fortune.* He wondered where law firm partners took their cars.

Chapter 6

After about half an hour, Guy finished the newspaper, neatly folded it up, and returned it to the top of the stack. The frequency of the clanging bell on top of the door began to increase. There still wouldn't be much traffic until church let out, but it would be enough to keep him occupied. As the sun peeked over the trees across the street, it burned off the rest of the lingering morning fog. Guy made pot after pot of coffee and engaged in the same idle but friendly chatter that he had for so many years:

"What's the good word, Guy?"

"Good morning, Guy."

"How's it hangin' man?"

"When you guys gonna get some good coffee in here, Guy?"

"Time to start raking leaves, huh Guy?"

"What time do the Bears play today, Guy?"

"Isn't it supposed to rain the rest of the week?"

"I hear it's gonna be sunny like this for another three or four days."

"Take it easy, Guy."

"Later dude."

"Have a good one."

"See ya tomorrow, Guy."

That last one never slipped past Guy without him wincing a little bit. *God*, Guy would think to himself, *I hope not.*

After checking the coffee and re-stocking Jacque's donuts, he stepped outside to have his mid-morning cigarette. Usually by this time, his mood had improved and he was no longer thinking about the fact that this was day number three thousand, one hundred and thirty-two. His mind wandered to the rest of his afternoon. The left headlight on his 1982 Pontiac Grand Prix had burnt out recently and because the Bears had a bye the previous weekend, his bar money was still in his pocket. He thought about spending it on his car. Guy didn't drive much during the week, so he was reminded of the dead light only in the mornings on his way to work. It didn't bother him for his five-minute morning commute, but over the weekend he had been out after dark and quickly got sick of "Hey, man. You know you got a headlight out?" That was the main reason he considered replacing it. Guy flicked his cigarette past the soda machine toward his car and headed back inside. He supposed he would make a run over to the auto parts store in McHenry after work.

It was almost time for the post-church crowd. They came for the big Sunday newspapers, gas, the rest of the donuts, milk, beer, or cigarettes—just the necessities. Guy dumped out all the coffee, save for one pot which would sit cooking and mostly untouched for the remainder of the day. He took the other pots to the bathroom and rinsed them out with foul-smelling water from the perpetually grimy sink. Then he wiped down the counter by the coffee maker. From the little supply cabinet underneath, he re-stocked the cups, lids, stir straws, creamers, and the little paper envelopes of sugar and Sweet-n-Low. After waiting on a couple of customers, he quickly checked the coolers. On Sundays, it was only milk and beer that needed to be re-stocked. During the week, however, it was the energy drinks that needed to be filled before lunch. They were an essential part of breakfast for so many of the high school students that stopped in on weekday mornings.

In the half hour before school began, about a dozen kids would rush in, grab their Amps, Monsters, or Red Bulls from the cooler, throw their money on the counter and say: "Box of Marlboro." Sometimes it was Marlboro Lights and sometimes it was something menthol, but it was always "box." Years ago, Guy knew all the kids coming in the morning and they knew him. They were one or two or three years behind him in school. Or they were the younger brothers and sisters of his friends. But, after a few years, he stopped recognizing their faces. One Saturday afternoon at the grocery store, some little kid he didn't recognize called out, "Hey, Gas and Go! You're that guy who's always at the Gas and Go in the morning."

"Yeah, that's me," Guy said, smiling weakly. Then he went home and drank himself to sleep.

The churches freed their flocks for another week and the traffic picked up a little as people stopped by for this and that. On weekdays, it was more hectic as people ran mid-day errands, and stopped in to buy the chips, soda, beef jerky, Slim Jims, cigarettes, and other assorted garbage they ingested for lunch. It was busy, and busy was good as time cruised along much like the morning with the same comfortably mindless tasks accompanied by the same comfortably mindless banter. They were days that Guy could have passed in a semiconscious state. Sundays were boring though, and left Guy too much time to think, to ruminate. And today, none of the topics were any good: spending money on his piece of shit car, Dean's success, and, thanks to Jacque, his looming birthday. He rarely left work on a Sunday in a good mood.

Finally, time inched along enough to the point where Guy's boss arrived to relieve him. At 6'5" and over 300 pounds, Big John, the station's owner, was an enormous man with a perpetually furrowed brow.

"Hey, Guy," Big John smiled. "What a gorgeous day, huh? It's heck comin' into work when it's this nice outside. I had to think about it real hard." He waited by the end of the counter so Guy could get out. There wasn't space enough for both of them to fit behind it at the same time.

"Well, I'm so glad you made it. It would have been a shame to have no one behind your counter on a busy day like this."

"What do you mean?"

"I was leaving at two whether you decided to drag your sorry butt over here or not." Guy was smiling as he walked past him.

"Yeah right, boy," Big John laughed. "Go stock the cooler."

After Guy re-stocked what needed to be re-stocked, he said so long to his boss and headed outside. He paused to light a cigarette. It actually is a pretty nice day out, he thought as he climbed into his car.

Big John's Gas and Go sat on the northeast corner of the intersection of Routes 12 and 31 on the southern fringe of Richmond, Illinois. Guy left the station but headed north in the opposite direction of McHenry. He was still planning on getting a new headlight, but he figured he would stop by his father's house first. He drove north along Route 12 with the 1,100 people of his tiny hometown strung out along either side of the highway for just over three miles as it traveled toward the Wisconsin border.

Richmond was small enough such that nearly all errands required a drive of ten or more miles through the countryside to get to another town. To the south was Guy's usual destination: McHenry. It had the nearest hospital, some fast food choices, a grocery store, and the auto parts store. Even further south was the largest town in the county, Crystal Lake. A forty-minute drive away, it had some chain stores for clothes, furniture, restaurants, and even a movie theater.

Guy passed through his downtown, dominated by a couple of dozen antique stores. They had come to prominence gradually. When the General Store closed, it became the General Store Antiques. The Richmond State Bank relocated and the building became The Bank Antiques. Then came the demise of Noisey's Tavern. Enough of its clientele succumbed to the rigors of a disciplined nightly intake of nicotine, alcohol, and BS to end its run. It died only to quickly be reborn as Tavern Antiques. And so it went. The antiques became a draw and ancillary businesses like Jacque's Not Your Average Bakery! popped up. He sold the strolling antiquers coffee, donuts, and pastries while down the street the Kandy Kone offered ice cream and a soda fountain for their bored, hostage children. That the quaint little downtown had survived was a function of what lay to the north and to the southeast.

Upon leaving Richmond, Route 12 turned southeast toward the vast suburban wasteland that buffered Chicago for so many miles. After a while, one town bled into another and the easiest way to discern the transition from one to the next was the sighting of another Walmart strip mall with an Applebee's in the outlot. Big box retailers and chain restaurants lined four-lane traffic arteries that seemed to have stoplights every hundred yards. Clogged with SUVs, they mirrored the actual arteries of their typical residents with their steady diets of drive-thru garbage washed down with super-sized sodas. Guy avoided driving that direction as much as he possibly could. On the rare occasions when he was compelled to wade into it, he always wondered how people could live in that kind of monotonous sprawl.

Although he didn't know how or why people chose to live a suburban Chicagoland existence, Guy understood that his town depended on them. Their lifestyle gave them cause to flee. And when they did, they fled through Richmond to the lakes of Southeastern Wisconsin and beyond. Less than an hour away were Twin Lakes, Pell Lake, Powers Lake, Paddock Lake, Lauderdale Lakes, Lake Como, Silver Lake, Camp Lake, Lake Edgerton, and the crown jewel of all of Southeastern Wisconsin, Lake Geneva.

All summer long, the denizens of Chicago and all of those cookie-cutter subdivisions that made up the Northwest Suburbs, full of streets named for trees leveled in trade, sought a temporary respite and escaped to Wisconsin. Leaving work early on Friday afternoons, they loaded their kayaks, dirt bikes, quads, and Jet Skis onto trailers, hitched up their boats and campers, piled into their Tahoes, Yukons, and other assorted oversized vehicles, put on a DVD for the kids, and tried to beat the traffic. Route 12 took them northward and as the population thinned, four lanes shrunk to two and funneled them past Big John's Gas and Go and past the antique stores of downtown Richmond. The increase in the little town's weekend traffic wasn't yet discernable as winter gradually relinquished its claims on the northern Illinois weather, but by the time spring finally began to look and feel like itself, it was. It built steadily toward Memorial Day Weekend, when Route 12 was transformed into the bane of traveler and resident alike. With no viable alternate route, the volume of cars slowed traffic to a crawl from the stoplight in front of Big John's on one end of town to the only other stoplight on the north end, two and a half miles away. From Friday afternoon through Monday evening, Route 12 was avoided at all costs by the locals.

It was October, though, and Guy quickly made his way to the north end of town. Just before Route 12 made its final push toward the Illinois/Wisconsin border, he turned left and drove the half mile westward to his boyhood home.

Chapter 7

Charles Bradford lived on seventy-five beautiful acres of oak and hickory savannah divided by the meanderings of the Nippersink Creek. Just off the highway as it accelerated out of the small town into the sea of farm fields, the property was a wooded oasis for all living things that weren't corn, cows, or soybeans. Charles purchased it shortly after he married. At the time, there was only a small, older house just off the road. Mr. and Mrs. Bradford made that their home for the first few years and Guy's older sisters were brought home from the hospital to that little two-bedroom place. But by the time Guy surprised them years later with his impending arrival, Charles had overseen construction of the brazen monument to his financial success where he still resided. Once home to a family of five, only Charles remained. Until recently anyway. First his wife passed, then his subsequent relationships failed, followed by his health, and Charles had been forced to hire a series of live-in caregivers.

Set almost in the middle of the property, the house was well hidden from the sights and sounds of the highway. An unassuming narrow driveway barely interrupted the greenery and burrowed through the dense foliage that grew alongside the road. If not for the ever-present rusting metal garbage can, it would be easy to miss on the first pass. After a hundred yards, the driveway ceased to be a tunnel and wound gently through a weedy, sporadically-mowed lawn presided over by several towering oaks. Surrounded by clusters of rocks in various sizes and arrangements, the house met the driveway and turned it away around a small hill back toward the highway and the culmination of a loop. To the right of the house, the overgrown woods threatened to engulf a detached two car garage while weeds filled the many cracks in the driveway and thrived next to the house among the rocks. Deadfall from a summer full of thunderstorms covered the patchy lawn, and if not for the enormous pale yellow Cadillac Eldorado parked in front, the house and property would have appeared vacant.

Guy parked next to his father's car and stepped out into the sunshine. He could hear the sound of an engine running behind the garage. Guy sighed and headed toward the back of the building. His father's tractor was there, seat vacant, the engine chugging along in idle. Charles was on his hands and knees in the dirt behind it.

"Hello," Guy called out over the noise.

Charles looked up. "You're just in time. Kill that engine. And grab the pick from inside," he ordered.

Guy walked over to the tractor, reached up and across to where the single key protruded from beneath the large steering wheel, and silenced it. As he went into the garage through the side door, he wondered what he was in for today. Guy looked around in the dim light. Resting against the back wall were a number of rusting shovels and rakes, a post hole digger, two pitchforks, and an axe. But no pick.

"It's not in here," he called out to his father.

"Sure it is. It's against the back wall."

Guy sighed before answering slowly. "Dad, I'm standing here looking at the back wall. There's no pick."

Charles didn't respond. As Guy scanned the rest of the room, the light dimmed even further for a moment. It was his father's bent figure temporarily blocking the sunlight as it shuffled through the door. He went over to the back wall and examined two or three tools before satisfying himself that the pick was not there.

"It must be down by the pond. Do you mind getting it?"

Guy fetched the pick and returned for instructions. The object of Charles's focus was a stone jutting out of the ground in one tire tread of the path around the garage.

"I want to get that rock out of there," explained Charles. "Use the narrow end of the pick and finish clearing around the edge. I started. I'm not sure how big it is though."

Guy obeyed and began. It appeared to be much bigger than what was showing.

"Keep all of that dirt piled up next to it. We'll need to use it to fill in the hole when we're done."

Again, Guy did as he was told.

"Don't get it in the grass though. Keep it on the side. It'll be easier if it's not in the taller grass."

Guy cleared the edges of the rock and piled the dirt in the correct spot.

"Now take the wide end of that pick and see if you can pry it out," Charles instructed.

"I'm going to get a shovel," said Guy setting the pick down.

"You don't need a shovel. Just drive that flat side in on the edge and pry it out."

"A shovel will work, too," said Guy heading toward the garage.

"I don't want you using one of my shovels," said Charles, raising his voice. "Shovels break. If you would just listen and use the pick how I told you, you wouldn't need a shovel."

Guy took a deep breath and silently returned to the pick. Its narrowness made the task awkward and the rock rolled off to the side more than once, but eventually and with several more pointers and directions from Charles, Guy pried the rock up and out of the hole. Using the pick.

"See," Charles gloated, "you didn't need a shovel. But now you do. Put that pick back in the garage and grab a shovel to fill that hole in and level it out."

Guy grabbed the shovel and, with more careful scrutiny and supervision, successfully put dirt back into the hole.

As Guy finished, Charles turned toward the house. "Now make sure you put those tools away where they go. I don't want you to leave them out in the yard. I've got to go sit down."

Guy put the tools away, turned off the single bulb, closed the door, and caught up to his father as he was opening the back door.

"Take your shoes off," ordered Charles as he leaned against the wall for support and kicked off his boots.

"They're off," he answered as he waited for his father in the narrow hallway.

Charles went into the kitchen and sat down at the table. Guy sat across from him. "Are you busy this afternoon?"

"I have to run down to McHenry today. I've got a headlight out," Guy answered.

"Do you think you could pick up a couple of bags of salt?"

"In McHenry?" asked Guy even though he knew full well that his father didn't mean McHenry. His father always bought 40 lb. bags of salt for his water softener from the Farm 'n Feed store in Twin Lakes. Over the border in Wisconsin, it was twenty-five minutes in the opposite direction of McHenry. The bags of salt were a few cents cheaper in Twin Lakes. And, just as important, a few years ago Charles had an argument over an expired coupon with the guy at the hardware store in McHenry. No one had a longer memory than Charles Bradford.

"That guy in McHenry is so expensive on everything. It's cheaper in Twin Lakes if you've got the time."

"Yeah. Sure."

Charles fished in his pants pocket for his money clip, found it, and put it on the table. Like always, it was stuffed with one-hundred-dollar bills. Sometimes there were a few smaller bills on the outside of the wad, but usually it was just the hundreds. Charles peeled one off and pushed it across the table toward Guy. "Bring me the receipt."

Guy pocketed the money. "Well, I'll be back in about an hour."

Chapter 8

Sophie rolled over in the bed and stretched out her legs. The strange sensation of being able to do so without bumping into anyone else or falling out of it woke her up. For a moment, she panicked and searched for the clock. It was just after one-thirty. Exhaling in relief, most of her calm returned. She still had over an hour to get back to Frannie's. Stretching out her arms and yawning, she allowed herself to savor the freedom of being alone in the queen size bed. No wonder she had slept for so long.

Sophie listened, but the apartment was quiet. Bear must have left for The Duke to work the Sunday afternoon football games. Too bad she couldn't take a leisurely shower here and get ready, she thought, but Bear's bathroom was the standard guy-bathroom gross. She decided to just put on her clothes from yesterday and head back. One of the few redeeming features of life at Frannie's was having a decent bathroom to herself. When she got back, she would have to check on Frannie and probably endure a bit of obligatory small talk with whichever family member had been stuck with her for the night. Once they gathered their belongings and fled for another week, she would be able to take her time and shower, get some clean clothes, and feel a little more human.

Well rested for a change, Sophie felt pretty positive for a Sunday. Normally, her mornings were spent brooding about her looming return to the confinement of another week stuck indoors with an old, nearly-dead person who was still either overly-damn-determined to continue drawing breaths or too afraid to do otherwise. But today she wasn't even really thinking about it as she used her feet to fish around at the end of the bed for her panties. Sophie found them, slipped them on, and located her shirt on the floor. As she pulled it over her head, the lingering scent of the bar and cigarettes hit her nostrils and she wrinkled her nose. Sophie smiled as she thought of the contrasts between her Saturday departures and Sunday returns. When she left work on Saturday afternoons, she was typically headed out on whatever the current "town" might be. Hair, makeup, maybe heels; looking her best. But when she returned on Sundays, it was a different story. Disheveled, ball cap to hide her hair, no makeup. Often the same clothes, but wrinkled as though slept in or piled on a floor. If she looked like she had just spent the night in her car somewhere, that might have been the truth. Anything to get out of the house, to get away for a day and a night.

After breakfast, she and Bear had fumbled back to the bedroom, to the bed. They were still tired, and neither was overly interested, but they both knew that it was their only opportunity for the week, so what the hell. He was decent and considerate. There was no great passion, but their parts did fit together nicely. Last week she was pretty bitchy about getting woken up by that guy's car and the dogs barking and nothing happened. Sophie figured that for a guy like Bear, being denied two weekends in a row might make him start looking for a reason to break it off. Then she would be either sleeping in her car again or risking a one-night stand. From what she'd seen of the locals hanging around The Duke, ugh, she didn't want to think about it. She had done well for herself with Bear.

Sophie sighed and forced herself to relinquish the bed. She finished getting dressed and threw the covers up over the mattress, not really making it, but making it presentable. Not that Bear would care. As she found her toothbrush in her purse and headed to the bathroom, her stomach grumbled at her. Those pepper and cheese omelets were hours ago and there was nothing left to eat here. She did have enough time to stop for food before heading back to Frannie's, but that would mean spending money. Sophie would have to wait for either a late lunch or early dinner. Bad food, but free food.

She inspected the apartment for any remaining belongings as if she was checking out of a motel. It was important to make sure she wasn't leaving anything behind. If she did, she would have to do without it for the entire week. Satisfied that she had everything, she stood by the entrance and looked into the kitchen. The morning's breakfast dishes still sat, egg remnants cementing themselves to pan and plate. Will they still be there in a week? she mused. Maybe the bears would come to life and lick them clean them after she left. If only. Digging her car keys from her purse, she turned off the lights and headed out the door.

Sophie squinted as her eyes fought to transition from the drab fluorescent lighting of the apartment building's common hallway to the brightness of the early afternoon sunshine. As she walked to her car, she felt a twinge of regret about sleeping all morning. It was a gorgeous day. She reminded herself that she must have needed it and that it was the best rest she'd had in a while. Her silver Nissan Sentra had been parked away from the shade of any trees and, despite the cooler weather, was almost hot inside. Generic pop jangled out of the speakers as she started the car, rolled down the windows, and found her sunglasses amid the clutter on the passenger seat. Turning toward the old section of town, Sophie turned up the radio just enough to drown out her own vocal imperfections and sang along as the wind tousled her hair around her face on the short ride back to work. Purposely trying to lose herself in the song and enjoy the moment, she pushed the unpleasant destination of her happy little car ride out of her head.

Just past the high school, Sophie turned onto South Street. It took her up the little town's one substantial hill toward a small neighborhood of large, old homes where the original local gentry had settled. The view of the town below was long ago obscured by the now mature oaks and maples they had planted along either side of the streets. On days like this one, turning right onto Washington Avenue where Frannie resided was like entering another world of color and light. The leaves were ablaze with infinite combinations of oranges, yellows, reds, and purples, radiant shafts of autumn sunlight broke through the canopy, and it was all set in dazzling motion by a gentle breeze.

This enclave of large Victorian style homes was a shadow of its former self. The growth of the trees inversely corresponded with the condition of the structures. Many were falling victim to the typical yet gradual neglect that comes with the inevitability of time passing. Others, however, had been partitioned into small, low-rent apartments. These tenements, witnesses to an endless parade of poverty, overcrowding, and struggle, were the worst. Any repairs or maintenance were hard won and shoddy. Their stately front porches and grassless yards were strewn with the cheap, faded plastic clutter of garage sale toys belonging to the children of single mothers and undocumented immigrants. Sandwiched between two of these especially blighted eyesores stood Frannie's still-magnificent home. As if with chest out and chin up, it wore its new coat of paint and manicured landscaping with a stoic pride; the house, along with its aging owner, still waging a futile battle against the onslaught of years.

In the comfort of the shade on Frannie's massive porch sat her son Dan. His belongings gathered next to him on the bench of the wooden table, he smoked a cigarette and flipped open his phone to check the time again and again. As the tires of Sophie's car eased onto the side of the street opposite the house and announced her arrival with the gentle crunching of leaves, Dan rose and stubbed out his cigarette into a small round ashtray. Before her car came to a complete stop, Sophie's eyes caught the blue LED lights on her dashboard clock: 2:53pm. Seven more minutes of freedom, she thought, and eased her car back into the street and past Frannie's. Dan stared after her and then looked at his phone again. Seeing and recognizing what she must have, he sighed and sat back down. Just as he didn't want to stay a minute longer than necessary, he understood why she would not want to return a minute sooner.

Sophie reached the stop sign at the end of Washington Street and turned left toward the edge of town. Past a small white clapboard church, past the grade school, past the cemetery and out into the vastness of the surrounding farm fields she drove, still singing along with the radio. After only a minute or two she turned right and right again to get to the highway that would take her back to town and complete her seven-minute rectangle. There was nothing to see out here, and she knew she was just wasting gas, but today she didn't care. The longer she drove, fumbling through the verses and hollering out the choruses with the wind in her hair, the better her mood became. By the time she returned to Frannie's at precisely three o'clock, she was feeling better than she had in a long time.

When he saw her car pull up a second time, Dan waited to stand. Sophie grabbed her purse and crossed the street toward him. Smiling, she hopped over the large root-buckled section of sidewalk in front of the house, hustled up the neatly edged walk, and jogged up the stairs onto the porch.

"Welcome back," said Dan greeting her as he rose from the bench. "You seem suspiciously happy to be here."

Sophie startled, then smiled. "Oh, hi Dan. I didn't see you sitting there. I guess I'm just in a good mood today."

"Well, don't let on," he cautioned, "or I'm sure she'll find some way to kill it."

"That kind of day?" she asked, her smile fading a bit.

"Is there any other with her?" he replied bitterly.

Sophie felt bad for Dan. He was the most frequent target of Frannie's abuse and seemed to deal with it the worst. She was almost as mean to Dan's younger brother Mark, but Mark seemed to handle it differently. For one, he wasn't around nearly as much and when he was, Mark got angry and vented about what a bitch his mother could be. Dan responded by clamming up and internalizing everything. It always amazed Sophie how parents could retain so much psychological power over their adult children. And how routinely they abused it.

"Well, I'm back now. You are a free man again. Anything specific I should know before I head in?"

"No, nothing out of the ordinary. I'd better go inside and say goodbye before I make my escape. Mark should be here next weekend. I'll be around though so you can call me if you need to."

Dan held the screen door open for her and Sophie headed in. "Okay. Thanks Dan."

"Mom!" Dan called from the foyer, "Sophie's back and I'm going to head out." There was no reply. He removed his shoes, walked past the dining room turned bedroom that Frannie refused to use, and headed up the steep and narrow staircase. Sophie followed behind. Down the hall were the childhood bedrooms of both Dan and Mark. With queen size beds, corner desks and dressers, and windows with curtains, they remained remarkably similar to what they were so long ago when they were still boys in high school. Dan and Sophie turned down the hallway opposite them, toward Frannie's room. On the left they passed a small room sparsely furnished with only an end table, a twin mattress lying on the floor, and a curtainless window. This was Sophie's room. Mark and Dan had both unsuccessfully argued that Sophie should be using one of their old rooms. Frannie had insisted that she wanted their rooms to be available for company. Pointing out that she hadn't had an overnight guest in several years only angered her and the conversations ended with her standard snipped refrain of "As long as it is my house, I will be the one making the decisions."

Opposite Sophie's room was a hall bath. This was specifically for her to use. It was, more than any other space in the house, given over to her completely by Frannie. Occasionally, when arguing with or simply belittling her sons, Frannie would suggest that they didn't understand because of their maleness. She would then knowingly nod toward Sophie in a gesture of feminine solidarity and superiority. Although Sophie understood she was primarily being used by Frannie to underscore the point she was making, or the dig she was giving to her sons, there did also seem to be a shred of sincerity in her words. It was, in fact, Frannie's years of being a lone female in the company of brothers, husbands, and sons that affirmed her belief in the sacrosanctity of a woman having her own bathroom. Even when Dan or Mark stayed in the house on Sophie's day off, they were forbidden from using "Sophie's bathroom." Although they each slept upstairs in their old bedrooms, they were required to shower and shave in the small bathroom in the basement.

Sophie followed Dan to the partially open door at the end of the hall. They could hear the sound of big band music coming from inside the master bedroom. Dan knocked gently. "Mom?" he called, but there was no response. Dan eased the door open and slowly entered. The large four-poster bed in the center of the wall facing the windows was unmade and empty. The music came from a small compact disc player that sat on a long, low dresser on the far side of the room. On the near side of the room, Frannie's chair sat next to an end table where stacks of tabloids and gossip magazines "borrowed" from her hairdresser competed for space with a reading lamp. Between the bed and the dresser was the door to the master bathroom where Frannie spent much of her time. Dan walked to within a couple feet of the bathroom door and called out again, "Hey Mom?"

"I thought you ran off already," came the sharp reply.

"Nope. I'm still here. Sophie is back now though, and I just came up to say goodbye," Dan explained.

"Well, you're going to have to wait. Can't you see I am in the bathroom?"

Sophie watched Dan roll his eyes and check the time on his phone again. He went to Frannie's chair and sat down. Back to work, thought Sophie as she began to make the bed. She wished Frannie would hurry up so Dan could leave, she could make sure Frannie was set for a little while, and then she could finally take a shower and maybe get some food. By this time, she was famished. Just as she finished the bed, Frannie emerged from the bathroom.

"What are you doing? Are you running out of here now or not?" she looked at Dan. "If you are going to be staying, you'll need to get out of my chair."

Dan stood. "I am leaving now. I just came upstairs to say goodbye." He moved toward Frannie and gave her a sadly perfunctory hug. "Love you. Call me if you need anything."

Frannie replaced Dan in the chair. "All right. Make sure you empty that ashtray before you go. And don't leave it sitting out there on my porch. You left it out there last time, and I don't like it."

"Okay Mom," Dan replied and turned to Sophie. "I'll see you. Have a good week."

"Thanks, Dan." Sophie smiled a sympathetic smile, "You too."

Dan started to head out of the room, but caught himself and turned to Sophie, smiling. "I almost forgot. You got some mail yesterday." He had put it in the kitchen, and knew she would find it, but he enjoyed watching her face light up as he told her. "It looked like a letter from someone in Sioux City. I left it out on the kitchen table for you."

Chapter 9

"Since when do you care about football?" Laura asked.

"Since never," Michele laughed. "I haven't even pretended to care about it since we were in high school and I started going out with Troy. What do you think?" She moved her chair back from the table and posed for her friend. Along with her tight jeans, she wore a too small Bears jersey that showed off her well maintained figure. It had been modified by cutting the neckline down into the space between the numbers. The cut made it appear that her breasts had burst the jersey open, just by their sheer magnificence. "Is it too much?"

"Uhh, it's barely enough," Laura laughed. "No, you look great. What's with the ponytail though?"

"I'm going for the sexy tomboy look." She pouted and turned her head from side to side.

"I see. Nice touch," Laura nodded approvingly. "You almost look like the cover of a Halloween costume package: *Sexy Football Player.* All you need is a mini-skirt, fishnets, and some of that black stuff under your eyes."

The two friends shared a table along the wall opposite the door. To their right was the large bar, surrounded on all sides by stools, most of them occupied. On an enormous screen to their left, the fourth quarter of the noon game was mercifully winding down. The Giants had nearly completed their drubbing of the Seahawks, but no one in The Duke really cared. The bar was on its way to filling up though, with the Bears game set to start in about twenty minutes.

"So, what are we doing here anyway?" Laura's eyes narrowed. "You're obviously up to something."

Michele smiled and sighed. "My maintenance from Carson and Son runs out at the end of next summer."

"Wow. Hard to believe it's been three years already."

"Tell me about it. I'm starting to freak a little bit here." Michele's smile faded.

"Why? What happens when the maintenance stops?" Laura asked.

"Ummm, I am basically fucked."

"You'll still get child support though, won't you?"

"Yeah. Only for a year though, and I won't be able to stay in the house on that. I'll have to find some kind of townhome or something."

"Oh, the horrors!" said Laura sarcastically as she thought of her own.

"I'm sorry, I didn't mean it like that," Michele apologized. "That's the only house that Carly has ever known. The basement is done, we have the pool, sunsets on the deck..." her voice trailed off. "It's not that a condo is bad, it's just that it would be so different from what she is used to."

"And what you're used to," Laura reminded her.

"Damn right." Michele became defiant. "Hey, you know how I grew up. You spent enough time in that ratty, gross little trailer with me. To this day, every time I smell mold or mildew or whatever, it takes me right back there." She took a drink of her beer. "Yeah, I want to keep my house. My nice house."

Laura softened. "I get it. I really do hope you can keep it," she smiled at her friend. "I think I've grown pretty used to using your pool in the summertime, too. So, what are you going to do for work?"

"Work?" Michele paused. "Seriously? Laura, I am thirty-two years old and I haven't worked since we both bussed tables at Andre's Steakhouse when we were in freaking high school. I have a high school diploma and I barely got that. What am I even qualified for? Some retail job at Target or Walmart? McDonald's maybe? Even if I was lucky enough to sport one of those colored vests with a name tag and stock shelves or don the drive-thru headset, that's not going to help me keep the house."

"You've gotta start somewhere, don't you? Maybe you could take some classes at MCC," Laura offered.

Michele laughed, "No. No way. It'd be too weird. Carly's a junior in high school. I know way too many of the kids there. But it's not just that. Classes, realistically, wouldn't pay off for at least a couple of years. And there is no way in hell I am going to take a remedial algebra class again just to start out."

"Well?"

"Well what?"

"No work, no school? What's your plan?"

Michele took another drink of her beer. "I'm going to try mining," she said, watching her friend's face with anticipation.

Laura stared back at her.

"Prospecting."

Again a blank look.

"Digging for gold?"

"What the hell are you talking about?" Laura asked.

"Jesus, do I have to spell it out completely for you?" Michele sounded exasperated. She'd thought about it carefully for a few months and had been able to justify it in her own mind. But now, having to flat out say it, well, it was different. "Gold digging. I am going to marry someone with some money," she said finally.

Laura paused. "Oh honey," she put her head in her hands and looked down. "Please tell me you're not serious."

"It's the only way. Come on. Give me an alternative," Michele challenged. "If you have a better idea, please, let's hear it."

Laura lifted her head and looked at her friend. "You really want another bad marriage? Really? You're young, you're beautiful. Go fall in love. Please don't do this to yourself."

"Do what? Take care of myself?" Michele began mounting her defense. "I'm not going to find some guy that I hate. I'm not going to make myself completely miserable. Who knows, I might even find someone I really like."

"So you're hoping to fall in like? Great. What about money? Unless you are planning to marry some old, wrinkled, creepy guy, I've got news for you: There isn't anyone around here, close to your age, who actually has any money."

"Look, they don't need to be sitting on a fortune right now. I don't need actual gold! But if they at least have a decent job and aren't up to their eyeballs in debt, Carly and I get to stay in the house. I get to continue to expand that giant gap in my resume and I don't have to get some awful McJob."

"What about Carly? She gets to stay in the house in exchange for a random step-father?"

"I'm not worried about that. She's got a year and a half left of high school and she'll be gone. She's so busy running around with her friends now anyway. And besides, she's started bugging me to get out of the house more. Even she knows that I am ready to date again."

Laura shook her head. "It's just wrong, Michele. What makes you think that this guy is even going to want to move into your house? What if he wants you to move into his?"

"I don't know, but it's not really even just the house. It's everything. I like having a newer car. I like going to Disney World. And when we go, we don't have to drive all damn day to get there. We fly. And we don't stay at my aunt's condo an hour away because it's cheaper. We stay in Disney. And in the winter, I get to escape the freezing cold for a week and go on a cruise with friends. I get to take Carly on spring break to a beach. Or we've been skiing in Colorado. When I go to the grocery store, I don't look at the prices, I buy what we like. I don't mow my own lawn, I don't paint my own nails, I don't clean my own house or maintain my own pool. I have people who do these things for me and that is the way I like it. You can call me spoiled if you want and I won't disagree. I know I am, and I don't care. It's the way I've lived pretty much since Carly was born and I really don't want to give it up. If I don't find a guy with some dough, it's all gone. Not just the house, my vacations, and whatever else, but my whole way of life."

"I don't know. I mean I get what you're saying and you're right. But it just…" Laura shrugged. "So what's your plan then? How are you going to find and land Mr. Moneybags? Is the sexy football player costume part of it?"

Michele laughed, "Yes, my 'costume,' as you call it, is part of it. I figure I need to work what assets I have and these may be two of my best," she answered, looking down at her cleavage. "I'm out now and working on getting noticed at least, but otherwise, I don't really have a plan. It was hard enough just to decide to do this. I was hoping you could help me strategize a bit."

Laura looked over at the bar and then back at Michele, "You are definitely getting noticed."

"Really!?" She grinned and sat up a little straighter. "Now what though? I haven't been on a date since high school."

"No kidding. And can you even really count going to prom and homecoming with your steady boyfriend as dating? I don't think so. It's not grown-up dating anyway."

"After the divorce I wanted to step back from everything and just be there for Carly. I figured I would get her through high school before I even thought about getting involved with anyone. But now I guess I need to modify that. It's time."

"Wow," Laura shook her head again in disbelief, "You went from not even thinking about dating until she's out of high school to this? To full blown marriage? To a guy you still haven't met yet? And that you may or may not even really like?"

Michele looked hurt. "I really wish you'd stop shaking your head at me. You're making me feel like shit about this. I need to do this. I was really hoping you would help me."

Laura rolled her eyes and exhaled, "I'm sorry. I'm worried for you. I come to meet you at a bar, which is weird to begin with, and you've got your boobs busting out of your shirt, weirder still, and you tell me you're getting married. Soon. You just need to find a rich guy first. I mean come on! It's weird. It's crazy. It's a lot for me to absorb in five minutes. You gotta to give me some time to get used to the idea."

"You're right," Michele reached across the table and held Laura's hand in hers. "I'm sorry. I'm just nervous and excited and I guess I want you to be too. I really need some support in this."

"Look. You're my friend, Michele, and I want you to be happy. But I don't know if I will get used to this idea. And even if I do, I still might not like it."

Michele let go of Laura's hand and they both sat back in their chairs considering each other for a moment. Michele spoke first, "I need another beer. Do you want one?" she asked as she stood up.

"I think I need something a little stronger than just a beer right now," Laura laughed. "Do a shot with me?"

"Sure," she answered, smiling and feeling a little better.

Chapter 10

Guy bent over and reached down into the bottom of his trunk for the last forty-pound bag of rock salt. Grunting slightly as he dropped it on top of the others in the overloaded, rusting, yellow wheelbarrow, he closed the trunk, turned, and gripped the weathered handles. Whenever Guy wheeled bags of salt down the hill in this ancient conveyance, he expected it to finally fall apart. But Charles Bradford didn't like to spend money on anything that wasn't specifically for himself and Charles wasn't the one who used the wheelbarrow. Guy dug his heels into the steep slope as he eased the heavy, creaking load down and around the side of the house to the basement door. From there he carried the bags through his father's little-used workshop and into the utility room. The first two got dumped right into the bin attached to the water softener. The rest were stacked on a pallet sitting next to it. Guy folded up the two empty bags and put them in the garbage. He then turned out the lights, closed the door tightly, and headed up to the garage to return the wheelbarrow that had survived yet another day.

The house was quiet when he entered. Guy removed his shoes and headed past the kitchen, through the dining room, formal living room, past the study, and down the long hallway toward his father's chambers. As he approached, he could hear first the television and then voices.

"Hello," Guy called out, announcing his presence as he walked into a bedroom nearly as large as his entire apartment. Sharette stood over Charles holding an IV bag as he sat in a large, brown leather chair.

"You needa sit up straightah Chahlie," she instructed him in her thick

43

accent that blended British and Caribbean.

"I'm trying. Give me a hand," he responded reaching up for her.

Sharette hooked the IV bag on the stand and grabbed his hand. Charles shifted and tried to use his legs to push himself back into the chair as she pulled him upward. Though not a big man, it was an obvious struggle for the both of them.

"I can help," Guy offered and hurried across the room to grab his father's other hand and pull up. The three of them got the one of them settled and Guy bent to move Charles's ottoman closer for him. Sharette thanked Guy and began to untuck his father's shirt.

"Late lunch today," Charles explained as he helped her with his shirt so she could access the clear plastic tube that protruded from a somewhat raw-looking hole in the right side of his abdomen. About eight inches long, the tube was taped to his side and had a little flip cap on the end of it, much like that of a beach ball. Officially called a gastronomic feeding tube, it had been surgically inserted into Charles early last spring. One of his more recently diagnosed maladies was called Progressive Supranuclear Palsy. Of all the chronic conditions he endured, this was the worst. In addition to a nearly constant low level of pain and discomfort, the palsy was also slowly degrading his muscle control. The feeding tube was intended as an answer to his corrupted ability to swallow properly. Deteriorating control and function of the throat muscles put a patient like Charles in danger of aspirating, or having food and fluid make their way into his lungs when he ate, thus putting him at an extreme risk for a lung infection. And in a body already weakened by heart disease, arthritis, multiple bouts with cancer, glaucoma, palsy, and a lifetime of diabetes, an otherwise minor infection could prove to be fatal.

As Sharette connected the IV bag to the feeding tube and eased open the valve, the creamy, tan, liquid lunch slowly began to drain directly into his father's stomach. "Dere you go Chahlie," Sharette stepped away. "Let me know if it a comin' too fahst."

Guy retreated from his father's chair and sat on the foot of his bed facing him, watching him. Charles put one foot up on the ottoman and shifted a little. His discomfort was visible as he reached around the IV line for the smudged eyeglasses that sat on the table next to him. He looked tired and he looked weak. Guy never liked seeing his father like this. He was used to arrogance and confidence, the manipulative, petty, passive-aggressive version of Charles Bradford, always on the offensive. When he went to visit his father, Guy had his guard up, ready to deflect the subtle attacks, the cheap shots. He worked very hard not to let his father get to him too much. In the yard on his tractor or in the kitchen cooking, it was obvious Charles had slowed, but his words were still razor sharp and with them he seemed to mask his failing health. But here, in his bedroom, squirming in his chair, his raised shirt exposing the grayed chest hair scattered about and the pale, sagging skin of his torso, he didn't look threatening; Guy pitied him.

"Dad," Guy reached out his hand, "Your glasses are filthy. Let me clean them for you." Charles handed them over. Guy exhaled onto each lens in turn and wiped them clean on his shirt. "There you go," he said returning them.

"I don't think I can tell the difference anymore anyway," Charles commented as he put them on. "You got my change for me? And my receipt?"

"Yeah, just a sec, the Bears game is starting. Do you want me to put it on?" Guy asked.

"Sure."

Guy reached across his father and found the remote.

"My change? And my receipt?" Charles repeated as Guy looked for the right channel.

"Just a second," Guy repeated, his chest tightening. He found the football game and returned the remote to the table next to his father before digging into the front pocket of his jeans. "Where would you like me to put it?"

"Leave it on the counter in my closet, would ya?"

Guy stood and took a deep breath. He forced himself to calmly walk into the closet and put his father's change on the corner of the dresser, along with the receipt so that his father could verify that he hadn't, after nearly thirty fucking years, began to cheat him. *Why?* he asked himself. *Why do I ever, even for a second, believe that I could mean anything to him? I can't be trusted, but I guess I'm useful?* Guy shook his head. It never failed. The second he softened, the second he let his guard down, the second his father appeared human, Guy ended up feeling like a dumbass. *"Wanna watch the game, Dad?" "Gimme my receipt." Fuck.*

"Did you make sure that door was shut tight this time? I don't need more mice getting in there."

"It's shut," Guy responded. "I've got to get going. I'll see you."

"You don't want stick around and watch the game?" Charles asked.

Guy chuckled to himself. *You have one chair,* he thought. *If you really actually gave a shit about anybody other than yourself, you might consider getting another fucking chair.* "No thanks, I've gotta run. Do you need anything before I leave?"

"Yeah," he twisted to look up at the mostly empty bag of food. "Tell the girl to come back in here. This thing is almost done."

"Will do. Call me if you need me."

"Yeah," his father nodded distractedly.

Chapter 11

"Ready for another, Jacque?" Mindy asked as she grabbed the empty bottle in front of him.

"Yeah, thanks. And hey, get Bear to turn off this shitty music and turn the sound up on the game."

Mindy laughed as she reached into the cooler for another bottle of Sam Adams. "Why do you even ask? You know he won't let me switch it until the game starts." She took his old, white cocktail napkin with the wet ring on it and replaced it before setting down his new beer.

"I don't know." He shook his head, picked up the bottle and re-filled his glass with beer. It was always the same thing. When Jacque sat down to watch the game, he wanted to hear it, too. It didn't matter if it had actually started yet or not. He liked those five minutes before the game. He liked to listen to the pre-game talking heads, in their Armani suits, building the hype and talking about match-ups and keys to the game. He liked to see the stupid graphics of random statistics, the crashing, exploding helmets, and all of the other bullshit. But whenever Bear worked, which was almost every single game, the music stayed on until the ball was actually resting on the tee. "I'll switch it when the game starts," was his standard answer. Jacque had made his arguments and lost. So, he sat there, listening to music he didn't like, reading the closed captioning, knowing he was missing out, and waiting for Bear to turn on the goddamn sound.

Mindy checked the time and tried to console him, "There's only a couple of minutes left. He'll be switching it soon."

"You know that's not the point. I am missing out on all of this glorious goddamn nonsense right now!" he complained gesturing toward the screen.

She laughed again. "If it's all nonsense, why do you even care?"

Jacque glared at her. "Don't you start with me now, too."

"Take a deep breath Jacque," she smiled as she moved down the bar to tend to other customers. "It's going to be okay."

The corner of the room brightened momentarily as the door opened and Guy entered. He stood there a moment, looking for a familiar face as his eyes adjusted from the sunlight to the standard dinginess of the bar. The Duke was crowded for the game, but he saw Jacque perched on his usual stool and headed over to him.

"Hey man," he said sitting down. "What's up?"

"Guy!" He turned to greet him. "Not much. I'm just sitting here *reading the words on the television because that stubborn prick Bear won't turn the sound on yet!*" He said the last part of his answer very clearly and loudly and looked toward Mindy. She was waiting on a customer across the bar but looked back over her shoulder and rolled her eyes at him.

Guy just shook his head. "Have you seen Tony in here today?"

Jacque looked around. "I don't think so. Maybe he got a flat on his bicycle tire."

Mindy had returned to their side of the bar. "Hey Guy." She gave Jacque a dirty look. "I think Tony's outside playing bags. MGD?"

"Yeah, thanks."

"Car trouble?" Jacque asked.

"Yeah, Bear said it's probably just loose belts. Nothing major."

"Why the fuck would you ask Bear about your car? He doesn't know anything about cars." His voice was full of irritation.

"Chill, Jacque," Guy laughed. "I didn't ask him. But we live in the same building and my car wakes up his girlfriend. He said he thought it was loose belts but that I should talk to Tony."

Jacque grunted.

"Jacque," Guy put his hand on his friend's shoulder with feigned serious-ness. Jacque looked at him. "It's going to be okay. Bear will put the sound on the game as soon as it starts." Mindy heard him and she and Guy burst out laughing.

"Fuck you. Fuck both of you." Jacque said sullenly. "A couple of fucking comedians."

"Come on, man." Guy said laughing. "You do the same thing every week. Why do you let it bother you so much?"

"Because every week I miss the beginning of the goddamn game!" he yelled and slammed his palm on the bar. A couple of people glanced over at the sound but quickly returned to their own conversations.

Guy shook his head. "I'm going to find Tony," he said, standing. In the back of the building by the parking lot, The Duke had a sizeable deck. There were some picnic tables, bags, and in the summertime, a beer bar. This afternoon the deck was crowded as people tried to soak up whatever remaining sun and warmth was left in the year. As soon as Guy stepped out the door, he heard his name.

"Guy!" Bear had called out. He was standing by the bags talking to a slightly swaying Tony. His hands filled with empty bottles and a stack of empty cups, he motioned with his head for Guy to come there. Guy nodded acknowledgment and walked over to join them.

"Here's the guy who keeps waking me up," Bear said as Guy approached them.

"You beat me to him. I just came out here to look for this guy," he said. "Hey Tony," Guy said shaking his hand.

"You two figure it out," Bear said holding up his full hands. "I'm working."

"You better get in there quick," Guy said with mock concern. "If you don't turn the sound on the game right away you might have a riot in there."

Bear looked confused for a second before it hit him. "Jacque can kiss my ass," he said and headed back inside.

"So wassup?" slurred Tony. "How you been Guy?"

"Good man. How about you? I haven't seen you in a while."

"That's cuz I don't gotta buy no gas no more!" Tony roared, laughing at his own joke. "Saving me a ton of dough, man."

Guy couldn't help laughing with him. And probably at him a little, too. "I'll bet. Stuff's not cheap."

"You know it man," he grinned. Then turning serious he asked, "Bear said you got a broken belt or something? What's the deal?"

"No," Guy corrected him. "Nothing is broken. It runs. It's just really loud in the morning when I first start it. Bear thought it might be just a loose belt."

"Yeah maybe," he thought about it. "How long does it make the noise?"

"Only until it warms up. Then nothing."

"What kind of car is it?"

"1983 Pontiac Grand Prix."

"You still driving that beast, huh? Yeah, it's probably just a belt. You gotta bring it to the shop though."

"Sure. Do you think you'll be able to look at it this week?"

"Probably. Call me tomorrow morning though. Cuz if my night goes as planned, I won't remember this conversation." Tony grinned stupidly as he steadied himself on the railing. "Right brother?" he reached out to shake Guy's hand again.

"Right on, man," Guy smiled and shook his hand. "I'll give you a call tomorrow. Thanks. Have fun Tony," he told him and turned to head back inside. *Wow*, he thought to himself, *how could anyone get that drunk that often? On a Sunday night, even. And that's the guy who's going to fix my car.*

Guy returned to his seat next to Jacque. The game had started. The music was turned off and the announcers could now be heard throughout the bar.

"Wow," Jacque exclaimed.

Guy looked up toward the television but saw only a commercial. He looked at Jacque, "Wow what?"

Jacque nodded toward the other side of the bar where Mindy was working. "Look at those things," he marveled.

There stood Michele, parts of her barely contained in her customized Bears jersey, waiting for Mindy to get her drinks.

"Yeah, that's a wow," agreed Guy. His eyes left her chest and scanned higher toward her face. "I think I know her."

"Really? She is really something, my friend."

"Yeah, wow, no kidding. I'm pretty sure I do. We went to high school together."

"No way. You look a lot older than she does. You look like shit compared to her." Jacque grinned at him. "She don't look like no thirty year-old," he continued.

"Gee thanks. Asshole. She's actually a little older than me. I think. And hey!" Guy turned toward his friend, "I ain't thirty yet."

"Yeah, yet."

"Screw you. Even when I do hit thirty, I've still got a long goddamn way to go before I catch up to you."

"You'll never catch up to me because you don't take care of yourself," Jacque smiled, hoping to piss his friend off. "You eat shitty food."

"I ate a fucking snack cake!" exclaimed Guy, throwing up his hands. "Get over it!"

Jacque just laughed. "So you know her, huh. You gonna tell me who she is?"

"I haven't seen her in years. And I don't think I've ever seen her out in a bar. I think her name is Michele. Michele Dasher or something. She married that douchebag Troy Carson."

"The Ford dealer?"

"The son. Total prick. He knocked her up in high school. But then I thought I heard they split. I don't know."

They watched her get two beers and two shots and head back toward a table along the far wall. As soon as Guy saw her sit down across from Laura he knew. "Yeah, that's gotta be her. She and Laura always hung out."

"Huh. It sure is nice to see her out now," Jacque commented before turning back to the game.

Chapter 12

Michele returned to the table clutching two long-neck bottles of Miller Lite with her left hand and two shots of Jägermeister with her right. She handed a beer to Laura and set her own on the table. Then, careful not to spill, she set the shots down, pushed one toward her friend, and sat.

Laura looked at the shot and grimaced. "Jäger?"

Michele smiled.

"I cannot stand the smell of Jägermeister," she complained.

"So don't smell it, dummy," she raised her glass toward her friend. "Drink it."

Laura hesitated, then lifted her shot to Michele's. "What are we drinking to? Marriage? Money?"

"Sure, both. To success. To having life not suck," Michele offered. "How's that?"

"Fine," Laura laughed. "All of it. Here's to marriage, money, success, and to life not sucking." They gingerly clinked their glasses together and threw back their shots. Laura banged her empty glass on the table and quickly grabbed her beer to chase the taste out of her mouth. After several gulps she set it down and shook her head quickly from side to side. "Yuck."

Michele gently set her glass down and smacked her lips, "Mmmmm. It's been too long since I've had one of those."

"Whatever. Let's get you married."

Mischief and excitement in her smile, Michele leaned in toward her friend. "Okay," she agreed. "Thank you so much for helping me. What do we do now? What's our first step?"

Laura looked around the bar. "Well, you're lucky. I don't think you are going to have a problem attracting guys. Like I said, you are getting noticed and I'm sure it's just a matter of time before you start getting hit on."

Michele looked around the room too and felt butterflies in her stomach. Was she really doing this? The Duke was filled with the noise of the TV, mixed with alternating cheers and groans, the clanking of dishes, and the jumbled drone of dozens of different conversations. There were groups of guys wearing Bears jerseys, sharing pitchers of beer and focusing on the game. They seemed to be on the younger side. There were a few couples about her age, she guessed, and older. Some tables were just a mix. She recognized a few of the faces from around town, but not too many. "So what? I just sit here now? And wait?"

"Yeah, I guess. For now anyway," Laura counseled. "It's only been thirty minutes, hon. Also, if you look around at most of the guys in here, they're watching the game. That's why they are here. If they were just here to drink and hang out on a Sunday afternoon, that's probably not someone you want to marry anyway." She paused and then sighed. "Unless of course they're rich. Then I guess it doesn't matter what they do on a Sunday afternoon. You may want them out of the house."

Michele ignored the dig. "Do you know a lot of them?" she asked.

Laura looked around again. "Yeah, or of them, I guess. And I'm pretty sure none of them are secret millionaires," she laughed.

"I said they don't have to be millionaires," Michele countered.

"Well how much then?"

"I don't know. I guess it depends on other stuff, too. Do they have kids? How old are they? I don't know."

"Well, maybe that's where we should start then," Laura suggested. "Let's set some guidelines and figure out who you are willing to be hit on by."

"Good idea! So we know money, but how much?"

"Like you said, it depends. I don't know how we can put any kind of exact number on it. It sounds like the most important things to you are being able to stay in your house and not having to go back to work."

"And vacations. I still want to be able to take Carly on vacations."

"Is that all? Are you sure there's not anything else?"

"Well," Michele hesitated.

"What?" Laura rolled her eyes. "You might as well say it."

"Well, I'd rather not have to buy a used car. I don't need a new car every year or anything, but when I do need a new car, I'd like it to be a genuinely new car."

"Okay, princess. No job, stay in house, regular vacations, and an occasional new car." She narrowed her eyes and glared at her friend. "I want you to know that if this somehow does work out for you, I am never going to feel bad about using your pool too much ever again. And I'm going to be showing up empty handed and drinking all of your wine."

"Honey, if you can help me make this happen I'll give you a key."

Laura laughed. "I already have a key!"

"Well then what do you want?"

"Nothing I guess," she said shaking her head. "I think you're realistically looking at six figures. Or close to it. Or more if he's got big child support."

"Okay."

"Now, what about deal breakers?"

"What do you mean?"

"What can you just not live with?"

Michele shrugged. "I'm not sure."

"Smoker?"

"I prefer not, but I suppose I could live with it."

"Drugs?"

"Drugs? What do you mean?"

"Do you care if he uses drugs?"

"What the hell, Laura? Are we still in high school?"

"You'd be surprised at how many people still get high."

"Really?" she paused. "I guess some pot might be okay. But I think that's gotta be it. Not like a total stoner or anything. And I'm definitely not going to marry some crack-head."

"I wouldn't worry about that. If he really does have some money, it would be coke. Not crack."

"I don't want either one!"

"Got it. Religion?"

"I guess I don't care. Church is fine, but I don't want a Jesus freak."

"Fine, no fanatics. What about Jews or Buddhists? Hindus? Muslims?"

"Come on Laura! We don't even have any of those around here!"

"Fine. Race?"

"Stop it." She looked around the room. "Do you even see anyone who isn't white?"

"Fine. Whites only."

"No! I really don't think I care."

"Got it. Divorced?"

"Don't care. As long as his ex isn't getting all of his money, I'm fine with it."

"Kids?"

"Kids? As long as they aren't little psychos, I guess. And he doesn't have like five of them or anything. Older would be great. Jesus, I don't think I want to start over again with little kids."

"What are you going to do if he's never had any of his own and he wants a couple?"

Michele's shoulders slumped. "Shit. I didn't really think about that. Oh, jeez. I don't think I want to do that again. I don't know. I just figured I was done with that, you know? I mean Carly's almost grown up and my mindset has been that I'm moving on."

"It could be big. If you don't want more kids, you need to be straight with the guy about that. I don't want any part of this if you are going to just tell the guy what he wants to hear and then 'change your mind' once he's married to you."

"No, no. I wouldn't do that. I guess I'm just not sure myself. I mean if I really love the guy…"

"Whoa there," Laura reminded her. "That love thing is not a luxury you have right now. Let's say you don't know about kids."

"Fine. What else should we consider?"

"Occupation. Do you care what he does?"

"I don't think so. As long as he makes enough money."

"Education?"

"Money's more important. I don't care."

"Pets?"

"Don't care. Within reason. I don't want a guy with like eight cats or something. Or a guy who kisses his dog on the mouth. That's gross."

"Check, no dog kissing. What about physical characteristics? Bald guys? Fat guys? Beards?"

"Preferably not all three! Bald, I don't care. Beard could be okay. As long as it's not some ZZ Top mountain man looking weirdo."

"What about fat?"

"I don't know. How fat?"

"Scooter fat," Laura laughed.

"Scooter fat? What's that?"

"You know," Laura explained. "Too fat to walk. So fat that he has to ride one of those little scooters around."

"Gross! Come on!"

"Might be good. Big, fat, unhealthy guy on a scooter might not live that long. Then you'd be set."

"No! Jesus Christ! I'm not that desperate. Yet. We can revisit that in a couple of months if necessary."

"Oh my god no! I won't let you do that!"

"Fine. No scooter fatties. I don't really want some big fat guy anyway, but I guess a little chubby could be acceptable."

"Okay. How about we say that his man-boobs can't be bigger than yours?"

Michele laughed again. "Fine. This is getting stupid."

"Not at all," Laura replied gravely. "This is important stuff, Michele. You have to set your parameters. You have to know this. You don't have that much time to be wasting on the wrong guys."

"Alright," she rolled her eyes. "Continue."

"Tattoos?"

"Not on the neck. Or his hands. I hate those!"

"Anal?"

Michele's eyes widened as she choked on her beer and began to cough. "What?!" she exclaimed.

"Anal," Laura repeated. "Are you willing to let him in the back door?" she asked, fighting to remain serious.

"Oh my god!"

"You sound excited. So that's a yes?"

"What?! No! I don't know! Why the hell are you asking me that?!"

Laura leaned in. "You gotta know this stuff. You've been out of the scene for a long time. That's like third date type stuff nowadays. You think about it while I go get us another beer."

Mouth agape, Michele just stared at her friend. Laura got up to get the drinks, but saw her frozen, panicked expression and stopped. "Hey. Relax. I'm kidding," she grinned.

Michele resumed breathing and shook her head. "You suck."

Laura smiled, laughed, and left to get two more beers.

When she returned, Michele took a sip. "I think this whole thing just might be a nightmare. Did we even resolve anything?" she asked.

"Ummm, that you want to marry a rich guy?"

Michele sighed. "I guess that's really the only thing right now."

"Yeah, I suppose when you have several rich guys lined up and fighting over you, then you can start to be a little pickier," Laura responded sarcastically.

Michele smirked at her friend. "Funny." She turned her chair a bit so she could take in more of The Duke and its patrons. "So, you know these people? Any possibilities in here today?"

"I don't think so. I'll start with the bar. Starting at the corner closest to us."

"Got it."

"That's Bill and Phil."

"Schmidt? Wow! I remember them from high school. They're cousins, right?"

"Yep. And they're both still single. They each took over their families' farms. I don't have any idea how much farmers make. But I do know they have not both had a legal driver's license at the same time in years. I think they take turns getting DUIs."

"Move on."

"I don't know the next guy, but the guy next to him drives a truck for Thelen Gravel, I think."

"Not enough money there."

"Okay, then you have two Ballard brothers. Plenty of money from their dad's business. They both work there. The older one is married and the younger one is closer to Carly's age than yours."

"Keep going."

"I don't know them, I don't know them. I know those women though. Are you open to lesbianism?"

"Are they really lesbians?" Michele whispered with surprise.

"I have no idea. Maybe you could turn them. Wait, never mind. Neither one really has any money anyway."

"Come on," she complained. "This is serious."

"Fine. That's Guy from the Gas and Go. Single, nice, but I'm sure that working at a gas station doesn't pay that much. Next to him is Jacque. He owns Not Your Average Bakery! and lives in the apartment above it. Single too. And a bit older. I don't know what bakers make."

"I remember Guy. He was always nice. Too bad he's broke. The baker guy? Tiny apartment? Too bad. He's cute in a weird sort of way. Skip the next group. Two of them work with Troy and one used to. The one who used to has some money. He was a finance guy, but he's married. Neither of the other two makes enough money. And besides, one of them's an asshole."

"I suppose if he's hanging out with Troy, he must be some kind of asshole. Okay. The last group is with their wives. That's it for the bar."

"Depressing."

"Not totally. There's a couple decent looking guys there. We just don't know if they're single or if they have any money."

"I suppose. And we do have the rest of the bar to check out." Just then Bear walked by with his hands full of empties. "I remember Bear! He's hot.

What's his deal? I don't suppose he bought this place…"

"Bear? No. I think he runs it for his uncle or something. I don't know. Single though. Well, not married anyway. I think he might have a girlfriend now."

"Are we even doing this the right way? I mean are we just going to meet here and go through everyone?"

"No. You're right," Laura agreed. "Look. It's Sunday afternoon. It's crowded in here, but it's all for the game. And once the game ends, this place will empty out right away. It's not really the right time anyway."

They both took a drink and considered their challenge.

"I kind of have a list going in my head. But I don't even know if the guys on it are available or have any money."

"That's a start. Who's on it?"

"There's a few guys from high school. A couple of other parents I see at school stuff. A super-hot guy I visited with once at the grocery store."

"Oh yeah? Who's the grocery store guy? What's his name?"

"I don't know. I don't even know his name. But he didn't have a ring on."

Laura laughed at her friend. "Nice. So what are you going to do, go buy a half-gallon of milk every day at random times until you run into him again?"

"I don't know. He was gorgeous. And really nice. Don't make fun of me!"

"Sorry. Maybe the list isn't a bad idea though. Maybe we should each make a list. Actual people though, with actual names. No random handsome strangers."

"Okay. And what about occupations? I was thinking about what kinds of jobs actually make enough money."

"That's a good idea, too. Why don't we do that? Let's brainstorm names and jobs this week. Write them down. I'll make Ron stay home with the kids Friday so we can go out."

"Cool. We'll need to compare lists before we go out though."

"Yeah. I'll try to come over to your house early. We can have a drink and go over what we each came up with."

"Alright! I think we have a plan!"

Chapter 13

Once Dan left, Sophie stood, distracted but polite, pretending to pay attention while Frannie disclosed all of the problems she'd had with him during Sophie's absence. How he did this wrong and that wrong and how she had to wait for her medicine and how he stayed downstairs and how he wasn't very pleasant and he spent too much time on his phone. What made him think he was so important that he needed to be on his phone all of the time anyway? It's not like he had a wife or kids to worry about. And she was sure his job didn't need him. And on and on. Sophie had learned to just play along. Frannie tolerated no defense of her incompetent children.

After what seemed like an eternity, the old woman's complaints tapered off and Sophie was able to verify that she was settled for the moment. Immediately excusing herself, she flew down the stairs to retrieve her letter. Even without the return address, the penmanship gave it away. It was from Abby, of course. Although the girlish, looping handwriting on the outside of the envelope belied her nineteen years, it always reminded Sophie of that too-brief time they had spent together when Abby was so young.

It was years ago, and she'd been living with a couple just outside of Waterloo, Iowa at the time. She remembered learning that she was going to be getting another sister. Sixteen at the time, Sophie wasn't looking forward to the power struggles that typically accompanied the sharing of a small bedroom with another hardened veteran of multiple placements. When she heard the door and the voices, Sophie put on her game face and went downstairs to meet her newest challenger. But there was no challenger, only Abby. Four years old, scared, sad, and shy, she stood next to her worn, pink backpack holding a gray and matted stuffed bunny. Dark curly hair spilled into her face and she kept her head low as if trying to hide her eyes behind it. Sophie was struck dumb at the sight of her. All of the confusion, fear, and anxiety in Abby's eyes had been in her own years ago. She sat on the stairs across the room, staring as the social worker explained that this was the first time she was being placed.

Sophie's ears perked up. She hated the language of foster care, especially that word: placed. Things got placed and misplaced, not people. It was so impersonal, like she was an object that someone needed to get out of the way. Foster kids got placed in foster homes. All her life, social workers had found placements for her. It was a constant reminder that there was no natural place for her, for Sophie Ross. Nowhere she truly belonged. Adults were always trying to figure out where she should be, always trying to find something that would work. And always, in their forced enthusiasm about the new placement, Sophie sensed their relief at being able to cross her off their to-do list. That was the other part of the system. So many adults worked hard to get to know the kids, to make them feel comfortable, and then they left them, or their file got passed to someone new. Over and over and over. All of this—her past and the little girl's future—blurred together as she sat there watching Abby, a knot forming in her stomach as she imagined the life that lay ahead of the little girl.

The grownups introduced them to each other and asked Sophie to take her upstairs, show her around, and tell her where she could put her few possessions. As they went up together, Sophie was suddenly aware that she was sounding like almost every adult she had encountered in her own life. She was gentle, she was friendly, she sounded positive, and she was asking Abby questions as she tried to make her comfortable and get her to talk a little bit. And none of that was bad, but it was always so goddamn temporary. That type of fleeting kindness just left scars and built calluses when the nice people all eventually moved on.

In that little bedroom with the low ceiling, they sat on the twin beds across from each other, Sophie's bare feet on the wood floor and Abby's little legs dangling off the edge.

"Do you have any brothers or sisters?" Sophie asked.

Abby kept her eyes lowered and slowly shook her head no.

"I don't either. But I always wanted to have a sister," she confessed. "I thought it would be really neat to have someone else to help me out, to look out for me and stuff." She could see Abby was listening. "And if I had a sister, I would do the same for them, too. Keep an eye on them and make sure they were okay, you know? Don't you think that would be cool?"

The little girl nodded slightly.

Sophie waited a moment before she spoke again. "You know what?" she asked. "I just had an idea. Since you're going to be living here and we'll even be sharing this room, maybe you could be my sister and help keep an eye on me and stuff."

Abby lifted her head a little and peered out through her curls at Sophie.

"And I promise I'll do the same for you. Like if you have questions or if you're ever scared or anything, you can talk to me and I will do whatever I can to help you out." *And I won't disappear on you*, she thought. "What do you think, Abby? Should we be sisters and help each other out?"

It was fifteen years ago that Abby nodded her head yes. As much as Sophie had promised Abby, she had also promised herself. She was determined that the little girl sitting across from her was not going to spend her life bouncing through the system without someone to hold on to. She was going to be there for her and be someone she could actually count on. She was going to be the big sister that she, herself, never had.

It was less than a year later that Sophie received a new placement and they were separated. But through letters, phone calls, and email once they had it, they kept in close contact. Whenever there was any semblance of a problem, either with Abby's foster family or even during the disastrous few months when Abby's mom was paroled and took her back, Sophie was on the phone with social services, threatening, bullying, charming, lying, whatever it took. After she graduated high school and was working and able to afford a car, it was easier to visit. She sent her birthday and Christmas presents and Abby sent her pictures she drew.

By the time Abby started high school, Sophie had been a caregiver for almost six years and had determined that her little sister needed to have the opportunities she hadn't had. That meant college, and so she saved whatever money she could. It was the only thing that kept her in this line of work that so mirrored her childhood. When she started out and was working with an agency, they even referred to jobs as placements. Now in her thirties, Sophie was still moving from one person's house to the next. She stayed, for a time, in the spare rooms, the extra spaces they had available. And when she arrived, they moved boxes and other things out of the way so there could be, yet again, a temporary place for her.

As Abby grew older and her focus shifted to friends and boyfriends, Sophie's work stretched into Illinois, the visits became less frequent, and the flow of mail slowed. The last time she actually saw her in person was at her high school graduation. For the entire year leading up to it, Sophie told her employers that she would need that time off. Driving back to Iowa for the ceremony, she could not have been prouder. When she bought coffee and filled her car with gas in Rockford, the cashier told her to have a good weekend. She thanked him and said that she would because she was going to her sister's high school graduation. At a café outside of Dubuque, where she stopped for lunch, she managed to let her waitress know that, once she graduated, her sister would be going to college in Sioux City and was going to major in psychology.

Now, a year and a half later, Sophie stood in Frannie's kitchen clutching her letter. Waiting to open it, she retreated to the one place where she knew she wouldn't be bothered. There was an unspoken truce between Frannie and Sophie while she was in the bathroom, which was only broken in times of great need. If, however, she ever sat down anywhere else to apply new nail polish, read, or write to Abby, Frannie was guaranteed to appear and be in sudden need of her help. Not with a big project, but just enough of a task to disrupt her. In the bathroom, however, she could lose herself for an entire hour with no interruptions and had learned to take full advantage of this.

Savoring the anticipation of news from her sister, she decided to wait to read it. Sophie closed the door to the bathroom, set the still sealed envelope on the corner of the sink, and took a long, hot shower. When she was done, she dried off and put on her robe as she thought about Abby's last letter from a couple of months ago. She had been excited about starting back at school and being out of the dorms. Along with two other girls, she was renting an apartment somewhere off campus. There was no boyfriend currently in the picture and Sophie was happy about that. She'd rather have her concentrating on school. Abby was worried about expenses. She'd been working all summer at a little restaurant but had some bad luck with her car and much of the money she'd made went toward that. Sophie had been happy she was able to send her a little extra money with her fall tuition.

Finally ready to read her letter, she made herself comfortable on the plush little bathroom rug in front of the sink and sat with her back leaning against the door. She held the envelope vertically and tapped it on her knee so that the notepaper inside shifted. Then, taking care not to damage the contents, Sophie tore off one end, reached in, and removed the treasure.

Abby started off by asking how she was doing and if she was still with Frannie the Grouch in the tiny little antique town. She hoped that she was getting nicer and said she didn't understand how anyone couldn't love her big sister. Sophie smiled and kept reading. She wrote about her classes. They were challenging and there was so much reading, but she felt like she was learning a lot and enjoying it. Work was going well. She was still part-time at Grumpy's, but she felt like that was enough. Between her job and school, she was very busy. The new apartment was good, even though utilities were more expensive than they planned. The girls were all getting along well. There were other students in the building and they had made friends with some of them. One of the guys from the apartment downstairs, Jake, was apparently very cute. They'd hung out together a couple of times with her roommates and his, and Abby thought they really hit it off well. She was definitely interested in him and hoped it was mutual. Lastly, Abby brought up Thanksgiving break. She wrote that she had been planning to make a road trip and visit her but was disappointed that she didn't think she could anymore. Between the extra utilities and an expensive graphing calculator for her statistics class, money was just too tight. She had decided that she was going to stay in Sioux City and pick up some extra shifts at work.

Sophie's shoulders slumped in disappointment when she read that last part. It would have been so special to be able to spend the holiday with her. But, she thought as she reread the letter, she was also very proud. She was working and keeping up with school. And if money was tight, Abby was doing the responsible thing, the right thing. Even before that very first time that Sophie had been forced to move away from her, they talked about being separated. She explained to her that it was never fun, but sisters were still sisters, even when they were apart. Seeing each other every day was not as important as having that other person looking out for you and knowing that they were thinking about you and that they loved you.

Chapter 14

"I hate this," Jacque complained. "One first down! They couldn't get one goddamn first down!"

Guy nodded and sipped his beer. Tampa Bay had the ball at the Bears forty-nine-yard line and the clock was stopped with 0:23 left in the game. Chicago was clinging to a 26-24 lead. The last two minutes of the fourth quarter had been more exciting than the whole rest of the game. Tampa was driving against a tired Bears defense. They kept chipping away, and The Duke let out a collective groan with every new first down. It was looking like the Bucs would score and take the lead with no real time left for the Bears to respond. But then, a Bears defender punched the ball out of the running back's grip and one of his teammates emerged with it from the bottom of the ensuing pileup. Chicago had recovered. That should have sealed the victory because they should have been able to run out the clock. Tampa was already out of time-outs and if the Bears had been able to get a single first down, they could have simply taken a knee a couple of times, watched the remaining seconds tick away, and headed to the locker room with the win. But, like Jacque lamented, they couldn't and were forced to punt it away. The return was as good as the punt was bad and now Tampa was already close to field goal range.

"I can't sit," Jacque announced and stood behind his barstool. "They're going to blow this game. They should have just run the goddamn ball right up the middle for the first down! But no, they always have to get cute and it never fucking works!"

Similar conversations spilled into each other around the bar. Then the

Bucs QB dropped back and threw right down the middle to a wide-open tight end at the 36-yard line. He was tackled immediately, but Tampa was still able to get to the line and spike the ball with 0:02 left. A chorus of profanity erupted throughout The Duke. Tampa would have a chance to kick a game-winning field goal.

"Dammit!" Jacque barked and turned away from the TV. "I knew it! How the hell is that guy left so wide open?! How?!"

"He's not going to make it, Jacque," Guy offered trying to calm his friend. "It's a 53 yard try. It's way too windy out there."

Jacque glared at Guy. "Don't try to calm me down. It's not that windy." He stood, hands on the back of his stool, staring at the big screen. "Come on! Block it! Miss it!" he urged.

The kick was up. The Duke held its breath and watched the ball arc down the field end over end. Straight and true, it sailed through the uprights and over the crossbar as time expired. But just as the deflated, anguished groans of the patrons were reaching a crescendo, before Jacque could even sneer at Guy with "See! I knew it," the clamor rose into cheers of relief and joy. The Bears had called their last time-out just before the snap. That meant that the play didn't actually count. Tampa would have to kick it again.

"Too windy my ass!" Jacque scolded Guy.

Guy laughed. "Relax, Jacque. It didn't count anyway."

"That's not the point! It wasn't too windy. That's a makeable field goal for that guy. He made that easy!"

"Ehhh, he won't make two in a row," Guy consoled. "The Bears are going to hang on."

"Don't even talk to me right now. You don't know shit."

The time-out over, Tampa lined up for another attempt. Again, The Duke inhaled and held its breath. This time though, as soon as the ball left the kicker's foot it was clearly low and wide. He shanked it. On the field, in the stands, and in The Duke, fans and players loudly raised their arms in triumph, rejoicing as the Tampa kicker hung his head and made his lonely way off the field.

"They can never do anything easy," Jacque observed as he returned to his seat. "I'll have one more please, Mindy," he gestured to the bartender with his mostly empty glass and turned to Guy. "And then I am done."

"I guess I'll have one more too," Guy called out to her.

She returned with their beers and Guy raised his to Jacque. "Here's to another uninspiring win in another uninspiring season."

Jacque clinked his bottle against Guy's but frowned as he drank. "What's the matter with you, man?"

Guy shrugged. "Nothing's the matter. What do you mean?"

"You're bleh. You're a slug."

"I'm fine. What are you talking about?"

"That was a great game, man. An ugly one, maybe, but it was exciting there at the end."

Guy shrugged, "Yeah?"

"That's exactly what I'm talking about! Since when do you just not give a shit? You sat there at the end like nothing. Like you absolutely didn't give a shit either way. Win or lose, whatever."

Guy shrugged again, "Okay?"

"That's not you, man! Where's the fire? What the hell? You just sit there. That's not my guy, Guy!" he looked at his friend.

Guy turned and tipped his beer back, "I don't know. I'm just tired I guess."

"That is bullshit, my friend. You're tired all the time lately. Something's goin' on." Jacque turned away toward the bar to sip his beer and waited. The two friends sat side by side in silence and stared straight ahead as the crowd in The Duke began to dissipate. Jacque knew he had struck a nerve and backed off a bit. In the couple of years since he moved to Richmond to open Not Your Average Bakery! and they started hanging out, Guy hadn't exactly been an open book about his personal life. Jacque assumed he had his reasons and didn't pry. He waited a couple of minutes, then leaned over toward Guy and said with false concern, "I hope Bear's okay."

Guy came out of his trance, and puzzled, looked at Jacque, "Why? What happened?" he asked.

"Well, the game's been over for almost five minutes and he still hasn't killed the sound on the TV and cranked up that shitty music."

Guy stared at his friend. Jacque wore a stupid, expectant grin on his face as he waited for Guy's reaction. That in itself was enough to bring a smile to Guy's face. "You're a freak," he chuckled. "I'm glad you at least have a sense of humor about it now."

"It's easy now. Game's over." He drained his beer and stood up, "and the Bears won."

"Speaking of Bears winning, I sold another one of Bear's bears just before I left today." Guy emptied his bottle and looked around The Duke.

"Seriously, man?" Jacque asked. "Who the hell buys those stupid things?"

"Hey now, Jacque," Bear scolded as came up behind them and put a hand on each of their shoulders. "There are plenty of people out there who appreciate fine art." He emphasized the words fine art and winked at Guy.

Jacque's hands went to his temples and he closed his eyes as if wincing. He took a deep breath and addressed Bear firmly and slowly. "Your bears are not art. And you are not a fucking artist."

"I don't know man," replied Bear easily, "I created 'em, people buy 'em, and they display 'em just like works of art."

"No. No," Jacque's frustration was clear. "You didn't create them. You made them. Those bears are a craft. You are a crafter. Crafters and hacks like you, you craft things. You make crude copies of other people's creations. You, yourself, do not create. You make. In fact, I don't know if you ever had an original fucking idea in your life. Except for maybe the idea that you are actually an artist."

Guy played along, "I don't know, Jacque. Those people who ponied up the money for one just today asked me if I was the artist. I told them no, but that the artist was a friend of mine."

"Fuck those people!" Jacque scowled at both of them. "Here's the difference you meatheads: Artists create. They create original works of art. Their artwork has a message. Their art speaks. And it says things other than 'Welcome to the Cabin' or 'Welcome to the Fucking Lakehouse.' Bear is a crafter because he makes the same fucking bears over and over and over and it wasn't even his idea to begin with. Now the guy who created that first bear might have been an artist, I don't know. If he's still alive, he is probably weeping about what you have done to those poor fucking bears."

Bear and Guy smiled at each other and let Jacque continue.

"Don't get me wrong, man, you got some skill. Those are some fine bears you craft. But Jesus fucking Christ, stop calling yourself a goddamn artist! If you want to be an artist, take your skills, use your talents, and try creating something. Make something other than a kitschy fucking cabin bear!"

"Like what?" Bear asked. "A cabin moose?" He and Guy burst out laughing.

"You go ahead, laugh it up," Jacque replied smiling now. "The artist and his agent, hawking their fine art on the corner at the fucking gas station." He made quotation marks with his hands when he said fine art. Then he bowed to them and then said, "Fuck both of you gentlemen. I'll see you next week. I'm going home."

They both said so long to Jacque and then Guy asked Bear, "So you heard that? You sold another bear."

"Sweet. What size?"

"$375 size. I took my cut and put the money in one of your envelopes and stashed it. Stop by tomorrow and I'll get it for you."

"Cool, thanks. I gotta go by there anyway and pick up my remaining 'works of art.' That's gonna be it for the year. Damn good year, too. That was my record," Bear reflected.

"Oh yeah? I guess I'm not surprised. It seemed like they were moving out of there pretty steadily all summer long."

"Yeah, a lot of the bigger ones, too. I love selling those guys. I call them retirement bears."

"Retirement bears?"

"Well you know what I get for 'em. That money goes right toward my retirement. I usually end up spending part of what I make on the smaller ones, but not those big bastards. Every dime I sell those for goes right into my IRA." Bear could see Guy doing some math in his head and smiled and nodded, "Yeah, dude. It adds up, doesn't it?"

Bear had been selling his cabin bears on the corner of the Gas and Go for almost as long as Guy had been working there. Say ten years. He got two grand for the big ones. How many a summer? Five? Ten? Ten seemed high. Say seven maybe? Jesus, that was still $14,000 a year. Cash. No taxes. Saved. Over ten years, with interest?

"Holy shit, Bear!" Guy's mouth was agape.

"Tell me about it," Bear grinned. "Don't say nothing though. I don't want Big John demanding a bigger cut. That's why I don't mind Jacque running his mouth about me not being an artist. I really don't give a shit. When I'm able to retire, which I figure should be around fifty, I'm gonna get a cabin way up north on a little lake somewhere with nobody else around. And I'm gonna make one last huge-ass bear. It's going to be holding a giant sign that reads 'Private Property: Fuck Off.' And that one, even Jacque's gonna have to admit, will be a work of art!"

Chapter 15

For the second time that day, Sophie found herself examining the contents of someone else's refrigerator in an effort to satisfy her hunger. Her disappointment with its meager stores was compounded by the degrading necessity of the task. With her son gone, Frannie had turned her attention toward Sophie. She recognized her high spirits and excitement about hearing from her sister and immediately started in, trying to chip away at it. Despite the wonderful letter, Sophie's mood degenerated back into the negativity of her early morning wake-up. The sparsely stocked fridges, Bear's bed, the lack of sleep, the lack of coffee, and the mattress on the floor upstairs were all reminders of her dependency. She was stuck. For now, anyway. On good days, she took deep breaths and reminded herself that it wouldn't be like this forever. That someday she would have a home of her own, her own place. That what she was doing was important, that her sister was depending on her, that it would all be worth it. On bad days, it was more difficult. She worried about Abby and her school. She worried about her next job. She worried about her age. She worried about keeping her current job. She worried about her status with Bear. She worried that it would never work out for her and she worried whether or not she was even doing the right thing.

Sophie grabbed the apple juice, bread, and cheese and set them on the counter. In the pantry she found one of the many cans of Campbell's tomato soup that would accompany the grilled cheese sandwich. In the bitchy, passive aggressive way that she had so mastered, Frannie asked her, "Will we be eating at five o'clock this evening? Or have you decided to surprise me again with a change in my schedule?"

Shortly after Sophie began working for Frannie, before she met Bear, she had passed her Saturday nights off mostly in her car. There had been a thunderstorm one evening and her sleep was fitful. Back at work the following afternoon, she dozed off on the couch. As a result, Frannie's dinner was delayed until almost five-thirty. Though Frannie rarely missed an opportunity to bring it up or complain about it, Sophie knew what was really going on. She had already decided that her mistake was perhaps one of the nicest gifts she could have given her. Frannie had been treasuring that small injustice for months. Although Sophie understood how much joy her indiscretion had brought her employer, she was careful not to present her with another.

She assured Frannie that her dinner would be ready promptly at five o'clock. Another grilled cheese sandwich and cup of tomato soup coming right up, she thought. Didn't that woman ever get sick of this meal? Grabbing a plate out of the cupboard, she longed for the days of grocery shopping without a list, the simple pleasure of walking up and down the aisles and filling her cart with whatever she wanted. She'd had jobs where she was given free rein to buy the groceries for herself and her "patient." That typically happened when the person's mind was fading, but they were physically still healthy. If the family had more money than time, necessity forced them into trusting Sophie. In cases like that, she worked very hard not to betray that trust. Even though the work was much more physically demanding, it was worth it because she was able to make so many more decisions on her own. She could be more independent.

This was not the case with Frannie. She was failing physically. Her mind was still very sharp, but her body was falling apart and shutting down. She never perceived Sophie as a valuable assistant. Instead, she saw her as a constant reminder of her own physical deterioration, of her weakness. Sophie represented her unwanted dependency and looming mortality, and as a result, her presence was only grudgingly accepted and continually resented.

An additional challenge for Sophie was that Frannie was the one with all of the money. Had it been her children who were supporting her and paying Sophie's wages, some of the bitchiness might have been mitigated by gratitude. No such luck. For Frannie, money was a source of power and control. And over the years it had also bequeathed to her ample measures of arrogance, entitlement, condescension, and pettiness. Sophie's responsibilities as a live-in caretaker were many, but they didn't consume her every waking moment. It grated on Frannie to see Sophie sitting on the couch reading a book or writing a letter. When the kitchen was clean and the laundry was put away and Sophie took time for herself, Frannie stewed. She wasn't able to reconcile that one of the reasons she was paying Sophie was simply for her to be available in case she was needed. So, she would nitpick, shuffling through the house looking for little tasks that she just needed a hand with, just for a moment. Sophie obliged these continual interruptions stoically. She knew Frannie's game and she knew fighting it would only jeopardize her position.

As Sophie took the toast and cheese out of the oven and turned off the broiler, she considered her life at Frannie's. It will be tough to mourn this woman's passing, she thought. Still though, it was a job. What a strange little underground she participated in. Cash only. And not a bad amount, at first glance. But no taxes also meant she wasn't paying anything into social security. There was no retirement plan, no 401k. No vacation days or sick days, and no health insurance. No stability either. She found her first gig when she was back in Iowa. It got her out from behind the bar and out of town, away from a bad situation. And then it seemed like the best way she could help Abby. Because she always received room and board, Sophie was able to minimize her living expenses. That made it easier for her to put away money for her sister's tuition.

It was hard for Sophie to believe that her Abby was already a sophomore in college, but she was also very grateful. All the years of moving around was wearing her down, but it finally felt like the finish line was in sight. Two and a half more years, she reminded herself. In January, she'd been near the end of a six-month job in Pecatonica. Then she spent three months in Stillman Valley. And now it had been about four months here in Richmond.

Before that was Rock Falls and a bunch of smaller towns on either side of the Mississippi. They all ran together in her mind. She was good at what she did, had excellent references, and, as far as anyone knew, she was also a certified nursing assistant. She rarely had trouble finding her next job.

Her role was primarily related to Frannie's health. She made sure that prescriptions were taken and refilled and was always available in the case of an emergency. Driving her to doctor appointments or to the drug store as needed was required as well. Other responsibilities were more fluid. She had been buying the groceries and other household supplies per Frannie's precise specifications. And she drove her to the beauty parlor once a week to get her hair done. Sophie usually prepared meals, washed the dishes, and did the laundry. Washing windows, scrubbing floors, raking leaves—that stuff was different. She was not a housekeeper, but she did keep the house as clean as if it were her own. Even though she'd never had her own.

Dinner was ready at two minutes before five and she went to tell Frannie. Just as she reached the top of the stairs, the old woman emerged from her room.

"I'm coming, I'm coming," she acknowledged Sophie.

"No hurry, Mrs. Bowers," Sophie smiled politely. "I just finished making it." She moved toward the top of the stairs and waited for Frannie to approach and grip the railings on either side. The stairs were old and steep, and she was a stubborn woman who resented any offers of help. Sophie's job was to hold tight to both railings as well but descend just a couple steps ahead of her. That way, if she stumbled, her fall could be arrested by running into Sophie's body. Dan had perfected this and showed her. It was important, he said, that his mother not catch on. Sophie agreed. The woman certainly didn't need anything new to complain about. She slowly walked down the steps, careful not to look back and careful not to get too far ahead. Once they were both safely on the main floor, she led the way into the kitchen and sat across from her at the little table.

Because it was affirmation rather than conversation that Frannie sought, dinner was the usual soliloquy of gossip and griping. In-between bites of sandwich and sips of soup, she droned on about her family, her neighbors, her aches and pains, and the current celebrity dramas being played out in her magazines. Sophie had learned that minor questions for clarification were tolerated, along with appropriate reactions of surprise or disappointment or whatever. It was always simpler if she just mirrored Frannie's emotions. She did so and was polite, but her mind drifted away to thoughts of being done with this life. Two and a half more years, she reminded herself, and Abby would graduate college. Two and a half more years and Sophie could stop having to pretend to care about nonsense like this. Two and a half more years and she could finally begin her own life.

Chapter 16

Bear woke up late Monday morning to an empty apartment. With Sophie having vanished for another six days, he was able to catch up on some of the sleep he missed out on Saturday night. It wasn't too long after the last football game ended on Sunday that The Duke had cleared out. Bear let Mindy close up without him and headed home. Now, he rolled out of bed, took a leak, and went into the kitchen. Damn. Still a mess. And still hardly any food. Last night he'd gone home, undressed and crashed without really paying attention to anything. He was hoping that Sophie would have cleaned up their breakfast dishes, but no such luck. Bear couldn't blame her though. I guess it is time to clean this place up a bit and get some groceries, he thought, and I even have some cash waiting for me at the Gas and Go. After throwing a jacket on over some fairly clean clothes, Bear headed out the door into the wet and cold. The season of thunderstorms had passed. Instead of a cloudburst, rain drizzled steadily down from a low gray sky that seemed to hint at the winter ahead. Before going to retrieve his bears and collect his money from Guy, Bear stopped by the Kozy Kitchen for a quick breakfast, some coffee, and the local news.

On the opposite edge of town as The Duke, the Kozy Kitchen had been there as long as Bear could remember. And it hadn't changed in all that time. It had a small room with a dozen tables and a long countertop with about as many stools. Up high in the corner, at one end of it, an old tube television with a bad picture remained on either cable news or Chicago sports all day. The regulars, mostly retired, semi-retired, or perpetually in-between jobs, idled away their mornings sipping coffee, gossiping, and commenting on the news. Bear found an open stool—more tape than upholstery—said his hellos, sat down, and joined them. By the time his breakfast arrived, he'd heard the headlines, sports, weather, and an analysis of how the rainy week would affect the fall colors. The county had approved funds for replacing the bridge over the Nippersink Creek out on North Solon Road. Work would start in the spring and there would have to be a detour around it for most of the summer. There was some concern that the current high school quarterback might be colorblind. Even though the Rockets won, he'd thrown three interceptions. And finally, it was going to be rainy most of the week, but should clear for the weekend, and there might be a bit of an Indian summer still to come. The only consensus reached on the influence of the rain on the color of the leaves was that it would affect it somehow. Bear did more listening than talking, finished up, and left to retrieve his bears and his money.

As he pulled out of the parking lot back onto Route 12, the lone active Richmond Police car pulled in. Bear checked his rearview mirror to confirm it was stopping, grinned and then hit the gas. Ever since high school, when one of his friends figured out that there was only one patrol car on duty at a time on weekdays, speeding through town had been kind of a ritual. If you were at one end of town and you saw the cop either parked or heading the opposite direction, you were free to floor it. Although the thrill had faded over the years, old habits died hard. It was almost out of a feeling of obligation that Bear took advantage of the situation. Downtown amongst the antiques, the speed limit dropped all the way to twenty for a stretch. He decided that fifty was a much more reasonable pace on a morning like this.

After zipping through town, Bear turned into the parking lot of the Gas and Go and backed up near his battered trailer and his bears. The only reason he even had any of them for sale in October was because of Columbus Day. The three-day weekend combined with a decent weather forecast was reason enough to run a couple out there and see if he could catch someone making a last pilgrimage through town for the year. And it had worked. Lots of people, it seemed, had made the drive north just to drive some more and enjoy the beauty of the changing leaves. He climbed out and hitched the battered trailer to his truck before unlocking the door and loading up the two smaller bears. Then he headed inside to collect his money and see if Guy could give him a hand with the big one.

"Hey Guy," he called over the jangling of the bell as he entered the little store.

"Mornin' Bear." Guy looked to the Miller High Life clock over the door. "This is more like it for you. I take it my car didn't wake you this morning?"

"Never wakes me," he reminded him, "only the girlfriend. But I'm solo again for the week so you're okay. Tony gonna look at it?"

"Yeah, I called him today. And he did actually remember talking to me yesterday!"

"Yeah," Bear observed. "Tony seemed to be taking it easy for Tony yesterday. He was gone before I left and I didn't even close."

"Well, maybe that's because he has a busy week. He said he can't even get me in to look at it until Thursday afternoon."

"No problem. Just so it's done by the weekend. Man's got certain needs you know…"

Guy rolled his eyes and laughed. "Whatever. You here for your money?"

"You know it. I got big plans for it, too."

"Oh, yeah?" Guy asked fishing around under the counter for the worn envelope. He located it, took out the cash, started to give it to Bear.

"Yeah. I'm thinking about getting a tank of gas and some groceries," Bear laughed. "Hang on to $50. I'll pump it after I get loaded up," he said.

"Wow, impressive! That still leaves you a lot of dough for groceries though. You going to buy a bunch of nice steaks or what?"

"Definitely or what. If I bought steaks then I'd have to cook 'em too. Then there'd be dishes and cleaning and stuff. Nah, I'll probably get some Cheerios and a couple of frozen pizzas. I pretty much eat at The Duke or the Kitchen these days. I suppose I'll just have to fatten up my IRA a little more with the leftovers."

Guy nodded his approval. "Keep doing that and you'll be making that giant 'fuck you bear' before you know it."

"I can hardly wait. Hey, you think you could give me a quick hand loading that big one into the trailer?"

Guy took a look out at the gas pumps. "Sure. Looks like the coast is clear for a couple minutes. How hard is it raining?"

Bear shook his head, "It's not. It's just kind of misting, really."

"Alright, let's go."

They headed out to Bear's trailer. Bear stood inside of it, reached up to the top of the statue's head, and tipped it back toward him. Once it was almost horizontal, Guy grunted as he picked up the base and moved it in the rest of the way.

"Man, those are heavy," he observed as Bear climbed out and closed the doors.

"Yeah they are. I can usually muscle them around when I need to, but they get slick when they're wet. People don't care if they are weathered, but they don't want 'em all banged up." Bear locked the trailer and patted it with his hand. "Go to sleep bears, it's hibernation time."

"I'm jealous. Think there's room in there for me? What do you say, Bear? Wake me up at the end of March?" Guy asked.

"Not a chance," he shook his head. "I say goodnight to them at The Duke," he motioned with his thumb over his shoulder to the bar just down the road behind him, "and you say good morning to them here at the Gas and Go." He pointed behind Guy to the little convenience store. "It's been that way for a long time now and you know how these small town folks handle change. It'd be chaos with one of us gone."

"I suppose," Guy sighed. "But one of these days..."

"I hear you, man."

Bear swung his truck around to get his gas as Guy headed inside.

Back behind the counter, Guy set the pump to stop at $50 and watched as the red LED lights raced toward it. *So, he's putting extra money into his IRA,* he thought. *Extra money? I wonder what the hell that would feel like. Maybe I would put it in my IRA, too. If I even had an IRA.*

Just then, a brand new, bright blue Ford F-150 pulled up at the gas pump across from Bear. Big silver letters painted on the driver's side door read

Schmidt Farms. Fuck me, thought Guy. Bill was driving and his passenger was, of course, his cousin Phil. He watched as they both climbed out and visited with Bear as he returned the nozzle and screwed his gas cap back on. They gestured at the truck together, nodding. Bill and Phil grinned proudly. Bill opened the hood and the three of them admired the engine. Then they walked around the other side. Bear was encouraged to sit in the cab and he did. Finally, Bear shook their hands, patted Phil on the back, climbed into his truck, and left the Gas and Go.

Bill started filling their new truck up with gas and Phil climbed back inside the cab. When it finally reached nearly twenty-nine gallons, Bill shut it off and came inside. "Mornin' Guy," he greeted him cheerfully.

"Hey, Bill," Guy forced a smile. "How's farming these days?" he asked, gesturing toward the new truck.

Bill's smile widened. "Oh, can't complain," he answered and looked out fondly at it. "Just picked her up this morning over at Carson's Ford. We bought her last week, but they give us a deal on putting our name on the door like that. Whaddya think?" he asked as he handed Guy the Schmidt Farms credit card.

"Looks good with the silver on the blue. They did a nice job."

"I like it. That was Phil's call. I let him pick colors since he's gotta wait about six more months before he's even allowed to drive it off the farm."

Guy handed Bill the charge slip to sign. "Well, he made a good choice. You can tell him I said so."

Bill signed and returned the Schmidt Farms credit card to his wallet. "I will do that. You take care, Guy." And he left.

Guy stepped outside to have a cigarette. *This is what I have to show for my twenties,* he thought. Sitting in the chair by the Coke machine, he glanced over at the piece of shit car he could barely afford to keep running. Dean made partner at his law firm. Bear's had a record year with his bears, has *extra* fucking money and a fat IRA. Jacque has his bakery. Even the drunks are kicking my ass. Tony's too busy to look at my car until the end of the week and the Schmidts just bought a truck that easily costs more than I make in a year. And I turn thirty in a week. *Yep,* he decided as he took a drag, *I pretty much hate my life. But I suppose that's only because I am a giant loser.* Bear's comment, "It's been that way for a long time," echoed in his head and he knew Jacque was right yesterday after the game. *I am tired,* he thought. A car pulled in for gas and he stood up, dropped his unfinished cigarette, and stepped on it. "I am so tired of this life," he said aloud.

Chapter 17

As she finished another chapter of her book, Sophie looked up to check the clock sitting on the mantle above the fireplace. Wow, she thought, I think this has to be the longest I have ever read in this house without getting interrupted. Her eyes tried to return to the page, but her mind would not allow it. Reluctantly, she closed the book, set it on the table next to her, and listened for a sign of her employer. Nothing. After lunch Sophie had driven her to the beauty salon for her weekly hair appointment. When they returned Frannie said she felt tired and might lie down for a bit. She said she thought it was the dreary weather. Sophie cleaned up the lunch dishes and started some laundry before parking herself in the living room to read. Frannie napped occasionally, but never for this long. It had been hours since she'd gone up to her room.

Sophie took a deep breath and rose from the couch. She walked to the bottom of the stairs and paused to listen again. Still nothing. No sound from the television and no big band music filtering down to her. With growing dread, Sophie climbed up the steep, wooden staircase to check on her. From the top she could see the door to the bedroom was partially open. That was a good sign. It was normally shut when she napped, so she must have gotten up at some point. Sophie peered inside. The bed was empty. She walked into the room and into a cloud of perfume. Coughing and blinking, she waved her hand in front of her nose and mouth and started toward the bathroom door. She had only taken a couple of steps when it opened. Out came Frannie, dressed in a once-elegant dark blue evening gown, matching elbow length gloves, and high heels. Sophie stopped short and stared.

Frannie glanced at her as she walked somewhat unsteadily toward her dresser. "Don't just stand there Louise, help me find my earrings," she commanded. "I don't want to keep your uncle waiting." She opened the top drawer and began to pick through her jewelry.

Louise? Sophie thought. Your uncle? What the hell was this? She had never seen Frannie dressed up. She had never even seen her in a dress at all. It was always slippers and pajamas or a nightgown around the house. Or pants and a blouse with old lady sensible shoes if they went anywhere. The outfit itself, though, was nothing compared to the madness of her face. Frannie had assaulted it with whatever makeup she still owned. Bright red lipstick poorly outlined her mouth, blue eyeshadow coated not just her eyelids but extended all the way up into her eyebrows, which had been penciled in heavy and dark. Her cheeks were bright pink with circles of rouge, and between the mascara and the eyeliner, well, Sophie couldn't decide if she looked like a little girl who found her mother's makeup for the first time, an aging drag queen, or just a clown. It was unsettling either way.

Frannie forgot things from time to time and repeated herself a bit too often, but actual dementia had never been an issue. That's not why she was hired. Sophie was there for other health problems—physical problems. This was positively creepy. Not sure what else to do, she played along. "Which earrings are you looking for?" she asked.

"The teardrops with the diamonds, dear. They're the ones that go with my necklace." She turned so that Sophie could see it.

Sophie tried not to look at her face. "Where is uncle taking you tonight?"

"We are going out to dinner at Andre's. Then he is taking me dancing," she smiled. "Oh, where are those earrings?"

"I think I saw them downstairs. Why don't I go take a look?" Time to call Dan, Sophie decided and hustled down the stairs for the phone.

Fortunately, she was able to reach Dan at work right away. He had more questions than she had answers and the concern in his voice was plain.

This was something new, unexpected, and clearly not good. He said he would get there as soon as he could. Sophie sat and fidgeted at the dining room table near the bottom of the stairs. She wasn't afraid to go upstairs, but she really had no idea what she would say. If she went back without the earrings, she wasn't sure how to play along. Saying the wrong thing risked bursting Frannie's bubble. She would leave that task to her son. Her best strategy seemed to be avoidance.

Dan only worked twenty minutes away, but it seemed like an eternity before she heard his car door slam and saw him quickly walk up to the house. She stood and greeted him at the door. "Nothing's happened since I talked to you. I snuck up and peeked in on her just to make sure she's okay. Otherwise I stayed down here. You can hear her moving around still."

"Okay, thanks. And thanks again for calling right away. Louise is my cousin, so her uncle would be my dad. But I have no idea what this is about." He took a deep breath. "I guess I'd better go talk to her and see if I can figure out what the hell she's doing." Dan started to head up, but just then, Frannie emerged from the hallway and gazed down on them in all of her garish glory. Fighting the deterioration of her posture, she posed, one hand on the railing, chin held high.

"You can stop looking for the earrings, Louise. I found them," she announced cheerfully.

"Wow, Mom!" Dan complimented her. "You look gorgeous. Sophie said you were getting ready to go out tonight."

Maybe it was simply the sound of Dan's voice, or being called "Mom." Maybe it was because he said "Sophie" instead of "Louise." Either way, as soon as Dan spoke, Frannie's fantasy began to dissolve. First she glared down at them, almost as if she were angry that they weren't the people who she wanted them to be. The makeup exaggerated her expressions as they shifted from joy, to anger, to shock, to confusion, and finally, sad resignation. Her bearing retreated under the weight of her realizations and she simply stared, first at Dan, then at Sophie, then slowly back at Dan.

"I'm glad you found those earrings," Dan continued, trying to stay pleasant and positive. "They really look beautiful on you."

Eyes locked on Dan, the defeated stare narrowed into a defiant, angry glare. The bright, happy clown face had taken a sudden and dark turn. "You," she said slowly, her voice dripping with derision.

Dan stood with one foot on the bottom step staring up at his mother, unsure of what to do. He could see the change, the recognition, the resentment, the return of Frannie. "Yeah, Mom. It's me, Dan," he said cautiously.

"What do you want? Why are you here?" She spoke menacingly, each "you" spat out with disgust.

He paused to steel himself before he answered. Then he began, calmly but directly, "Sophie called me. She told me that you were getting all decked out for a night on the town. It's nice to see you all dressed up, Mom."

"You're lying," she spoke sharply, pointing a gnarled finger at him.

"I'm not lying to you, Mom," Dan countered. "I just wanted to come and see you dressed up." He started up the steps.

"Stop," she commanded. "You stay down there. You stay away from me."

He paused where he was, put his hands up, and said patiently, "Come on, Mom. Let's just sit and visit for a while. Why don't you tell me where you're headed this evening?"

Frannie made kind of a choking, sobbing noise, lowered her head and held the railing with both hands. Her voice was ragged. "I'm not going anywhere tonight." They could see her shoulders begin to shake.

Dan froze, unsure of what to make of this sudden, unexpected vulnerability. He looked over at Sophie. Dumbfounded as he was, she silently put her hands up, shrugged, and shook her head. He returned her shrug and looked up at his mother again, searching for some way to comfort her. They waited in silence. When it seemed Frannie's sobs had abated and her shoulders stilled, Dan spoke. Quietly, patiently, compassionately, he said, "Mom, it's okay to need help once in a while. I know you had a rough day. I know you're tired. I know it's not easy."

The old woman's head rose; dark eye makeup bled with the bitter tears down into the exaggerated flush of her cheeks. Any trace of sorrow was displaced by fury. "You, Daniel Robert, will not tell me what's okay and what's not okay. This is still my house! You are not eighty-four years old! You are not in charge here!" she practically shrieked.

This time Dan reacted, frustration getting the best of him. "I'm not trying to be in charge, Mom!" he shouted back. "I am trying to help you!"

"You stay away," she raged. "You and your brother are just going to have to wait to buy your new cars and your boats and go on your big vacations because I'm not going anywhere!"

"What the hell are you even talking about?" Dan fired back. "Who's buying a boat?"

"Not you! I know why you are always hanging around here. Don't play innocent with me! Neither one of you can even stand it that I'm still around! You hate the fact that you can't ship me off somewhere and sell this place!" Dan slumped, defeated as the hateful words rained down on him. "The only reason you ever come here is to check and see if I'm still alive! You can't wait to start spending my money! Well that's just too goddamn bad, Daniel, because I don't intend to go anywhere!" With that, Frannie turned. It seemed as if she were intent on storming back into her bedroom. But it had been a very long time since she had worn heels. Or maybe the gloves prevented her from getting a good grip on the railing. If she hadn't been perched right at the top of the staircase when one of her ankles buckled, she might have come away with just a nasty sprain.

Chapter 18

"Jacque," Guy called out, "over here."

Jacque saw him across the room. "What the hell, my friend?" he asked as he walked over to the table. "Since when don't we sit at the bar?"

"Since I gotta talk to you."

"We don't talk at the bar?"

"Not like that. Not regular bullshit. You were right yesterday."

Jacque considered his friend for a moment, then sat down. "Alright. I wondered what was so fucking important about this game tonight."

"Nothing."

"Yeah. I can see that now."

"I got your first one. Sam Adams?" Guy asked as he got up.

"Sounds good," he nodded. "Thanks."

Guy took his empty MGD and walked over to the bar to order their drinks. Getting together for the Bears game on Sundays was pretty routine for them, but Monday night games only mattered if the Bears were playing. They both had to get up too early for work on Tuesdays. Guy returned and handed Jacque his bottle of beer.

"Hey," he scolded, "where's my glass?"

"Seriously? It comes in a glass."

"No. It comes in a fucking container. Do you eat your soup out of the can? Or do you eat it out of a bowl?"

"Fine. You know you're a pain in the ass, don't you?" Guy asked as he got up again. He returned and firmly set a glass down in front of his friend.

"Satisfied?"

Jacque tilted his glass slightly and slowly poured the dark beer into it. "Yes. Don't hate me because I have standards. You can drink that swill out of the container if you want and I'm sure it won't make a damn bit of difference. But if I am going to drink a beer, I want to taste it and enjoy it. My consumption is beyond ritual and boredom." He took a drink. "Ahhhh. That's good stuff. I know I'm a fucking snob. And so should you by now."

"I don't know what the hell you are." Guy laughed and took a swig of his swill out of its container.

"So I don't have to stay and watch this entire game, do I?" Jacque asked.

"Not if you solve all of my problems before it ends."

"Shit." Jacque's head dropped. He raised his glass and took another sip. "Big stuff?"

"Big stuff," Guy nodded.

"You want ass kissing and understanding? Or do you want brutal honesty?"

Guy winced. "Both?"

Jacque shook his head. "Doesn't work that way. Can't work that way."

Guy took a deep breath and let it out slowly. "I suppose not." He looked away. Jacque waited patiently. "So you know yesterday, as the game was ending, how you asked me what was the matter?"

"Yeah," Jacque nodded.

Guy hesitated and took another drink. "Well, it's pretty much every single thing. I hate my life. I'm lost. And I have no idea what to do about it."

Jacque grimaced and then nodded, understanding. "That's a shitty place to be my friend. I'm sorry."

"You know why I come here on Sundays and watch the Bears game?"

Jacque shook his head.

"Me neither," Guy shrugged. "You were right yesterday. I really don't care. It just seems like a good way to piss away an afternoon. One more Sunday laid to waste sitting on a bar stool."

"But you'll be back next Sunday, won't you?"

"I suppose."

"You know you don't have to."

"What the hell else am I supposed to do?"

"I don't know. What the hell else do you want to be doing?"

Guy shrugged again. "Doesn't really matter, does it? I don't have any money to do anything anyway."

"Money's not your problem, Guy."

"Oh? Really? I've been living on shit wages at a shit job for the last twelve fucking years. And money's not my problem?"

"Absolutely not."

"Well then, for fuck's sake, please tell me. What the hell is my problem if it isn't money?" Guy demanded.

Jacque stood up. "I'll be back. Big stuff needs big medicine."

Guy waited as Jacque headed to the bar. He took another drink of his beer and watched the game without watching it.

"Here." Jacque placed a rocks glass containing a couple of ice cubes and a golden brown liquid in front of him.

Guy had calmed down. "What is this?" he asked, inspecting the drink.

"Big medicine. Sip it."

Guy raised the glass to his nose.

"Take a sip. It's just whiskey."

"And what?" He tasted it.

"Right now, just ice. When the ice melts, it will be whiskey and water."

"Funny. Where's yours?"

Jacque smiled, "I don't have big problems. And you might need a ride home tonight."

"Uh-oh," Guy's shoulders sagged. "How bad is it Dr. Jacque?"

"I've seen much worse, my young friend. You're going to live, but you've got some work to do. Let's start with this shitty job that you say you hate so much. I think if you really hated it, you wouldn't still be there."

"I am an almost-thirty-year-old clerk at a convenience store. I get up at five every morning to make coffee, ring a cash register, empty garbage cans, and stock coolers. What's not to hate?"

"Almost thirty," Jacque repeated the number. "Do you think that's bothering you?"

Guy hesitated a moment before nodding. "I guess I didn't think it would, but the closer it gets," he shook his head, "the worse I feel about everything."

"It is a milestone, I suppose. But I also think that it's more of a symptom of what's eating you. Let's get back to your job and your mundane tasks. What the fuck do you think I do all day?" Jacque challenged him.

"What do you mean? You own your own business."

"Yeah, sure, but just like you I am up early every morning. Just like you I do the same fucking things every fucking day. I make coffee, I make the donuts, I take out the garbage. I even clean the goddamn toilets once in a while. I know you don't do that at your place. Nobody does."

Guy laughed. "But it's your bakery, man. It's different."

"Why do you think that makes such a big goddamn difference? All that means is that I just got more problems to deal with. When something breaks at the Gas and Go, what do you do about it? What do you do when the compressor in the cooler is fried on a busy summer weekend?"

"I call Big John," Guy acknowledged.

"Yeah. I can't call Big John to come deal with my bullshit." Jacque scolded him. "Because it is all my bullshit. Our work isn't that different. But you can walk away from yours anytime you want. I've got my life savings tied up in my ovens and in that old building. I'm the one who's really stuck, not you. Trust me, it's not your job you hate."

"Sure feels like it."

"No. It's not your job. It's the idea of your job that you hate. You hate that you have worked there forever. You hate the idea that you are turning thirty and still there. Look, any job can start to suck when a person starts to feel like they can't leave if want to. It's not the job, it's the feeling of being stuck, trapped."

"So hating my job is different than hating the *idea* of my job?" Guy was skeptical.

"Absolutely!" Jacque was emphatic. "We all have to work. And all jobs are full of bullshit. It's really about freedom, my friend. When the job is your choice, when you own that choice, then you're on to something. When you make your job your bitch, then you can be happy with it. Because that bitch is yours. But when you let yourself be the bitch," Jacque shook his head, "it won't matter what the fuck you do. You can be the goddamn king of the world and still be miserable."

Guy drank more of his medicine and chased it with a swallow of beer, thinking. "Well," he observed finally, "I'm pretty confident that, at this point, I don't like the *idea* of spending my life staring at that same stupid intersection through neon beer signs, selling gas, beer, cigarettes, and lottery tickets to people."

"Okay, fair enough. So what is it you want to do?"

Guy stared, took another sip, looked around, and shrugged. "I don't know."

"Bingo!" Jacque fairly shouted and slammed his hand on the table. "Now we are getting somewhere! It's always easier to figure out what we don't want to do than it is to figure out what we do want to do."

"Alright, so how do I figure out what I want to do?"

"I don't know. But at least now we know what the problem is. That's half the battle right there."

"Why do I feel like that was the easy half?"

"Because it was," Jacque grinned. "You want another beer? I'll buy."

"Yeah, sure," Guy laughed. "I know that what I want to do right now is to have another beer."

"Huge progress!" Jacque laughed with him and stood up. "Pretend you can do anything you want. Anything at all. Think about it. I'll be back. I gotta take a leak."

Guy watched his friend go up to the bar. Anything I want? His mind wandered back in time to the types of things he thought about as a kid. He laughed to himself thinking back on those ancient dream jobs, that at one point in time, he was so certain he was going to pursue. Let's see what Jacque can do with these, he thought.

Jacque returned with their beer. "What did you come up with?"

"You're gonna laugh."

"Of course I am, but so fucking what? Let's hear it."

92

"Cowboy."

"Cowboy?"

"Cowboy."

"Can you ride a horse?"

"I think so."

"Get the fuck out of here with the cowboy shit. What, are you nine? You don't even know if you can ride a horse? Have you ever ridden a horse?"

"I rode a horse once on a trail ride I went on during a vacation with a friend of mine. And yeah, I was about nine at the time."

"What else you got?"

"River guide."

"What the hell is a river guide?"

"It's the guy who steers your boat down the river when people go whitewater rafting."

Jacque put his head in his hands. "Let me guess. You went rafting once on a family vacation when you were a kid."

Guy nodded. "Same trip."

Jacque shrugged. "You could do that, I guess. Where do people go whitewater rafting?"

"Places they have mountains. We were in Tennessee. But I suppose out west, too. I don't really know."

"Okay, save that one. That's got possibilities. What else?"

"Truck driver. Like a long-haul trucker."

"That's better. That's easy enough to do. Why a trucker?"

"When I went on that vacation, we drove. I saw all those giant semis with the sleeper cabs out on the highways and I thought it would be a cool way to see the country."

"Not bad. I can see that." Then Jacque hesitated.

"What?"

"Do you ever want to get married?"

"Yeah. I suppose. What's that got to do with it?"

"Can't be a long-haul trucker and be married."

"Why not?"

"You hit the road and your wife will start banging your best friend right away. Haven't you ever listened to country western music? That's all those fucking rednecks sing about."

"You'd bang my wife?" Guy asked, pretending to be hurt.

"Maybe. If she was hot and you were dumb enough to leave her all alone just so you could go drive your fucking truck all over the country."

"This is stupid," Guy laughed.

"It's fun though, isn't it? Do you have one that doesn't involve you going on a vacation as a kid?"

"Stuntman."

"Shut the fuck up. Next."

"Garbage man."

"Bullshit. Nobody wants to be a garbage man.

"And nobody wants to be a convenience store clerk either."

"You got a point there," Jacque acknowledged.

"Actually, I don't really want to be a garbage man anymore. When I was a kid, I thought it would be cool because I would get to keep all of the cool shit that people threw away."

"Too bad you can't just ride around on a fucking horse and pick through people's trash. You'd be in heaven. What else?"

"Rock star."

"You don't play an instrument do you?"

"No."

"Can you sing?"

"I think so."

"Can you sing in front of people?"

"Maybe," Guy answered, although he privately doubted it.

"Do you have friends who know how to play any instruments?"

"I don't know. Can you play anything?"

Jacque just stared until he realized that he was the friend. He shook his head, "No, my friend. I don't know shit about music. You and I are not starting a band."

"You're killing my dreams, man."

"Those aren't dreams, my friend. They're fantasies, mostly. If you want to be a rock star, then learn how to play guitar or drums or something. It's not just going to magically happen. You could drive a truck and maybe do the river guide thing. I don't know much about that one. But in all seriousness, trucking is a marriage killer. You could drive locally."

"Forget trucking. Locally is just sitting in Chicago traffic. That might suck worse than working at the Gas and Go. What about a smoke jumper?"

"Where the hell do you come up with this shit? What's a smoke jumper?"

"Smoke jumpers are the guys who get flown in or parachute into the backcountry to fight forest fires out west."

"Holy shit man! Who are you? Mild-mannered Guy with the big adventure dreams. Wow!" Jacque leaned back from the table, shook his head, and looked across the table. "You think you know a guy."

Guy smiled and shrugged.

"I don't think we figured out a job for you, but we have clearly established a theme. Why the hell did you stick around this town? Why didn't you ever move? Somewhere you could actually do some of this shit?"

Guy sighed. "Oh, I thought about it. I even kinda had it all planned out for a while. I was saving up money and everything. I had a friend who was going to let me stay with him in Colorado until I got on my feet." Guy smiled without feeling and sipped the whiskey. "But that was like a hundred years ago."

Jacque could see the clear change in his friend's demeanor. "What happened? Why didn't you go through with it?"

Before he could answer, Guy's phone buzzed. He flipped it open to see who was calling and held it up for Jacque to see, "That's what happened."

Chapter 19

I t didn't take long for the rescue squad to arrive. Frannie was loaded onto a gurney and carried into the back of the ambulance. She wasn't conscious, but she was breathing, and as they took her away under the watchful eyes of curious neighbors, Dan followed in his car. The paramedics had offered to let him ride with her in the back, but he was afraid that she might regain consciousness and start screaming at him again. Sophie stood alone on the porch in the chill of the evening air watching them drive away and wondering what the hell had just happened.

Shot full of adrenaline and suddenly alone, she didn't know what to do with herself. Although she had quit smoking a few years ago, right then, all she wanted was a cigarette. She went back inside and rummaged through the places she suspected Dan might have stashed an extra pack. Upstairs in his bedroom she got lucky and found one with three left in it. Sophie was out on the front porch before realizing she had nothing to light it with. Back inside she went to repeat her search. This time, nothing. By now the craving was making her antsy. She just wanted to light the goddamn cigarette, sit her ass on the porch, and decompress. Standing in the kitchen, racking her brains for where Frannie might have some matches, she thought of the stove. She could turn on the burner, light it, and quickly walk outside. Better not, she thought. Even if she did light it, run like hell to the porch, and leave the windows open all night long, Frannie would probably still smell it. And there was no way she was going to deal with that.

Then it hit her. Frannie was not coming back. Her arms dropped to her sides and she stood there looking around the room. *Slow down, Sophie, think about it for a minute,* she told herself. *Could she come back?* The fall was horrific, and she was certain she heard the cracking of bones. Dan even told her as much when she called 911. Wooden stairs just didn't give. She figured Frannie would fight to get back here so she could continue to make Sophie and her sons miserable, but no amount of meanness and determination could mend those old bones. *Holy shit,* she thought, *this might really be it. No, it has to be. Even if the physical stuff magically does heal, something in her mind had snapped. That was some crazy shit with the evening gown and those old-timey gloves like Audrey Hepburn. And the makeup!* She shuddered at the image. *Yeah,* she nodded, *it's over.* Sophie returned the unlit cigarette to her mouth, ignited one of the burners, and leaned in to touch the end of it to the flame. Then she turned off the burner, took a drag, and exhaled as she slowly walked through the house out and to the front porch.

Chapter 20

J acque sat and waited for Guy to return. They always sat at the bar and it felt weird to be sitting at a table. The Duke looks strange from this perspective, he thought as he sipped his beer, watched the game, and wondered what was up with Guy's dad. Finally, the door opened and Guy walked back over to the table. He carelessly tossed his phone down. Then he sat, elbows on the table, and rubbed his face with his hands.

"That," he gestured to the phone, "is the story of my life."

"How so?" Jacque asked.

"That was Sharette, my dad's live-in caretaker. He's got a nosebleed and she's taking him to the emergency room. They want me to meet them there."

"For a nosebleed? What the hell?"

"You don't understand. Nothing is ever simple when it comes to him. He's had the nosebleed now for almost two hours. They can't get it to stop. Sharette's starting to freak a little and my dad's not real comfortable with it either."

"That's fucked up, my friend."

"Tell me about it. I swear, he's been dying ever since I was a kid."

"So he's like a hypochondriac or something?"

Guy shook his head. "Not at all. It's all legit stuff. His body is fucked up in more ways than you can imagine. It's always something. And it's always something major. That's why I never moved out west."

"Because of him? What happened?"

Guy shrugged and sighed. "A new spot on his lung. More cancer, more chemo. But he beat it, just like he always does."

"Wow. So you're it? You're the only family? I thought you had sisters or something."

"I do. But I'm the only family that will still have anything to do with him."

"That sucks. Why you? Why'd you get stuck?"

Guy sighed. "You know, I've thought about that a lot. I know why all of my relatives hate him. He was business partners with his older brother," he explained, "and when my Uncle Ed died, my dad screwed over his family and forced them to sell out for a fraction of what they should have received. He actually bragged about it, so I can't really blame them." He shrugged before continuing. "When my mom died, I was only four. Both of my sisters were in high school, though, and they pretty much hated him by that time anyway. I don't remember really, but I guess he was a dick to my mom. Just controlling bullshit. I don't know. But neither one of them have talked to him in years."

"Wow," Jacque shook his head in wonder. "That's crazy. I didn't realize your sisters were that much older."

"Yeah," Guy nodded. "I was a mistake. I guess he was pissed at my mom for getting pregnant, and then even madder that she died because then he was stuck with me on his own."

"Jesus. It seems like you would be justified in leaving."

"I know, but it's not that easy. You know, when a situation is bullshit, it's easy to be the first one out the door. Those first people to run away, well, they know there are other people still there who will deal with it. It's a lot harder to be the last one out the door. If I leave, there's no one. That's it." He finished the whiskey. "Besides, I never thought he would actually live this long."

"Wow."

"Tell me about it. Here I sit, going on thirty, life on hold. Whatever, I gotta get going. I told Sharette I would meet them there as soon as I could."

"You okay to drive?"

"Yeah, it takes me more than a shot and a beer." Guy stood up. "You know, Colorado wasn't the first time I made plans to do something with my life. I actually registered for college classes once."

"And?"

"Heart attack, followed by quintuple bypass surgery. It's funny really, in a demented sort of way. Here we are tonight, just talking about me doing something else, and it's like he senses it. And somehow, he reaches out through space and time to fuck with my life yet again."

Jacque stood up with his friend and put his hand on his shoulder. "Well, I hope it goes fine tonight and that he's okay."

Guy laughed bitterly, "Oh, I'm sure he will be. I don't doubt that for a minute." He turned to go as his friend sat back down.

"Hey, Guy!" Jacque hollered before he got out the door. "Bears game on Sunday? I'll save you a seat," he grinned.

Guy looked back toward the table, smiled, and shook his head. "Yeah, sure."

Chapter 21

Halfway through that first cigarette, Sophie wished she had a jacket and remembered why she had quit smoking. As bad as the craving was for that nicotine hit moments before, it quickly turned inescapably stale and disgusting. But it had been hours since Dan left and here she was again, out in the cold, smoking that third cigarette. *Good thing there were only three left in that pack,* she thought. When she was done, she stubbed it out in Dan's little ashtray which he had, of course, left to blight Frannie's porch. *Poor Dan,* she thought. It was times like these that made her feel a little less bad about not knowing her own parents.

Headlights lit up the porch momentarily as a car turned onto the street. It was Dan. He parked in front of the house behind Sophie's car, slowly climbed out, and walked up the steps to the porch.

"Hey," Sophie stubbed out her cigarette and stood up. "How is she?"

Dan sighed. "Not good. She fractured her hip. Her elbow is shattered. She has a concussion. She's covered with bruises already. All they did was get her stabilized tonight. She's on morphine and not feeling any pain right now, at least. Tomorrow the orthopedic surgeon is going to look at everything. And the cardiologist. And the neurologist. They don't know why she was acting so strange. They think maybe she had a stroke or something." Dan fished in his pocket for a pack of cigarettes. "And then," he shrugged, "who knows?" He lit his cigarette and offered the pack to Sophie.

"No thanks. I quit a few years ago, but I dug around and found a couple of yours after you left. Sorry."

"Don't worry about it." He slumped in the chair next to her.

"How about you? How are you doing?"

He took a drag and exhaled slowly. "You know, when my dad died, it was a total shock. Car accident. Mark and I were both little. She was so strong. She was awesome. He had a trucking company and she didn't know shit about it. Really nothing. It was his business and she ran the house. Very traditional. But when he died, she got in there and figured out what she needed to know and she ran it. She probably made it bigger and better than he ever would have. And all the while she was doing that, she was still there for me and Mark. When I got older and understood more about what that must have been like, I really respected what she did. You know, there weren't a whole lot of women in that business. I don't know if I could have done that. When it was clear that Mark and I weren't interested in becoming involved, she found a buyer and got out. But whatever. She was a hell of a woman and I loved her. I was proud of her and I respected her." He took another drag from his cigarette. "And I am really trying to hang on to that. But it's so hard. I don't see her like that anymore. I see her as a selfish, mean, old bitch. She's manipulative, controlling, scheming. Even dishonest! I catch her in these little self-serving lies and denials all the time. And sometimes...sometimes I wonder if that's all she ever was, you know?" He shrugged. "Maybe that's why she did so well with the business? Because she was a ruthless bitch? I don't know. I wonder if I was just always blinded to how she was because I was her son, you know?"

"I've been around a lot of old people Dan. A lot of them have a real tough time. It's got to be hard to lose control. Not just of your body, but your life, everything. It's especially tough for the ones who are so used to being independent."

"But they don't all act like that," he pointed at the house where the stairs are. "I know they don't."

"No," Sophie agreed softly. "No, they don't."

They sat in silence as Dan finished his cigarette. Then he perked up a bit. "You up for a drink? Because I sure am. Come on."

Sophie laughed and stood up with him. "I could definitely go for a drink. Good thing I didn't know there was any booze in there or I probably would have finished that off, too!"

"I keep a little stash. I'm sure you can understand why."

They entered the house and passed through the front hall with both of them avoiding looking up at the stairs. Once in the kitchen, Dan asked her to get some glasses and ice while he went to the basement to retrieve his hidden bottle of scotch. They sat down at the kitchen table and he gave them each a generous pour.

"Scotch, huh?" she asked and took a drink. "Phooo," she made a face and shook her head.

"Let the ice melt a little," he advised. "It'll soften it. Yeah, my dad wasn't a big drinker, but I do remember him ordering scotch once in a while. So when I got older, I guess I started drinking it as a way to try to connect with him in some way. I don't know."

"That's cool."

"It wasn't cool when I was eighteen," he laughed. "It was just odd."

Sophie smiled. "It was precocious."

"You weren't there. Trust me, it was just odd. Scotch is an acquired taste though, that's for sure. I know I made a worse face than yours when I first drank it. But I was pretty determined. Now I really enjoy nursing a glass of it once in a while."

Sophie was glad to have some company. And she could tell Dan was too. She knew he lived alone and probably wasn't in a big hurry to get home. "I just realized that you must have missed dinner," she said abruptly and went to the fridge thinking about what she could get him. "Can I get you something to eat?"

"Nah. Thanks though. I don't really have an appetite right now."

"You sure? Not even a snack?"

"No really. I'm fine."

"You should eat something." Sophie busied herself in the kitchen and found some crackers and a jar of spreadable cheese. She put them on a plate in between them. "You don't have to eat anything, but it's there if you change your mind."

"Scotch and cheese and crackers. Hmmm," he teased. "What a delicacy."

"Cheese and crackers goes with everything. Trust me." She took another sip of her drink and made much less of a face than the first time. "Yeah, the ice melting is helping." Then she took a cracker, spread some cheese on and popped it into her mouth. "Oh yeah," she exaggerated, "that really goes well with this scotch. Mmmmmmm."

Dan laughed out loud. "Fine, you win. I will have some food," he said reaching for the knife. "Not bad," he acknowledged after trying one.

Sophie watched Dan lean back in his chair and look around the kitchen. He sighed and she could see that his mind had returned to his mother.

"This house used to hold such good memories for me. It's the only home I remember from growing up. And these past couple of years, she's even destroying those. I don't even like this place anymore. I get stressed just walking in the damn door now. I can feel my whole body tense up. It shouldn't be that way."

Sophie nodded and let him continue.

"Years ago, when she had her first bout of cancer, I can remember taking her to this cancer doctor's office. In the waiting room there was this inspirational needlepoint framed on the wall. I guess one of the patients made it to inspire the other patients with cancer. It had this line from a poem by Dylan Thomas. It said: 'Do Not Go Gentle Into That Good Night.' I looked up the poem and thought it was pretty cool, that idea of raging against the dying of the light. Not going out without a fight, you know?"

Sophie nodded.

"But I tell you," Dan shook his head. "I think I hate that poem now. I don't care anymore if she goes gently into that good night. Or not gently. Or screaming bloody murder, like tonight, and cursing everyone in the room. But I am ready for her to go, one way or another, into that good goddamn night already."

Chapter 22

"It's open!" Michele hollered from the kitchen. "Come on in!" She heard the door open and Laura call out a hello. "I'm in the kitchen."

"Big night tonight," Laura said dramatically as she took off her coat and put it on the back of a chair. "Here," she handed Michele a bottle of Captain Morgan. "Appetizer."

"Cool! Thanks! I'm just cleaning up. Tanya and Carly ate and made a mess. You just missed them. They're headed to the football game."

"Uhh, I passed the high school on the way here and there's nobody there."

"No, it's not a home game. It's in Marengo. I'm sure they'll go out afterwards or something. She said she'll text me and let me know. What do you want me to mix this with?" she asked holding up the rum.

"Do you have any Coke?"

Michele looked in the pantry and produced a 2-liter bottle. "Ta-daa." She grabbed a couple of glasses and filled them with ice. "Here. You be the bartender," she told Laura as she set them on the table and sat down.

Laura filled hers mostly with soda and Michele's only about halfway. Then she topped them both off with the rum.

"Jesus!" Michele exclaimed. "I still have to get to the bar, you know!"

"It's just one big one to start you off. And don't worry. I am your chauffeur tonight. Cheers." She raised her glass.

"Here's to single, rich, handsome, lonely men," she laughed.

"Who aren't fat, bearded, bald and don't make out with their dogs," Laura added.

"Oh yeah! That, too. May one actually exist!" They clinked their glasses together and took a drink.

"So, should we compare our lists? Or do you want to get ready to go first?" Laura asked.

Michele started to protest and then stopped. She cocked her head slightly and glared at her friend. "Nice try bitch. I look damn good and you know it."

Laura laughed. "I almost had you. No, you look awesome. I love your top. That blue brings out your eyes so much. It almost makes it look like you have colored contacts in."

"Thank you. You look great, too."

"So where's your list? Let's see it."

Michele hung her head. "I don't have one."

"What?! How can you not have a list? You don't have anything?"

"No, I tried, but it's hard. Everyone I thought of is either married, has a girlfriend, or is just gross."

Laura shook her head in disappointment.

"I did go to the store every day and bought just a half-gallon of milk, like you said. I even went at random times."

"Oh my god! You're not serious. You went looking for the hot grocery store guy?"

"I totally did! And then Carly asked me why I was buying half-gallons of milk all of a sudden. Look." Michele jumped up and opened her refrigerator. There on the shelf sat five half-gallon containers of milk.

"You are crazy!"

"Not crazy, desperate. I had to lie to Carly and I felt like an idiot. I told her I wasn't sure if we had any and I was going to be doing some baking."

Laura almost spat her drink out. "Baking!? Baking? Why the hell would you need so much milk for baking?"

They both laughed. "I don't know. It was all I could think of. I'm a horrible liar."

"You didn't see the guy, did you?"

Michele pouted. "No. And I'll probably end up dumping most of that milk out."

"Well, you didn't have to *actually* buy milk, you know! You could've bought other stuff that you would actually use."

"Whatever. I don't even care. Let's see your list, smarty pants."

Laura lowered her eyes.

"You don't have one either!" Michele shouted and pointed at her friend. "You are a hypocrite!"

"I know. But I had the same deal as you. There is a lot of gross out there. I told Ron that he better not ever leave me. Sorry to say it honey, but I would hate to be single right now. Too young, too old, too broke, too drunk, or taken. I did have a couple of possibilities, but when I got more information, they were no good."

"What was wrong with them?"

"The best one is gay. He's one of the salesmen that Ron works with. He's gorgeous, great shape, super nice. He makes good money, too. I've met him a few times at work functions. I asked Ron if he was single. He said yes and asked me why. I told him I wanted to set him up with a friend. Then I told him it was you and he just laughed at me. I had no idea the guy was gay."

"Damn."

"Yeah. I thought I really had a good one for you. Another guy is a bit on the older side, but I know he has some money. He has a nice house anyway and drives a pretty nice Mercedes. But he's already been divorced three times."

"That could be good!"

"Yes and no. Supposedly, he has been very, very vocal about never getting married again. He always talks about how much money the first three cost him."

"Ehh. Yeah, probably not good then. Too bad I wasn't the third wife."

"The last guy could be Troy's long-lost brother. Charming, good looking, but really an asshole with severe control and jealousy issues. My friend Denise said he hit his last girlfriend."

"Yeah, been there, done that. Great," she said.

"I don't think it's panic time yet though. I've got feelers out there. Ron knows and the ladies I work with know that I have a beautiful, wonderful, divorced friend who is interested in starting to date again. I didn't tell them that she really just needs to marry a financially secure guy with a good job within the next few months."

"You better not have!"

"I told my mom we were going out tonight and that you were ready to start dating again."

"What'd she say?"

"She said it's about time, but that we shouldn't be going to a bar."

"Where are we supposed to go?"

"She said if you wanted to meet someone nice, you should go to church."

Michele straightened up in her chair and shook her head. "Oh, don't even get me started. I am so done with that. Troy's family are all big church goers. His dad is even like a deacon or elder or something, but they are the biggest bunch of phonies. You know that Pastor Winke took me aside one Sunday after his sermon and gave me a little talk about divorce and how wrong it is and what a great guy Troy is? He didn't even ask me anything about what happened. Someone, I don't know, maybe Troy's mom, who would never believe anything bad about her little angel, went and talked to him and told him a bunch of shit. Who knows? But the whole thing caught me so off guard that I just stood there and listened to him lecture me. Afterwards I was so angry and I thought of a million things I should have told him, but whatever. That was the last time I went there. I don't even like the fact that Carly still goes once in a while."

"Okay, settle down. Give me your glass." Laura poured them each another drink.

Michele took a deep breath and exhaled slowly. "I've still got some baggage I guess."

"Don't worry about it. Look, we are going to go out tonight and have a good time. Let's not stress about finding someone for you right now. You don't need the pressure. It hasn't even been a week, for Christ's sake. We'll go, we can take a look, but really, let's just go have fun, alright? A good girls' night out. Deal?"

"Yeah, deal."

Chapter 23

"You sure you don't need a hand?" Dan asked.

"No thanks. I travel pretty light," Sophie answered, closing her trunk. "If it won't fit in my car, then I figure I don't need it. I just have a suitcase and some makeup left in the bathroom. I still need to shower though, and I want to take a last look around to make sure I have everything."

"Hey, you are more than welcome to stay here again tonight," Dan offered.

"That's sweet of you, but I'm good. I'm gonna go hang out with my friend and just crash at his place. Besides, I already put fresh sheets on my bed and cleaned up the house. I'd like to be able to leave it that way. I want to hit the road as soon as I wake up tomorrow morning and I'll be able to leave a mess for my friend without feeling bad about it," she joked. As if Bear would even notice.

"You really didn't have to clean the house like you did either. Thank you though."

"Well, you didn't have to pay me for the full week either. Thank you for that. I am going to set the key on the kitchen counter when I leave, right?"

"Yeah, just lock the door behind you. And you have my number. Please use me as a reference if you need to."

"Yeah, I will. I have your work and your cell."

"I guess this is goodbye then," Dan gave her a hug. "Thanks for having that drink with me Monday night. I needed that."

"I did too. You hang in there, Dan. You're a good son."

"Thank you for saying that."

109

Dan got in his car and drove away, leaving Sophie on the sidewalk waving. She turned and headed back into the house. No matter how many times she'd moved on like this, it was always strange. Often times at the end of a job, there was a funeral, the house was full, and she was nudged out the door pretty quickly to make room for other family members. Not this time. She really enjoyed having the house to herself all week. She switched to the queen size bed in Mark's old bedroom the night after Frannie left. She put a set of clean white sheets on it and slept right in the middle—no arms or legs hanging over the edges. When she woke up late the next day, she didn't want to get out of bed. So she didn't. She just stayed there dozing off and on until early afternoon and it was wonderful.

Once she was showered and dressed, Sophie finished packing, zipped up her suitcase, and set it by the door in the front hall. Then she took one last walk through the house. Satisfied that nothing was left behind, she picked up her suitcase to leave. She put her hand on the doorknob, but something made her turn and look up at the staircase one last time. An involuntary shudder ran through her and she hurried out the door.

After spending the week looking through Frannie's freezer and pantry in the futile hope of finding something different to eat, Sophie was looking forward to a big juicy hamburger and French fries at The Duke. Bear was working but told her that he would buy her dinner as a going away present. Big spender, she laughed to herself. He did offer to let her stay with him for a little while, at least until she found another job. Sophie was relieved that he didn't really mean it, but it was nice to be invited. If she did stay there and they started playing house, well, she had seen enough people fall into long-term relationships just because. She didn't want that.

It was late for dinner but early for a night out and the crowd at The Duke reflected that. There were still a few families with kids sitting at the tables while the bar was populated with holdovers from the Friday Afternoon Club. Some of them would inevitably say to hell with it and decide to just stay out all night, burning through a sizeable chunk of their paycheck before they even made it home. Sophie found an open stool and sat down at the bar.

"Hey," Mindy teased as she hustled over to wait on her, "it's not Saturday. What do you think you're doing in here?"

Sophie laughed, "I got special permission tonight."

"Ohhh, I see," Mindy nodded conspiratorially. "Vodka grapefruit?"

"Not just yet. I'm going to eat first. Can I get a big burger, medium, with cheddar and some fries? And I'd like a Miller Lite to wash that down, please."

"Bottle or draft, hon?"

"Bottle."

Mindy fetched the beer, popped the cap, and set it in front of her. "Burger will be up in a few," she said and went to turn in the order.

As she took that first drink of beer, Sophie turned her stool a bit and took in the rest of the bar. The Duke was pretty good, as far as small-town bars went. It reminded her of the ones back in rural Iowa where she grew up. And a dozen others from the different little towns she worked in over the years. If she hadn't jumped at that first opportunity to be a caregiver, she reminisced, she might be on the other side of the bar with Mindy. Sophie tended bar briefly, in a place not too different from The Duke. When the caregiver opportunity came along, it was a chance to disappear from a bad relationship. But it seemed so boring and she was hesitating. One of the older bartenders, Barb, had laid it out for her and practically demanded that she take the job and leave.

Barb had nailed it, Sophie thought as she watched Mindy hustling back and forth behind the bar. Probably just into the second half of her twenties, she was busy making drinks, wiping counters, and engaging in the endless playful flirtations with her overwhelmingly male customers. She was likely transitioning into the middle phase, according to Barb's analysis. The first phase was when the girls began tending bar at a place like this. They'd just turned twenty-one, and in the smallness of their small-town universe, the local bar was the epicenter. It had the cool people, the cute guys, all a little older, and it was the place where so many stories they'd grown up hearing about took place. Working there, tending bar, it had a certain glamour to it at twenty-one. They were young and cute and the older guys smiled and joked around with them. And leered whenever they turned around or bent over to reach into the cooler. They'd never had so much attention in their lives. Plus, they were making money. Cash tips from busy Friday and Saturday nights sure beat the hell out of the fast food or retail jobs they could get with only a high school education.

In the second phase, the late nights started to wear on them a little. For the past few years they drank more than they should've and started smoking, too. They'd slept with a couple of the wrong guys, maybe had an abortion. And they found the money didn't go quite so far as it used to. It wasn't long before there were babies or bad marriages or both. The marriages usually didn't last more than a few years. "If you marry a bar rat," Barb had said, "don't expect too much from him. Sure, they're fun," she had pointed out, "but they're fun because they don't have any responsibilities. You start giving them responsibilities like a wife and a baby or, god forbid, a mortgage payment, and you'll see, they ain't quite so much fun anymore." After the babies, the girls returned to work, not nearly as perky in body or spirit. Many of their good-money Friday and Saturday night shifts had been taken over by someone a little cuter and a little younger. They settled into their day shifts and weeknights and complained about trying to collect their child support payments. By the end of the second phase, the job—that's all it was anymore—had lost any trace of its glamour. The universe of the bar was rife with dysfunction and they had fully assimilated.

Barb said she was well into the third phase. She knew the way it was and made the best of it. Her kids were grown and although she really didn't have much in savings, her finances were a little easier. She made enough to live on. She didn't work at the coolest place in town until 2am every weekend and liked it that way. Barb enjoyed kidding around with the customers and didn't really mind that none of them stared at her ass anymore. "Even though it's a lot harder to miss these days," she joked. She liked the rhythms of the bar, the football season and the pools, the gossip, the guys comparing notes during hunting season, when the shake-a-day pot got really big and, when they had a good winter, folks coming in on their snowmobiles. The local bar was her big, messed up extended family. It was the work she knew and the life she knew and she was okay with it.

Sophie sighed. *Messed up family*, she thought. *Is there really any other kind?*

Bear came up behind her, put his arm casually around her, and gave her a little squeeze. "Hey, Sophie! Last night out in big city Richmond, huh?"

"Yeah. This is it, I guess."

"You all packed up? Everything loaded?"

"Yep. I'm planning on just leaving as soon as I wake up tomorrow morning."

"Damn," he laughed. "Why can't all women be like you?"

Sophie smirked and rolled her eyes. "By the way, you're buying me a cheeseburger. I already ordered."

"No fish fry?" Bear sounded surprised.

Sophie shook her head. "I need a cheeseburger today."

"Alright, I'll let Mindy know. I gotta get back to work. I'll see you later."

Guy climbed into the van. "You didn't have to drive you know, but thanks."

"Bullshit. If anyone needs a night out, it's you. Drink up and don't worry about it. I've got it tonight. And who knows, maybe we can even find some poor desperate woman with no taste whatsoever and get you laid." Jacque cackled.

"Funny."

"Hey, when a doctor does not have a cure ready, he at least tries to make his patient more comfortable. A heavy dose of alcohol will release some tension. And the affections of a woman are always big medicine. There's nothing like the tender, healing hands of a woman, my friend."

"What if they're around my neck?"

Jacque shook his head and sighed. "Always with the negative." He pulled his van with the big Not Your Average Bakery! logo painted on the side around the building and into the gravel parking lot behind The Duke. "I don't like my work van parked by the road where everyone who drives by can see it. It looks like I'm always here."

"Uhh, maybe that's just because you are always here," Guy teased as they got out.

"Fuck you, my friend," muttered Jacque as they waded through the familiar faces that comprised the collection of smokers out on the deck and went inside to find a seat at the bar.

The back door opened and Sophie glanced toward it. She smiled as she recognized a familiar face. "Hey, Jacque," she called, putting a hand up and giving a little wave. She was happy to see him change course and head toward her.

"What the hell?" he asked as he and Guy claimed the two stools to her right. "Do I have my days confused?"

"No, it's really Friday."

"Hi," Guy leaned over and introduced himself, "I'm Guy."

She smiled and nodded, "Sophie."

"You two haven't met?" Jacque seemed surprised.

They both shook their heads.

"This is Bear's girlfriend," he explained.

"Yeah, for lack of a better description I guess," she shrugged.

"Oh, hey. Good news," Guy said to her. "I got my car fixed yesterday."

Sophie looked puzzled.

"You're the light sleeper and I'm the guy who's been waking you up early Sunday mornings," he explained.

"Ohhh," she said narrowing her eyes and pretending to be angry, "you're the one!"

Guy put his hands up. "Yeah, but don't worry. It's fixed. I promise. You'll be able to sleep in this weekend."

"Well, thanks," she said, "but you're a little late. I won't be over there anymore."

Now it was Jacque's turn to look confused.

"Frannie fell," she explained. "She's in the hospital."

"Who's Frannie?" Guy asked.

"She's the old lady I work for."

"Bad?" Jacque asked.

"Yeah. When an eighty-four-year-old woman falls down a flight of wooden stairs, it's pretty bad."

"Oooh," both Jacque and Guy winced.

"Hip?" Jacque asked hesitantly.

Sophie nodded. "And elbow, and head, and who knows what else."

"That's too bad. Poor lady," commented Guy.

Sophie thought about correcting him, but let it go.

"MGD and a Sam?" Mindy interrupted as she grabbed Sophie's empty burger plate and bottle.

Guy and Jacque nodded while Sophie added, "I'm ready for that vodka grapefruit, too, please."

"Got it," she said, hustling away to get their drinks.

"So tonight, I'm out enjoying the freedom of unemployment," Sophie explained. "I'm heading back to Iowa tomorrow morning."

"Oh wow, you're leaving us?" Jacque asked disappointedly.

"Unless you know of anything around here."

"What was your job at Frannie's?" Guy asked.

"I was her live-in caregiver. I stayed there and helped take care of her and drove her around."

"Ohhh. My dad's had somebody doing that for him for the past few years."

"A few years, huh?" She frowned. "That's a pretty long time. What's his disability?"

"His disability seems to be that he's immortal," Jacque interjected. "Apparently, nothing can kill him."

"Yeah," Guy agreed. "It's actually pretty impressive. He's been diabetic since he was a kid. When I was in grade school, he had a spot on his lung and went through chemo. He was good for a while, but then there were more spots and more chemo. About ten years ago he had quintuple bypass surgery. He's had multiple angioplasties since then. He's got Parkinson's disease. A couple of years ago they said he had prostate cancer, so that was another surgery. He's also got cataracts and a severe arterial sclerosis which is basically really bad arthritis in his back so he's constantly uncomfortable. His heart's bad again, but nobody's willing to operate on him anymore.

And then, last fall, he was diagnosed with supranuclear palsy and he had a feeding tube implanted in his abdomen."

Sophie's jaw dropped.

"And nosebleeds!" Jacque added.

Guy laughed and nodded. "Oh yeah, can't forget about the nosebleeds. You know they had to cauterize that thing the other night?" he said to Jacque.

He made a face. "What's that?"

"It's when you burn it to stop the bleeding."

"Jesus Christ!" he exclaimed, imagining cowboy movies, gunshot wounds, and hot irons.

"Yeah," Sophie added, "they numb up the whole area with a local anesthetic and then they use this little cauterizing tool on the vein. That poor man."

Guy thought about correcting her, but let it go. Instead, he asked, "So how long have you been a caregiver?"

"Too long." She rolled her eyes and shook her head.

"You don't like it?"

"Eh. I don't hate it."

"I can relate to that. It's a job though, right?"

"It is a job."

"So," Jacque asked her, "what's back in Iowa?"

"My little sister is a student at Morningside College in Sioux City," she said proudly. "I am going to take a road trip and surprise her. It's been too long since I've seen her. Then I'll work all my contacts and try and get another job."

The three of them hung out and made conversation as the volume of people and noise in The Duke gradually increased. Jacque bought them each a shot of tequila and they all drank to his standard toast: To the best times of yesterday and the better times of tomorrow. Bear stopped by a few times to visit and they all made fun of him and talked about his bears. Bear repeated his usual assertion of being an artist and that, predictably, set Jacque off so then they all made fun of Jacque for a while. And so it went in turns.

With the bar filling up, Sophie slid off her bar stool and told them "Don't let anyone take my chair. I'm going to the ladies' room."

"I like her," commented Guy as he watched her walk away. "She seems pretty cool. And she's gorgeous."

"Yeah, she's great. She was only in here on Saturdays. That was her night off. And you're always such a pussy on Saturday nights."

"Whatever. I can't really afford to be out two nights a week anyway," Guy sighed.

"Hey, quick, give me some quarters," Jacque said suddenly.

"Why, what's up?" asked Guy digging through his pockets.

"That's what's up." Jacque nodded toward the pool table.

Guy looked over and saw Michele inspecting the cue sticks while Laura racked the balls.

"She's out for a reason," Jacque grinned, taking the quarters from him. "Let's find out if it's one of us." He hopped off the stool and walked over to put the coins up. Guy watched him say something to them, they laughed, and he started back toward the bar. "Damn," he said as he sat back down, "those might be the bluest eyes I've ever seen."

"You're funny. How do you know she's out for a reason?" Guy asked.

"Are you kidding? How do you not know? What the hell man? What is wrong with you? Look at her." He turned toward the pool table and then back to Guy. "You said she's divorced. You said you haven't seen her in years. And now she's out twice in a week? And both times," he glanced over at her again, "she looks phenomenal. You don't have to be a fucking detective to figure that out, my friend."

"Huh," Guy thought about it. "That makes sense I suppose. I guess I just don't pay attention to that kind of stuff."

"And that's another problem Dr. Jacque needs to talk to you about! When's the last time you got laid? When's the last time you even asked anyone out? What the fuck man? You're still young enough that you should be doing some chasin'. Mix it up a little bit, have some fun."

"Hi, I'm Guy," he smiled stupidly and spoke in a dumb voice. "I work at the convenience store. Want to go out with me?"

Jacque just shook his head, "Man, you are messed up."

"Who's messed up?" Sophie asked rejoining them.

Guy turned away, but Jacque answered, "Guy is. He wants to get laid, but he says he hates his job."

"Thanks asshole," Guy turned back to Jacque. "Do you want me to call Bear over here so he can announce it to the whole bar?" he said sarcastically.

"Wait," Sophie asked, "What does hating his job have to do with getting laid?"

Jacque put his hands up and stood. "I will let him explain it to you while I go take in the scenery." He headed toward the pool table.

"So what's this job you hate sooo much that it's preventing you from getting laid?" Sophie was intrigued.

Guy rubbed his face with his hands and ran his fingers through his hair as he let out a groan. He turned to face Sophie, "I work at the Gas and Go," he confessed.

She shrugged. "So what?"

"I've worked there for twelve years."

She raised her eyebrows slightly as she processed that part of the story. She took a drink and turned back to Guy. "Twelve years?"

He nodded.

"Okay," she acknowledged, "I guess that makes a little more sense. So if it's making you crazy now, why don't you quit? Do something else?"

"Well," he said slowly, "that all comes back to my immortal father."

"Okay. Now we're getting somewhere." Sophie scooted over onto Jacque's stool so they could hear each other better. "Tell me more."

Guy explained the situation the way he had to Jacque earlier in the week. "So I am kind of stuck," he shrugged.

Sophie didn't say anything. She just looked at him with a big smile on her face.

Confused, Guy slowly smiled back. "What?" he asked. "Why are you smiling?"

"Because I think you and I are the same."

"How so?" Guy was confused.

"We're both waiting to start our lives."

Guy was still unclear. "I don't get it. How are you waiting?"

"This is too funny. I've been working as a caregiver forever because I can't beat the money anywhere else right now. I've only got a high school education," she explained. "And other than tend bar, I've never really done anything else. The only reason I do this job is because I can afford to pay for my little sister's tuition. She's got two years left. As soon as she's done, I get to start my own life."

Guy nodded in understanding. "I get it now. So, are we crazy?"

"Are we crazy?" she laughed. "Everybody's crazy. But I don't know if this makes us any crazier. I do know that I am really looking forward to Abby being done with school."

"Yeah," he hesitated a moment before continuing. "I say this knowing how horrible it sounds, but I think you'll understand. I am really looking forward to not waiting for my dad to die anymore. I mean, I don't want him to die, but..." he started to explain, but she cut him off.

"No, no, no," she put up her hand. "Stop. You don't need to justify that or explain it. I totally get it. I've been doing the caregiver thing for over ten years now. There's a lot of long good-byes and I don't think people need to feel guilty. It can really grind a person down."

They were both silent for a moment as they reveled in their mutual understanding. Sophie took a drink of her vodka grapefruit and then turned back to Guy. "So, what's your plan? When you do get start your own life? What are you going to do?"

Guy sighed and put his hands on his face again before solemnly shaking his head and confessing, "I have no fucking idea."

Sophie burst out laughing. "Me neither!" she said excitedly, "Not a clue!" Then she shook her head. "How is it we don't know? What's wrong with us?"

"I don't know. You know I've made plans in the past, but..." he shrugged.

"Yeah. Yours is different. You've got an excuse. Your situation is so much more open ended. That's hard to plan."

"True. But you've still got a couple of years at least don't you? You have plenty of time to make a plan."

"Yeah. I suppose I should get busy with that. It's just weird to think that I might finally get to start something for myself."

Guy shook his head. "I never thought it would last this long." Sophie nodded in understanding and turned to pick up her glass. As she took a sip of her drink, he stared at her. He felt something and wasn't sure what it was. When Jacque told her how screwed-up he was about his job, he was angry and embarrassed. But now, talking to her, those feelings had vanished. He noticed that he didn't care anymore. He had been exposed and he was vulnerable and it was okay. She hadn't pounced, she didn't make him feel stupid. She simply smiled and said she understood. She got it. The transition from shame to complete comfort was so abrupt that Guy was confused. The whole encounter was so surreal, but it felt really good. It felt...right.

"Hey," Jacque interrupted as he returned, "we're almost up for pool."

Sophie shook her head. "No. Can't you find a different partner? We're bonding right now."

He stared at an unusually happy-looking Guy. "Seriously? Come on. One game. I need you."

Guy made a face and stood up reluctantly.

"Are you really going to steal my new best friend?" she asked Jacque.

"Just for a little while. You two can bond more later. We're up for pool."

"You can play pool later," she countered.

"Hey," Jacque said subtly tilting his head toward Michele and Laura. "I don't really even want to play pool right now, let alone later."

Sophie looked confused.

"Jesus," he was exasperated. "You're just like him. It's not about the pool, it's about the opponent. I'd go play fucking tiddlywinks right now if that's what she was playing," he said, nodding his head over at the table.

Guy laughed as Sophie caught on.

"Come on, I need my wingman. Who knows, maybe one of them will help him overcome his occupational constipation and he'll get lucky," he teased.

Guy was reluctant to end his conversation with Sophie. Then he reminded himself that she was leaving for Iowa tomorrow. And even if she wasn't, she was with Bear. Two ships, he thought. "Hey, thanks for listening." He shrugged and stood up. "But duty calls." Guy paused and smiled at her before following Jacque. "I suck at pool. So does Jacque. This shouldn't take too long. When I come back maybe we can help each other figure out what to do with our lives."

"Maybe," she smiled at him hopefully. Then she looked toward Michele and Laura. "Maybe not."

As they walked over to the pool table, Jacque leaned in toward Guy. "You know you can hook up with someone or mess around once in a while without having a whole big relationship."

"Ehhh," he shrugged.

"Jesus, Guy. I bet even those two drunken bastards have gone home with more women than you," he observed gesturing across the bar to Bill and Phil.

"Probably," Guy agreed fatalistically. "I know they have better jobs and drive a nicer truck than me."

"Hey, Guy," Laura greeted him as they approached the table. "Are you two up next?"

"Yeah. This is my friend Jacque. Jacque, Laura."

They said hello to each other and Guy nodded toward Michele who was talking to the waitress, "Is that Michele Dasher?"

"In the flesh."

"Wow! Where's she been hiding? I haven't seen her in years."

"She's been around, just doesn't get out very much."

Just then, Michele came up, "Is that you, Guy Bradford?" she asked excitedly.

"How've you been Michele?" he smiled as he nodded.

"Oh my god! I haven't seen you since high school!" She threw her arms around him, giving him the great, happy embrace of the intoxicated.

He startled, but recovered to hug her back. When he had been released, he said, "This is my friend Jacque."

"Jock?"

"Jacque," he corrected her.

"Shock?" she tried again.

Laura rolled her eyes and said quietly to Guy, "Like I said, she doesn't get out much." Then she turned to her friend, "Michele. It's French," she tried to explain. "It's like that explorer guy, Jacque Cousteau."

"Ahhhh," she said, thinking she had it figured out. "Oui, oui, Inspector Jacque Clouseau. It is an honor to meet you, sir." She held out her hand

Laura and Guy burst out laughing, but Jacque played along. He bowed his head, took her hand, and kissed it gently. "Merci beaucoup, but zee pleasure eez all mine, Madame," he said in an exaggerated French accent.

Guy put in the quarters and Jacque set the rack. Laura had a decent break and the game was underway. Michele and Jacque were laughing and being silly while Laura and Guy made small talk and caught each other up on their lives. That was always painful for Guy. The few people who didn't see him regularly at the Gas and Go would always ask, "What have you been up to, Guy?" He would always be vague and say something like "Oh nothing" or "Same shit, different day," which were both absolutely true in his case. No new job, no girlfriend, same apartment, same car, no dog. Nothing. Nothing was new and nothing had changed since they last saw him. But people would press and ask him for details that really didn't exist. And then finally they would ask, "So where you working these days?" And, feeling like a giant loser, he would have to say, "I'm still working over at the Gas and Go." When he ran into people he hadn't seen in a while, he avoided eye contact and hoped they didn't notice him. Fortunately, he thought, Laura knew he worked there so she wouldn't ask and he wouldn't have to say it. He was right about that, and as they visited, he was grateful that she did most of the talking. Suddenly, while in the middle of a story about her youngest son's Little League exploits, she put her hand to her mouth and said slowly, "Holy shit."

Guy could see that she was staring past his shoulder toward the door and he turned around. Troy Carson had just walked into The Duke. "Is that bad? Didn't Michele divorce him?"

"Yes. But he's always such an asshole. He just can't get over the fact that any woman dumped him." She looked to see if Michele had noticed. No, she was watching Jacque take his turn.

"I'm surprised to see him in here."

"No kidding. I didn't think he really hung out in town anymore. Too many of the women around here already know what a dick he is. He had to expand his range."

"I guess so. I don't know the last time I saw him in here. It's been years," Guy added.

They watched him put his arm around a cute little redhead. "No way!" Laura exclaimed. "Is he really with her? Oh my god! I wonder where she got her fake ID. She looks like she's Carly's age. Oh, that poor girl has no idea what she's in for."

"Who's Carly?"

"His freakin' daughter! She's in high school."

The redhead did look pretty young, thought Guy. And she did appear to be his girlfriend. At least for tonight, anyway.

"Shit. He's coming over here." She walked over by Michele and tried to nudge her subtly so they could flee into the bathroom, but it was too late.

"Hey Michele," he greeted her with exaggerated sweetness, "Laura. You ladies are looking fine tonight. My boy Matty said he saw you over here on Sunday for the Bears game."

Michele just looked at him with a combination of surprise and drunken bemusement.

Laura spoke up. "Hello Troy. Been going to the gym much?" Clearly ripped, his tribally-tattooed biceps stretched the sleeves of his tight white t-shirt.

"You bet." He seemed to stand up a little straighter. "Gotta break a sweat every day, baby. Even though, lately," he nodded over toward the little redhead, "I've been breakin' one at night, too."

"Really? You're in your thirties and still bragging about getting laid?"

Laura didn't mask her disgust.

Troy ignored her. "Exercise is healthy. All kinds. You know, Michele, working out a little wouldn't hurt you. Hittin' that gym's not a bad idea," he suggested. "Especially if you're going to start going out and hitting the bars like this. You ain't as young as you used to be honey."

Jacque had finished taking his turn and stood up. He heard Troy's dickish comment to Michele and decided to have a little fun. He walked up right next to Michele and put his arm around her waist. "It's your turn sweetie," he told her. Then he kissed her. He turned and grinned at Troy. "Hey buddy. How's it goin'? I'm Jacque." He stuck his hand out. "You a friend of Michele's?"

Troy stared at him, trying to process what he just saw as Jacque's extended hand waited patiently. Finally, he reached out, shook it, and muttered quietly. "Uhh, yeah. Troy."

He nudged Michele. "Take your turn hon. I think you've got a shot at the seven." Dazed, she moved to take her turn. Jacque turned his back on Troy and started talking to Guy and Laura about the game as if he wasn't there. Troy stood dumbfounded for a moment before walking away. Laura and Guy stared wide-eyed at Jacque, not paying any attention to what he was saying. He followed their eyes as they watched Troy walk away over his shoulder. "Is he gone?" he asked and broke into a mischievous smile.

"That was so awesome!" Laura exclaimed.

Michele came over with her mouth hanging open. "I can't believe you just did that. Thank you so much." She gave him a long hug.

"Well thanks for playing along and not slapping the shit out of me," he laughed. "That's the ex I take it?"

"You know," marveled Guy shaking his head, "you have some huge balls."

They finished their game of pool, rehashing the little drama, their shock, and making fun of Troy's stupefied expression.

"And now you two have to stay and hang out with us." Michele smiled and grabbed Jacque's arm. "At least until he leaves. Come on, let's find a table."

"I guess if we have to," he said with false reluctance as she dragged him away.

Laura and Guy dutifully followed as Sophie watched from her perch over at the bar. *Good for them,* she thought. Guy looked over, caught her eye, and gave a little wave. He then looked toward Jacque and the ladies, looked back at her, and shrugged as if to suggest he was stuck. Sophie was disappointed. There was something about him that she couldn't put her finger on, and even though she would have liked him to come back, Sophie smiled and waved him off. *Really,* she thought, *what difference does it make? I'm leaving tomorrow. And even if I was staying, well, there's Bear.* Raising her glass, she gave him a little nod. Guy smiled and was gone.

Michele, Laura, Jacque, and Guy hung out together long after Troy had slunk out of The Duke. For Laura, the rest of the evening brought about an unexpected kind of déjà vu. In junior high, she and Michele used to go to skate night at the roller rink in Twin Lakes and that's where she found herself once again. Her friend was blissfully chatting with the boys, laughing and generally being fun, beautiful Michele. Laura was once again reprising her role as the friend. She was there but not there, included but ignored. She laughed to herself as she recognized it and was entertained watching how Guy and Jacque vied for the attentions of her friend. When she was young, it wasn't so amusing. It hurt. But now, well, as genuinely attractive and charming as Michele was, Laura was the one who was happily married. It was all less competitive and far subtler, but it was still happening, just as it had when they were younger. The jokes, the eye contact, the helpfulness, the casual contact, and all of the other infinite little ways in which men and boys compete for the approval and affections of a beautiful woman were on full display. She wondered how aware of it they even were.

As it got close to midnight, Laura began dropping hints about heading home. She had to get up early for a soccer game the next morning. Michele was oblivious, but Jacque and Guy caught on and helped a clearly fading Laura get her friend moving toward the door.

"Got an extra cigarette?" Laura asked Guy as they all stepped out into the cool air on the deck.

"Sure." He shook the pack so a couple of them were sticking out and offered it to her. She took one, as did he, and then Guy lit them both. Michele and Jacque scolded them and wandered into the parking lot, separating themselves from the smokers.

"What's Jacque's deal?" Laura asked. "How do you guys know each other?"

"Just from work and The Duke. When he first opened the bakery, I think the Gas and Go was one of the first places to have one of his cases," he explained. "For a long time he made the deliveries himself and I'm always the one working in the mornings so we used to visit and he would ask me questions about where everything was around here."

"So where's he from?"

"Chicago. I guess his parents had a bakery there, but he wanted to get out of the city. Anyway, we just started hanging out."

"That's cool."

"Yeah, he's a good guy. He's funny. Really smart, too."

As they finished smoking, Michele and Jacque returned. Then the women said goodnight and were gone.

"Wow," Laura commented as they climbed into her car, "you just kissed a guy in a bar tonight," she teased. "You don't waste any time."

"Hey," she protested, "he kissed me! And it was perfect. He saved me from Troy."

"I'm not so sure he was just interested in saving you..." Laura countered as they drove away. "And wow, you're drunk."

"Maybe. But I don't care."

"I can probably guess how much Guy makes, but do we know how much money bakers make?"

Michele's shoulders slumped. "Please don't make me think about that right now," she complained.

"It was your idea!" Laura protested.

"But tonight was just supposed to be about going out and having fun! That's what we said."

Michele was right and Laura backed off. "Well I am glad you had fun." She started laughing. "I still can't believe the look on Troy's face when

Jacque kissed you like that."

"Oh my god, I know!" Michele's face lit up. "It was so perfect. I can't believe he did that!"

Laughing about it all over again, they made the short drive back to her house. After a hug goodnight, Michele climbed out of the car and fumbled with her keys as she walked in a not-so-straight line to her front door. Once she was safely inside, Laura backed into the street. Before she could drive away however, Michele came running back outside, yelling and carrying something.

"Wait! Wait!" she hissed trying to get her friend's attention without waking up the neighborhood as she ran down the driveway.

Laura stopped and rolled down the window while Michele hustled up to the car. "Here," she said reaching in and dropping a heavy bag on her lap. "Take some of this with you or I'll just have to dump it out." Laura looked in and saw two half-gallons of milk.

Sophie had watched Guy and Jacque exit out the back door to the deck with their new friends.

"More water? Or do you want another drink?" Mindy asked.

Bear was still busy and she found herself alone in the dwindling crowd, thinking about her long drive all the way across Iowa in the morning. "Just my tab, I guess." After settling up, she took a last look at the back doors for Guy and Jacque, then left The Duke.

"How about that, my friend?" Jacque beamed as they watched Michele and Laura drive away.

"That was fun," admitted Guy as they headed back inside. "I am impressed. You still got some game. For an old guy."

"You just gotta take a chance once in a while. You never know."

As they returned to the din of the bar, Guy looked to the spot where Sophie had been stationed. Seeing it vacant, he scanned the room. Nothing. He followed Jacque to a couple of empty stools and Mindy came up and put coasters in front of them.

"Water for me and an MGD for my friend." Grinning happily, Jacque put his hand on Guy's shoulder. "Not the first time, but it has been a while since I kissed the hottest lady in the place."

Second hottest, thought Guy.

Chapter 24

Even without setting an alarm, Sophie was up early and on the road by eight o'clock. Bear had gotten up when she did and milled around awkwardly while he watched her get ready and finish packing up the few remaining items that weren't already loaded into her car. He had offered to help, but there wasn't anything for him to do.

"Keep in touch," he told her.

"You really going to write me letters?" she asked skeptically. "None of these old people that I take care of have entered the 20th century yet. Without a computer or any kind of internet access in the house, I'm pretty much off the grid for a few more years. At least until I get settled somewhere."

"Yeah," he admitted. "That's probably not going to happen."

"How about this?" she offered. "If I ever get back to Richmond, I will stop into The Duke and you can buy me a beer?" Sophie was used to these goodbyes and they didn't bother her too much. She learned years ago that expecting to stay in touch with the few acquaintances she made along the way only led to disappointment. Even when people had good intentions, well, it just didn't happen. Out of sight meant out of mind.

"Deal."

They hugged without kissing and she left Bear and his bears alone in his apartment. Sophie checked the time, set her odometer, and put on her right blinker as she coasted toward the exit of the apartment parking lot. She started to make the turn, but then abruptly changed her mind and went the opposite direction. Two minutes later she was parked in front of Big John's

Gas and Go and, she told herself, just grabbing a quick coffee for the road. When she went inside and actually saw the coffee pot she paused, but then bravely filled a small Styrofoam cup and fitted it with a lid. On her way to the register, Sophie also saw Jacque's donut case and smiled to herself as she used a piece of wax paper to pick out a chocolate frosted éclair.

"Good morning," the woman behind the counter greeted her. "Just the coffee and the donut this morning?"

"That'll do it." Sophie put a five-dollar bill on the counter as she looked around the little store. "Guy's not working this morning?"

"Oh no, hon," she replied handing back her change. "He's always off on Fridays and Saturdays."

"Oh. Would it be possible for me to leave a note for him?" she asked surprising herself.

"Well sure, hon. Do you need a pen and paper?"

"Yes, thank you," came her reply. She took the pen and the sheet of paper from the cashier and stared at it. *Okay, genius*, she asked herself, *now what? What are you going to write?* Then, before all the doubts and second guessing cascaded down upon her, she wrote her name and her post office box number in Waterloo. She quickly folded it in half, put his name on the outside of it, and hustled out the door.

The drive from Richmond, Illinois to Sioux City on the far border of Iowa was almost 450 miles straight west. It also put her right in-between I-70 to the South and I-80 to the north. Sophie did not miss the convenience of an interstate though. Traffic was light and Route 20 traveled well enough. She enjoyed the endless fields and farms and passing through the small Midwestern towns she had known all her life. The sky was clear and her journey into the hills around Galena, across the Mississippi into Dubuque, and finally out into the gently rolling hills of her home state, was a relaxing one.

Sophie was trying to reach Waterloo before noon and did so with twenty minutes to spare. Leaving Route 20, she detoured into the old downtown, parked on the street across from the post office, and hurried inside while the counter was still open. The little post office box she rented there offered the illusion of stability in her otherwise unstable life because, although she moved continually, her mailing address had not changed in over a decade. After Frannie's accident, she put a hold on her mail. Once she got settled again, she would begin to have it forwarded to wherever she happened to be. It was always either holds or forwards; she never actually checked her box for mail. Sophie waited in the short line, and when it was her turn the clerk disappeared into the back for a few moments before returning with the few items that had accumulated. She requested that the hold continue and, leafing through her mail, slowly walked back outside.

As she approached her car, Sophie's stomach reminded her that it was time to eat again. After trading the mail for a light jacket, she left it parked where it was and started walking the couple of blocks down toward the river and her old tavern. It had been ten years since she heeded Barb's advice and chose to duck out from behind the bar at Smitty's Tap. It was busy inside, but she found an open stool at the bar, looked around, and appreciated how little it had changed. Sophie ordered a Coke and one of their enormous Italian beef sandwiches with extra hot peppers and visited with the bartender while she waited for her food. She identified herself as a former Smitty Bitty, as the female employees were called. They reminisced and were able to find a few people in common. He told her that his brother-in-law bought the place about three years ago. Smitty was still around though and stopped in every once in a while. She asked about Barb, but the name didn't ring a bell with him. Sophie ate her meal quickly, paid, and returned to her car.

Back on the road, her mind wandered. She was looking forward to surprising Abby. It would have been fun to spend Thanksgiving with her, but, oh well, she thought, this would be even better. No holiday stress; we can just hang out. She wondered what Jake from downstairs looked like. Sophie was excited about seeing the college and Sioux City. She'd never been that far west before. *Who knows*, she thought, *maybe I can even find a job somewhere nearby*. She didn't know anyone in the area, but maybe some of her contacts had contacts there. Either way, she decided, it was time to be closer to her sister. Eight hours away in Illinois was just too far. There had to be plenty of old, sick people around in Iowa, too.

Sophie considered her next job. Normally, she would be almost set up already. But the trip to see Abby was throwing everything off. She'd notified the placement agents she worked with but told them she was going to take a short break to visit family. They were good about getting her work, but if she stayed with just them, she was going to be stuck in Illinois. That had been the whole reason for her eastern migration. In and around the cities of Waterloo and Cedar Rapids and Des Moines, where Sophie started, the market for caregivers was controlled by a creepy assortment of bullying Eastern European men. They called themselves brokers, but they were more like pimps. Each had their stable of women, mostly fresh from Eastern Europe. They got them the jobs but took a sizeable cut out of every paycheck. Most of the women didn't know any better and were essentially trapped. The nature of the work was isolating, and they were in a new country. It was difficult for them to understand that there were other ways of doing business. Sophie started out working with a Polish guy, Stan, who hung out at Smitty's once in a while. Then she found a job on her own near Galena. It was through the family she had worked for in Rock Island. They really liked her and recommended her to some friends who had a need. Stan was furious at the idea of losing one of "his girls" and demanded his cut. He harassed her and even threatened her. After her tires had been slashed, she ended up paying him a bullshit finder's fee just so he would leave her alone. From there she found some decent people who worked with social service agencies, churches, and meals on wheels type stuff. They took a decent chunk out of the first month's wages, but then that was it. They weren't predatory and they found her jobs throughout western Illinois. It'd been years since she'd gone more than two weeks without one. That was important for two reasons. First, she was still focused on paying for Abby to go to college and second, even cheap hotels weren't very cheap. When she wasn't working, she was basically homeless. She had to pay to stay somewhere.

Sophie stopped for gas one last time before the final push into Sioux Falls.

After using the bathroom, she cleaned the accumulated garbage from her travel snacks out of her car. Along with the gum wrappers, soda bottles, napkins, and empty Corn Nuts bags, she tossed out the Styrofoam coffee cup from the Gas and Go. Shaking her head and laughing, she imagined Guy's face looking at her name and address scrawled across the paper. What would he even think? And where the hell did that even come from? She thought about their too brief conversation the night before.

Sophie had never really talked to anyone about the idea of waiting to start her life before. She wasn't even sure she had thought about it too much herself. She supposed it was there, lingering in the back of her mind, but her focus was always on the next job and saving up the money for Abby. When Guy was talking about it though…well, it was all right there. They've both been slogging along for years. At least she'd had some variety, she thought gratefully. He'd been at that gas station forever and it really seemed to be wearing him down. And, he was the only one dealing with his dad. She thought back on the different placements she'd had over the years. There wasn't one she could recall where it involved only one, relatively younger, child who was also single. That was a tremendous burden for just one person to bear. There always seemed to be families involved, even if it was an aunt or uncle or cousin. There was always someone else and they all took turns and helped each other out. Granted, some always did more of the work than others, but everyone got some kind of relief from time to time. They didn't always have to be the one.

She wondered if he would write. She hoped he would. What would he write about? His dad? Work? The Duke? The only letters she ever got from anyone were from Abby. They were always full of little tidbits about her life. It didn't even matter what she wrote about, really, it was all interesting to Sophie. She guessed it would probably be the same if Guy wrote. Maybe, she mused, they could help each other figure out what to do with their lives. They could find out more about each other and then make suggestions. That could be cool. Her thoughts returned to last night again. She'd really hoped that he would come back after playing pool but understood why he didn't. Jacque needed him, and what difference did it make? She was leaving anyway. Sophie wondered if he actually left with that other woman and then wasn't sure how she felt about it. Part of her was happy for him if he did, but part of her didn't really like the idea. She caught herself and laughed. *Wow! Get a grip Sophie. Yes, he was a nice guy, but come on. You don't even know him. It's done.* She looked out the window and thought about her note. With a measure of disappointment, it dawned on her. *He's probably just going to think I am looking for a job, dammit. I should have written something else on that paper.*

Telephone poles, silos, tiny towns, partially harvested fields of corn and soybeans, gently rolling hills, hours, and miles all flew past as she contemplated her way across the state. Once the mileage signs for her destination dropped below fifty, she stopped thinking, she stopped trying to figure out her life, and simply reveled in the anticipation of her visit and the coming excitement of the surprise. As the lights of Sioux City blended into the setting sun, she turned on her radio and, losing herself in the feel-good nonsense of a top forty station, sang her way into town.

Chapter 25

Guy slept in, woke up to pee, returned to his bed, and slept in some more. *Why not*, he thought, *I don't really have anything to do today anyway.* As the clock approached noon, hunger finally coaxed him up and into the kitchen. He poured himself a bowl of cereal, plopped down on the couch, and turned on the television. Without cable, his choices were limited to college football, golf, and something about modern American poetry on PBS. He chose football and, despite his complete disinterest in doing so, began to wake up.

When he finished his cereal, he set the bowl on the coffee table in front of him and continued watching a game he didn't care about until halftime jarred him out of his stupor. Still sitting on the couch, he scanned his apartment. On the counter was a stack of mail. It had been piling up and he knew there were at least a couple of bills in there. Past that, he could see an accumulation of dishes in and around the sink. The last clean bowl had just been used for his breakfast. Into the bedroom, he could see a couple small mounds of clothes on the floor. He imagined his closet for a moment, hoping to find a reason to delay that task, but found it wanting. *I guess this is my Saturday*, he thought. *Bills, dishes, and laundry.*

Guy grabbed some jeans and a t-shirt and got dressed. Gathering up his clothes and towels, he tossed them toward a broken plastic laundry basket and retrieved the detergent from under his bathroom sink. He was grateful to find a decent supply of quarters remaining in the plastic cup on his dresser. Then, he grabbed a hat and a flannel off the back of a kitchen chair, found his cigarettes and lighter in one of the breast pockets, picked up his laundry, and left. Despite some sunlight peeking through the clouds, the concrete was cold on his bare feet as he followed the sidewalk from his building to the little room in the next that housed the sporadically functioning washing machines and dryers.

Guy went through his clothes, checking pockets and turning them right side out before tossing them into the basin of one of the machines. It was full before his basket was empty. He paused to check his supply of quarters and counted enough for two washes, but only one dry. Or, he thought as he stuffed in the rest of his clothes, two dries and one wash. Once the machine was running, he stepped outside to light a cigarette. It took him a couple of tries as the corridor in-between the buildings acted like a little wind tunnel. Moving to the front of his building, Guy found a spot that was both out of the breeze and in the sunshine. He closed his eyes and tilted his head toward the sky, trying to absorb some of the warmth as he smoked. When he was done, he flicked the butt into the parking lot and returned to his apartment.

Back inside, he picked through his accumulation of mail. Most of it, the junk, went right in the trash. The rest were bills, and although he worked to keep their totals low, his paycheck was pretty low as well. Guy prioritized by due date and wrote what checks he could. Using a magnet, he stuck the couple of unpaid ones on his refrigerator so he would see them and be reminded. The paid ones were sealed in envelopes and put on the counter next to his car keys. Then he turned his attention to the dishes. He cleaned them off his coffee table, kitchen table, and dresser, and brought them into the kitchen. He emptied the sinks, filled one with soap, and forced himself to slog through cleaning the dishes while he wondered why he routinely neglected to rinse them and allowed food to dry and harden on them. *I just can't seem to do anything the easy way*, he mused.

Guy checked the time on the microwave clock and, with the dishes drying on a towel on the counter, grabbed the paid bills and his car keys. He stopped by his car on the way back to the laundry room and put the envelopes on the dashboard. Hopefully, that would be enough to get him to stop by the post office for stamps on Monday. After moving his clothes to the dryer, he lit another cigarette and wandered back to his spot in the sunshine. Stepping off the concrete, he felt the significantly warmer black pavement of the parking lot on his still bare feet and enjoyed that little victory while he smoked. When he was done, the second butt landed close to the first, and again, he went back inside.

His chores mostly completed, Guy put a frozen pizza in the oven and returned to his couch. *So this is my day off*, he thought. *Holy fuck, do I have problems.* He looked around his apartment. He considered the effort it took to get himself out of bed, to find the energy to do his laundry, pay bills, and wash the dishes. Out loud he said, "I just don't want to do anything." *And this is just the most basic shit necessary to perpetuate my existence*, he thought. *It's a Saturday. It's my day off. It's pretty nice out for October. And I am sitting here, on my ass, putting in time, waiting to get through the day. I'm just ticking off the hours trying to get through another fucking day.* He looked at his bike in the corner and tried to recall the last time he rode it. The timer went off and he got up to get his food. *Even this*, he observed shaking his head as he took the pizza from the oven, *how much of this shit have I been eating lately?*

He took a soda from the fridge and carried it with his food back to park himself in front of his TV. He found another college football game and sat there waiting for the pizza to cool. Taking a deep breath, he tried to assess his situation. He thought about his conversation with Jacque earlier in the week. *Do I really hate my job?* he wondered. Guy thought about Big John and the regular customers and how he'd spent so much of his life to this point. Grudgingly, he acknowledged that while he was sick of it, he didn't really hate what he did. But he did hate that he was doing it. It was brutalizing his self-esteem and he was, like Jacque pointed out, feeling stuck.

His mind drifted to the previous night. He thought it was cool how forty-two-year-old Jacque had the balls to go after Michele. She was gorgeous. He knew there was no way he would have done that. Once they started hanging out with her and Laura, though, it was easy. *So why don't I ever do that kind of thing on my own*, he wondered. His mind returned to the Gas and Go. *I know why I don't ever talk to women anymore*, he decided. *It's because I'm a loser and I know it. I know I have nothing to offer. I don't need anyone else to know it, too.* He thought about Sophie and sighed. It didn't matter that she was with Bear or that she was leaving, there's no way he would have hit on her anyway. But, damn, it just felt good to be talking to her. He perked up a little and half smiled. It was weird. She didn't seem to really care about the Gas and Go.

He leaned forward to take a slice of pizza and cautiously bit into it. It was hot, but not burning. *Okay,* he started over, *I need to find something.* Guy stood, trying to spur some motivation, and turned the volume down on the game. Pacing, he tried to focus. *I need a different job. I don't even know if I care what it is or that I even have to like it. I mean, really, who actually likes their job anyway? I just want some kind of a job that, when someone asks me what I do, I don't feel like such a loser answering them. A little more money wouldn't hurt either,* he thought. Guy recalled the jobs that he mentioned to Jacque. Were those really it? They did mostly seem like adolescent bullshit. But when was the last time he really thought about stuff like that? Probably when he was about that age. *What do I want to do now?* he asked himself. *Do I want to move? Could I be a river guide? Could I actually become a smoke jumper? I could probably do both of those. And there are commercials on television all the time for truck driving school. I could do that, too. I'm single and they always say they can help with student loans and stuff.* Then Guy thought about his father and everything ground to a halt. *I can't move. I can't be on the road for days at a time. I can't just leave him at this point.* Deflated again, Guy dropped back onto the couch. Leaning forward, he put his elbows on his knees and rubbed his temples with his hands. *I should leave,* he thought, *I know I should just fucking leave. But I know as soon as I try to, something will just happen again. Some crisis will suck me right back in.* He felt completely powerless over anything in his life and slumped backward into the cushions. Taking a deep breath and letting it out slowly, Guy wondered out loud, "When? When does this end?"

Chapter 26

Sophie saw the signs for Morningside College and drove past them as she double checked her directions. It was disappointing that the apartment was so far away from the campus, but she assumed that Abby must have a good reason for it. Probably cheaper, she guessed. A few miles later, she found Fairmount Street and finally turned off Route 20. Fairmount turned into 6th and took her past a semi-occupied industrial area, over the canal that pretended to be the Floyd River and into the aging downtown. From there, she headed north past a refinery and a rail yard, both of which tempered her excited anticipation with concern over the neighborhood. She anxiously re-checked her directions, slowed down, and began looking for her sister's street.

Abby's address was only a couple of blocks away from her turn down Royce Street, and although she found it quickly, she was puzzled. Parking under a streetlight, Sophie looked out at what appeared to be a ranch-style duplex instead of an apartment building. She examined the address she had written down and found that it matched the numbers clearly displayed on the house. Sophie scanned up and down the street for Abby's car, but did not see it anywhere. Jake, the guy she was interested in, lived downstairs, according to the last letter. Maybe there was a basement apartment? It sure didn't look like it. She tried to consider her options but didn't feel like she had any other than going up to the house and finding out. Without a phone, she was kind of stuck. Besides, a call would give away the surprise.

Sophie turned on the interior light and checked herself in the rearview mirror. Then, after taking a deep breath, she got out of the car, walked with some trepidation up the sidewalk to the porch on the left-hand side of the duplex, and rang the bell. Still uncertain that she was in the correct place, her pulse quickened as she heard footsteps approaching. The door was unlocked and partially opened by a skinny guy who looked to be in his early twenties. He had a patchy, thin beard, a shaggy mess of dirty blonde hair, pale skin, and a tired looking face. His feet were bare and he wore long, dark blue corduroy shorts that clashed with his plain greenish blue t-shirt. Sophie's first thought was that she woke him up.

"Hi," she smiled. "I'm trying to find Abby Stewart. I'm not sure that I'm in the right place though."

"Are you her probation officer?" he asked in a voice that sounded groggy from sleep.

Staring blankly, Sophie tried to process the question—tried to find a way that she misheard it, a way that it didn't make sense. But she couldn't. Her stomach knotted, her chest tightened, the smile on her face vanished as the man stared back at her waiting for an answer. Finally, she found her voice and managed a quiet, dazed, "No. I'm her sister. Sophie."

"Oh, wow," he apologized, "my bad. I didn't even know Abs had a sister."

Her smile returned, weak and pained, as she absorbed that second blow. They stood on either side of the door in awkward silence, confused, as they both tried to incorporate the new information into their understanding of Abby.

He spoke first, "Uh, well, hey, Abs isn't home right now, but," he hesitated while he checked his pockets for his phone. Not finding it, he asked, "Do you know what time it is?"

"Almost five-thirty."

"I can text her if you want, but she should be home in about an hour."

"Please don't text her. I was hoping to surprise her. Is that okay?"

"Oh yeah, that's cool," he smiled. "She was working today, but then her and Kara were gonna stop by the boat afterwards. They're supposed to come back here and get me when they're done. We were gonna go out."

"The boat?" she wondered aloud.

"The riverboat, the Argosy," he tried to explain. Seeing nothing register on her face, he continued, "It's one of those floating casinos. It's downtown, on the Missouri River."

"Ohhh," Sophie nodded. "Well, is it far from here? Can you give me directions?"

"I could, but you'd probably just miss her. She'd be on her way back by the time you'd find it and get parked and everything."

"Okay." Sophie waited on the porch.

"Uhh, I guess if you want, you could wait here for her."

"Are you sure you wouldn't mind?"

"No, no, not a problem," he started to open the door wider, but caught himself. He turned his head and looked back into the apartment. "Just give me a couple seconds, okay? It's pretty messy right now. It'll just take me a minute, promise." And then he closed the door on her.

Sophie stood on the porch, alone in the dim light and took a deep breath to try and settle herself. Who was this guy? What was he doing in there? Probation? She wondered how Abby could have gotten into trouble. Who was she associating with? Was it this guy? She started to wonder if she should even go inside. Would she be safe? Should she go for a drive and find a restaurant and come back later? But it was too late. The door swung wide open.

"Sorry about that," he extended his arm, "come on in and have a seat."

Sophie cautiously entered the apartment. The smell of air freshener couldn't quite mask the scent of old carpet and cigarettes. Inside the doorway was a small area of faded yellow linoleum that gave way to some very worn, very dated shag carpeting. The walls were dark paneled wood, and on one end of the room was a large flat screen television showing cartoons. Video games and controllers dominated a coffee table that separated it from a battered green couch. On either side of the couch was an end table. One had a lamp and was adjacent to a wing-backed chair that appeared to have been upholstered long ago in a rust colored velour-type fabric. Past the television and against the wall near the entrance to a darkened hallway, a medium size fish tank rested on another taller table. On the far side of the room was a counter with three mismatched stools that opened into a small kitchen. Squeezed into the corner of the kitchen near a sliding glass door was a small table with just two folding chairs. As she moved to sit down on one of the stools, she noticed that there were no dirty dishes in the sink. There were no crumbs on the counters, no clutter even. In fact, from where she sat, the entire apartment appeared to be in order. He either just miraculously cleaned everything in about ninety seconds, she thought, or he was lying.

"I'm Jake, by the way," he said extending his hand, "her boyfriend. What's your name again?"

She shook his hand, "Sophie."

He stood across the counter from her in the kitchen. "You want something? Like a soda? Or a beer or something?"

Screw beer, she thought, *I want some vodka right now*. Instead she said, "Sure, I'll take a beer."

He opened the refrigerator. "All we have is PBR," he looked at her expectantly.

She tried to smile and sound pleasant, "Sounds good."

Jake took out two sixteen-ounce cans, "I guess I'll join you," he smiled and returned to the counter opposite her. "Here you go." He slid one of the Pabsts toward her and popped the tab on the other.

Sophie followed his lead, opened hers, and took a long drink. "Thank you." There clearly wasn't a downstairs apartment and it was obvious that Jake was living here. *Why would Abby lie to me about him or her living arrangement?* Sophie wondered what she might have said or done that made Abby feel like she couldn't tell her. "So how long have you two been seeing each other?" she asked.

He thought a moment, "I guess it's been about ten months. Wow, it doesn't seem like that long."

"Did you meet at school?"

"No, I grew up in South Dakota," he answered, shaking his head. "I didn't move to Sioux City until after high school. We met at Grumpy's. When Abs worked there. I was a line cook."

I didn't mean high school, dummy, she thought. *And since when is she gone from Grumpy's? That's another lie!* Anger crept in to join her shock and she fought to hide them both. "Oh," she replied, trying to sound nonchalant, "I didn't realize she wasn't still working there."

Jake looked a little uncomfortable, "No. Not for a long time. They wouldn't give her any time off last spring when we went down to Mexico so she bailed. She started at T-Bird's when we got back. They're pretty chill about that. It's easy to trade shifts and stuff. And it's almost full-time now."

Reeling, Sophie put her hand over her mouth, frozen, and just stared at Jake. They went on a vacation? To Mexico? She didn't know what to feel. There was too much to understand, to piece together. And every time he opened his mouth, it all got worse.

A moment passed before he asked, "Are you okay?"

Snapping out of it, she blinked, exhaled, and took another deep breath. "Yeah, sorry," she lied, "I guess I'm just wiped out. I've been driving all day."

Jake wasn't convinced but played along. "Where did you drive from?" he asked.

"Illinois. Kind of by Chicago."

"Oh yeah," he agreed, "that'll do it, sitting all day in a car. What a drag."

Sophie didn't respond. Her thoughts raced from lie to lie, grasping, desperate to assemble some framework where they could all make sense, to find the simple explanation that would tie it all together. She wanted to hear something that would make her smile and say, "ohhh, okay," and then she could breathe again. Abandoning the charade of calm, she put her elbows on the counter and lowered her head into her hands, thinking. Looking down at the counter, she spoke, more to herself than to Jake, "So she's working full time now? Why? How is she keeping up with all of her schoolwork?"

Jake understood that she was no longer talking to him and he was grateful. "Look, uhh, I think I'm gonna go get in the shower now. They should be back pretty soon." He waited for a response, didn't get one, and quietly walked out of the kitchen and down the hallway, leaving his troubled guest to her thoughts.

Sophie ignored him and continued to fumble through the surprises. *Abby has a probation officer. She's had a boyfriend for almost a year and instead of an apartment with girlfriends, she is living with him. They went to Mexico. She's working full-time, and it's not even at the place she said she was working.* Sophie tried to be objective. *Is any of it really that big of a deal? The probation officer, definitely. And I can understand why she wouldn't tell me that. The rest of it though? Not really. So she has a boyfriend, so what? Different job, so what? Mexico? Did they go on spring break with friends? Jesus,* she thought as she grudgingly came to terms with it. *I guess I can see that. But why all the lies?* She started through them again and began to calm down. Individually, she could see how they all made sense, but it was a lot to process all at once. And even though she could see why a kid might lie about stuff like this, it still hurt to be the one getting lied to.

Sophie stood up and took a deep breath. On the end table without the lamp was an ashtray, cigarettes, and a lighter. *I am so stealing one of those,* she thought as she laughed nervously and walked over to do so. After considering for a moment whether or not to light up in the house, she decided to step out front. Darkness had fallen as she sat down on the front step and lit the cigarette. Every so often, a car approached, and anxiety gripped her as she wondered if it was Abby returning. Sophie was still excited to see her little sister. And she was hungry. *Hopefully we can go get a bite to eat,* she thought. *I don't want to press her on anything right away. We can just catch up and, who knows, maybe she'll fess up on her own.* The more the minutes slipped by, the more her mood improved.

When she stood to go back inside, Sophie stretched and checked the time on her phone. It was almost twenty after six. She knocked lightly on the door figuring Jake was probably still getting ready. There was no sign of him as she slowly opened the door and peeked in. Returning to her seat at the counter, she finished off her beer and looked around for a magazine or something to read. Nothing. As she rose to inspect the fish tank, the front door opened and in walked Abby and her friend. Sophie turned and smiled, waiting to be recognized.

The reunion was short and painful. Jake might have texted to warn her, or maybe she just noticed Sophie's car parked on the street. Either way, Abby didn't even bother to act surprised. She smiled with her mouth only and put her things down to give her sister an obligatory hug. She didn't introduce her friend and spoke without any trace of enthusiasm or excitement. Instead, she seemed barely able to mask her irritation. She wanted to know how long Sophie was planning to be in town and where she was staying. The second question carried the implication that it wasn't going to be there, with them. Heart sinking, Sophie fumbled through a response about a hotel she had passed on the way into town. It was immediately clear that her visit was simply an inconvenience, an intrusion. *Where is my Abby from my letters?* she wondered. They stood there, with Abby using the silence like a weapon to drive her away. At first it was working and Sophie wished she could snap her fingers, disappear, and pretend the visit never happened. But then, the big sister, the guardian, rose up within her and she felt anger and the urge to scold.

"When I got here, Jake asked me if I was your probation officer," she challenged.

"And?" Abby remained defiant.

"Why do you have a probation officer, Abby?" Sophie demanded.

She shook her head and rolled her eyes. "I got busted for having a little pot. It's stupid. It's legal in like ten states now anyway."

"Legal or not, it's still a drug," she scolded. "You can't study when you're stoned. You're supposed to be concentrating on school right now." As Sophie finished her sentence, she saw the friend's expression change. It was subtle, but she caught it. It was her eyes. They narrowed and the eyebrows came together ever so slightly and, for a fraction of a second, she glanced at Abby. It was confusion. It was confusion at the word school. Abby didn't respond and Sophie suddenly felt numb. She scanned the living room and the kitchen. No textbooks, no notebooks, no folders, no backpack, no desk. Turning, she walked quickly toward the hallway that led to the other rooms in the little duplex.

"Where are you going?" Abby called out behind her.

Ignoring her, Sophie opened the door to the first bedroom and found the light switch. There was a twin bed against one wall and a dresser on the other. A few clothes and shoes littered the floor, but no books, no desk. She closed the door and continued down the hall.

"Hey!" Abby yelled and followed her. "What are you doing?"

The next door opened into the bathroom and she moved past it. Abby caught up with Sophie by the time she arrived at the end of the hallway and had positioned herself in front of the last door. Kara had trailed behind them and stood dumbfounded, watching.

"What the hell do you think you're doing?" she repeated insolently. "Jake's in there."

Sophie shoved past her and opened the door. A queen size bed. Clothes, clutter, a television. But no desk and no books.

"What the fuck?" Abby was angry now.

Jake, who had been sitting on the edge of the bed putting on socks, stood up quickly. "What's up? What's going on?"

Sophie turned to her, furious. "Where are your books, Abby!? Where are all of your fucking textbooks!? Where is your goddamn graphing calculator, Abby?!"

Abby met her gaze, but was silent, defiant.

"Are you fucking kidding me?! Are you even in school?" She was shaking now.

Ignoring her, Abby retreated back down the hallway toward the living room.

Sophie followed her, "Don't you walk away from me! Answer me goddammit!"

Jake followed, "Hey! Chill!" he shouted.

She whirled, jabbed her finger at him, and through gritted teeth, said "You stay out of this."

"Excuse me?! This is my fucking house! Who the fuck do you think you are?"

Behind her, from the living room, Sophie heard Abby's voice. "She thinks she's my sister."

Chapter 27

"Uhhhnnnggg," Guy's hand flopped down on the top of the buzzing alarm clock buying another eight minutes of silence. Again. And the yellowish glow from a security floodlight still filtered in through bent and grimy venetian blinds. His three thousandth, one hundred and thirty-eighth morning of getting up early to open the Gas and Go was starting out just like all of the rest. The number ran through his head as he rolled out of bed to use the bathroom, splash some water on his tired face, and throw on some clothes before heading out into the cool of the dawn.

Guy made the same drive and parked in the same place. He unlocked the same door and readied the store in all of the same ways he had for so long. About the only thing different in the store that morning was the sheet of paper with his name on it, folded in half and tucked in-between a couple of bank bags underneath the counter. The letters were facing down though, and it didn't really stand out, so he didn't notice it. Jacque's delivery kid was back on the job and brought in the donuts. He told Guy that he had been given orders to check and see if he had eaten anything else or if he was waiting.

Rolling his eyes, Guy tiredly held up his coffee cup and gestured toward the empty countertop. "Just coffee, I swear." He smiled. "You can report back to Jacque that I did actually wait for one of his donuts this morning."

Although the rest of his shift passed in the same manner with the same flurries of activity and the same idle conversations, Guy made an effort to approach it differently. He tried to enjoy the banter and tried to smile more. Jacque talked about making his job his bitch. Even though he wasn't exactly sure what that meant or how to do it, he tried. He tried not to focus on money. He tried not to be jealous when people younger than him filled up gas tanks on nicer cars than his. He tried not to dwell on the people towing their dirt bikes and quads up to Wisconsin to go and play. He read about the Bears game in the paper and tried to get excited about watching it later that afternoon. But even though he tried, he couldn't quite shake the feeling that he was still just idling away another morning, staring out at the same intersection, waiting for his life to begin.

When his shift was over, he had a little time to kill between work and the Bears game. Feeling the familiar tug of obligation, he drove to his father's house to check in on him. Near the entrance to the driveway, blocking any further progress toward the house, sat the tractor belonging to Charles Bradford. Guy stopped his car, got out, and looked around to see if his father was anywhere in the vicinity. Seeing no sign of him, he climbed up into the seat of the old Ford. Leaning over the steering wheel onto the engine cover, he unscrewed the gas cap and peered inside. Nothing. He climbed down, went back to his car to get a cigarette, lit it, and then started walking up to the house. As it came into view, he could see two beat up, six-gallon gas cans sitting just outside the door of the garage. Guy walked over and lifted them to see if any fuel remained. Nothing again. He picked them up, walked back to his car, and put them in his trunk. After driving back through town and filling them up at the Gas and Go, he drove back to his father's, filled the tractor with gas, drove it into the garage, and parked it. Then he returned to get his car and drove it up to the house. He got the gas cans out of his trunk and carried them to the shelf in the garage where his father kept them. Finally, after making sure he had the receipt in his pocket, Guy went into the house.

His dad was sitting at the kitchen table with Sharette. He greeted them, sat down, and turned toward his father. "I got gas for you and filled the tractor. It's back in the garage now." He slid the receipt over toward him.

"I heard you. I don't know why you always rev that engine so much.

That's why I don't like you driving it. Did you put the cans back in the garage on the shelf where they go?" His father picked up the receipt and, extending his arm, squinted at it. "I can't read this."

"Yes. The cans are back on the shelf. It was $47.80."

Charles reached into his pocket for his money clip. "Do you have any change on you?" he asked as he leafed through the bills.

"No, I don't," Guy replied. *Just another reason to hate my job*, he thought. *If I actually had any money, I could just buy him the stupid gas and not have to deal with this petty bullshit.*

Wait, he caught himself and made sort of a half-smile. *I don't really hate my job*, he reminded himself, *I only hate the idea of my job.*

Charles finished looking through the wad of large bills, peeled off a fifty, and pushed it toward his son. "You owe me $2.20."

Chapter 28

He was in the back when she entered the bakery, and before he even saw her, he noticed how well she had learned to pronounce his name.

"Is Jacque working this morning?" she'd asked the girl at the counter.

He came out in front by the display cases to greet her. "Bonjour, Mademoiselle Michele," he smiled.

She smiled back and said she was just stopping by to get some donuts. He went behind the counter and got a box and some wax paper. Michele said she wasn't sure what she liked, so Jacque selected a variety of what he thought were his best donuts and put them in the box for her.

She thanked him and paid, grateful that he didn't try to give them to her. Jacque handed her the change from a twenty. They both agreed that they had a lot of fun on Friday night. Jacque said that The Duke was his usual hangout. In fact, he noted, he and Guy were planning on going there that afternoon to watch the Bears game. She told him that maybe she would see them later.

Feeling like she hadn't felt in, well, ever, Michele stood on Laura's front porch holding the donuts and rang the doorbell. The racing of footsteps preceded the fight to open the door and the fight to be the first to get at the treats. About an hour ago she had called Laura to see if it was okay if she stopped by. She told her that she was going to check out Not Your Average Bakery! Laura had told her kids and they had been waiting.

She came down the stairs still in a robe and slippers. "Look at you!" she commented to her friend, "pretty spiffy for an early Sunday morning."

"Do I look stupid?" Michele's face grew concerned. "It's not too much, is it?" Although she was dressed simply in jeans and a snug fitting blue long-sleeve t-shirt, her hair was done and she was wearing a little makeup.

"No, no, no. I'm just teasing."

"Well I didn't want to just climb out of bed and run over there in sweats and a hat. But I didn't want to look like I overdid it either."

"You're fine. You want some coffee? I need some coffee." Laura headed for the kitchen and Michele followed. "So how was it?"

"Wonderful and weird. He did look a little older than I remembered, I guess. I felt so awkward, but he was really sweet. He said he was going to watch the Bears game at The Duke this afternoon." Michele sat down at the kitchen table as the kids were busy dividing up the donuts.

"Hey," Laura interjected while she busied herself with the coffee, "you can each have two. Get a plate, get Michele a plate. Napkins, too. And get yourselves a glass of milk." She talked over the objections and bickering of her children. "Leah, you pour it. Pour one for your brother. Do you want a glass of milk, Michele?" She held up one of the half-gallons given to her Friday night. "It's yours."

Michele looked embarrassed. "Oh my god. No, thanks, just coffee."

"He looked older because he is older."

"How old do you think he is?"

"I don't know, early forties? Mid-forties?"

"Well I don't really care either way."

With the kids settled for the moment, Laura sat down. "You want to go watch football this afternoon, don't you?"

Michele smiled. "Maybe."

"And you want me to go with you?"

"Maybe," she smiled hopefully.

"Is Guy going to be there?"

"I think so. Yeah." she answered slowly.

"Younger, better looking Guy?"

"Younger, yes, obviously. But better looking? I don't think so."

"Really?"

"Really. I think Jacque's more handsome."

"But Guy's in better shape. Can we call it a tossup?"

Michele was confused. "Fine, I guess, but I don't think I like where this is headed."

"Yeah, I didn't think you would." Laura stood up and filled two mugs with coffee. She handed one to her friend. "Come on. Let's go sit in the other room."

Michele followed her and they sat down on the couch out of earshot of the kids. "Okay already. What's the deal? Why are you asking about Guy?"

"I don't want you to pick the wrong guy. Guy is the right guy. Jacque," she shook her head sympathetically and winced, "is the wrong guy."

Michele's shoulders slumped. "Are you serious?" she sighed, disappointed. "What's the deal? What's wrong with Jacque?" Then she added, "And what is right with Guy? I thought you said he worked at the Gas and Go?"

"It's not that simple, hon. First, nothing is really wrong with Jacque. From everything I can tell, he seems to be a pretty decent guy. But," she smiled weakly, "he lives in that tiny little apartment above his bakery. He can't be making that much money."

"He's got to be making more than Guy though," Michele protested.

"Probably," Laura acknowledged. "That's not the whole story though." She took a sip of her coffee.

"Well?"

"You know how Ron's sister works in the ER over at the hospital in McHenry?"

"Yeah."

"Well, last Monday night, Guy was in there with his dad. Do you know who his dad is?"

"No. Wait, who was in the emergency room? Guy? Or his dad?"

"His dad, Charles Bradford."

"Okay."

"So I guess Charles had a seat on the Chicago Board of Trade for years.

152

He was some kind of trader, broker, or finance guy or something. I'm not sure exactly what he did, but he's loaded. Big time. Have you ever seen his house?"

Michele shook her head. "I don't think so. Where is it?"

"He lives off 173, just as you leave town heading west. It's this ginormous stone mansion that sits on…I don't know how many acres. But you can't see it from the road."

"Okay, I think I know where you mean. I've never been back there though."

"I was. Once, like in junior high, I think, my mom was driving a bunch of kids home from some school thing and we dropped Guy off. We drove in there and everyone was like 'Holy shit! Nice castle!' and Guy was all embarrassed. The thing is huge."

"Well, okay. So his dad has money."

"A lot of money," Laura corrected her.

"Okay, a lot of money. So what?"

"His dad was in the emergency room because he's basically dying."

"Oh no! What's wrong with him?"

"I don't know," Laura shrugged. "What difference does it make?"

Michele's jaw dropped. "Wow. You are cold."

"What?" Laura was shocked but laughed out loud. "You're one to talk! You're the one who put me on this mission. I'm supposed to find you someone to marry who has some money. Just so you can stay in your house and not have to work!"

"Shhhhhh!" Michele scolded, looking over her shoulder toward the kitchen, "your kids are going to hear!"

Laura lowered her voice. "Well then don't tell me I'm cold. This whole thing is cold and it was your idea."

"I'm sorry. You're right. Can't we be compassionate and cold, though?" she laughed.

"No way. It's too hard on you. When you are using people and grinding them up and spitting them out, you can't look back. Never look back. The ends justify the means. Keep your eyes on the prize."

"Oh my god," she rolled her eyes. "Thanks coach. I think I created a monster."

"Hey. I want to swim in your pool again next summer. Let's get this done. Guy is a good person."

Michele sighed. "When Troy came over and was being a dick, Jacque is the one who said something. Guy just stood there. Don't get me wrong, Guy's nice too, but…" she shrugged.

Laura shook her head. "I knew it. This is what I was afraid of. You're not thinking with your head. Or your purse. Which you shouldn't really be anyway, but that was the whole point of this."

"I know, I know." They sat in silence. Finally, Michele spoke again. "I was with Troy forever. I was sixteen. And when I look back now, I can see that he was a dick even then. But I was a kid, and then we had a kid, and then I thought I was doing the right thing, not just for me, but for Carly. And it really did make her life a whole lot easier. Even though our marriage wasn't perfect, there weren't screaming matches every day and she wasn't stuck with me in a trailer park struggling to get by on food stamps." She paused, remembering what that was like and sipped her coffee. "But whatever. That's not the point. Last Friday, that was the sweetest a guy has ever been to me. He was funny, he was considerate, he was genuinely interested in me, he listened, he didn't try to make me feel stupid. And it was the same this morning at the bakery!" she shrugged. "I like Jacque."

"But Guy is the one with the money," Laura reminded her.

"No," Michele corrected her, "his dad is the one with the money."

"Yeah, but not for long."

Michele put her head in her hands. "I think I hate this."

"Well," Laura sighed, "I guess being a cold, calculating gold digger doesn't come naturally to you. There's nothing to be ashamed of about that."

Chapter 29

"You're early," Michele protested as she answered the door. "I'm not even ready yet."

"I know, sorry. I was hoping to run an errand before we went over there," Laura explained.

"Okay, good. I didn't want to get there like right when the game starts. I don't want to seem desperate."

"Don't worry," she assured her, "I will keep your desperation a secret."

Michele smirked. "Give me five minutes." She retreated back up the stairs.

Laura walked past the stairs and the powder room into the spacious kitchen. From the cupboard she grabbed a glass and helped herself to some ice water from the dispenser on the refrigerator. It was a beautiful house, she mused as she sat down at the table. The Sunday edition of the *Chicago Tribune*, almost completely intact, rested in the middle of it. She giggled a little as she noticed which part of the paper was the only one that appeared to have been touched. Spread out before her was the sports section. It was open to the Bears Game Preview Pages. There were keys to the game, players to watch, key matchups, injury reports, lineups for the Bears and the Arizona Cardinals, how each team was doing so far this season, picks by the experts, and more. Laura looked through it and felt bad for Jacque or whoever Michele ended up going after. *They're not going to stand a chance,* she thought.

"Where'd you go?" Michele called, coming down the stairs.

"Kitchen!"

Michele came in wearing the same jeans she had on that morning, but instead of the blue shirt, she had changed into an orange Bears t-shirt worn over a plain white long sleeved shirt. "How do I look?"

"You look fine. Are you ready?" Laura asked standing up.

"Fine? Like fine, whatever? Or fine, like hot, like 'she looks soooo fine'?"

"You look good. Come on, let's go."

"No. Which fine?" Michele wasn't budging. "You can't just change it to good now. You said fine like I was presentable. Like I don't have dirt on my face and it's okay for me to be seen in public. I don't want to look fine like that. I don't want to look adequate. I want to look like damn fine. I want to turn heads."

"Now you are just being neurotic."

"Said the happily married woman. Bullshit. I haven't dated in forever. I know this isn't a date, but I'm nervous. I want to make a good impression. Now come on," she instructed, "give me more than a glance and a generic 'fine.' Give me an honest assessment." She stood up straight and turned slightly to the left and to the right. "How do I look?"

Laura looked her over, thinking. Then, after a moment, frowned, shook her head and said, "You look terrible."

"I hate you," Michele pouted.

"Oh, you know I'm kidding," she laughed. "I don't know what you want from me though honey! You are gorgeous. You're in great shape. Your boobs aren't even close to your waist yet. You've got great hair. As far as your outfit goes, it's jeans and a t-shirt. You look like you are going to a bar to watch a game. You're someone who could crawl out of bed, put on a garbage bag, and still turn heads."

"Okay, now you're overselling it."

Laura threw up her hands. "I can't win. Come on already, let's go."

"Fine. Who's driving?"

"Me. My errand, I'll drive."

"Fair enough. Where are we going?"

"I have to run down to McHenry. Leah needs poster board for a school project," Laura lied.

They drove through town, past The Duke and the Gas and Go, and headed south on Route 31. There was a Walmart in McHenry that was only about fifteen minutes away and it wasn't long before they were parked and walking into the store. On the way there, Michele had insisted on listening to sports talk radio for the pre-game show, and as they strolled the aisles, they talked about how repetitive all the analysis was.

"I actually like watching football games," Laura said.

"Right," Michele agreed. "Me, too."

"But I don't see how people obsess over every little detail. It just gets crazy."

"Totally. Troy used to watch the game and then all of *SportsCenter* just to see the highlights of the game he already saw! And then he would get up the next morning to read about it!"

"Ron's not too crazy. He knows way more about it and all the players and stuff than I do, but he doesn't obsess like that."

Michele stopped. "Hey, what are we doing anyway? We've been up and down almost every aisle here."

Laura shrugged. "Leah doesn't really need any poster board."

"What the hell are we doing here then?" Michele put her hands out to her sides.

Laura lowered her voice and spoke slowly. "I thought, that before you continue with Jacque, it might be a good idea to visit the place where you will be likely spending your days."

Michele's shoulders drooped and she tilted her head down. "You dragged me down here for nothing? What time is it?" She found her phone in her back pocket and flipped it open to check the time. "The game started like twenty minutes ago," she complained.

"Now hang on. Look, I know you like Jacque. But let's take a little reality check. He lives in a tiny apartment and works seven days a week. If you want to chase him, that's fine and I will support you. But, let's be clear about what you are going to need to do. Look around. You want a job when you have no resume? This is the place. This is who will hire you." She gestured to an older, heavyset woman wearing a familiar blue vest with

Always Low Prices! printed on the back. She was stocking shelves in the next aisle. "Behold the future."

"This is low. You are low."

"You asked for my help. You wanted a guy with money. I found you Guy. And he is going to have money. A shitload of money."

Michele's face sagged. Her mouth was open slightly as she looked around the store, thinking.

"Don't worry though," Laura continued, "you won't be spending all of your time here because they don't hire anyone full time. That's how they will avoid paying you any benefits. You'll work here, but you won't get any sick days, vacation days, or insurance…certainly no pension. No holiday pay or overtime either. Plus, the good ol' boys who run this place have a well-established reputation of discrimination against women so forget about a promotion." She could see Michele absorbing it all and pressed on. "But it's not all bad. You'll be able to qualify for food stamps. You can come here on your days off to buy low-cost groceries with them. Assuming you have days off, that is."

"Wait a minute," Michele sensed a flaw. "You said no overtime and no full-timers. Why wouldn't I have a day off?"

"You'll have days off here, hon. That won't be an issue. But because they won't ever give you enough hours, you'll need to find another part-time job somewhere else to try and make ends meet. It can be tough to juggle both schedules so you'll have days where you don't work at either place. But the other job won't have to be that much. You see, your expenses are all going to be much lower because you won't be in your house anymore."

Michele just stared.

"The way I figure it, you'll get some money when you sell your house. That should be all retirement money. Just invest it and don't touch it until you're sixty-five or whatever. You don't want to be one of those old people who counts down the days until their Social Security check arrives every month. You don't want to be squinting at a pill cutter trying to split your prescriptions in two because that's all you can afford. No, save the house money for your retirement. Work your ass off now and live within your limited means, but let yourself have a decent retirement someday." Laura could see she had her on the ropes and went in for the kill. "With that in mind, you'll probably want to get a two-bedroom apartment until Carly leaves for school. And after that, you're going to be tempted to keep it. You know, a little extra space and Carly can still have her room when she is home from school. But really, when she leaves next year, downsize to the one-bedroom. Get a pullout sofa and she can sleep on that when she comes home on breaks. You won't be sweating your expenses as much and it'll be easier to miss a little work so you can spend some time with her. It wouldn't really make any sense to work all that extra just so she can have her own bedroom when she visits if you hardly get to see her when she's here."

"Stop already! You're really scaring the shit out of me." Her knees weak, she looked for a place to sit. The aisle across from them was populated with cheap office furniture and Michele found a desk chair to collapse into with her head in her hands. "I feel sick right now."

Laura waited for her friend to collect herself. She found another chair, wheeled it over, and sat down. Then, gently, she suggested a change in plans. "Look hon, let's not go to The Duke today. Let's just chill. Friday night was cool. It was a lot of fun and I'm really glad you had a good time. But don't jump at the first guy who pays attention to you. Especially not an older guy who lives in a tiny apartment over a bakery."

Chapter 30

"Hey, you made it!" Jacque greeted him. "I was starting to worry that you actually found something better to do!"

"Yeah, right. What did I miss?" he asked checking out the big screen.

"Not much. A couple of punts. And the Bears' tight end just dropped a gimme first down when the pass hit him in the hands. So, what's up? Where the hell you been?" asked Jacque as Guy sat down.

"I got stuck in my father's gravitational pull again."

"What? Does he have a fucking tractor beam or something?"

"No, but he does have a tractor."

"What do you mean a tractor? Like a lawn tractor? A riding lawnmower?"

"No, no, it's a real tractor tractor. It's big, with big tractor tires. He can barely drive it anymore, but it's one of his favorite things to do. He drives around his property and imagines projects. And then, when he runs out of gas, he just leaves it where it stops because he can't lift the gas cans to put the gas in it."

"Interesting. And you get to be the gas man?" Jacque asked.

"Yes. And the gas cans were empty today so I had to run back to the Gas and Go to fill them before I could fill the tractor."

"You are being a good son, my friend," he smiled, trying to make Guy feel better about it.

He shook his head. "I'm the only son."

"Still though, it is nice of you to do that stuff for him."

"No," he continued shaking his head. "It's really not. The only reason I ever do any of this stuff for him is because I know there's nobody else. I go by his house a couple of times a week to see if he needs anything because I know he usually does. If he doesn't, I get to sit and listen to him complain about what I did the last time I was there and how he would have done it differently. Or he complains about his caregiver and how he would do things differently from her. That's like his hobby or something. He sits around and watches other people do things and then thinks about how he could or would do it better. I've actually received an instructional lecture from him on the best way to hold a broom and dustpan when I sweep dirt into it."

"Seriously?"

"Yes. Seriously. It's insane. I mean, I get it. He can't really do much anymore. And he ends up spending so much time stuck, sitting, watching other people do stuff. Most of the time, though, because he isn't the one actually doing the job, he doesn't really understand why it's being done that way. But he'll insist that the person tries it his way and he'll sit and pick and give pointers. I used to argue with him and get all worked up. Then, one time, I found myself trying to defend the positioning of my hands while I was carrying a heavy garbage can with a partially broken handle and all of a sudden, it was like I was outside of myself, listening to our conversation. And it was the stupidest goddamn thing I ever heard."

"Wow."

"Tell me about it." Guy was on a roll. "Imagine listening to that! Dumbest fucking conversation ever! It doesn't matter how small or inconsequential the task is, he can always tell me a better way to do it. And then insist I try it his way. And then be irritated if I don't perfectly follow his half-assed instructions. He can never just be like, 'Oh, hey, this person is doing me a favor. Maybe I should shut the fuck up and just appreciate that he is helping me.'"

"Well, I guess the important thing is…is that you don't let it bother you anymore," said Jacque sarcastically.

"Fuck you." Guy took a deep breath and tried to calm himself down again. "Where's Mindy, dammit? I need a beer."

"She's coming," Jacque pointed out as she worked her way down the bar toward them.

Guy got his beer as the final seconds of the first quarter ticked away. "There's a reason I don't usually talk about my father. Now I want a fucking cigarette. You coming out?" He stood up.

"Fuck that. You think my lungs are too pink? That I need to darken them up a bit by voluntarily spending some time in a cluster of people spewing carcinogens?"

"Come on," Guy coaxed. "You're the one who got me talking about my father."

"Oh, I see," Jacque countered. "If I inadvertently distress you, I am then somehow obligated to attend your pity party and hold your hand while you spend seven to ten minutes poisoning yourself as a way of coping with your momentary upset."

Guy laughed, "I promise I won't make you hold my hand."

Jacque rolled his eyes and shook his head.

"Look," Guy pointed toward the window, "it's nice out. And we can go stand on the side, away from the poisonous cloud."

"Fine." He grudgingly got off his stool and followed his friend out back onto the deck.

In the winter months, the smokers all tended to huddle right near the door, but the days were still warm enough for them to be somewhat dispersed around the deck. Jacque and Guy moved toward the railing upwind of most of the others. Guy lit up, took a deep drag, and exhaled. "Hey, I did better at work this morning," he said with some pride.

"Oh yeah? How so?"

"I think you were right. I thought about it and I decided that I don't really hate my job. I don't love it, and I'm not even sure I like it, but I don't hate it. It's a job, it pays my bills, barely. And the work itself really isn't so bad. I don't know, I guess I was just generally trying to be more positive about it. I was thinking about the difference between hating it and hating the idea of it. I do definitely hate the idea of it," he laughed.

"Hey, that's progress, my friend."

"I suppose."

"It is. I don't care what your job is, you have to find a way to make it your bitch. Like it or not," he shrugged, "the Gas and Go is your job right now. You spend way too much time there to be letting it make you miserable. And if you can't change it right now, you need to change the way you think about it."

"I am trying to do that. And yesterday, while I was living large on my day off by hanging out, alone, in my apartment doing laundry, I was trying to think of other jobs. Trying to figure out what I really want to do."

"Did you look at old photos of vacations?" Jacque teased.

"Funny. No. But it doesn't really matter. Everything comes back to my father."

"How so?"

"While he breathes, I am stuck. I could get another job, but I think it would end up being the same thing. I've got to have flexibility. Big John has been great with me about dealing with him. Two years ago, when he was up in the ICU in Milwaukee, I missed a bunch of work and it was no problem. When I am randomly running off to the emergency room in McHenry, he's cool with it. Plus, I can be up all night dealing with some crisis and still be able to get to work and muddle through the next day with a pot of coffee. I can basically do my job in my sleep if I have to."

"So it works for now."

"True. But that's what I've been basically saying my entire adult life."

"Man, that's fucked." Jacque thought about it. "And you can't just walk away? I mean if he's really such an asshole and everyone else abandoned him, it seems like you'd be justified. You won't do it?"

Guy sighed and shook his head. "No. I've left his house so pissed off so many times. But he is going to die at some point. And even though he is a petty, selfish, manipulative prick most of the time, there is this other side to him. Whenever he has a major health crisis and he begins to fade and he believes that his life is truly in jeopardy, when his own mortality is shoved into his small-minded, arrogant face, and he can't be in control, he becomes human. He's scared. He's kind. He's appreciative. He's patient. He's considerate. He listens. He is a fellow human being. He is real. He stops playing mind games. There is a real person in there. A decent person." Guy finished his cigarette and flicked it into the parking lot. "And then, every time he recovers, that person retreats, or is beaten back into submission. That's how I always know that he is feeling better."

"How?"

"He becomes an asshole again and I feel like shit for getting suckered. But then I catch myself and realize that he's out of the woods—that he has beaten the reaper one more time."

As they went back inside, Jacque scanned the bar but didn't see Michele. She'd only said maybe, he reminded himself. They sat back down at the bar. "Guess who stopped in this morning for some donuts?" he asked Guy.

Guy thought for a moment and shrugged. "I don't know. Who?"

Jacque grinned. "Michele."

"Ohhh, nice! How did it go?"

"I wasn't expecting it, but it went well. I am a charming son of a bitch. She got some donuts, we talked a little, only a couple of minutes. I told her we'd be here for the game and she said she and Laura might come by."

"Wow. That's great." He leaned back and looked his friend over. "So that's why you don't look like shit today."

"Fuck you, my friend. At least I have the option. You look like shit every day."

Chapter 31

The car ride back from McHenry was a quiet one. They didn't listen to the game on the radio and Michele spent a lot of time looking out the window. As they drove back into town and approached The Duke, Laura felt compelled to speak up and break the silence.

"I'm sure Ron's got the game on at the house. Why don't you come on over and watch it with us?"

Michele looked out the window as the bar and its mostly full parking lot passed by on the left and sighed. "I don't know. Maybe you should just drop me off at home."

"What are you going to do if you go home now? Sit by yourself and brood? No," she insisted. "I'm taking you home with me."

"Why? So I can brood at your house instead? This just sucks."

"I'm sorry, hon." She forced enthusiasm into her voice. "Come on, I've got some new cheap screw-top wine. It's supposed to be really good and I haven't tried it yet. I'll make some snacky food and we'll sit and watch the game and see if we like the wine."

Michele knew her friend was right. She didn't really have anything to do at home. Carly had spent the night at a girlfriend's house and they were supposed to be working on a school project today. She would probably end up pouring herself a glass of wine anyway. And then, instead of watching football, she would end up sitting on the couch by herself watching some sappy movie on Lifetime and feeling even worse about her life. "Fine," she said reluctantly. "But you should drop me off at my house so I can get my car. Otherwise you or Ron will have to give me a ride home later."

"Good thinking," she agreed as she slowed down and put her turn signal on to head into her friend's neighborhood.

They pulled up in front of the house, but before Michele got out of the car, Laura stopped her. "You're not bullshitting me, are you? I better not get home and then get a text from you telling me that you're tired or some other garbage. You *are* coming over?"

"Yes." She rolled her eyes. "I said I'm coming, I'm coming. I'm just going inside to switch my laundry. I'll be right over."

"That's it? So like ten minutes?"

"Yes," she said with exasperation. "I promise."

Michele keyed in her garage code on the small panel next to the door and waited for it to open. She stopped at her car to toss her purse onto the passenger seat before walking up the couple of stairs and inside. The door from the garage led into an oversized mudroom that also doubled as a laundry room. She pulled the wet clothes from the washing machine, stuffed them into the dryer, and then decided to take a quick look in the kitchen for something to take with her to Laura's house. From the fridge, she grabbed an unopened container of spreadable cheese and found a mostly full box of crackers in the pantry. Setting them on the kitchen table, she went into the dining room to get a bottle of her standard red just in case Laura's new screw-top wasn't any good. Returning to the kitchen, she took a plastic bag out of the pantry to put her things in. The newspaper and the still spread-out sports section caught her eye and stopped her. *Dammit,* she thought, *I should be at The Duke watching this game.* For a split second, she considered blowing off Laura, hopping into her car, and driving right over there all by herself. But just as the butterflies began to take flight in her stomach, she noticed the Walmart logo on the bag in her hand and the unpleasantness of Laura's earlier ruse quickly grounded them. Feeling defeated, she turned off the light and left.

Twenty minutes later, Michele sat on the loveseat in Laura's family room, sipping a glass of wine and watching the game. Next to her, on a matching sofa, Ron slouched, his feet propped against the side of the coffee table in front of him.

"I see she talked you out of going," he observed after they exchanged hellos.

Michele sighed and nodded. "You knew about her plan?" she asked.

Ron nodded and smiled. "She's on a mission for you. She's all over this."

"I can see that," she laughed. "I think I'm a little afraid."

"I think maybe you should be. That woman is relentless when she makes up her mind."

"Ruthless, too."

Ron nodded in agreement, but before he could reply, they were interrupted by Laura entering the room with a tray of food.

"Here you go," she announced. In addition to Michele's cheese and crackers, there was a bowl of large pretzels, an open jar of spicy mustard, and a half dozen little southwestern egg rolls. She set the tray down on the coffee table. "Do you want another beer before I sit down?" she asked Ron.

"Sure, thanks," he said putting his feet down and sitting up to grab an egg roll. "Grab some napkins too, would ya?"

Laura returned with his beer and some napkins and the bottle of wine. Before she sat down next to Ron on the couch, she topped off Michele's glass. They watched the game for a little while before the conversation turned back to her friend's quest. She brought it up.

"Michele," Laura began, "how much gas do you have in your car?"

"I don't know. Maybe a quarter of a tank, I guess."

"Good. You'll need to fill up this week. Guy works in the mornings. I think he leaves a little after lunch so make sure you go there before that. Go in the morning. And don't pay at the pump! Go inside. Buy something else so you can say hello."

Michele and Ron exchanged a quick glance before Ron spoke up. "What if she doesn't need anything else?"

Laura gave him a blank look. "What do you mean?"

"Why should she buy something if she doesn't need anything?"

"She's buying something so she can go inside and talk to Guy." She replied as if the answer was obvious.

"Yeah, but why can't she just go inside and pay for her gas? Why does she have to buy something else?"

"Because if she is only getting gas, then she would pay at the pump. She wouldn't have any reason to go inside."

"Other than to talk to Guy."

"Right."

"But she doesn't want Guy to know that she is only inside to talk to him?"

"No! Of course not!"

"Why the hell not?" Ron laughed.

"I would feel weird. I always pay at the pump," Michele chimed in. "One day I show up and just start going inside to pay?" She made a face and shook her head.

"Why would you be going inside to pay?" Ron asked her.

Michele shrugged. "To see Guy, I guess."

"Ron," Laura was shaking her head, "she can't just go in and only pay for her gas. It would be too obvious."

Ron paused and considered the two women. He took a drink of his beer before he spoke. "Let me get this straight. You would be going inside the gas station just for the purpose of seeing Guy. But, you don't want him to know that. So when you go inside, you are going to buy some gum or a soda or some other shit that you don't really want or need."

They both nodded.

"Are you going to ask him out?"

"I wasn't planning on it."

"Then I think you are both insane."

They protested and demanded to know why.

"Look," he explained, "if you go and get gas, and you go inside to get some gum, or whatever, and then pay, the only thing Guy is going to think is that you wanted some stupid gum. You can't expect him to read your mind. If you want him to know you're interested, make it obvious. Go in there and smile and pay for your gas and visit with him for Christ's sake. Don't make a fucking game out of it."

They thought about it for a moment before Laura spoke. "He's right, hon. Get in there and take what you want."

Michele thought about Jacque but sighed reluctantly. "I suppose you're right. Do I have to go this week though?"

"Why not?" Laura asked. "Why would you wait?"

"I need to psych myself up. I don't know. Maybe I just want a little time to get Jacque out of my system."

"That makes sense," Ron offered. "I am sorry to hear that guy doesn't have any money. Laura told me about the thing with Troy. I laughed my ass off. He's gotta be a pretty cool guy to pull that off."

"Hey!" Laura shot him a look. "You're not helping."

"That's the other thing," Michele continued ignoring Laura. "I think I should at least wait a week anyway. Won't it be weird if I start coming on to Guy right away? I didn't go to the Gas and Go this morning. I went to the bakery to see Jacque. And now they are sitting there at The Duke watching the game together. I'll feel stupid."

"What!" Ron's voice was sharp. "Who's watching the game together?"

Laura looked at her husband. "Guy and Jacque. I told you Jacque asked her to go to The Duke to watch with them."

"Yeah," he replied. "I knew that. But Guy and Jacque are friends?"

They both nodded and Laura scolded, "I told you that!"

"Unh-uh," Ron argued. "You did not tell me that."

"Yes I did! That's who we played pool with!"

Ron shook his head. "I don't think so. I know you played pool with them, but you didn't tell me they were friends. No. I don't remember you telling me that at all."

"That's because you don't listen half the time! I told you that," she complained. "Why else would they be playing pool together?"

"Because one of them wanted to play pool and needed a partner. Whatever. How good of friends are they?"

"Pretty good I think. They hang out together at The Duke quite a bit."

"Well then," Ron shook his head. "Don't bother with the gas. You're screwed."

"What do you mean? Why is she screwed?"

"Guy won't go out with her."

"Why won't he go out with me?" asked Michele. She wasn't sure if she was disappointed or relieved.

"Because he knows his friend likes you."

"They never even went out though," Laura protested.

"Doesn't matter. And I'll say this, too. If he does go out with you, then he's a dick and you shouldn't be with him anyway."

"What? Why not?"

"Because, you can't just screw your friend over for a woman. It would mean he's not a very good friend."

"This is crazy."

"It's not crazy. It causes a rift."

"A rift? What's a rift?" Michele asked.

"A rift is like a little divide between them," Laura explained.

"Or a big divide," Ron added. "It just changes the friendship. It's hard to explain, but it's not good."

"This is stupid. They never even went out!"

"That doesn't matter if they are good friends."

The frustration was clear in Laura's voice. "So what? Is this forever?"

"Well, it's not forever, but it could take a while. What's your time frame, Michele? A few months or something?"

She nodded.

"Don't waste your time."

Laura wasn't ready to give up. "What if Jacque doesn't like her anymore?"

"What do you mean?"

"What if, I don't know, what if she's like a bitch to him?"

"Well then, Guy will stay away because she was a bitch to his friend."

Laura groaned. "This sucks! This is stupid," she repeated.

"I don't think so. Besides, you both know how women interact with each other with the backstabbing and the gossip and all of the other bullshit that goes on. I hear all of the shit you two talk about. I don't think either of you have any room to be criticizing these rules."

"Give me a break with your Bro Code bullshit," Laura scoffed. "You really think that Guy would turn down Michele?"

"Look, I don't know Guy. I don't know if he would or not. But he should." Ron took a drink and shrugged as he looked over at Michele, "It is what it is. Bros before hoes."

Laura rolled her eyes and Michele protested, "Hey, I'm not a hoe!"

"No, of course not," Ron answered sarcastically, "You're just a woman trying to marry a man for his money so you don't have to get a job."

Michele pouted. "You make it sound so bad when you say it like that. I'm not just about the money. I want to love the guy, too."

Laura ignored their bickering and racked her brain. She was sure there had to be a way to get Michele and Guy together. It was just too perfect to have it not work.

"The kind, loving, compassionate whore," Ron laughed. "Too bad you can't just cash in that heart of gold you have there."

"Whores are slutty, too. And I'm not slutty. Troy is the only guy I've ever been with," she continued her protest. "Whores have multiple sex partners."

"Fine," he laughed throwing up his hands, "you are not a whore. Yet. How many guys do you have to be with in order to earn your whore badge?"

"I don't know," Michele smirked. "Why don't we call your mom and ask her?"

Ron's mouth fell open, but before he could return fire, Laura interrupted, "Both of you, knock it off. I think I've got it."

"Got what?"

"How we can make it okay for Guy to go out with Michele! What the hell have we been talking about?"

"Whores?" Ron asked jokingly and he and Michele started laughing.

"Come on. I'm serious here. What if we hooked Jacque up with somebody else? If he was with someone else, then he couldn't really complain about Guy going out with Michele. Could he?"

Michele and Laura both looked at Ron expectantly as he mulled it over. "Are you talking like a hook up? Like a one-night thing for Jacque? Because I don't think that would work."

"I really don't know what I'm talking about," she shrugged. "You tell me what would work."

"I guess I think if it is just a hook up, then Michele is still off limits. I think it's got to be some kind of a relationship. Then Michele would definitely be fair game for Guy because Jacque would have clearly moved on."

"Well that sucks. How the hell am I supposed to find him a girlfriend?"

Michele followed their exchange like a tennis match and felt grateful to have others figuring it out for her. It was all so much more complicated than she wanted it to be.

Ron sympathized. "I don't know. That could take a while."

"Because you," Laura pointed a finger at Michele, "waited too long. Now we're forced to hurry this thing up."

"I'm sorry. If I knew you were such a schemer, I would have brought it up earlier. Or not. I don't know. I had a hard enough time convincing myself."

"Wait a minute," Ron interjected. "I don't think it really needs to be an actual relationship, like official boyfriend girlfriend thing. I think you'd be okay if it was just something that stretched into a few dates."

"That could work. I could probably find someone to go out with him a few times."

Ron shook his head again. "Yeah, but she's going to have to vanish for a while anyway." He nodded toward Michele.

"Why?" they both asked.

"Who are you going to find for Jacque that is going to compete with this gorgeous piece of whoreflesh?"

Laura looked confused and Michele rolled her eyes. "Whoreflesh?" she asked.

"Jacque just got sat at the grown-up table for an evening."

Laura gave him a blank look.

Ron tried again. "He's just had a cup of coffee at the show."

Now Laura glared at him. "If you make one more stupid analogy without explaining yourself, I am going to punch you."

"Michele is way above average," he explained. "Who are you going to find that can compete with her? Anyone you try to set him up with is going to

172

pale in comparison. You just gave him a taste of steak and now you want to tempt him with ground beef. It's not going to work. He just got spoiled."

Michele brightened and sat up a little straighter. "I'm steak, huh?"

Laura looked at her and was discouraged again. "Yeah," she acknowledged, "you're steak."

"Whore steak," Ron grinned.

Michele made a face at him and extended her middle finger.

Laura continued. "But now we're back to the time issue. If she's got to disappear and Jacque's got to go on multiple dates and whatever the heck else, we are going to kill a month just like that."

"I think you need to be working more than one front here. Why can't you try doing what you need to do to set the stage for Guy, but be working on other stuff, too?"

"Ron's right." She looked at her friend.

"Oh my god," Michele groaned. "It's taking us three people just to try and figure this out. How are we going to manage multiple scenarios?"

"Come on, they can't all be this complicated. So where else should we go? Lake Geneva? There's people up there with money."

"No way," Ron interjected. "Go up there and you'll get hit on by a bunch of douchebags with wedding rings in their pockets. They have the cash, but they also have a fat wife and two rotten kids back in Chicago."

"What about Crystal Lake then?"

"I would be up for that," Michele agreed.

Ron considered it for a moment. "Why not? They've got some bars. Go check it out. Just stay away from The Duke for a while."

"Wait a minute! I think that's the key!" Laura exclaimed.

"What?" Ron and Michele asked together.

"Just staying away from The Duke for a little while. Look," she explained, "I can go over there with Lisa or somebody and make a point of running into Guy and Jacque. I casually mention something about you starting to date some other guy. Then we disappear for a while. When we come back, she'll have a clean slate!" She looked expectantly at Ron.

"Okay," he said slowly as he nodded his head. "If they think she is dating someone else, then that makes it obvious that Jacque wasn't really anything."

"Right!"

"And if Jacque wasn't really anything, then she should be fair game for Guy."

"Because she had this other relationship. When she comes back to The Duke, she'll be coming back in as fresh meat on the market again. Just like before. It'll be like a do-over."

Ron was deep in thought. "That sounds like it might work," he agreed. "But give me a minute to think about it."

"Do you need to consult the Bro Code?" she teased. "Want to call some bros and ask them?"

"Shut up and let me think."

Michele raised her hand meekly. "I'm confused. Am I going to Crystal Lake to find a guy or am I just going to pretend to have already found one?"

"Both. We are going to start going to Crystal Lake to hang out and try and find you a man. And, as of right now, you have an imaginary boyfriend. What do you want his name to be?"

"How about Mark?"

"Perfect. I will go to The Duke and let it be known that you are out again with Mark and that he is this guy you started seeing." She turned back to Ron. "Well? Do we have a ruling?"

He shook his head and shrugged. "I can't find a problem with it. If Michele is just coming out of a relationship with…" he paused.

"Mark."

"Right, Mark. If she just stopped seeing Mark, then she should be fair game for Guy. Jacque would have no standing to be upset with Guy. And it wouldn't be a dick move for Guy to go out with her. I think you've got it."

Chapter 32

"Well, I guess that's it," acknowledged Guy. The two friends had nursed their beers, harassed each other, and watched the Bears and Cardinals slog through a boring defensive struggle. Tied at six for most of the game, a pick six followed by a fumble recovery late in the fourth quarter sealed it for Chicago. "What an ugly game."

"You know what the worst part was?" Jacque asked.

Guy shook his head.

"Watching you crane your neck to look at the door every single time you heard someone open it."

"What are you talking about?" Guy knew but asked anyway.

"I am forty-two years old. I know who I am and I know what I have to offer. You will never see me stewing over a woman, my friend. She only said maybe. Maybe she would stop by."

"Well, I was seeing if, maybe, it was her."

"Yes, for the first part of the game, I can understand that. After halftime though, I figured she wasn't coming so I tried to forget about it and tried to enjoy the damn game. But you kept looking." He shook his head. "Easy come, easy go, my young friend. There are many other fish in the sea." Jacque grinned. "And fishing can be a lot of goddamn fun."

"Okay, fisherman Jacque. And hey, don't blame me for not enjoying that game. That game sucked. What's the record for punts in a game? How many three and outs were there?"

"A win's a win," Jacque countered.

"I suppose. Who we got next week?"

"I don't know," Jacque shrugged and looked around. "Hey, Bear!"

Bear walked over to them and put his hands on their shoulders. "What's up gentlemen?"

"Who do the Bears play next week?"

"Broncos, on Monday night. Bears are now 5-3 and the Broncos lost earlier to a weak Kansas City team, so they are 3-5. But it is in Denver, so who knows."

When he said it was on Monday, Guy and Jacque both made a face and looked at each other. Jacque spoke first. "I hate Monday night games. The Bears suck on Monday Night Football."

"They've actually been pretty decent on Monday nights for the past four or five years," Bear pointed out. "They're like 6-2 or something."

"Doesn't matter," Guy interjected. "He's never going to get past 1985. That was a Monday night game when the Dolphins beat them to ruin their perfect season."

"That was the best defense the NFL has ever seen! They destroyed teams." Jacque shook his head. "And fucking Marino just picked them apart. On Monday Night Football."

Bear rolled his eyes. "That version of Marino is long gone, and so is that best defense ever. We'll see what happens next Monday."

"Any good games on Sunday?" Guy asked.

"I'm pretty sure Minnesota and Green Bay is the noon game. That should be decent. And I think in the afternoon, it's Oakland and Kansas City. I know that's supposed to be a big rivalry, but they both suck right now. You guys going to come by on Sunday? Or just wait for the Bears on Monday night?" he asked.

"Probably both. Somebody's got to keep this place in business," replied Jacque.

Bear looked around at The Duke. Like last week, it wasn't packed, but it was almost full. With the game over, customers were either settling their tabs or having one more drink. "Yeah, I don't know what we'd do without you two. Well, maybe I'll see you. You guys have a good week," he said and resumed his endless meander through the bar.

Guy and Jacque each ordered another beer, and as Guy drank his, he watched Bear pick up empties and bus tables. As he did so, he visited briefly with almost everybody. Mindy called him over to the other side of the bar to tell him something and then he hustled into the kitchen and returned with a handful of limes for her. After that, he went out to the deck for a few minutes and returned with more empty beer bottles and glasses.

"You think Bear likes his job?" he asked Jacque.

Jacque looked around the bar and found him talking to a couple in their forties. The woman said something and Bear and the man both laughed. Then he took their dishes and went into the kitchen. "I think, yes. I think he decided to like his job."

"I've been watching him," Guy began, "and I know he's the bar manager. But really, he's a busboy and a garbage man a lot of the time. He's Mindy's helper. He's the cook's assistant. When it's slow during the week, he *is* the cook or the bartender. But I think you are right. I think he has decided to like his job."

"You are figuring things out, my friend," Jacque smiled.

"Yeah," he sighed. "I've been working on it. And, like I said earlier, this morning at work wasn't so bad."

"That's good. Some days will be harder than others. Especially if you've been deciding to hate it for as long as you have. But as long as you keep working on it, it will get better."

Guy nodded and took another sip of his beer. "I think I can. But I've also been thinking, that's probably the easier part. This dealing with my father is what's killing me. It all starts there."

Jacque put his elbow on the bar and his chin in his hand and thought about his own parents. It had been about five years since they retired and moved down to Tennessee, near his sister and her family. Fortunately, they still had their health and they still had each other. He wondered how he would deal with them when they got older. And how they would deal with him. "That's a tough one, my friend."

"*He* is a tough one," Guy shook his head.

"Yeah, and even if he wasn't, it's always harder with families. Those emotions are so strong and run so deep. Nobody can piss you off like a member of your own family."

Guy laughed. "And that's true when they aren't even trying. Imagine if they were!"

Jacque was skeptical. "He tries to make you mad?"

"Yep," Guy nodded matter-of-factly. "That's what he does. He's always poking and prodding and looking for some kind of weakness. Then when he finds something, he's a bully. He's mean. He knows how to get under people's skin and push their buttons. He's like a marionette guy. What do you call the guy who does that, who controls one of those marionette things, makes it dance around?"

"Is it a puppeteer?"

"Is a marionette a puppet though? I always think of a puppet like a hand puppet."

"I don't know. I think it has more to do with being controlled. Maybe it's a kind of puppet?"

"Maybe. Whatever. I don't know. But that's what he does. I finally figured out that whenever I tell him anything about my life, he'll find a way to use it against me somehow. So I don't talk to him about anything except sports and the weather. I refuse to give him the satisfaction of seeing me get mad or upset or whatever. But he is relentless. I think my not reacting makes him try harder. And the crazy thing is that even though I don't react outwardly, he still gets me, and I think he knows he does. But without the outward reaction, he's not certain. So he keeps yanking on those strings. If I blew up at him or something, that would make his whole goddamn day."

"Wow."

"You know," Guy continued, "I know everyone's parents are crazy, right? And sometimes I second guess myself about my father, like it's not him and maybe we just don't get along. But then I look at all of his other relationships. He doesn't have any! The man doesn't have any friends."

"Really?"

"Really. So I know it's not just me. He's not nice and I think he's afraid that someone might ask him for a favor. He lives in fear of having to do something for someone else. No friends means no obligations. Nobody's ever going to ask him for help."

"What did he do for a living?" Jacque asked.

"He and his brother had a securities firm in Chicago. They dealt with bonds. It's funny. I think all those psycho traits he has really helped him at work. He was a master at reading the markets and people and anticipating what they would do and how they would react. But, you know, he was in that industry for thirty-five years and he doesn't have a single friendship from it. Nothing." Guy paused. "Not nothing I guess," he observed bitterly, "he does have his precious money."

"He made good money?"

Guy nodded. "Yeah. I don't know why though. He won't spend any of it. I guarantee that he's walking around in his big stupid house right now wearing a winter coat because he won't turn the heat up."

Chapter 33

The little alarm clock on the table next to the king size bed showed 6:22pm as Sophie entered the hotel room on Sunday evening. She was tired but managed a smile at the enormity of the mattress and flopped down in the middle of it. Taking a deep breath and letting it out slowly, she stared at the ceiling and pondered her next move. It had been a long day of driving from Waterloo, into Davenport, and then down alongside the Mississippi on Route 61 into St. Louis. This was the farthest away from Waterloo she'd ever been. She was in uncharted territory and it felt strange.

Since it was around dinnertime, she considered getting something to eat, but then decided against it. Too many late-afternoon Corn Nuts, she guessed. She thought about showering and dressing up a little. There was a fancy restaurant in the hotel and there looked to be a few more nice ones within walking distance. Plus, the Arch was close by. I should be able to walk over there, too, she remembered. Sophie supposed that she would be hungrier after she got cleaned up and went for a stroll. Then she would also know what her options were.

The bed was comfortable though, and for a moment she considered staying put and letting her eyes close for a while. But the idea of waking up hungry in a couple of hours, still in her clothes, and being stuck ordering pizza because everything was closed forced her to her feet. Standing and stretching her arms over her head, trying to wake up a little more, she remembered that she was on the fourteenth floor and quickly crossed the room to pull back the curtains and check out her view. The entirety of the Gateway Arch, accented with golden-hued spotlights, stretched into the night sky before her. It was impressive and it was beautiful, and for a few moments she drank in the scene. Near the bases of the Arch there appeared to be a well-lit park with groups of people walking, craning their necks, and taking pictures. Beyond that she could see the dark swath of the Mississippi River bracketed by two lofty, well-traveled bridges. In the daylight, she thought, cities were ugly and dirty, all gray and strewn with garbage. But when the sun went down, even the traffic set in motion with all its lights had a kind of beauty to it. Sophie couldn't remember the last time she was in a real city after dark and simply looking out over the dazzle of electricity and activity spurred her into action.

After a quick shower, she dug through the one suitcase she'd brought inside and found a nicer pair of jeans to go with the bright red top she picked out. Her first impulse was to simply put her hair up in a quick ponytail and head out to explore, but then she changed her mind. *No one is waiting for me,* she reminded herself, *and I don't have to hurry. I can stay up and out all fucking night if I choose. As long as I am out of here by eleven-thirty tomorrow morning, I'm fine. I can even stay here another night if I want to.* Then she caught herself and took a deep breath. Her attitude was defiant, bitter, petulant, angry, and she didn't like it. *Let it go and get to acceptance, Sophie,* she reminded herself. *Enjoy yourself. You're on vacation.*

Last night, fighting to breathe, fighting to steady herself, she walked out of Abby's apartment and to her car. Hands shaking, she managed to find her keys, let herself in, and drive all of three blocks before the sobs flooded her eyes with tears and forced her to pull over. When she recovered enough to resume driving, she made it out of the neighborhood and ended up downtown. Not knowing what else to do, she located Route 20 and fled Sioux City the way she'd come in only a few hours earlier. Sophie bawled her way back across the state and into Waterloo. She found a cheap motel a couple of blocks from Smitty's and, after checking in, spent a minute in front of the bathroom mirror splashing water on her face and trying to make it look like she hadn't just spent most of the past three hours crying.

181

Then she put on a baseball cap, pulled it low over her eyes, and walked to Smitty's.

Hiding alone at a table in the corner of the bar, she lit a cigarette from the pack she'd purchased an hour outside of Sioux City, sipped her drink, and tried to sort through her feelings. The urge to say "fuck it" and drink away the confusion and the pain was strong, but she'd been down that road enough times in the past to know that the relief it brought was so fleeting. Besides, she had let Abby, or rather her idealized version of Abby, rule the past sixteen years of her life. She was determined to not let her control any more of it, not even for one more night. She was sick of crying and sick of nursing the hurt.

After she left Abby's and the lights of Sioux City faded in the distance, her tears subsided for a while and she began to play the "What if?" game. What if she misheard Abby? What if she misunderstood what she meant? What if she had a gambling problem? What if she was too quick to walk out? What if Jake was really the problem? What if something was going on that she just couldn't tell her about? What if she had a serious problem and really needs help? These questions and others like them tumbled through her mind. She tried all of them on in turn but couldn't make any of them fit. Then, Sophie tried to fix everything. What if I go back and talk to her at work? What if I just wait a couple days and confront her when she is alone? What if I write her a letter explaining the importance of education? What if I talk to somebody at the college and can get her back in? But it was all just more of the same. Deep down, she knew she was just flailing and that there was no good explanation, no justification for all the lies. There was no excuse for how Abby had treated her. And there was really no solution.

After exhausting the what ifs, Sophie quit thinking about Abby and started to think about herself. She thought of the sacrifices, the horrible jobs she didn't dare quit, the bouncing around from house to house all the while desperate for her own, but waiting, saving every penny she could for Abby's tuition. And her trip to Mexico, she reminded herself bitterly. She thought about how she had put her life on hold for so many years and began to get angry. That's when she stopped for cigarettes. They jacked her adrenaline and she drove on, shaking with rage, pounding both her steering wheel and her dashboard as she screamed "You fucking bitch!" over and over until she was hoarse. Then the screams dissolved into choking sobs and anguish over the callousness of the betrayal and she descended again into overwhelming sorrow. And so it went: tears, questions, rage, over and over and over.

Sitting alone at Smitty's, replaying the shock and drama of Abby's, and the emotional roller coaster she had ridden back across the state, it dawned on her that she was in full on Kübler-Ross grieving mode. Years of working with terminal patients had familiarized her with the five stages of grief, but until then, she always associated them only with death. Sophie took stock and realized that she'd been storming back and forth between the stages since she walked out of Abby's apartment. She was devastated and felt hollowed out inside. Have I gone thirty minutes without crying or fighting to stop myself from crying? she wondered. That's obviously depression. She'd been negotiating the what ifs of both denial and bargaining off and on all night. Smiling a little, she considered that screaming "you fucking bitch" until her throat hurt definitely qualified as anger. The only stage left was acceptance. She sighed and dug out another cigarette.

According to what she'd read about Kübler-Ross, people couldn't get on with their lives until they were able to accept their loss. If they didn't accept it, they were stuck, ruminating over their fate, and never moving ahead. She didn't want that. As far as Sophie was concerned, she'd been stuck for her entire life. Her adolescence was spent waiting for adulthood so she could stop being a guest in someone else's home. She longed to be on her own, independent. But following the little taste of that kind of freedom while she worked here at Smitty's, she had put it all on hold again for Abby. Her little Abby. Her throat and chest clenched at the thought of her sister and she was forced to concentrate on taking a few deep breaths in order to keep the tears at bay. She got through it only to have the anger race back. She was pissed over the hold Abby had on her, how it was making her a wreck. *The little bitch is probably out with her friends right now not giving a shit about me and I am sitting here hiding in the corner of a bar, in fucking Waterloo, all by myself, like a goddamn basket case. Okay,* she thought as she laughed a little and sighed again, *I guess that would be the anger returning.*

Sophie knew that everything she was feeling was both normal and justified, but she resented it. She resented the idea that Abby was controlling her emotions, or, rather, that she was allowing Abby to have that control. *I've got to get to acceptance,* she thought, *I've got to move on, I've got to let it go. There really isn't a good explanation. There isn't a solution. It's not even my problem,* she thought. *It's Abby's life and Abby's problem. I'm just collateral damage.*

Leaning back in her chair, she surveyed the bar and marveled at the idea of being back after so many years. When she left Smitty's the first time, she was a kid on a mission. She had a plan to work, to save, to help her little sister. Sophie fished out another cigarette, lit it, and took a deep drag. *I sure don't feel like a kid anymore,* she thought, *and as far as a plan goes,* she shrugged. *Why am I even back here?* she asked herself. *My post office box? That's my home? My anchor? Thirty-two years and that's it?* Sophie didn't like the way that felt. Then she considered that maybe, that was the wrong question. *Instead of asking why Waterloo,* she wondered, *maybe I should be asking myself where else would I go?* And that one question ushered in a complete paradigm shift. In one terrifying and exhilarating flash, Sophie realized that she could finally start her own life. Not even that she could, but that she was, right then. This was it. The waiting was finally over.

She sat frozen while her mind carefully but futilely searched for anything she might have missed or hadn't considered. Nothing. This was really it. Dumbfounded, Sophie leaned back in her chair and let this new understanding of her own reality wash over her. It was as if she just flew forward in time two and half years to when Abby would be done with school. For so long, she'd kept her head down, working and saving. It was the only way she knew how to get through it. If she'd spent her time dreaming about her own future, well, she didn't think that she could have made it this far. *But here I am,* she mused, looking around Smitty's, *here I finally fucking am.* Sophie raised her glass to herself and paused before draining the contents, "Welcome to your life, Sophie Ross," she said quietly.

For the next couple of hours she nursed vodka grapefruits while in her head her past and future wrestled for control. The heartache of losing Abby and the sting of having been played for a sucker was so raw and painful, but the realization of finally being able to live for herself and actually have a place of her own was a powerful salve. Shortly after midnight, she polished off another cocktail and was grateful to feel a weariness beginning to take over. Hopeful that she drank enough to hasten sleep, she settled her tab, slowly walked back to her motel, crawled into bed, and crashed.

It was the next morning over breakfast at a diner down the street from her motel when she made the decision to drive south. Sipping her coffee while waiting for her eggs, Sophie's mind wandered back to Kübler-Ross and the idea that she had to accept what happened with Abby. *If my future really is right now and I can finally begin my life, well, it's going to get off to a very shitty start if I spend all day either crying, questioning, or raging,* she thought. Then, unexpectedly, the words "huevos rancheros" intruded into her consciousness. She looked to the table next to hers and saw the waitress taking an order. Some guy was ordering huevos rancheros for his breakfast and in an instant, Sophie's mind jumped to Abby's trip to Mexico and she was angry again. Abby and Jake hanging out on a beach in Cancun, on her dime no less, was an especially bitter image for her. For years she had longed to visit the ocean somewhere, anywhere, and just sit and watch the waves. But she'd never done it. She'd never even seen the ocean. Instead, she'd worked and she'd saved.

Sophie took a deep breath and gradually coaxed her mind back around to the necessity of acceptance. Acceptance gave her a future and she began to think about what that future would be. In the short term, she had about an hour to finish eating and walk back to her motel to check out. And go where? she wondered. Her first thought was that she should get in touch with her placement contacts and go ahead and start another job while she figured out what to do with her life. That meant holing up for a few days or a week in a motel like the one she was just leaving until they had a job for her. Her savings were limited and she started to calculate how long she could afford to pay for temporary housing. Then, for the third time in less than twenty-four hours, her entire world shifted again. *Her* savings were limited, but she wasn't counting any of the money in Abby's college account. She always kept that money separate, both mentally and physically. A stupid smile gradually spread across her face. As it was, she already had most of the money set aside for Abby to finish her undergraduate degree. That didn't count books or other expenses that always seemed to come up, but there was almost two full years of tuition in the account. She was sitting on close to $30,000.

The number was staggering. Sitting in the college savings account, it had never really seemed like that much because the withdrawals she made from it for tuition were always so substantial. But now, with no more of those bills to pay, it suddenly seemed like a whole lot more money. She started to become overwhelmed by the possibilities and her attention ricocheted from one idea to the next as fast as they entered her head. When her breakfast arrived, she tried to get a grip, to slow down and organize her thoughts while she ate. Getting a place of her own was the only certainty so far. After that, it seemed to come down to work or school or both. It was exciting to think about going to college herself, but she didn't know what to study. She could stick with what she knew and go with nursing. Or try something completely different. As far as work went, her qualifications were limited. She could go back to the bar or be a nurse's aide somewhere. She knew the bar was a dead-end, but she was so ready to be done with old people and sick people. And it would probably be easier to accommodate school with bar tending hours. She mentally started to run through the colleges in and around Waterloo, Cedar Rapids, and even Des Moines as the waitress returned to the adjacent table and announced, "Here you go, huevos rancheros," as she set the plate down. Sophie glanced over and all of her thoughts of higher education vanished. She decided that, for the first time in her life, she was going to go on a real vacation. She was going to find a beach.

After rushing through her meal, Sophie hustled back to her motel, packed up, checked out, and drove to one of the big gas stations southeast of town near the Interstate. After topping off her tank, she went inside for a Coke, some Corn Nuts, and an atlas. Opening up to the map of the whole nation, she quickly saw that the shortest route to the ocean was straight south and plotted a course from Waterloo to Davenport to St Louis to Memphis to New Orleans and then east to Florida. Giddy with excitement, she exited the gas station, found the I-380 on-ramp, and waved goodbye to Waterloo.

Chapter 34

The noise from his alarm assaulted the early-morning quiet as Guy's brain fought its way to consciousness and clung there while he silenced the buzzing and found the light switch. He shifted to a sitting position and leaned his back against the wall where a headboard would be if he had an actual bed instead of just a frame. Blinking and rubbing his eyes, the day and the room gradually came into focus. It was Tuesday morning, October 20. It was his birthday. He was now thirty years old.

Guy sat there for a moment as he considered this fact without excitement. Patient, reflective, self-aware Guy, the one who had been listening to Jacque, took a deep breath and reminded himself that it was just another day and that he shouldn't worry about it too much. He should go to work, check on his father, the usual stuff. But that wasn't the only voice in his head. There was also the loud complaining of bitterly disappointed, self-loathing Guy, and together they argued.

It's just another day at the Gas and Go. It may be day number three thousand, one hundred and forty-five, but I know this won't last forever.

Whatever. You've been saying that for a long time. You're a fool. And you're thirty now.

So what?

So what!? Thirty!

And?

And you're still there! Loser!

That's only because Charles is still alive. It works for now.

188

For now?! How long has 'for now' lasted, genius? Twelve years! That's a copout.

Bullshit. He can't live forever. Besides, I don't hate working there.

Now that's some real bullshit! You're a thirty-year-old clerk.

No shit. I'm definitely not thrilled about that. But, really, my job isn't too bad.
Remember what Jacque said? There's a difference between the job and the idea of
the job. Anyway, fuck off. It's my birthday.

Whoopee. Why don't you celebrate by doing nothing? Because remember,
you're broke, birthday boy.

I pay my bills and I'm not in debt. So fuck off.

Fine. Have a nice day at work at the gas station, thirty-year-old loser.

Fuck off.

Unsure of the winner, Guy stood up, went to the bathroom, and got ready
to go to work.

Leaving his apartment building, he walked through the parking lot, took
a deep breath of the cool autumn air and, looking toward the eastern
horizon, even paused for a moment. The sky was glowing pink and orange,
backlighting a couple of thin bands of clouds. Guy climbed into his car,
turned the key, and the engine quietly came to life. His neighbors and their
dogs continued dreaming and he recalled with relief how little Tony had
charged him to tighten that loose belt.

Five minutes later, Guy was at work, cruising through the morning setup,
and waiting for the coffee to finish brewing when Jacque burst through the
door.

"Good morning, my friend!"

"Morning, Jacque. Kid's mom need his car again?" Guy asked as he moved
to give him a hand.

"Nope. It's all good there. I am here today for a different reason," he said,
grinning mischievously.

Guy was immediately suspicious and tried to imagine why he was making
the rounds this morning. "I think I'm afraid to ask."

"So, don't," Jacque shrugged coyly as he put his donuts in the case.

They finished quickly and Guy took one for himself before throwing away the empty boxes and walking back behind the counter to get the check for his friend. Jacque waited for him on the other side of the counter, still silent, still grinning. The stalemate continued while they exchanged check for receipt, but even when they were done, a Cheshire-like Jacque remained. Guy laughed and relented, "Okay. I give. What's up?"

"Stay here."

"Okay," he said uneasily as Jacque went back outside. The windows in the Gas and Go were fairly high off the ground and Guy could only see his friend from the shoulders up as he turned to the right, walked toward the back of his van, and opened up the doors. His head vanished for a moment before it popped back up, the smile on it bigger than ever. He appeared to be carrying something as he closed the doors and hustled to come back inside.

"Happy birthday motherfucker!" he practically yelled, bursting through the door. "I found you a present last weekend!" In one hand he held an acoustic guitar. The other held a present wrapped in newspaper.

Guy's jaw dropped. "Seriously? Oh man." He moved out from behind the counter to take it from Jacque.

"I was in Fox Lake on Saturday morning and I was cutting through that subdivision behind the drug store to get over to Morning Joe to make a delivery and this old guy was setting up a yard sale. I wasn't even looking or anything, but as I was driving by, he came walking out of his garage with that baby and I practically slammed on the brakes."

Guy held it awkwardly as if he was going to play and laughed. "Oh man. I don't even know how to hold it! Dude," he looked at Jacque for a moment, "this is so cool. Thank you."

"It's not the best. It's definitely a starter guitar, but it's really in pretty good shape."

"Are you kidding me? I wouldn't know the difference. I guess I need to figure out where I can get some lessons though."

"No you don't! That's the best part. Check this out!" He handed Guy the other present. It was about the size of a large book.

Gently, Guy set the guitar on the counter and took the package from

Jacque. "What is this?"

"It goes with the guitar," he explained. "Open it."

He tore the paper off to reveal a large softcover book with a spiral binding. On the cover was an odd-looking man sitting by a brick fireplace and playing a guitar. To Guy, he appeared to be some sort of bizarre, disco/cowboy hybrid. His plaid, western-looking shirt was undone one button too many in order to show off the large gold chain nestled in his abundant chest hair and he wore a matching bracelet on his right wrist. The shirt was tucked into tight-fitting blue jeans, and although his view was obscured by the guitar, Guy could only imagine that he was also wearing a great big belt buckle. He looked tan and his smiling, round, cherubic face was framed by a fuzzy, almost afro-looking hairdo that seemed to extend down into his long and equally bushy sideburns. Across the top, in a large and very groovy, very seventies font, it read, *Roy Clark's Big Note Guitar Songbook.* Next to the title was the square, red and white "AS SEEN ON TV" icon. Guy laughed out loud. "What the hell is this?"

"That's Roy Clark!"

"Who the hell is Roy Clark?"

Now Jacque's jaw dropped. "You know, that guy from the show *Hee Haw!*"

"*Hee Haw?* What the hell is *Hee Haw?*"

Jacque's smile faded a bit and he shook his head. "You are making me feel very old, my friend."

"I'm sorry man. I'm not trying to."

"*Hee Haw* was this weird country-western variety show. Forget it though. It doesn't matter. You have to check this out," he said excitedly and took the book from Guy. "This thing is mint. And it has everything you need in here to learn how to play the guitar!" Resting the book on a stack of Budweiser twelve-packs he opened it up and began leafing through it. "Total beginner step-by-step instructions," he explained. "And this is the coolest part!" Flipping to the back of the book, he found the sticker page and the poster. "Look. It's got these colored stickers that you can put right on the neck of the guitar to help you learn. And this, even!" Gingerly, he removed and unfolded a poster showing how to play a bunch of different chords. "I don't think anyone ever used this stuff."

"Oh wow, that is pretty cool. Hold that poster for a second," Guy instructed as he grabbed the guitar off the counter. He studied the simplest looking chord, an "A" chord, placed his fingers on the frets and pressed down as he carefully studied the poster. After double checking his positioning, he used his other hand to strum the guitar, gently at first, then faster and harder while they both grinned at each other like little kids. "Dude, check it out, I'm playing the guitar."

"Nice! The guy I bought it from even had the old VHS instructional tape that came with it, but it looked like it was partially melted."

"I don't have a VCR anyway." Guy continued to strum the guitar and experimented with moving his fingers around on the neck. "This is so awesome."

Jacque laughed. "You're on your way, my friend. Look out, Eddie Van Halen."

Guy stopped playing and pretended to be confused. "Who's Eddie Van Halen? Was he a *Hee Haw*, too?"

"Oh, fuck you, you're not that young. Listen, I've got to get back to work and make my deliveries. Happy Birthday, my friend," he said extending his hand.

Guy stopped playing and set the guitar down. "Thank you, man." His tone was serious. "You really have no idea. This means a lot to me. I don't know the last time I even got a present like this. Thank you." He shook his hand and gave him a quick hug.

"Don't worry about it. Just don't forget about me when you are a rich and famous rock star, okay?"

"Yeah, right."

II

Part Two

Chapter 35

Guy winced as his hand found the snooze button and silenced his alarm. Rolling onto his back, he blinked his eyes open and stared into the darkness. The surprise stab of pain from his fingertips helped chase away the sleep. He muttered the day's number, "Three thousand, one hundred, and eighty-seven," but his discomfort kept him from dwelling on it. Flexing his left hand, he thought about what a fool he was and smiled a little. He'd practiced his guitar nearly every day since getting it almost two months ago for his birthday. Holding his hand out over his face, he checked the condition of each finger by pressing it against his thumb. The pinky, although still tender, was the least damaged. The other three were all very sore and seemed to be in equally bad shape. The white medical tape had stayed on through the night though, and that was good. Guy made a mental note to buy some more on his way home from work, climbed out of bed, and headed into the bathroom to get ready to leave.

After washing his face, he peeled the wet tape off the fingers of his left hand and threw it away. The bandages underneath were mostly off already. That was the reason for the tape. Once he put the Vaseline on, they didn't stick very well and kept coming off. The tape did a good job of holding everything together. Guy carefully inspected each finger. Eh, he thought, not too bad, but come on, how long was it going to take to get some calluses going? Next, he washed his hands and gently dried each finger. Then he took four bandages out of the box on his vanity and unwrapped them. The jar of Vaseline was open and he got a little bit on his pinky before putting one of the bandages on and then wrapping the whole fingertip with the medical tape. He repeated the task with each finger and inspected his work. He guessed it would last through his shift as long as he didn't have to get his hand wet.

Guy observed that the tape was holding up well as he brushed his teeth and got dressed. He also noticed that it barely affected his ability to grab the laces on his shoes and tie them. And that gave him an idea. Before he grabbed his coat and headed out into the cold, he decided to experiment. There were still a few minutes before he absolutely had to leave for work. *I've got time,* he thought. Picking up his guitar, he sat down on the edge of the coffee table facing the *Roy Clark's Big Note Guitar Chord Chart* that was tacked up on the wall. It looked out of place in-between the stunning redhead in the bright green, extremely low-cut blouse holding a bottle of Killian's Irish Red and the always blonde and buxom St. Paulie Girl with her hands full of frothy steins, but it commanded Guy's attention in a way they never had.

He put his fingers on the frets and strummed a few different chords. They did hurt as he moved them around and pressed them firmly against the strings, but it really wasn't too bad. They weren't cracking anymore because of the Vaseline and that seemed to be the big difference. Cool, he thought, I'll still be able to practice when I get home tonight. He continued through the chart, playing the different chords and then running through some of his exercises where he went from chord to chord. After a mistake, he restarted and played through the transitions a couple of times to be sure he had them down. He was about to move on to another exercise when it dawned on him that he was actually supposed to be on his way to work. "Shit," he said out loud as he set his guitar down and jumped up. Grabbing his coat, he put it on as he raced out the door.

Between his apartment and car, he checked the time on his phone and swore again when he realized that he was going to be late. Guy unlocked his door, hopped in, and started the engine. After cranking the front defrost and hitting the button for the rear, he dug around on the floor for his ice scraper. Finding it, he quickly scrambled out of his car and scraped just enough ice away from the driver's side of his windshield so he could kind of see the road. He jumped back in the car and threw it in reverse, blindly backing out of his spot. Then, leaning forward to peer through the little ice-free rectangle, he sped out of the parking lot onto Route 12 toward the Gas and Go.

He imagined a collection of irritated customers, idling in their cars and trucks, repeatedly checking the time as they waited for him to open the store. Moments later, though, Guy was relieved to pull into the still-deserted gas station. He parked and hustled inside to get ready for the morning. Once the coffee was going, the drawer counted out, the lights turned on, and the newspapers brought inside, he paused to check the time. It wasn't even ten minutes after six. He smiled and guessed it wasn't really that big of a deal. As he poured himself a cup of coffee, Guy tried to remember the last time he had been late to work, but couldn't. Then he tried to decide if that was either very good or just really messed up.

Before he came to any conclusions, the customer parade was underway. It was almost mid-way into December and the weather, Christmas, and the tape on his fingers dominated the conversations.

"Morning Guy."

"Brrr. Sure is cold out there."

"What happened to your fingers?"

"Hey, are we supposed to get more snow before Christmas?"

"I'm heading out to the mall tonight. You get all of your shopping done yet?"

"What did you do to your fingers, Guy?"

"It'll be nice to have a white Christmas this year. It's been a while."

"Have you been naughty or nice, Guy? Naughty's always more fun."

"I hope Santa brings you something good."

"What's up with the tape?"

"What's cheaper, reindeer food or gas?"

"Stay warm."

"Hey, Guy, if I don't see you before then, you have a Merry Christmas."

Despite the stress of the holiday season, people were typically in better spirits and a little friendlier. He enjoyed visiting with all of the familiar faces but felt awkward when they asked about his taped-up fingers. Embarrassed to tell anyone he had been practicing guitar so much that they were cracked and raw, he lied and said he burned them. It seemed simpler, but it really wasn't. They were concerned and wanted to know how badly, and what he burned them on, and what he put on the burns. Then they teased him and offered sarcastic advice about pot holders and serious advice about treating burns, and so on. Guy was reminded of exactly why he didn't lie very often and marveled at how quickly one little lie could spawn a hundred others. It went from the simplicity of "I burned them" to an entire story about making spaghetti noodles and the burner light out on his stove and getting distracted by a phone call and picking up a spoon and how he didn't know how his thumb escaped damage, but, yes, he was lucky it did, and he really wasn't even sure what else. Every concerned follow-up question seemed to lead to another uncomfortable and awkward lie. He was glad it was Thursday and decided to be extra vigilant in doing everything he could to make sure they were healed by Sunday morning so he wouldn't have to wear the stupid tape to work again.

As he slid into the mid-morning lull, Guy's mind, as usual, wandered to the rest of his day. All of the holiday talk had him thinking about Christmas shopping and he considered making his annual pilgrimage to Spring Hill Mall. It had been years since he exchanged gifts with his sisters, but he hadn't really gotten used to it. It wasn't that he missed receiving presents because he did not. Although well-intentioned, they were typically as useless to him as he supposed his were to them. It was difficult to find appropriate gifts for people he rarely talked to and almost never saw. It was like shopping for strangers.

Guy liked the mall at this time of year. He liked hearing the generic Christmas music playing over the department store speakers. He enjoyed seeing the oversized mall decorations hanging from the second floor and the enormous chalet covered with fake cottony snow set up in the center court. Guy liked to see the anxious children and their mothers, all possessing varying degrees of patience, as they lolled in the gated, serpentine queue coiled around where Santa and his elfish photographers held court. There was always such electricity in the air. The longing, excitement, and frustration of kids as they were towed, tugged, and scolded in and out of stores past the endless displays of toys and candy mixed with the elevated levels of stress from their parents as they strained to balance their financial well-being with the guilt and obligation wrought by the consumer's Christmas season. And all was set against a ticking clock. Hurry! Only two weeks left! Amidst this cacophony of agony and ecstasy, Guy would calmly stroll, sip his coffee, and alternately bemoan and revel in his detachment from the absurdity of it all.

He himself had no memory of ever sitting on Santa's lap and nervously making his requests. There was an old photo, in a paper frame decorated with candy canes, of him doing so. When or where it was taken, he did not know. Guy did remember writing letters, but after his mom passed away, he was pretty sure that they didn't get read because he no longer received anything he asked for. Over time, he and Charles settled into their own dysfunctional tradition of gift giving. His dad gave him a check for a couple hundred dollars, and he gave his dad an Old Spice gift set. To Charles, money was appropriate because it was the only thing he believed had any real value. For Guy, Old Spice was the only thing he was certain that Charles would neither complain about nor blatantly dispose of.

It didn't matter that Guy hadn't cashed one of his father's checks in years. Charles continued to write them, and when the time came, Guy would play his part, open the card, take the check, and politely say thank you. Then he would take the check home and stick it in a drawer with the others. Every birthday and every Christmas, Charles kept writing them and Guy kept filing them away. He stopped cashing them when he realized that they weren't really gifts. Charles never actually gave money away. He invested it. Instead of giving him a gift, he was purchasing a stake in him, like buying stock in a corporation. But Charles wasn't really expecting a return on his investment, he just wanted some control. He wanted a say. Once Guy understood this, he stopped selling shares of himself to his father.

He thought about his guitar and his wounded fingers and decided that he wanted to get a present for Jacque. But he didn't want to get him something just to get him something, he wanted to get him something really good. He considered what he knew about his friend. Jacque liked to savor things. He liked quality stuff, but not stuff like tangible stuff. More like his beer or his coffee. And once in a while, at The Duke, he would order a top shelf whiskey. Guy also heard him talk about steaks and cigars on occasion. He laughed as it dawned on him that Jacque was right. He really was kind of a snob.

While he was busy trying to imagine what kind of gift a snob would appreciate, Mrs. Schultz came in to pay for her gas and purchase her lottery tickets. She saw his fingers and the lying began again.

"Oh, Guy," she asked with concern in her voice, "what happened to your fingers?"

"Oh, nothing. I got a little burn."

"Well, you've got them all bandaged up. That must not be a little burn. What did you do? Did you burn all of them?"

"Not my thumb." Guy smiled and gave her a thumbs up in order to show off his one undamaged digit. "I got lucky there."

"What happened? How did you burn them?"

"I was trying to cook myself some dinner."

She looked at him, confused, wanting more information. She waited. He waited. Then she asked, "So what happened?"

Guy sighed and proceeded with the story he had concocted over the course of the morning. "I turned on the wrong burner on my stovetop. The burner lights on my stove don't work anymore so I didn't notice. Anyway, I had the pot of water on one burner and a metal spoon on another. But I screwed up. I wasn't boiling the water; I was really just heating the spoon. Then when I went to pick up the spoon, I burnt my fingers on it because it was sitting on the burner that was actually turned on."

"Oh my gosh," she winced. "That must have hurt."

Guy shrugged. "It wasn't too bad."

"Did you put anything on them?"

"Just a little Vaseline."

"Oh, Guy," she shook her head. "No. No, no, no. Don't use that. Listen to me. Last summer, one of my granddaughters burned her little hand on the grill. It was awful. It was almost her entire palm. Her daddy was cooking some burgers in the backyard and he let her get too close to the grill." Mrs. Schultz shuddered as she remembered. "And then I think she kind of stumbled a little bit. She tripped on something and her daddy wasn't paying attention. She's just a toddler, you know, and she lost her balance, I think. She reached out to catch herself and she put her poor little hand on that hot grill." She winced. "It was awful. The poor dear burned her little hand something terrible. When Jenny, my daughter, took her to the pediatrician, he recommended a very specific burn ointment. It was called silver something." She thought for a moment. "Silvadene! That's what it was, Silvadene. That's what you need for your fingers, Guy. It was really a miracle cream. I want you to write that down. Silvadene."

"Silvadene, huh?" Guy nodded. "I think I can remember that."

She looked at him somewhat skeptically. "You get me a piece of paper and I'm going to write it down for you. I want you to ask the pharmacist about it."

Obediently, Guy fished around underneath the counter for paper, found some, and set it in front of her along with a pen.

Mrs. Schultz wrote down the name of the cream on the top sheet. "Now, you need to go and get some this afternoon. The sooner you get it on those burned fingertips of yours the sooner the healing will start. What pharmacy do you usually go to?" She pushed the paper toward him.

"Uhh, I guess the Osco in McHenry."

"They should have it there. That's where my Jenny goes." Then she locked on to his eyes with hers and demanded, "I want you to promise me you'll go this afternoon."

Feeling guilty, but helplessly drowning in his own ridiculous story, Guy promised her that he would go to the pharmacy in McHenry to get burn ointment to treat the burns that he did not actually have. "I promise I will go there after work." He held her gaze until she seemed satisfied. She told him that she was going to be back next week and check on him. Then, finally, she said goodbye, he thanked her, and she left. He watched her get into her car and turn onto Route 12 before breathing a sigh of relief and cursing his injured fingers, the tape, and his stupid lie.

He looked at the piece of paper in front of him. "Silvadene," he said out loud. *At least I'll know what to use if I ever really do burn myself,* he chuckled. Guy took his prescription from Mrs. Schultz, crumpled it up, and tossed it into the garbage can. When he turned back to the counter, he was greeted by his own name written on the sheet at the top of the little stack of scratch paper. It was folded in half and "Guy" was written on it in a very unfamiliar handwriting. Curious, he picked it up and unfolded it. It read:

Sophie Ross
PO Box 83711
Waterloo, IA 50701

Chapter 36

Sophie turned away from the comfortable running surface along the water's edge to make the hard charge across the loose sand that separated her from the entrance to the long Mexico Beach Public Pier. Thighs burning, she fought to maintain her pace for the entire one hundred or so yards. Although winded by the time she reached the parking lot, she made a sharp left under the sign, onto the wooden planks, and willed herself on a final sprint all the way to the end of the pier. Far out over the water, she came to a stop and walked the perimeter of the large rectangle terminus with its benches and scattered fishermen while she tried to catch her breath. After a couple of minutes, she was still breathing hard, but had mostly recovered. Sophie locked her fingers together, put her hands on her head, and began walking back toward shore and the rising sun.

Although she was sweating from her run, it was a cool morning and the sunlight felt warm on her face. At the end of the pier, she turned and trudged back through the loose white sand to the shoreline. Being up early and jogging along the nearly deserted beach was in itself a sublime experience, but it was the walk back that she truly savored. With nowhere to be, with no one waiting for her or depending on her, Sophie was able to take her time and she did. She drank in the thick, humid, ocean air that smelled like fish and saltwater, and well, she guessed, the ocean. It was so unlike any place she had ever been. Strolling along, she scanned the tumbling blend of sand and shells behind the retreating waves and often bent to examine the ones that caught her eye. After rinsing them off, she would turn them over in her fingers, marveling at the detail. Sometimes, she removed her shoes and socks and walked back in the surf line, allowing the waves to splash over her feet and calves. And perpetually leading the way for her was some kind of little bird. As she moved up the beach, so did they. There were small ones that ran ahead, chasing the waves back into the sea and stabbing their little black beaks into the sand as they scurried. Others, slightly larger, waited until she was closer and then noisily flew ahead a few dozen yards only to wait for her to approach anew. Her favorites, though, were the pelicans. Huge, silent, stoic, and barely seeming to move, they somehow managed to stay just inches above the water as they glided past her either up or down the coast. And it was quiet. Other than the occasional faraway drone of a fishing boat heading out to sea from the canal, the only sounds were the crashing of waves and cries of gulls. It was all so relaxing and serene, and it was these mornings, as much as anything, that were helping to repair her wounded heart.

When she reached the walkover just before Toucan's, she used it to cut through the protected strip of vegetation, over the small dune, and across Highway 98 into the little neighborhood where she had been living for most of the past couple of months. Two streets in, Sophie walked up one of the short, sandy driveways, through the gate next to the garage, and into the little backyard. Sitting down on the bench of a weathered picnic table, she removed her shoes and socks and shook the sand out of both into the sparse coastal Florida scrub that made up the backyard. The picnic table itself sat next to an equally battered grill, and both were on a small, rectangular slab of concrete that served as a sort of detached patio. A half dozen large stepping-stones led to a sliding glass door on the back of the house. It was unlocked and she went inside.

Wiping her feet off on the little rug, Sophie wondered if she could ever get used to the sand. Being extra careful with her shoes hadn't mattered—neither had frequent vacuuming and sweeping. There always seemed to be a few grains sticking to the bottoms of her bare feet. *I guess that's just life*, she mused. *Sometimes, no matter how well things are going, there are these annoying little distractions trying pull my attention away from all of the good that surrounds me.* She sighed and thought about Abby. *Is she just an annoying little distraction now? No, not hardly. Not yet.* That was the goal though, and Sophie felt good about the progress she'd made. She was also appreciative of all the good fortune that had come her way.

When she left St. Louis, her only goal was to get to the ocean and walk on a beach somewhere. She didn't know where and she didn't really care so she headed south on I-55. Along the way, she enjoyed overnight stops in Memphis and New Orleans and decided that both cities would be worth a few more days if she weren't on a mission. But she was on a mission and each morning Sophie dutifully checked out of her hotel, gassed up her car, and continued her journey southward. She thought that she might be able to at least get a glimpse of the Gulf when she got to New Orleans, but that wasn't the case. Instead, she had been an hour outside the city, cruising along Highway 90 in Mississippi when the sky and the sea finally met out her passenger side window. It was on the long bridge over Bay St. Louis and she struggled to keep her attention focused on driving. Fortunately, the road delivered her right to a beach less than a mile after crossing the bay.

Sophie turned into the parking lot, found a spot facing the beach, and stared out at the calm waters of the Gulf. She started to get out of the car but stopped. The ever and always responsible part of herself, the voice inside of her that she had obeyed for so many years, wanted to know what came next. "You made it to the ocean," it asked, "now what? What happens next?" She leaned back in her seat and took a deep breath. *I don't know what comes next,* she admitted. And she decided that she didn't really want to think about it right then. Right then, she simply wanted to get out of her car, walk across the beach, dig her toes into the sand, and get her feet wet in the ocean for the very first time in her life. She just wanted to enjoy the moment and not, for once, worry about the next. And that's what she did.

Sophie opened her car door and stepped out into the sunshine and the ocean breeze. Removing her shoes and socks, she left them in the car before walking gingerly across the rest of the parking lot and into the warm sand of the beach. There, she paused and smiled broadly, enjoying the fact that she had actually arrived. For a moment she felt a little silly and self-conscious and wondered if other people could tell that she'd never been to the ocean before. Not that there were many other people around. After all, it was midday on a Thursday in October. A few scattered people sat reading, one guy was throwing something out into the water for his dog, and there were some walkers and joggers. None of them paid any attention to the grinning, solitary woman near the cars as she started across the beach toward the water. It was in the low 70's, the only clouds were far out over the Gulf, and Sophie was comfortable in a pair of shorts and a t-shirt. The steady breeze was coming off the water and it fluttered her hair behind her as she made her way down to the shoreline. She hesitated a moment on the very edge of the damp spongy sand where only the biggest waves reached and watched some smaller ones collapse and race toward her before they inevitably retreated back into the sand and the ocean. Then she took a couple of steps forward and let them wash over her feet and ankles. She marveled at the way they tugged the sand out from around her feet each time they washed back into the sea. Sophie ventured out a little further into the water, past the gritty line of shells and pebbles. The waves climbed up over her knees, causing her to gently sway each time they passed her. The bottoms of her shorts were wet and she could smell the salt. She dipped a hand into the water and brought it up to her face. Cautiously touching her finger to her tongue, she tasted the salt and laughed at her own childish curiosity.

She stood there for a while, filling her lungs with the fresh air and taking it all in. Then she came out of the water and walked back up onto the shore. The wind cooled her legs as it dried them, and she decided to walk down the beach for a while. Once her car was almost completely out of sight, she turned around and slowly started back. As she did, she reluctantly allowed herself to begin thinking about what came next. Her initial thought was that she might as well head back to Iowa now. Then she surveyed the sun and the sand and the water that surrounded her. As beautiful as the leaves were back home in mid-October, she knew they were falling fast and would soon be gone. Months of the cold, overcast, drab, industrial ugliness of a Midwestern city in the winter lay ahead. Iowa, she mused, shaking her head. For so many years, that's where she retreated and regrouped, and that habit was hard to shake. It was an effort to remind herself that there was nothing back there for her other than a post office box and the mild comfort of familiarity.

So, if not Iowa, she wondered, then where? Sophie thought back to her trip down here and the stops she'd made in St. Louis, Memphis, and New Orleans. No, she shook her head. Big cities were interesting, but only to visit. She couldn't imagine herself living in one. They seemed so impersonal and anonymous. *Maybe that's why I don't like them,* she thought. *Too much of my life has already been like that, impersonal and anonymous.* In a city she would feel like a ghost, she decided. She was almost across from the parking lot again when she looked up and noticed. She stopped and sighed. "When you get back in your car, where are you going to go?" she asked out loud. A few short days ago, the same question had been exhilarating. But it wasn't anymore. It wasn't liberating and it wasn't exciting. But it wasn't upsetting or stressful either. It wasn't really anything other than a question.

Sophie walked back across the beach to her car, sat on the hood, and used her feet to brush the sand off each other. It wasn't even noon yet. She got the atlas out of her car and returned to the hood. Before opening it though, she stopped. *I don't have to go anywhere right now,* she reminded herself. *This is supposed to be a vacation, not just an hour-long trip to a beach. What the hell is wrong with me that I don't even know how to go on a vacation?* she wondered. *Plus, I don't have to make any decisions today. Or tomorrow, or the next day. I should just be enjoying a vacation. That's it, nothing more.*

Looking back down the beach, Sophie saw a solitary man sitting on a lawn chair. Next to him was a cooler with a drink resting on it. He appeared to be reading a book. *That's what I need,* she thought. *I need a cooler, and a lawn chair, and a book, and I need to sit on the beach and do nothing. For like a week.* She looked across the parking lot to the other side of the road that ran along the coastline. There were no motels. There weren't any restaurants or bars either. She couldn't even see any shops. There was a condominium complex and some vacant land. Nothing she could see looked very vacationy. The beach itself looked nice, but she knew she didn't really have anything to compare it to. *If I am going to take a vacation at the beach,* she thought, *I should do it right.* Sophie decided to get back into her car and keep driving.

Unimpressed, she cruised through the rest of Mississippi. The beaches were almost always nice, but the other stuff just wasn't quite what she had in mind. She wasn't even really sure what she was looking for but was hoping to know it when she saw it. In Alabama, the road took her away from the coast and up and across Mobile Bay. Sophie was unconcerned though because she knew Florida lay ahead and people always talked about going to the beach in Florida. She was certain that there had to be something good waiting up the road. After all, who ever heard of anyone talking about going on a beach vacation to Mississippi or Alabama anyway?

By midafternoon, she crossed the border into Florida and was in downtown Pensacola. It didn't take long to find the beach and it was beautiful and it was busy. It was vacationy. There were bars and restaurants and hotels and beach stores and gift shops and music and big broad sidewalks. This was definitely more like it, she thought. She cruised along, checking it all out, and as the city faded into the distance behind her, Sophie debated whether or not to turn around and find a hotel. She knew she liked it, but there was plenty of daylight left and part of her thought that it would be foolish to pick the first city that stood out. She also found that she was enjoying the drive along the coast and checking out the different towns. Sophie decided to keep going, knowing it wouldn't be a big deal to retrace her steps if she wanted.

For a while Pensacola was her favorite and nothing else measured up. Then she hit Panama City and liked how it didn't feel quite as touristy. It had a lot of the same stuff, but it was a little smaller and seemed a little less hectic. *Maybe that's just because it's later in the day, though,* she thought. Daylight was fading and the sun was going to be setting soon. She started to think it might be time to make up her mind. As she drove out of Panama

208

City and tried to reach a decision, she suddenly noticed that, for possibly the first time since entering Florida, one town stopped bleeding into the next. She was out in the country and it was a welcome respite from all of the busy beach towns. Then, just as she began to doubt the existence of another town worth examining and just as she was about to turn around, Sophie saw the sign for Mexico Beach. She rolled her eyes thinking about Abby's Cancun vacation and the huevos rancheros the other morning in St. Louis that had started this whole adventure. *Fine*, she thought, *I'll check it out.*

Stretched out for a couple miles in a narrow band along the Gulf, Mexico Beach was home to just over one thousand people. It did have a surf shop full of swimsuits, towels, and touristy t-shirts, a handful of motels, and a couple of restaurants and bars, but it was nothing like either Panama City or Pensacola. It was vacationy, but not in an obnoxious way. It didn't have the endless billboard assault of all of the activities a tourist needed to partake in. There wasn't the not-so-subtle drumbeat of go and do and see and so on. To Sophie, it seemed more like a regular small town that happened to be located on the beach and she liked that. About halfway through Mexico Beach, as Sophie was appreciating the differences, she saw an enormous weathered, wooden, multi-tiered beachfront restaurant and bar advertising fresh seafood and a happy hour from 4-6pm. Briefly considering her stomach, she found it wanting. She checked the clock on her dash and saw that only five minutes remained before the end of happy hour. It was fate, she decided, and simultaneously hit her brakes and her turn signal. After parking, she slipped her shoes on without her socks and hustled inside Toucan's Beach Bar and Grill.

She sat on the deck, alone in the small crowd, and, for the very first time in her life, watched the sun disappear into the Gulf. It did not disappoint. The restaurant wasn't very busy, and while she ate the delicious, spicy bowl of shrimp gumbo, she fell into easy conversation with the bartender, Rick, who had recommended it. A couple of the locals joined in and they teased a little bit of her story out of her but didn't press, and she appreciated that. She listened to their gossiping and they provided context for her when necessary. By the time she left, it was almost ten o'clock and she was feeling tired. She had learned the names of a half a dozen people and they had made her promise to stick around for at least one more day. Then, before she could leave, they had insisted on calling Dorothy, just down the street at the Buena Vista Motel, to verify she had a room available for her. Feeling very full and very comfortable and very welcome, Sophie drove there to spend the night. That was almost two months ago.

Chapter 37

Guy stared, his mind as blank as the inside of the card on the table in front of him. It was a Christmas card that he had spent way too long picking out at the drugstore yesterday afternoon. When he left the Gas and Go, he'd gone to check on his father and re-shovel the drifted-over pathway from the house to the garage. Charles sat in the kitchen and watched him out the picture window. Guy knew his father was there, analyzing every aspect of what he did. He finished up and went inside for his performance review. After listening to a critique of his shoveling strategy and answering queries as to why he piled the snow the way he did and where he did, Guy assured Charles that the shovel was put away where he wanted it and that the garage door had definitely been closed tightly. With his mind still trying to process the sudden re-appearance of Sophie, or of her address at least, into his life, his father's nitpicking didn't bother him very much. Charles sensed his son's distractedness and seemed to double his efforts at provoking a reaction, but Guy weathered the assault and left.

He drove down to the Osco in McHenry to buy some more medical tape for his damaged fingers and felt a little pang of guilt as he walked past the pharmacist without inquiring about Silvawhatever for the burns he didn't have. The tape was near the bandages and he figured he should probably get an extra box of them, too, and he did. On his way to the register to pay, he walked down the card aisle, thought about Sophie, and got stuck. The idea of sitting down with a pen and a blank sheet of paper to write a letter felt intimidating. Sending a note in a Christmas card seemed like it might be a little easier and less weird. So he began trying to find the right one and it took him a while. They were all either too corny, too religious, too cheesy, too pretty, too cutesy, too clever, too stupid, or just too something. But then he stumbled on a couple of blank ones and decided that was the way to go. The one he chose had a photograph of a simple rural scene on the front. There was snow on the ground and a few trees. One lonesome fir grew slightly apart from the rest, but it was decorated with lights and red and silver ornaments and had a star on top.

At home, Guy put the card on the table in front of the television and went into the bathroom to re-bandage and re-tape his fingers. While he worked on them, he thought about Sophie. When he first saw the note, he wondered if she might be back in the area, but then decided that the Iowa address wouldn't make any sense. Besides, if she was around, she could have just stopped in while he was working or gone to The Duke. Or called. *Unless, maybe she thought it would be weird to call?* No, he decided, that didn't make any sense. Calling would be less weird than a cryptic note. When Big John arrived to relieve him, Guy showed it to him. He looked at it and said he had no idea where it came from. He guessed she must have given it to one of the weekend girls. Then Guy tried to figure out just how long ago she'd left town. After looking at the Miller Lite Bears schedule taped to the bottom half of the door, he remembered watching the Arizona game with Jacque and Jacque being mad at him because he kept checking the door to see if Michele was going to show up. That was the weekend he met her. They'd been talking and she called him her new best friend. Then Jacque dragged him away to play pool and he was stuck. And then she was gone. That was over two months ago.

When he was done with his fingers, Guy found a pen and sat down on his couch. He took her address out of his pocket and re-examined it yet again. No matter how many times he looked, though, there were no clues to be found. It said Guy on the outside and there was nothing more than her name and address on the inside. No "Hi," no "write me," no smiley face, no nothing. He opened up the card on the table, leaned forward, pen in hand, and realized he had no idea what to write. For a moment he just sat there, thinking. Then he set the pen down and leaned back onto the couch. The ceiling was almost as white as the inside of the card. Feeling frustrated, Guy picked up his guitar and practiced until the tape started to slide around and make it difficult. It was also becoming worn and soft enough that his fingertips were starting to hurt again.

Reluctantly, he put down the guitar and picked up the card again hoping to be seized with some sort of inspiration. Then he looked at her note and it struck him that maybe she just wanted a job? She was out of work, he recalled. That was the whole reason she was leaving town. Again he put the card down and leaned back. This time he closed his eyes and tried to remember as many details as he could of the night they met. He could clearly see her face. It was beautiful and she smiled a lot. She had on blue jeans and a long-sleeve black top. He thought it might have had a couple of buttons, but he wasn't sure. He knew it wasn't low cut like Michele's. She wasn't drinking beer. It was vodka and something, maybe? Grapefruit? That sounded right. As best as he could, Guy replayed the evening and decided he would be very disappointed if she just wanted a job. He also decided that he would very much like to see her again. Such thoughts, however, only served to make it much more difficult to figure out what to write. So he didn't. Instead, he settled for the illusion of progress by neatly writing her name and address on the envelope. Then he carefully wrote out his name and return address in the top left corner.

Surrendering to his writer's block, Guy made himself some dinner, ate it while he watched television, and cleaned up. He would have liked to continue playing his guitar but remembered the endless questions at work and his promise to himself to get his fingers healed by Sunday. The Christmas card lay open next to the envelope on the coffee table taunting him. He thought about just writing Merry Christmas or something. Then he could be done and get it in tomorrow's mail. But that seemed lame, too. Nothing for two months and then a generic Merry Christmas? No, he couldn't do that. He found his phone and texted Jacque. "TNF?"

The response was quick. "Wtf?"

"Thursday night football. The Duke. Interested?"

This time there was a delay. Then "4 football? Or counseling?"

Guy laughed, typed "football" and hit send. After a few seconds he added, "And advice. No counseling" and sent that.

"Knew it."

An hour later Guy was sitting at The Duke waiting for Jacque. When his friend arrived, he flagged Mindy down and ordered him a beer. With a glass.

Jacque sat down. "You know, the only reason I am here is because I want to know what the fuck the difference is between advice and counseling."

Guy laughed. "With advice you get to sit at the bar. When I needed counseling, you had to sit at a table."

"That's something, I guess," Jacque acknowledged as he poured his beer. "All right, let's hear it, my friend. What's going on?"

"You ever write letters?"

"I used to. I used to write my parents. But now I email them. Who the hell writes letters anymore?"

"I think me. I'm going to start."

"Who the hell are you going to write a letter to?"

"Sophie Ross."

Jacque's face was blank. "Am I supposed to know who that is?"

"Bear's Sophie. Remember her?"

"Oh yeah. Really? How did that come up?"

"I just found her address at work today. I think she left it there for me."

"Huh. You just found it?"

"Yeah, I went to get some scratch paper from under the counter and there it was. It must have been sitting there for the last couple of months."

"Yeah, it's been a while, I guess. So no email? No phone? Just an address?"

"Yep."

"So you going to write her?"

"Yeah, but I don't know if I've ever written a real letter in my life. What am I supposed to write?"

"Write about your life. Tell her what's going on. Ask her how she's doing?

Where is she anyway?"

"I don't know. I only have her PO Box in Waterloo. What am I supposed to tell her about my life?"

"What do you mean?"

"I don't have a life. "

"Doesn't matter."

"Why not?"

"Because she likes you, my friend."

"What? She's Bear's girlfriend."

Jacque laughed. "No she's not. She was just hanging out with Bear for the hell of it. He moved on the week after she left. She's definitely not his girlfriend."

"You really think she likes me?"

"She wouldn't have left you her address. She didn't leave me her address and I hung out with her a lot more than you while she was in town. On Saturdays. She was always in here on Saturdays."

"That's true, I guess.

"You, you charming motherfucker, you hang out with her for about an hour and a half one night and she's all yours."

"Yeah, right."

"Good thing she left or you would have had to throw down with Bear for stealing his woman." Jacque cackled.

"Shut up. Seriously though, what the hell am I supposed to write?"

"It really doesn't matter."

"Bullshit."

"I'm serious. Write about your damn day. Tell her what you did."

"I don't do anything though, that's the problem."

"Yes you do. Tell her how work was. Tell her about your dad's latest health whatever. Tell her what you are going to do for Christmas or New Year's. Ask her what she's doing for the holidays. Trust me, she'll just be happy to hear from you."

"It's going to sound stupid."

"So what? She's in Iowa. You've got nothing right now. Take a leap. The only way you fuck this up is by not writing a letter."

"Yeah, I suppose. Just tell her stuff, huh?"

"Just tell her stuff. You'll be fine. "

"This is weird."

"It's not weird. Well, I guess it is weird because nobody writes letters anymore, but otherwise it's not. It actually seems kind of romantic in a way."

"Romantic? I don't know."

"Jesus Christ, Guy! Write the goddamn letter! Here you've got a little good that's fallen into your lap. Quit analyzing it and embrace it!"

That was last night at The Duke. Jacque left at halftime, but Guy stuck around to nurse a couple more beers and finish the game so he wouldn't have to go home and actually write the letter. But today was Friday. He'd already eaten breakfast, cleaned up the kitchen, showered, shaved, taken out the garbage, and put in a load of laundry, but the card was still blank. "Shit," he said out loud. *Fine,* he bargained with himself, *one more cigarette and then I will sit down and write this damn thing.*

Ten minutes later he was back inside, sitting at his kitchen table. He took a deep breath and wrote, "Dear Sophie." First off, he apologized for not writing sooner and explained that he did not find her note until yesterday. He wrote that he was still working at the Gas and Go and still waiting for his life to begin. He told her that his dad had only been in the hospital once since she'd left, and it was brief. The more he wrote, the easier it became. He asked about the visit with her sister. He asked about her new job and told her he hoped it was going well. And he took Jacque's advice and asked about her holiday plans. Finally, he told her about Jacque buying him a guitar for his birthday and how he had been learning to play it. He even told her about his damaged fingers. It was the first time he told anyone about either one.

Chapter 38

Michele looked at her phone and saw it was Laura again. Reluctantly, she answered it.

"Hey, where have you been?"

"I just got home. I had to run Carly over to a friend's house and then I did a little grocery shopping. I didn't have my phone with me," she lied. It wasn't a total lie though. She had dropped Carly off on the way to the grocery store, but her phone was with her and she had been ignoring the texts from Laura.

"Oh. So, what's the plan? Are you still up for doing a little Christmas shopping before we head out?"

"I don't know. That's fine, I guess."

"Wow. That sounded enthusiastic. What's up? What's the matter?"

Michele hesitated before answering. "I don't think I want to go out in Crystal Lake again tonight."

"Ohhh." Now Laura paused. "I thought we were going to give it a little more time?"

"No. I think I'm done."

"Really?"

"Yeah. I just don't think it's worth it. And I'm sick of driving down there."

"There's been a lot of guys though," Laura pointed out encouragingly. "And it really hasn't been that long."

"It's been long enough for me."

"Because of the drive? I'll drive. It's not that far."

"It's not just the drive. And I know there have been a lot of guys. But you've seen what's out there. And we keep running into the same people now anyway. They're either too young or too old. I think maybe we're just at this weird in-between age. I'm thirty-two. This is when people are either already married or, if they're not, there's usually a good reason."

"That's true," Laura admitted. "They have all been either younger or older or so not even a consideration."

"And the younger ones, Jesus, some of them still live at home. The ones that don't, I think they have an apartment with a couple of their friends. It's not really that they're that much younger, but maybe just immature? Not really immature. I don't know. I was married for over ten years and my daughter's almost out of high school. I think I'm just at such a different place in my life than they are, you know?

"Yeah, I can see that."

"The older ones have been great. They've been way better. I can talk to them, we have things in common. And there has really been some potential there," she admitted. "There's a few of them I'm sure I would have gone out with. That is if you weren't doing such a good job at screening them for me."

They had developed a system. Michele was always just her normally friendly and flirty and beautiful self. If they met someone and it was going well, if she was interested, she would excuse herself for the ladies' room. Then Laura would be able to perform her background checks. She was upfront with them about what she was doing. She told them nicely that she was just looking out for her friend. She asked pretty specific information and they usually obliged her. If they didn't, that was okay, but they were done with them. Laura and Michele had decided that they didn't have time to play games and be three dates in before figuring out what was wrong with them.

"Yeah, there were a couple of them. I really liked that guy Bill. I thought he would have been great for you. He seemed like a good guy. He was nice and good-looking. And he was fun, too."

"He was. And he had a decent job. He was some kind of financial guy, I think. But he had a needy ex and four kids. That's a huge child support commitment. His youngest was only like six."

"Yeah."

"All of the older ones who I would even consider have been divorced or were in the process. All of them. But it's not just the divorces. I don't care about that. It's all the shit that goes along with it. I don't want to deal with that. And their kids are way younger than Carly. None of them are even in high school yet. They are going to be writing checks to their exes for quite a while yet."

"Yeah, I guess you're right. But still, we won't know what's out there unless we go and see for ourselves. And hey, what about me? I've been planning on going out all week."

"I'm sorry."

"Maybe you just need a break," Laura suggested.

"Maybe. This was so much easier in my head. I don't know what I was expecting. Like I was going to go out a couple of times and then allow myself to be swept off my feet by some rich Prince Charming. Like it was going to be that easy."

"Look, it's not a bad idea. It's just not necessarily a quick thing, you know? I think the time factor is what's getting you down. I mean, really honey, you have to remember that it's only been a couple of months. I think you need to be more patient. Hang in there."

"I know."

"And every time we have been out, we've met people. You clearly don't have a problem attracting suitors. Something is going to click. You can't get discouraged yet."

"I am, though. I get knots in my stomach every time I drive by a Walmart. I hate going there now. I was there today, and I walked around watching all of the employees and it freaked me out. It just freaks me out, Laura. I imagine them all having these horrible, desperate lives and see myself headed there. But I don't know what else to do."

"Oh, honey, I'm sorry. I didn't mean to ruin Walmart for you," she apologized. "I guess I oversold that just a little."

"Maybe. Look, I know it's not the end of the world if this doesn't work out and I have to get a job, but it would be the end of my world the way it is now. It scares me."

"Hey, it's okay. Let's take a break this weekend and not worry about it. But I still want to go Christmas shopping with you tonight. Are you up for that?"

"Yeah. I'm sorry to bail on your night out, but I am just, I don't know what I am. I don't think I am in the mood to go out. But I would like to go shopping."

"Sounds good. We'll go to the mall. And I promise we won't stop by Walmart."

Chapter 39

Michele and Laura got lucky and found a decent spot in the crowded parking lot just outside the entrance to the Wickes furniture store that anchored one wing of Spring Hill Mall. Ditching their coats in the car, they hustled inside to the warmth and bustle of the Christmas season. Winding through the labyrinth of master bedrooms, living rooms, dining room tables, and china cabinets, they avoided eye contact with lurking salespeople and strategized.

"What's the plan? Anywhere specific you want to go?" Laura asked.

"Not really. I still have to get something for my mom, but I am fine to just wander. What about you?"

"I do have a couple stores I want to go in, but if you're not in a hurry, we can just go with the flow and stop when we get to them."

"Sounds good to me," Michele replied as they reached the alcove where Wickes spilled out into the mall. Before them coursed a lazy river of shoppers meandering their way around the interior perimeter. After pausing for an opportunity to merge, they fell in behind an older couple. Both were heavily laden with a variety of colorful shopping bags emblazoned with the holiday versions of various store logos.

"I think she needs to have him make a trip to the car," Laura observed.

"Yeah," Michele agreed. "No kidding! Unless, maybe, they're just going for it in one shot. When they can't carry anymore, then they know it's time to go home and start wrapping."

Laura laughed. "I wonder how many grandkids they have."

"I don't know. Quite a few by the looks of it."

"Or maybe they have only one. One that they spoil rotten."

Michele started to speak again but was interrupted. "Oh!" Laura exclaimed, grabbing her friend's arm. "Quick! Come on!" she commanded, pulling her into the bench and kiosk-strewn center area that separated them from the opposite flow of people on the other side of the mall corridor.

"What? Where are we going?" Michele asked, trying to keep up. Her eyes searched ahead for a clue as to what had caught Laura's attention.

"Just come with me. Trust me." Laura positioned them along the edge of the crowds on the other side.

"What are we doing? What's going on?" she asked, but Laura was ignoring her and looking behind Michele at the people walking toward them. Frustrated, she turned to see what Laura was fixated on just as her friend spoke.

"Hey, Guy," Laura called out waving, "Merry Christmas!"

To her surprise, when she heard Guy's name, Michele found herself immediately looking instead for Jacque. She was dismayed to see only Guy casually strolling along with nothing other than a cup of coffee to keep him company. He glanced around for a moment trying to locate the source of the greeting. Then he smiled as he spotted a waving Laura and angled over toward them to say hi. They hugged their hellos and he wished them both a happy holiday.

"Hey," he stepped back and looked at them. "Where's all of your bags? Aren't you two Christmas shopping?"

"We just got here," Michele explained.

"Yeah," Laura assured him, "just give us some time and I'm sure we'll have our arms full."

"What about you? Where're all your goodies?" Michele asked.

Guy held his arms open and gestured with his cup of coffee. "This is it. I don't really have anyone to buy for."

"Really?" they both asked, clearly fascinated by the very idea.

"No one?" Laura was in disbelief. "What about your dad?"

"I guess that's one person," Guy acknowledged. "But I don't really do a whole lot of shopping for him. All he wants is a bottle of his aftershave from the drugstore. It takes me a whole five minutes to shop for that."

"I can't imagine what that would be like," Michele wondered out loud. "I'm not sure if I would love it or hate it."

"Aftershave, huh? What kind does he use?"

Guy whistled the theme from the once-ubiquitous Old Spice commercials of their childhood.

"Old Spice!" she exclaimed, recognizing it instantly.

"You got it."

"So if you don't have any shopping to do, what are you doing here at the mall a week before Christmas?" Michele asked.

Guy shrugged. "I don't know. I guess it just doesn't quite feel like Christmas without a trip to the mall. You know, all the decorations, and the cheesy music, and the kids, and the Santa Chalet and everything." He seemed a little embarrassed.

Laura smiled. "I think that's sweet," she said leaning into Michele in a marginally subtle attempt to draw attention to it.

"Yeah," Michele agreed. "I can see that. I guess I take it for granted and complain about the crowds. But I suppose I would miss it if I didn't have to come down here."

"You would," Guy assured her.

"Do you have any plans for the holidays, Guy?" Laura asked. "Are you going anywhere?"

He shook his head. "Nope. I don't ever go very far. My dad's health isn't good. I pretty much need to stay close to home so I can help him out."

"I'm sorry to hear that," Michele sympathized. "That must be rough."

Guy shrugged. "What about you two?" he asked. "Are either of you going anywhere?"

Michele answered first. "I wish. But no, not this year."

"We meet Ron's family at the Kalahari Resort in the Dells for a few days in-between Christmas and New Year's," Laura said.

"That sounds cool. I bet your kids love that."

"Yeah. It is a nice set up. They get to see their cousins and swim all day. And Ron's parents pay for our room and dinners. That's our Christmas present from them." She smiled.

"Even better!" Guy exclaimed.

The conversation had reached the point of pause and Laura sensed it. They'd said hello and made a little requisite small talk. Now it was either going to end and they would go their separate ways, or someone would say something else and keep it going. Michele wasn't saying anything and her own mind was blank. Shit, she thought, come on Michele! This is a golden opportunity! Guy shifted his feet and took a sip of his coffee. He was getting ready to move on. She tried to think, but nothing came.

"Well hey," Guy spoke up. "It was great to see you two. I'll let you get on with your shopping. Enjoy. Merry Christmas."

As Laura's mind raced for a way to keep him talking, she and Michele said thanks and told him it was good to see him. Then he turned to walk away.

"Guy!" Laura called out abruptly. "Wait a second."

He stopped and turned back to face her. Michele was looking at her, too.

"Do you have plans for New Year's Eve?" she asked.

He shook his head. "No, not really. I'll probably just head over to The Duke."

"Well, Ron and I made reservations to go out to dinner up in Lake Geneva with another couple. But they canceled on us. We still want to go, though, and the reservation is for four people. Anyway, I was trying to get Michele to come with us, but she and Mark are through and she said she wouldn't do it without a date. But she's not really doing anything to get a date. So, what do you think?" she asked. "Why don't you come out to dinner with us and be Michele's date?"

Chapter 40

It was almost nine when Guy made it back to Richmond, pulled into the parking lot behind The Duke, and found a spot next to Jacque's van. When he went in, Jacque was in his familiar spot at the end of the bar and he joined him.

"Hey Romeo," Jacque teased, "did you write your letter?"

"Yes. And I even mailed it this afternoon," he answered confidently. "Thanks for the help. I actually did just what you said to do. I wrote about my life. I told her about my day, what was going on with my dad. I even told her about learning to play the guitar. And I asked her about her plans for the holidays, too. Once I got started, it was pretty easy to fill up the inside of the card."

"The card?"

"Yeah. I bought a Christmas card and wrote inside of it. That seemed easier than just a plain letter."

"That's cool. Nice work. Now you wait, huh?"

"Yeah, I guess so." He caught Mindy's eye for a second and motioned for a beer. She mouthed MGD and he nodded. Turning back to Jacque, he asked, "Do you remember that Michele girl? The one we played pool with?"

"Are you kidding? The hottie who got a boyfriend and vanished as soon as she appeared? Yeah. What about her?"

"I'm having dinner with her on New Year's Eve."

Jacque took his elbows off the bar, sat up straight, and turned to look at Guy. "Shut the fuck up."

Guy faced him and shrugged. "I'm serious."

225

"I thought she was seeing someone. You asked her out? What the fuck, man? When did this even happen?"

Mindy set his beer in front of him and Guy grabbed it to take a drink. "Dude, it was really weird. It happened just over an hour ago. I ran into her and Laura at the mall."

"And what, you just asked her out?"

Guy shook his head. "No," he laughed.

"She asked you out?" Jacque was incredulous.

"No. That's what was weird. Laura asked me if I would be Michele's date. I don't know. The whole thing was just weird."

"I don't get it."

"Dude. I don't either. I was wandering through the mall, minding my own business, and I see her and Laura and they wave me over. I go over, we say hello, talk about Christmas shopping for a minute and then I say 'see you around' and I start to walk away. But Laura was like 'Hey, wait a second. Do you have plans for New Year's Eve?' I told her I figured I would just be here. Then she's like 'We are going out to dinner and Michele needs a date. You should be Michele's date.'"

"What did Michele say?"

"She seemed into it. The first thing I did was look at her like…are you okay with this? But she was like 'Yeah, that'd be great. Come on, be my date. We'll have fun!' and she was all smiling and everything. Then we exchange numbers and she tells me to give her a call."

"You're fucking kidding me."

Guy laughed again. "It's crazy, right? I don't know what happened with the other guy, but Laura said something about them not being together anymore."

"You are one lucky son-of-a-bitch, my friend."

"I don't know. I think I might be just a warm body. Laura said she and Ron made plans with another couple but they had to cancel. So she was trying to get Michele to go but Michele didn't want to go without a date and then they saw me and whatever."

"Hmmm. That makes sense, I guess. But she told you to call her, right?

That sounds like something more than a warm body."

"Yeah. The whole thing was just weird. At first it was so random, but then she did seem like she was really into it and everything. I don't know what I'm going to do."

"What the hell do you mean you don't know what you're going to do?" Jacque hollered. "A fun, beautiful, single woman gives you her number and tells you to call her after making plans to go out with you on New Year's Eve. I'll tell you what," Jacque's voice grew serious. "If you don't call her, I am going to go buy a gun and then I am going to shoot you so I can put you out of your misery."

Guy laughed. "Okay, okay. I'll call her. Just don't shoot me."

"You know," Jacque mused. "I've always heard it was true, but I've never seen it work quite like this."

"What?"

"Chicks dig musicians."

"Yeah, right," said Guy rolling his eyes.

"I'm serious," said Jacque, although he clearly wasn't. "You get the guitar, you start practicing. You must have reached some magical level of proficiency. Women can sense it now."

"Give me a break."

"No. Think about it. First Sophie, now Michele. I think you must be giving off sexy musician vibes. You've been practicing a lot, haven't you?"

Guy held up his taped fingers. "That's kind of all I've been doing. My fingertips are shredded right now. But I do feel like I have been making a lot of progress."

"Well, it's definitely working. You've crossed over into musician chick-magnet territory. I think this is only the beginning. Your life is about to get very interesting, my friend."

Still skeptical, Guy took another drink from his MGD. "Whatever, Jacque."

"You don't believe me!" said Jacque taking mock offense at the slight. "Check this out. Hey Mindy!" He called the bartender over.

She came over to them and checked their beers. "Ready for a couple more?" she asked.

"Yes," Jacque answered for both of them. "But I have a question first. Does Guy seem different to you?"

"Dude, shut up," Guy scolded.

"Different how?" Mindy asked looking at Guy.

"Just ignore him Mindy."

"Sexier. Does he seem sexier to you? Do you find yourself wanting him?" Jacque asked.

"That's it," said Guy standing up. "I'm going to have a cigarette."

Mindy caught on and began to play along. "Yeah, he kinda does. Hey Guy," she said in a sultry voice, "whatcha doin' later?"

"And look at him walk!" Jacque raised his voice so Guy could hear him as he walked toward the door. "Wooo," he called out as Mindy whistled a catcall after him. "Look at that swagger!"

Without looking back, Guy raised his hand with his middle finger extended as headed out onto the deck.

Chapter 41

E ven though she'd been there for well over a month, it took Sophie a moment to process her surroundings when she opened her eyes. The slats of the top bunk were not that far above where she lay and although the feelings of claustrophobia had waned, after another night of deep, uninterrupted sleep, she still needed that fraction of a second to recall where she was. She was lying in the bottom bunk in the spare bedroom of Artie's cottage, two blocks from the ocean in Mexico Beach, Florida. In addition to the bunk beds, a long, low, oversized dresser that easily held all of her clothes had been squeezed into the small room. The remainder of the house consisted of another slightly larger bedroom that Artie used when he was in town, a little kitchen and dining area, a small living room, and a bathroom.

She lay in bed for a few minutes and just listened. It was strange to her that there was nothing to hear and she wondered if she could ever get used to it. Artie was gone and said he probably wouldn't return until New Year's. Most of the neighbors weren't full-timers and the ones that were tended toward the geriatric and genteel. There wasn't even much traffic noise. The house sat far enough away from the main drag that only the sounds from an occasional truck or loud motorcycle carried through the thick gulf air. Sophie climbed out of bed and went to the kitchen in her underwear to turn on the radio. Usually, by the time she had washed her face and dressed, there was a weather report.

Ever since she started working behind the bar at Toucan's, she had been paying closer attention to the forecasts. She'd learned that the tourism here tended to be pretty local. Far more people drove down from Atlanta, Tallahassee, or Birmingham than flew in from Chicago, Detroit, or Minneapolis. Even though sixty degrees and sunny was a great December temperature for someone living in the Upper Midwest, it took more than that to coax those already in the South to make the drive down. She listened to the weatherman explain that the low clouds and rain were expected to move out of the area by late Thursday and the weekend was going to be sunny with highs in the low eighties. If that held true, it would motivate people to head for the coast and a quick getaway. And that meant Toucan's would be busy, and she could continue to avoid dipping into her savings.

It hadn't taken her long to appreciate what an insignificant sum $30,000 was when she had no money coming in. She hadn't spent very much of it but could see how quickly it would be drained if she continued living in a motel and eating every meal at a restaurant. Ever since she arrived in this little town, though, it seemed as if the fates were taking pity on her. Her luck had definitely turned. She had a job, a ridiculously convenient and cheap place to live, and even a handful of people she was beginning to consider friends.

On her first morning here, Sophie had woken up at the Buena Vista Motel. After splashing some water on her face and throwing on shorts and a t-shirt, she opened the door to her room and squinted into the bright mid-morning sunlight. Two doors down, outside of the small motel office, Dorothy, the owner, was having a cigarette as she watched her little white dog sniff around for a suitable place to relieve itself in the small patch of grass near the entrance. When she spotted Sophie, she waved her over and insisted that she sit with her and have a cup of coffee. Barefoot and barely awake, Sophie joined her host in a lawn chair under the shade of the weathered fabric awning that extended out over the office door and gratefully accepted a mug of hot, fresh coffee. It seemed that whoever called her from Toucan's the night before tipped her off that Sophie might be a bit wounded. Prying, but well-intentioned and compassionate, a very motherly Dorothy succeeded in learning most of Sophie's tale. By the time they were done having coffee, she had laughed, cried, been hugged, consoled, and counseled, and had agreed to stay at least through Sunday night. It was as crazy as it was cathartic. Even though she'd been spilling her guts to a total stranger, it felt good to share her burden with someone.

Dorothy told her, "You just need a little R&R honey, some time to recharge those batteries. We'll get you fixed up in no time. That's what this little town is for." Sophie wasn't sure if that was all she needed or not, but she welcomed the opportunity to find out. She left Dorothy and walked down the road to the beach shop where she bought herself a blue, two-piece swimsuit, an oversized beach towel, sandals, and some sunscreen. When she got back to the Buena Vista, she changed into the swimsuit top, put on the sandals, and headed to the beach to stroll and explore. It was almost noon by that time and the hint of a breeze coming off the water was not enough to keep it from feeling hot. Gradually, she made her way up the beach, and when she found herself in front of Toucan's, she was thirsty and hungry. She went upstairs and claimed an open barstool outside on the deck. It was Friday and much busier than the night before. Families and couples filled most of the tables. The single people sat alone together at the bar. That's when she met Artie.

Charming and charismatic, Arthur Bergsman was sixty-six years old and mildly and harmlessly lecherous. A functioning alcoholic and attorney who lived and lobbied two hours away in Tallahassee, he considered Toucan's specifically and Mexico Beach generally as his hideout. When he could, he fled the sordid political machinations of Florida's capital city to spend weekends at his little, almost oceanside cottage. From there, he tottered back and forth to Toucan's where he sipped away his afternoons and evenings enjoying the bikini-topped waitresses, customers, and occasionally the view out over the Gulf. She spent that afternoon on the barstool next to his, laughing at the endless trove of stories he'd gleaned from a lifetime in and amongst barrooms, girlfriends, courtrooms, and ex-girlfriends. They featured lives more disastrous and dysfunctional than even her own and it proved a therapeutic respite from the drama of the previous days. For Artie, it wasn't simply a fresh audience to entertain, it was a fresh audience that was dressed in shorts and a bikini top and beautiful to look at.

He was there with some other locals again on Saturday night when she returned after a day idled away on the beach with a book borrowed from Dorothy. This time, however, she was the topic and they peppered her with questions. What was she doing in town? Where was she from? How long was she staying? There were few of them she could honestly answer and she told them that. They all sang the praises of Mexico Beach and suggested she stick around for a while and give it a chance. They knew she would just love it. Walking back down the beach to her motel that night, it was hard for her to imagine how she couldn't.

On Sunday night, Artie showed up at Toucan's with an extra set of keys to his house and insisted that she take them. He said he would be back the following weekend. If she liked it, they could set something up. He said he'd made similar agreements off and on through the years. In the winter, when he wasn't able to be around as often, he liked having a low maintenance tenant to keep the little bungalow hospitable, secure, and maintained. He made it sound like she would be doing him a favor. She moved in the next day and by the end of the week had started picking up a few shifts at Toucan's.

Sophie enjoyed tending bar again. Unlike working as a caregiver, she was able to leave it behind at the end of the day and go home. So far it had just been lunch shifts and helping out randomly on the weekends when they got a little busier, but it was as close to a perfect setup for her as she could imagine. She got a discount on food and drinks and the tips were good when the weather cooperated. Although she wasn't going to be able to save up any money working there, it was low stress, and as long as she was close to breaking even, she was happy.

It was Thursday morning and clearer skies were still some hours away, but it wasn't raining. Dressed in shorts and one of the jogging tank tops she had to go to Panama City to find, Sophie put her hair in a ponytail, tied her shoes, and went into the backyard to stretch a little before beginning her run. After experimenting with different routes, she had settled into a meandering loop through her own neighborhood before crossing the main highway and heading down the beach toward the pier at the end of town. As she ran, she considered the growing number of palm trees strung with Christmas lights and shorts-clad, sunglass-wearing Santa Clauses adorning the yards where locals lived. Less than a week to go, she reminded herself, and it would be over. The holidays had never been an easy time for her, but at least she'd had Abby. Abby had given her a reason to go Christmas shopping and a reason to be excited about checking the mail as she waited for the package or card from her little sister. Abby gave her a reason to feel that, in some small way, she was part of it all. As tough as it had been to not be able to spend the holidays with Abby, not having any family to miss was proving to be brutal.

Instead of walking back along the beach like she usually did, she pushed herself, running hard until she reached the end of her driveway. Thoroughly winded, she was aware that physical exhaustion was only a fleeting distraction, but she was happy to have it. The pack of cigarettes purchased on her way out of Sioux City back in October was long gone and so far she had been able to resist buying another. Running and walking up and down the beach had facilitated a measure of acceptance, sometimes for days at a time. But when the depression and anger crept back in, well, nothing could replace cigarettes as a full embrace of the "fuck everything" attitude that accompanied them. Maybe that would be her Christmas present to herself, she thought bitterly, another pack of Marlboro Lights.

Back inside Artie's little house, she started a pot of coffee and hopped in the shower. She had about an hour and a half before she needed to walk over to Toucan's to set up for lunch. It was unlikely to be busy enough for her to lose herself in the work and she would be forced to visit with customers and co-workers alike. At any other time of year, that would be fine. But today, all of the talk would revolve around Christmas and Christmas shopping and Christmas cookies and Christmas dinners and family traditions and visiting relatives and on and on and on. It was going to be a long, depressing shift. She could feel herself becoming tense just anticipating it all. Breathe, Sophie, she reminded herself, you can get through this.

She did get through it, but just barely. By the time she had punched out and was heading down the stairs toward the parking lot, she was fighting the urge to start running. Instead, she forced herself to walk and used her hands to try and stifle the sobs that overcame her before she'd even crossed the street. A block away was a little gas station with the restrooms on the outside of the building. Sophie picked up her pace and made a beeline for the ladies' room. It was empty and she locked herself in, lowered the lid on the toilet, sat down, and bawled. When she was all cried out, she splashed water on her face, found her sunglasses in her purse, and went inside to buy cigarettes. Then she continued her walk home.

Toucan's had been slow and, as expected, the conversations all revolved around Christmas. She had been managing to tune most of it out. It was when Sharon, one of her co-workers, invited her to spend the day with her and her family in Pensacola that it became significantly more difficult. Sophie thanked her for the invite and then declined. But Sharon, do-gooder, kind, caring, generous fucking Sharon wouldn't let it go. The only thing worse than spending Christmas alone, in Sophie's experience, was to spend it in the presence of a big, warm and loving family that was not, and would never be, her own. She'd made that mistake in the past with the family of an elderly man she was caring for. One of his daughters asked what her plans were and when she found out that Sophie didn't have any, she insisted that she join them on Christmas Day. It was a nightmare and she ended up pretending to be ill and leaving before dinner. People like Sharon and the old man's daughter meant well, but they just didn't get it. When she was at a family gathering like that she felt like a ghost. She was there in the room with everyone, but only a few of the other people had any awareness of her. Most had no idea who she was. She was there, but apart from it all. Everything that she was missing out on was shoved in her face. After that year, she simply lied and told people she had plans. With Sharon, though, she couldn't. Sharon knew her story, knew that she was alone. And Sharon would never be able to understand why she wouldn't want to spend Christmas with her.

As she walked, she tore the cellophane off the pack of cigarettes, fished one out, and not really expecting to find one, dug through her purse for a lighter. She did not have one and added that minor insult to the list of things that was making it feel like a truly horrible day. When she reached the end of her driveway, she checked the mailbox for advertising flyers and junk mail that she could add to the pile for Artie. But the only item in there was for her. It was a green envelope with a Christmas stamp on it. It was from Guy.

Chapter 42

Michele looked at her phone and groaned. She answered by saying, "No Laura, he hasn't called yet."

"Damn."

"Do you really think that if he did call, I wouldn't tell you?"

"You better tell me if calls!"

"I will, don't worry!"

"What the hell is he waiting for?"

"I don't know, but it *is* Christmas weekend, Laura."

"So what? It's been a week. And Christmas isn't until Monday. That's really not a reason to not at least call."

"Maybe he's just freaked out. Maybe you scared him away. I still can't believe you asked him to be my date. I felt like I was in freakin' junior high again."

Laura started laughing. "Oh my god. I wish I could have seen your face when I asked him."

"Go ahead, laugh it up. It would have been nice to have some warning, but I get it. I know it wasn't planned. He probably thinks we're just a couple of weirdos."

"No. I think you did a good job of saving it and playing along. You seemed into it. I was impressed that you actually gave him your number and told him to call you."

"And you were lucky to actually get a reservation at Donavan's. You're too good of a liar. You scare me. I couldn't figure out who canceled on you and Ron, you faker."

"I would never lie to you, honey."

"Whatever."

"Not unless I had a very good reason."

"Whatever."

"And it was for your own good."

"Whatever. You sure he's not calling because of Jacque?" Michele wondered.

"I really don't think that matters anymore. Ron said we're covered. Because of your boyfriend, Mike."

"Mark."

"Whatever. Listen. I didn't really call you to find out if he called. I know you would tell me. I think we need to make a move. We need to go to The Duke tonight."

Michele sighed.

"You've got to figure that he'll be there. He's had a week and he hasn't done anything."

"Yeah," she said without enthusiasm. "I guess you're right."

"Hey. You need to be up for this. You keep thinking like prey. You need to think like a predator."

"Oh my god! Turn off the nature channel!"

"I'm serious, Michele. It's like the gum thing. You can't just sit around and be all coy and wait for him to come after you. It's not going to work with him. You need to be direct. You need to get it in your mind that you are the aggressor here. I don't know if you've ever had to do that before."

Michele's phone beeped. "Hang on a second Laura. I have another call." She looked at the screen. "Finally! It's him. It's Guy. I'll call you right back."

Chapter 43

The weatherman had been right. It was only nine o'clock on Friday morning, but the skies were clear and Sophie could tell it was going to be hot. She'd just returned from a quick trip to the grocery store where she went to find something to write a letter on. The only paper in Artie's entire house was the small pad of sticky notes on the fridge. Her choices at the store had been postcards or spiral notebooks. She found a pen, and then took it, her new notebook with the yellow cover, Guy's letter, and her coffee out to the picnic table in the backyard. She already had decided to skip her run because she wanted to write him back and be able get to the post office before work. She was scheduled for lunch. If the weather stayed nice and it got busy, she was going to return after dinner to help out with any late crowd that materialized. She might not have a chance to mail it later.

Sophie smiled and picked up her Christmas card. Her only Christmas card. She thought the scene on the front with the snow and an evergreen with ornaments and lights and a star on top was a lot more like it. That's how Christmas is supposed to look. How can you even put a star on top of a palm tree? she wondered. Sophie opened the card, read it again, and felt good inside.

"Dear Guy," she said aloud as she wrote the words. She began by telling him how happy she was to hear from him and that she'd kind of given up hope. She said she was glad that his dad was doing okay and that she knew how lucky he was to have Guy around helping him out. She knew how tough it could be on him and encouraged him to hang in there. It won't last forever, she promised. She said that she thought it was really cool that he was learning how to play the guitar and she hoped he got some calluses soon. She said it reminded her of that Bryan Adams song, "The Summer of '69," and she wrote the line "I got my first real six-string / bought it at the five and dime / played it 'til my fingers bled / was the summer of '69." She told him that she never figured that was a real thing, that she assumed it was just an exaggeration. She asked if it was too soon for her to request songs for him to learn and said she was looking forward to hearing him play.

Sophie debated whether or not to mention Abby and decided against it. There was just too much to explain in a letter. She did tell him though that she was no longer waiting to start her life. Check out my return address, she wrote. She told him how she had decided to visit the ocean for the first time in her life and how she was renting a room in a cottage in Mexico Beach from an old guy who only came into town on the weekends. She wrote about working at Toucan's and running on the shore in the mornings. She also confessed that she really didn't have a clue what she was doing but that for right now Mexico Beach seemed like a nice place to take her time and figure it out.

Finally, she wrote how perfect the timing of his letter was. She told him that she'd been having some up and down days and wasn't looking forward to Christmas. And the day his letter arrived had been one of the worst. In fact, she admitted, even though she hadn't smoked in months, she'd bought a pack of cigarettes on her way home from work. She already had one out and was heading inside to find a lighter when she stopped to get the mail. His letter saved her from smoking it. She had put it back in the pack. So, she thanked him for keeping her lungs clean. She told him that she'd gone inside, poured herself a glass of wine, sat on the couch, and read his card. It made her day.

She instructed that if he wrote again, and she hoped he would, that he should mail it to the address in Mexico Beach so it wouldn't have to be forwarded. She stopped and took a drink of her now lukewarm coffee as she considered how to sign it. The only letters she'd ever written were to Abby and she always signed them "Love, Sophie." What were the other options, she wondered. Sincerely? Yours Truly? Lame. Regards? Your friend? They all sounded dumb. She looked at the card from Guy again. He just signed it with his name and she hadn't really noticed anything about it. She shrugged and wrote her name. Then she quickly added, "P.S. Say hi to Jacque!"

Sophie sat back and read what she wrote. Then she tore it out of the notebook, removed the little paper fringes, and read it again. She liked it. She liked the way she felt right then, and she liked Guy. She folded the letter, picked up her things, and went back inside the house. It was later than she thought and she realized that she'd better hurry up if she wanted to get it to the post office before work. Her shower was quick enough that the mirror on the back of the door wasn't completely steamed over. As she dried off she paused to check out her reflection. The sun had made her hair a little blonder and her skin a little darker. Running every morning hadn't hurt either. She'd even lost those last few pounds that didn't seem possible to lose. She was fit, tanned, toned, and liked what she saw. "Damn," she smiled approvingly. Then she laughed to herself and thought about what a difference a day could make. And what a difference a letter could make.

Chapter 44

Shit, thought Guy as he walked in to The Duke. Bar or table? Table, he decided. With so many people back in town for the holidays, the bar was busy and he was lucky to get one. Taking off his coat, he set it on the back of the chair and checked the time on his phone. It was a quarter after. Michele said she would be there at about eight-thirty. He was glad he arrived a little early. One of the waitresses, Beth, came by and he ordered a beer. It felt weird to be sitting there at a table by himself and he fought the urge to go outside and have a cigarette.

"Hey Guy," Bear greeted him. "Happy holidays. Where's your amigo tonight?"

"Hey Bear, you too. Merry Christmas. Jacque's got his parents in town this weekend. I don't expect to see him. Plus, he'll be pretty slammed at the bakery the next few days."

"Yeah, I can imagine. Hey, what are you doing tomorrow night?"

Guy shrugged. "I don't know. Probably nothing. What's up?"

"You should come by. Dean and his family are going to be staying with mom and dad for Christmas and I'm going to make him come out with me. I'm even going to be taking the night off work."

"That is a big deal!"

"My parents are going to babysit so he can take his wife out in Big City Richmond. You know, show her the town," Bear laughed.

"That should take all of five minutes. What are they going to do for the rest of the night?"

"What does anybody do?" He looked around the bar. "They're going to

241

hang out here. You should really come by. I know Dean would love to see you."

"I don't know. I have to open on Sundays, you know."

"So, come early and don't stay out late. Come on, I'm going to start a tab and give it to Mr. Law Firm Partner at the end of the night," he smiled mischievously. "Help me run it up. You know he can afford it."

Guy shook his head and laughed. "Nice. Be careful you don't get sued though."

"Good point," Bear laughed. "So what do you say?"

"I'll try. I'm not promising, but I should be able to come by and stick him for at least a couple of drinks. How's that?"

"Sounds good, man. And if you think of anyone else who he might want to catch up with, pass the word. I gotta get back to work. See ya tomorrow, Guy."

Bear left and Guy checked the time on his phone. It still wasn't eight-thirty. Beth had brought his beer and he took a drink and thought about whether or not he would actually try to come by The Duke tomorrow night. Dean was a good guy and it would be nice to see him. He just wished he had something else going on in his life to talk about. Lost in thought, he didn't notice Michele come in.

"Hi. Mind if I join you?" she asked. She was across the table from him taking off her coat.

"Oh, hey, I didn't see you come in," he said standing up. She put the coat on the back of her chair and gave him a quick hug which he awkwardly gave back. "Have a seat. Thanks for coming out. It's great to see you again. What would you like to drink?"

"How about a Bud Light?" she said sitting down.

"Sounds good." He looked around for Beth. "I have a waitress. She should be back in a minute."

"No hurry. So how's it going?"

"Good, good. Listen, I wanted to say thanks for asking me to go with you guys on New Year's Eve. It's been forever since I spent New Year's anywhere other than here. I'm looking forward to it."

"I am too. But I guess we should both thank Laura," she laughed.

"Yeah," he smiled. "That was kind of funny I guess."

"She's been pushing me to get out more and get on with my life, you know. My divorce was finalized a while ago and I guess she's right. It is time."

"Yeah," he lied. "I suppose." He had no idea what it might be like to be either married or divorced and he suddenly felt like a little kid. She'd been married for a long time and her daughter was in high school. *I had a girlfriend once*, he thought. *Jesus.* He caught Beth's eye and she came by to take Michele's order. He asked for another MGD. "So what's the name of the place where we're going to for dinner?"

"Donavan's. It's kind of new. It's right on the lake just down from the Riviera."

"Oh yeah. I've heard of that," he said, trying to play it cool. He had heard of it. He heard it was fancy and he heard it was expensive. "It's supposed to be great." He wondered whether or not he still owned a tie and if he did, how old it was?

"It is. They have a special deal for New Year's Eve," she said as if reading his mind. "So it shouldn't be too bad. You know they do the limited menu kind of thing. But everything is supposed to be really good there."

"That's cool."

"Oh, I almost forgot to tell you. Ron volunteered to be the designated driver. He's going to pick us up. If that's okay with you?" she asked.

"Yeah, that'd be great," he assured her. *Thank god I don't have to drive up there in my car. They probably have valet parking.* He imagined himself pulling up in front of the restaurant in the biggest piece of crap they would see all night. *They'd probably fight to see who got stuck parking it.*

"Laura wants us to go out up there after dinner. Maybe to Hogs n Kisses or something. Somewhere we can dance."

"Wow," he laughed. "This is really going to be an adventure for me."

"It'll be fun," she smiled and reached her hand out and put it on his arm. Then she feigned seriousness and looked him in the eye. "You *are* going to dance with me, aren't you?"

Holy shit, he thought, *she is absolutely gorgeous.* And she was touching him. "Yes," he met her gaze and tried not to betray his nerves. "I will dance with you." As he said it, he noticed that Jacque was sitting at the bar behind her. He was watching them with a big stupid grin on his face and raising his eyebrows up and down suggestively. And then his phone rang. "I'm sorry. I'm kind of always on call." He took out his phone and saw that it was his father's number. "Shit." He hesitated for a moment trying to find a reason to ignore it. But he knew that any call at nine o'clock on a Friday night was going to be one he needed to answer. "I'm sorry," he apologized again. "I have to answer this. It should just take a minute. It's my father's house. It's probably his caregiver."

"Go. Go ahead. It's okay. Really." She looked concerned.

Guy said hello as he got up and walked toward the exit. Outside in the cold, he stood on the deck and learned that once again, his father must have somehow sensed that something good was happening to him. So, of course, he needed to have some kind of fucking crisis and fuck it all up. He told Sharette that he was in the middle of something but would get there as soon as he could. Then he hung up, took a deep breath, tried to compose himself, and went back inside.

Michele's back was to him. On the table in front of her were two full beers that Beth must have delivered while he was on the phone. *Shit,* he thought. He had meant to pay for those. Guy saw Jacque sitting at the bar and quickly walked over to him.

"Hey," he said coming up to him. "What are you doing out? I thought your parents were in town."

"They are. But they're old and are pretty much done for the night." He looked at his watch. "They are probably already asleep. My place is small. I had to get out of there and get a break."

"Can you stay for a little while longer?"

"Sure. What's up? Is everything okay?" He could see that his friend was stressed.

"I'm sitting over there with Michele and I have to go. My dad's having a problem and I have to go over there. We just got drinks. Can you hang with her? I don't want to just leave her sitting there by herself."

"Yeah, sure," said Jacque grabbing his glass and standing up. "Is it serious?"

Guy was already walking toward the table. He got there several steps ahead of Jacque and started explaining. "I'm really sorry Michele, but I have to go deal with my father." That sounded kind of dickish, he thought. Whatever. "You remember Jacque, right?" He turned to his just-arriving friend.

"Yeah, absolutely. What's going on? Is everything okay?"

Guy took a deep breath and let it out slowly. "I'm sure it will be. There's just a minor crisis right now."

"What happened?" asked Jacque.

Guy hesitated as he tried to find a succinct way to describe the complex, ongoing clusterfuck that was his father's health situation. Then he said, "His feeding tube is clogged and it's been clogged. Sharette hasn't been able to flush it. She's been trying for a while and now she's starting to freak out because she can't feed him. He exerted himself earlier today. That messes with his diabetes. Now he's not just hungry and crabby, his blood sugar is crashing too. Sharette is not a nurse. She's scared." He paused. "You want more?" he said wearily.

Although their expressions said *Holy shit*," their words were kinder and calmer. After a moment, they both spoke, "Go. Go take care of your dad. We're fine. Let us know if you need anything. Don't worry about it."

"Thanks. I'm really sorry. Jacque can explain more. I'll call you."

Chapter 45

Michele looked at the time when she pulled into her garage. It was almost ten-thirty. Laura would still be up, she figured, and thought about calling her. Then she hesitated. She wasn't sure what she wanted to tell her. Was she supposed to say that meeting Guy out for a beer turned into meeting Jacque out for a beer? And it was great? No. No way. Her friend would flip. It would have to wait. Laura would probably be calling first thing in the morning anyway.

When she went inside, the extra shoes in the mudroom told her that Carly was home and had friends with her. There was more evidence in the kitchen. It sounded like they were in the basement. She could smell popcorn and guessed they were probably watching a movie. She wasn't tired and thought about heading down to join them but decided to get ready for bed first and went upstairs.

She turned on the light in her bathroom, stood in front of the mirror, and took off her jewelry. She thought about Guy's dad and wondered if everything was okay. *What if he died?* She hesitated, trying to calculate how it would affect her plans. She supposed it would be okay because they already had a plan to go out. *It's not like he would die and then I would hurry over and try to go out with him. No, I'm okay,* she reassured herself. *But, wait,* she thought, *if he does die, like tonight or something, would Guy still want to go out on New Year's Eve?* She counted the days in her head. *Maybe. The funeral and everything should be done by then. He might be ready to go do something. Unless he's like really depressed and everything. Then, again,* she reminded herself, *it doesn't really matter. I could still start going out with him without coming off like an obvious gold-digger because we already had a plan to go out before his dad even died. And we kind of went out tonight anyway.*

She thought about their "date." He seemed a little uncomfortable. Like he was kind of nervous. And a little awkward. Laura had told her that, as far as she could tell, he didn't really date. She had consulted her "sources" and they told her that he hadn't had any kind of girlfriend for years. That was kind of weird, she thought. He was a pretty good-looking guy. He wasn't dorky. He didn't seem like a weirdo or creepy or anything. He just seemed like kind of a nice, regular guy. Maybe a little boring. Maybe that's it, she thought. Maybe he's just really boring. She went into her closet to change her clothes and imagined what it would be like to be married to a boring guy. Troy wasn't boring and that sucked. Maybe boring would be good? Then she wondered if she was boring. What makes somebody boring anyway? What makes somebody not boring? Jacque wasn't boring. Shit, she thought. Why did things have to work out like that tonight?

Michele reflected on her time with Jacque while she put her hair up, started to take off her makeup, and washed her face. When Guy ran out, Jacque sat down and they talked while she drank her beer. He told her what he knew about Guy's dad's health problems and how Guy was kind of stuck taking care of him. He also told her how they joked about him being immortal. That wasn't good. If he did live for a bunch more years, well, that would suck. They talked about his parents being in town. He was really funny telling her about them. They sounded like a cute old couple. By that time, she was done with her beer but didn't want to leave. It was her who suggested that they stay for another. Both times. After the third one, he apologized and said that he really had to get going. She cringed a little thinking about it. She knew she probably shouldn't have done that. But she really liked hanging out with him.

She thought about the differences between Guy and Jacque as she headed back downstairs. Attractiveness-wise, they were about the same. Jacque was older, but not old. She already knew she didn't care about that. Jacque had a better job. She didn't know if he actually made any money, but at least it had potential. Guy's job? Well, how the hell could anyone do that for so many years? she wondered. Then she thought about his dad, what Jacque had told her, and tried to give him a pass. She thought about her conversations with both of them. Guy just seemed kind of unsure of himself. Jacque, she realized, was just Jacque. He was relaxed. He was confident. Was it a maturity thing? Maybe. It wasn't that Guy was childish or anything, but he wasn't grown up in the same way that Jacque was. It was hard for her to put her finger on it, but she understood what she meant. And she understood who was more appealing.

Michele stopped in the kitchen to get herself a glass of ice water before going downstairs to check on the girls. The stack of mail on the counter caught her eye. Carly must have brought it in today, she thought as she casually flipped through it. She recognized the envelope with the Carson and Son return address and her heart sank. Only eight more of these, she thought as a very anxious feeling swept through her. She thought about Jacque and Guy again. "Dammit," she said out loud.

When Michele woke up on Saturday morning it was already after nine. She took her phone off the nightstand and saw that she had a text from Guy and three missed calls from Laura. She read Guy's text first. "Really sorry about last night. Everything is fine with my father. Maybe we can try again next weekend?" So, the old man was still alive, she thought. She realized how callous that was and swore to herself. Shit. She wished she could just fast forward everything and it could be a year from now and she could already be re-married and done with all of this. Then she thought about the check on the counter in her kitchen and the idea of working multiple part-time retail jobs and losing her house and everything else that would go along with it. She reminded herself why she was doing what she was doing and tried to convince herself that she was still a good person and that she would be a good wife for Guy. *Like I'm doing him a favor?* She sighed. Then she called Laura.

"About damn time," she said when she answered the phone. "Unless of course you were making him breakfast this morning. Then I forgive you."

Michele rolled her eyes. "Not hardly. It didn't really work out last night."

"Why not? What happened? Did you go?"

"Yes. I went and we sat down at a table. He ordered me a beer. And then he had to leave."

"What?!"

"Something happened with his dad. He got a call and he had to leave."

"No way. Is he in the hospital? Is he okay?" She almost sounded excited.

"Settle down Laura. I guess he's fine. I got a text from him this morning."

"What was the text?"

"He just apologized, said his dad was fine, and asked about trying again next weekend."

"Alright. That's good, I guess. How did you respond?"

"I didn't yet. I just got up. I stayed up late watching a movie with Carly and her friends."

"What are you going to say?"

"I don't know yet. I need some help. We did get a chance to visit for a few minutes before he had to leave."

"And?"

"I don't know. He seemed pretty nervous. Just kind of unsure of himself."

"Well, yeah. He doesn't date and you're a whoresteak. Remember?" she said laughing. "What would you expect?"

"Whatever. And by the way, Donavan's? What the hell were you thinking? He's broke, Laura. He doesn't go to steakhouses."

"Excuse me! That was the only place that I could even get a reservation up there and it's only because they had a cancelation. We got lucky."

"Yeah, but I feel bad if I make him pay for me. I know he can't afford it."

"Hmmm." Laura was quiet for a minute. "Okay, so normally, you would definitely make the guy pay for something like this. But really, it was more like you asked him out. But," she continued talking through the problem, "you can't pay for him because that would be too weird. Plus, then you risk getting into a whole emasculation issue."

"Emascu-what? What the hell is that?!"

"Emasculation is like you taking away his manhood. If you pay for him then he won't feel manly and that can piss guys off."

I definitely can't do that, then, Michele thought. *I don't know how much he has to spare.* "So what am I supposed to do?"

"Well, you could tell him that since you asked him, you're willing to pay for yourself. Give him the option. Just don't make a big deal out of it. If he decides to pay for you, then whatever. It's his choice."

"Okay. That makes sense. But I need your help otherwise too."

"How?"

"Like for a second date. After New Year's."

"You want me to ask him out for you again?" Laura laughed.

"No. Not like that. Help me figure out what he would want to do. I mean we can't just go hang out at The Duke all the time, can we?"

"I don't know. If that's what he wants to do, why not?"

"I don't know. I guess it doesn't really seem like dating."

"But he doesn't date, remember?"

"Yeah."

"I think you should invite him over for dinner and screw his brains out."

"Oh my god!"

"I bet it would work!"

"Oh my god!"

"Look, honey, at some point you're going to have to get naked with him."

Michele groaned. "You're right. I know you're right. I don't know. I wasn't planning on seducing him. I guess I just thought that part would happen naturally."

"It might normally, but this isn't normally."

"I know."

"Listen, between you, me, and Ron, we'll figure this out. Don't worry about it."

"I hope so. I just got my check from Troy. There's only eight checks left."

"Plenty of time. Especially with how you sound about everything now."

"How do I sound?"

"Like you are starting to get the right attitude. You are on the hunt. You're in predator mode."

"Like I said, eight checks left."

Chapter 46

G uy turned just before Not Your Average Bakery! and parked on the side of the street. It was a cold morning and he got out quickly to hustle inside. All six tables Jacque had been able to squeeze inside the limited space were occupied and the girl at the counter was busy helping a man and his young son as they decided on which donuts they wanted to fill out their dozen. When they were finished, Guy ordered a large coffee and a chocolate donut. As the girl gave him his change he said, "Thanks. I'm going to sneak in back and say hi to Jacque if that's okay."

"Sure," she replied, moving out of his way.

He stepped behind the counter and walked through the storage area to the back. It was always hotter there than he remembered. Jacque looked up when he saw him enter.

"Hey, Guy. How's your dad doing? Everything okay?"

He smiled half-heartedly and shrugged. "Of course. He's fine. I mean, why wouldn't he be? He's immortal, right?"

"Stay over there unless you want me to put a hairnet on you. And don't touch anything. So tell me, what happened? What was the problem?" Jacque asked.

"It really wasn't a big deal. It only took me a few minutes to get the tube unclogged. You just have to flush it with water and kind of massage it to break up whatever is blocking it. If you run water through after every time he eats, it usually stays clear. She says she did, but who knows? Once it was clear, we got him some food and got his blood sugar back in line pretty quickly. I wanted to head back, but Sharette is pretty young and she was shaken up. I think she's like 22. I know she hasn't been doing this kind of work for very long. I don't even really know if she ever has. This could be her first caregiver job." He paused. "You know, now that I think about it, it probably is."

"Seriously? You hired someone with no experience to do that job?"

"I didn't. My father did. But it's such a shady business. I'm sure the agent told him that she had experience. They all lie. They'll tell you whatever they think you want to hear."

"Man, that's messed up."

"Yeah. It is. But it isn't up to me. Charles makes all the decisions. I just pick up the pieces. Hey, tell me about my date already. How was it?"

Jacque grinned. "Excellent. I dropped her off at home on the way to work this morning."

"Nice try. You live upstairs. Seriously, how was it?"

"It was good. We sat and talked for a while. She's a sweetheart. We ended up having a couple of beers. She said she'd just gotten ready to go out and it seemed like a waste to turn around and go right back home. We were there for about an hour."

"That's cool. Thanks for doing that. I swear my father knows when I'm doing something. Or even about to do something."

"Yeah. I'm a believer now, my friend."

"This is the way it's been for years."

"It's creepy."

Guy sighed. "It's fucked up is what it is."

Jacque winced and pointed to the wide opening that led to the front counter and the customers. He hissed, "Language man!"

Guy held up his hands apologetically. "Sorry, sorry," he whispered. "Hey, I'm going to head out. I have to go buy some decent clothes. Something I can wear out to dinner on New Year's Eve."

"Oh yeah," he laughed. "She told me about that. Donavan's, huh? Nice!"

"I went through my closet this morning. The only things I own that would be dressy enough are a belt, dark socks, and I do have a pair of very uncomfortable dress shoes."

"I don't think they'll let you in like that," Jacque deadpanned. "Plus, you'll freeze."

"Funny. I am going to buy a pair of pants and a dress shirt. Do you think I need a tie?"

Jacque thought about it for a moment. "I don't know. You could ask if Ron's going to wear a tie. Either way, don't buy one. I've got a bunch. You can borrow one of mine."

"Cool. Thanks. See you Sunday for the Bears game?"

Jacque tilted his head toward the ceiling and his apartment that sat over the bakery. "I don't know. I am going to try and get mom and dad to go over there and watch the game, but," he shrugged, "we'll see how it goes. If I don't make it, you have a great Christmas, my friend."

"Thanks, man. You too."

As he drove home from the mall, Guy felt pretty good. He was happy with the clothes he bought and they were on sale so it didn't cost him as much as he worried it might. Standing in front of the mirror in the dressing room, he thought he looked pretty good. No one would know that he worked at the Gas and Go. He didn't look like a loser at all. When he passed The Duke on his way back into town, he thought about Bear's invitation to stop by and see Dean. And then he thought about Michele. *If I show up tonight with her, that could actually be pretty cool. Any heterosexual boy who went to high school with her would remember her. Some of them probably still fantasize about her,* he laughed to himself. *And she's still as smokin' hot now as she was then. It might actually be enough to keep anyone from bringing up the Gas and Go.* The more he thought about it, the more he liked the idea.

Back inside his apartment, he removed the various tags and stickers from his new clothes, threw them in with his laundry, grabbed his detergent and re-stocked quarter supply, and went to start a load. When he returned, he set his oven to 400 degrees, took a pizza out of his freezer, and sat down with his guitar. Without looking at either the poster or his fingers on the frets, Guy ran through his warm-up exercises. The tape was gone and his fingertips were pain free. He finally had some calluses. The oven beeped and he got up to start the pizza. He sat back down on the couch but picked up his phone instead of his guitar. Finding Michele's number, he took a deep breath and called her.

"Hi Guy." She sounded happy to hear from him.

"Hey Michele. I heard you had a great date last night," he joked.

She laughed. "Not hardly. The guy bailed on me right away and stuck me with some loser."

He laughed. "I'm really sorry about that. I'm pretty much on call all of the time though."

"Don't worry about it. Really, it was no problem. I'm just glad everything was okay with your dad. And I'm kidding about Jacque. He was great. He was a gentleman. He told me some of the stuff about your dad. That's got to be tough. He's lucky to have you around."

Sure, he wanted to say. Everyone tells me that. When is somebody going to tell my father that? Instead, he responded the way he usually did, "Yeah, I suppose," before continuing. "Anyway, before you got there last night I was talking to Bear. He said his brother Dean is in town for Christmas and they are going to be out tonight. I was thinking about stopping over there. I haven't seen him in years. I was wondering if you were up for going with me? I have to work tomorrow morning so I can't make a big night of it or anything, but I would like to go by for a bit and say hi."

"I remember Dean. That sounds like fun. What time?"

"How about I pick you up around eight?"

"That sounds good."

"Cool. I have no idea where you live though," he laughed.

"I suppose that would help." She told him that she lived over in Sundial Farms and gave him her street number.

He said he knew where it was and that he would see her about eight. Then he closed his phone, tossed it on the table in front of him, and sank back into the couch. "Fuck me," he said out loud as his confidence wilted. The homes in Sundial Farms were huge. *What the hell am I doing?* He leaned his head back and stared at nothing until the timer in the kitchen told him the pizza was done. Then he forced himself to get up. He sat on the couch and ate without turning on the television. When he was done, he cleaned up his dishes, found a plastic garbage bag in the kitchen, and went to clean out his car.

When Michele got off the phone, she texted Laura. "Round two tonight." Her phone rang almost immediately.

"Hey. I can't talk now. I have to get busy and clean my house. He's coming here to pick me up at eight."

"Okay. Sorry. You've gotta tell me what happened though. Did you just call him?" Laura asked.

"No. He called me."

"Awesome! That's great! What are you going to do?"

"Guess," she laughed.

"The Duke?"

"Of course."

"Doesn't matter. You can't worry about that. Just go, be sweet, and have fun."

"I know. I will. Look, my house is a mess. I really gotta go. I'll talk to you tomorrow." She put down the phone, started loading the dishwasher, and thought about Guy's phone call. He didn't sound nervous that time. That was good.

Guy took the trash bag to the dumpster and went back inside. From under his kitchen sink he found an extra roll of paper towels and some Windex and went back to his car. After using up almost half of the roll, he switched his clothes from the washing machine to the dryer and took his remaining laundry money to the self-clean car wash. When his money ran out, he decided that he was done. Appraising his newly clean car on the way back to his apartment, he was pleased. Even though the exterior left something to be desired, the interior really didn't look too bad. And it would be dark outside when he picked her up.

When he returned home, he folded his laundry, put it away, and straightened up his apartment. Then he sat back down on the couch and picked up his guitar again. The *Roy Clark's Big Note Guitar Songbook* was open on the table in front of him. He flipped through it. The songs in there were good practice, but they were all old and corny. He couldn't imagine a time or place where he would ever break out "She'll Be Comin' 'Round the Mountain." He thought about the music he usually listened to and considered what he might actually want to learn how to play. Maybe some Tom Petty? He wondered what kind of music Sophie liked. That's something he'd have to ask her in his next letter. Guy tried to remember when he mailed her the Christmas card. When he calculated that she must have received it already, a brief wave of anxiety swept through him. He hoped she didn't think it sounded stupid. He really hoped that she would write back.

Chapter 47

You're not going to ruin this for me tonight, thought Guy with hopeful determination. His headlights found the lonely garbage can and he braked to make the turn into his father's driveway. An hour ago he'd been sitting at home, guitar in hand, trying to come up with some songs he'd like to learn to play. As he struggled to isolate the guitar chords, his thoughts drifted to his impending date with Michele and then to his father's uncanny ability to disrupt every bit of progress toward something good in his life. *Not tonight though*, Guy shook his head unconsciously. Then he hesitated. He turned off the music as a feeling of dread began to build. *Why wouldn't he ruin tonight?* Guy wondered. *Why would this be any different? Just because it would be two nights in a row? Shit.* Guy set down his guitar and slouched back into the couch. *Why wouldn't it be two nights in a row? What's so damn special about tonight that's going to keep him from pulling his usual bullshit?* He shrugged. *Not a fucking thing.*

Sick and tired of being resigned to reacting and the overall helpless feeling wrought from his circumstances, Guy mulled his options for responding to a crisis. It didn't take long as there were only two choices: end his date and deal with it or simply ignore it until his date was over. If he ended his date again, well, it wouldn't be the end of the world, but...*fuck that*, he thought, *I already did that last night.* If, on the other hand, he chose to ignore calls from his dad or Sharette... He shook his head. *I don't know*, he wondered. *Could I really get myself to do that?* As much as he wanted to and felt justified in doing so, it didn't change the fact that he knew he only got calls in a legitimate crisis. If he ignored it, well, that really put Sharette in a tough spot. And, he grudgingly supposed, his father, too.

On the verge of surrendering to his fate, Guy picked up his phone to check the time and came up with an idea. It was only a little after five o'clock and he wasn't picking Michele up until eight. If he got ready now, he'd have plenty of time to head over to his father's house and check in. He could make sure he'd eaten dinner, checked his blood sugar, taken all his meds, and make sure that Sharette didn't need anything; that nothing was building toward a crisis. He knew that it might not make a difference, but it felt good to be doing something other than waiting, hoping, and dreading. Guy rose from the couch to shower and get ready.

Feeling a sense of purpose, Guy parked next to his father's car and hustled inside. Removing his shoes in the dim hallway, he called out a "hello" to announce his presence. Although the television was on in the living room, it had no audience so he headed toward his father's bedroom. When he reached the slightly opened door, Guy knocked and again called out, "Hello? Dad? Sharette?"

From the usual setup in the far corner of the room, they both looked up. A clearly tired Sharette acknowledged him with a weary, "Oh, hello Guy," while his father's weakened voice was lost in the noise of the television. Charles Bradford sat uncomfortably in his chair, shirt open, connected via plastic tubing to the bag of liquid nourishment that hung from the metal IV stand in the corner behind him. Sharette sat on the foot of the bed, patiently waiting for the meal to end so she could flush the bag and tube with the large glass of water she held in her hands.

Guy crossed the room and found the remote on the small table next to his father's chair. "I couldn't hear you," he said as he lowered the volume.

"I said, what are you doing here?" his father repeated.

"I was on my way home and I just thought I would check in," Guy lied. He looked to Sharette and asked, "How's it going?"

"It's going okay," she answered quietly, avoiding his gaze.

"She's leaving," said Charles.

Guy looked at Sharette. "Leaving? Like quitting?"

Meekly, she lifted her head to meet his eyes. "Yah. I'm going to go home. I'm sorry."

Are you fucking kidding me? thought Guy. He looked at his father, blaming him. You just sit there like it's nothing, he said to himself as he felt the stress building within him. "Okay," he said, recovering slightly and turning back to Sharette. "Well, that's too bad. I'll be sorry to see you go. Is everything okay? Or are you just ready to go home?" he asked her sympathetically.

"My family needs my help," she said without conviction.

"Oh," said Guy, nodding and playing along. It didn't matter anyway. They all left. Nobody could live with Charles Bradford for very long. "So," he started to ask, "do you have-"

"A week," Charles interrupted. "She's leaving in a week."

Guy froze. A week? One fucking week? Are you kidding me? He took a deep breath and gritted his teeth. "Dad. You do know that it's going to be almost impossible to find a replacement right now?" he asked. "It is Christmas on Monday." He looked at Sharette.

"I told Chahlie I would stay longer, but he said it t'was fine."

Guy looked at Charles. He didn't look back. "Oh," he said finally. Then he left the room.

Sitting on the hood of his car in his father's driveway, Guy took another drag of his cigarette and exhaled slowly as he continued to collect himself. She told him she would stay longer, but he said it was fine. Today is December 23rd, he thought, and the chances of getting someone to replace Sharette right away, in the middle of the holidays, were not good at all. He said it was fine, Guy replayed Sharette's words in his head yet again. *Of course it was fine—for him. Because he knows that I'm here and I won't let him die. I may not have much of a life,* Guy mused, *but I sure as hell don't want to give it up and come here and be his nurse and whipping boy.* "God dammit!" he swore out loud.

In the past, when one caregiver left before another was hired, Guy was stuck filling in. Sometimes it was only a day or two, but once it had been nearly two weeks. It had been a nightmare of complaining and nitpicking, and the possibility of being forced to repeat it made him feel ill. He checked his watch and wondered if his father had bothered to get in touch with the service that supplied him with Sharette. Guy put out his cigarette, stood up, and headed back inside to find out. He figured he could at least make the phone call and get the ball rolling on finding her replacement.

Chapter 48

On his way to pick up Michele, Guy appreciated his newly clean car and wondered how long it had been since it looked and smelled this good. *Maybe I don't actually hate this car*, he mused and smiled, *maybe I just hate the idea that it's all I can afford.*

Guy saw the glow from the spotlights that illuminated the enormous stone walls bracketing the entrance to Sundial Farms, took his foot off the gas, and put on his blinker. As he slowed to make the turn, a wave of anxiety passed through him and he felt very much out of his element. Once inside the gates, he stopped at the stop sign, recalled Michele's instructions, and worked to suppress all of his doubts about this entire situation. Women didn't ask him out. Really hot women didn't ask him out. Really hot women who lived in really big houses didn't generally even acknowledge his existence let alone ask him out. *Yeah*, he thought, *it's Michele, and I know her, but still...* He thought about Jacque and his advice to not overthink everything and just enjoy the evening. He thought about going to The Duke with her and seeing Dean. The clock on his dashboard read 8:00pm. Guy looked at the reflection of his own eyes in his rearview mirror and shrugged. Then he took a deep breath and made a left turn.

Two minutes later he found the brick and stone mailbox column with the decorative metal plate reading "Carson" adorning the end of a driveway. It was a driveway that arced toward an elaborate entrance and then exited onto the street again just ahead of him. Since it was blocked by cars, Guy pulled onto the shoulder in front and got out. The homes in Sundial Farms were spread out and it was generally dark and quiet. Michele's house sat

261

on a slight rise and the steps leading up to her oversized front door were bathed in light from an ornate fixture in the alcove above them. Again, Guy felt uneasy and he longed for a cigarette. Pausing for only a moment, he took another deep breath, let it out slowly, and began walking up the driveway.

Just as he reached the wide steps leading up to the porch and the door, it opened and Michele stepped out like an actor onto center stage.

As she shut the door quickly and quietly behind her and moved forward to come down the steps to greet him, the light above the porch silhouetted her remarkable figure. At the same time, that small decorative bulb served to illuminate her beautiful blonde mane like a halo. For a split second, it was as if an actual angel were descending from the heavens toward him and Guy felt his jaw drop slightly in awe.

"Hi Guy," she said excitedly but quietly as she gave him a quick hug, "Carly has friends over and I'm trying to sneak away without all of them gawking at us through the windows. They don't know I have a date."

"Ohhh," said Guy nodding and whispering conspiratorially, "Come on then, let's get out of here." They walked quickly to his car and made their escape unnoticed.

"Thank you for understanding," Michele said as they drove away. "I haven't really dated since the divorce. Carly has some friends over tonight and I didn't want your picking me up to turn into a big show for a half dozen teenage girls."

"No problem," Guy assured her. Then he smiled, "That *would* be something, I suppose," he said, imagining all of the not-so-subtle peeking from the various windows in the front of the house. "What about..." he paused. "I thought you were seeing someone for a little while. How was that? When he came to pick you up? Were the kids all goofy about it?"

Oh shit, thought Michele. *My made-up boyfriend! Mike? No, Mark!* "It wasn't an issue," she said recovering. "If he picked me up, either Carly was at her dad's or it was just her, not all of her friends," she lied.

Guy and Michele made small talk about the holidays during the ten-minute ride to The Duke. The parking lot was fuller than usual, but there were still a couple of open spots in the back.

"When's the last time you saw Dean?" Michele asked as they got out of the car.

"Maybe five or six years ago, I guess." And it sucked, as Guy recalled. It wasn't Dean's fault though. Dean was fine. Dean was always nice. But just seeing him from behind the counter of the Gas and Go made Guy feel like shit. He looked at Michele and smiled. It's going to be a little different tonight, he thought. "How about you?"

She shrugged. "High school, I guess. I didn't really know him. I just knew he was Bear's little brother."

"That's funny. I was pretty much the opposite. I didn't really know Bear back then. Other than that he was Dean's older brother."

The deck behind The Duke was adorned with holiday lights that looped around the railings and dangled from the eaves of the roof over the entrance. As Guy reached out to open the door for Michele, he smiled at her in the dim glow from the colored bulbs and thought, *just wait until Dean sees her.*

When Guy lay down in his own bed a few hours later, sleep eluded him and he was grateful. There was nothing about the evening that had disappointed him. Lying on his back with his hands folded behind his head, he stared into the darkness and tried to recall as much of his night as he could.

It was a surreal experience to enter a bar with a woman as stunning as Michele. Every head turned—first to stare at her, and then to see who she was with. Guy had never been that guy before, and it felt incredible. Especially when he spotted Dean among the gawkers. On the far wall, there'd been a couple of tables pushed together and his old classmate was holding court on the one end. Along with his wife and Bear, the table was populated with several other familiar faces. When Guy followed Michele into the bar, he could see that all of their eyes, especially Dean's, were locked on her before they began shifting to him. It was exhilarating. Then Bear called out his name and waved them over.

After a flurry of hugs and handshakes, people grabbed chairs, moved over, and then fell back into the easy conversations and reminiscences of old friends. Between he and Michele, they knew everyone at the table and nearly everyone who stopped by to say hello throughout the night. It turned out to be the closest thing to a high school reunion they'd ever had. Bear and Mindy made sure there was always a pitcher or two of beer somewhere on the table and people enjoyed catching up, gossiping, and just hanging out together. Guy's job at the Gas and Go did come up a few times, but it was fleeting and he didn't dwell on it or let it derail his good mood. Being there with every guy's high school fantasy made that so much easier.

Maybe the best part of the night though was when he and Michele were playing darts with another couple. After taking his turn, Guy had returned to the table to pour himself another beer. Dean was doing the same.

"Dude," Dean had half-whispered as he leaned in and motioned with his head toward Michele. "Get the fuck outta here. Are you really hitting that? Holy shit! She's ridiculous! I was so in love with her in high school."

Guy grinned. "Come on, Dean," he deflected, "you're not doing so bad yourself. Your wife is awesome, man." Which was true. Marlene was attractive and intelligent and nice. But she also looked like a woman who'd just had a couple of kids and was settling into marriage, homemaking, and motherhood. She was a Chrysler minivan. Michele was a Ferrari. And they both knew it.

"How long have you two been seeing each other?" Dean asked.

"Oh, we're just kinda hanging out," Guy replied.

Just then, a very buzzed and affectionate Michele came up. Smiling blissfully at him and completely ignoring Dean's presence, she put her arm around his waist and spoke softly with her face very close to his, "It's your turn, partner."

Dean's eyes narrowed and he gave Guy a look that conveyed just how completely full of shit he thought Guy was about "just hanging out" with her. Guy smiled so big his cheeks hurt as he took the darts from Michele. He knew there was nothing anyone could possibly say to persuade Dean that he was not actually "hitting that" and it was absolutely beautiful.

The more Michele drank, the more affectionate she became, and Guy started to wonder if he might actually be "hitting that" later. He still couldn't get his head around the fact that she might genuinely be interested in him so the idea that he might be having sex with her that night was not something he had previously considered. But, on the way back to her house, he had definitely started doing some considering.

There were still cars in the driveway when they arrived and she'd told him just to park in front like he had when he picked her up earlier. He slowed to a stop and turned off his headlights.

"I'm sorry," she said taking off her seatbelt, "but Carly's having a sleepover." Before he could respond, Michele Dasher leaned over, placed her hand tenderly on his cheek, and briefly looked him in the eye before closing hers and kissing him fully and slowly on the mouth. "I had a lot of fun tonight," she said softly. "Thanks, Guy." And then she was gone.

Chapter 49

Guy pulled into the unusually empty parking lot of The Duke shortly before the noon kick-off. He grabbed the small green and red gift bag off the seat next to him and tucked it inside his coat. Walking quickly through the cold December air, he surmised that Christmas Eve must be trumping the Bears game for quite a few of the regulars. Inside, a clearly engrossed Jacque barely looked away from the television as Guy sat down on the stool next to him. He caught Mindy's eye and motioned for a beer.

Setting an MGD down in front of Guy, she turned toward Jacque. "How about you? Are you ready for another one?" But Jacque was staring at the ex-jocks in suits as they talked about the game and gave no indication that he had even heard her. She turned to Guy, "He's really enjoying his Christmas present," she said, shaking her head and rolling her eyes before walking away.

Only then did it dawn on Guy; kick-off was still ten minutes away and instead of music, the bar was filled with the sounds of those ex-jocks in suits previewing the game. Bear must have turned off the music and turned up the volume on the television already. He laughed out loud as a commercial came on and Jacque finally turned to him.

"Isn't this great?" he grinned at Guy. "Pre-game hype! Keys to the game! Players to watch! Match-ups!"

Guy raised his glass to his friend, "Merry Christmas, Jacque. I'm glad you are enjoying it."

"It's awesome! It's my Christmas present. Best one in a while," he called out toward Bear on the other side of the bar.

Bear laughed as he walked over. "It's kind of slow today and I thought... what the hell. I had no idea you would really enjoy it this much."

"Are you kidding me? It's the best. Thank you, my friend!"

Bear turned to Guy. "Hey, thanks for coming by last night. That was great."

"Yeah," Guy agreed. "No kidding. I haven't talked to a lot of those people since the day I graduated high school. Hey, how much did Mr. Law Firm Partner's bar tab come to anyways? Did he pay it?"

Bear laughed, "Oh he paid it, alright. That rich son of a bitch didn't even blink. Just filled out the tip and signed it. It was over $300 and he signed it like it was nothing. And there I was feeling a little guilty about it when I gave him the slip to sign. Nothing though. No reaction." Bear shook his head. "I tell you, I better be getting a good Christmas present from him this year. If he can drop hundreds at a bar without batting an eye, I should be getting more than a new flannel shirt every year."

"Yeah," agreed Guy, "No kidding."

"Or at least he could buy you some that aren't so damn ugly," Jacque said making a face and looking up and down the green and blue flannel that Bear was currently wearing.

"Fuck you, man," Bear said defensively. "I like this shirt. And I picked it out."

Jacque just grinned.

"Watch yourself, smart ass. You know I can always turn the music back on. There's still some time before kick-off."

Jacque put his hands up in front of him. "My apologies. It is a beautiful shirt. And it looks great on you." Then he turned back around on his stool to face the television again.

Bear rolled his eyes as he departed for the kitchen.

Guy took Jacque's present out of his coat and set it on the bar in-between them. It was a moment before his friend noticed.

"What's this? Is this for me?"

Guy nodded. "Yep."

"Get the fuck out of here. I didn't get you anything."

"Bullshit. My birthday present. That guitar is seriously the best gift I've ever gotten."

"Well I'm glad you liked it. But I just found that thing. I wasn't even looking. It's not like I went shopping for you. You didn't have to get me anything."

"Shut up and open it."

Jacque reached into the bag and pulled out a cigar and a small white box. "A cigar! Hey, thanks. I haven't enjoyed a good cigar in a while."

"The guy said it was a good one. I hope it is. I don't know anything about cigars."

"It's a Macanudo. Nice." Jacque held it up to his nose and inhaled deeply. "Mmmmmm. Smells good."

"There's more."

Jacque picked up the small white box and removed the lid. Inside was a Zippo lighter. "Hey, alright. I had one of these many years ago. I don't know what happened to it. Thank you!"

"Read it."

Jacque turned it over in his hands and found the inscription. *Not Your Average Friend*, he read. "Aw, man. That's pretty fucking cool."

"Well, it's true. I really appreciate all of your help."

"Thank you, my friend. Thank you very much. I won't lose this one." He opened it up and lit it. "I love these lighters."

"I'm glad you like it. Hey, did your parents leave?" he asked.

"This morning," Jacque replied. "They'll get home late this afternoon and then head over to my sister's tomorrow for Christmas Day. Christmas with their grandkids is much better than Christmas with me—for everyone. Plus, I will be very busy baking."

"Makes sense. It's cool that they made the trip up here, though."

"True. I am grateful. It was different saying goodbye to them this morning when they stopped by the bakery."

"How so?"

"Over the past few days, all of your bullshit with your dad was on my mind."

Guy laughed. "I'm sorry, man."

"No," Jacque countered. "It was actually good. I was thinking about them as generic parents, not specifically as my own mom and dad."

"Okay."

"And I was able to see them differently, almost objectively maybe. And I think they did a good job raising my sister and me."

"Well that's cool."

"Yeah, it was," continued Jacque thoughtfully. "I mean, they are my parents and I love them, but this was different. It's not like everything was perfect, but I think overall, they did a really good job parenting. And I appreciated them in a different way."

"That's really cool, man."

"It was. But it was strange, too. Your dad's health issues had me thinking more about their age and health. And when they were leaving, it struck me." Jacque paused. "I might not see them again. They are old. Old people die. I know that, but still, it was very different to be thinking about it with my own parents. And I didn't like it."

Guy laughed again. "Oh, I get it. Every time I leave my father's house, for the last several years, I wonder if that will be it. He's been so unhealthy for so long, it crosses my mind whenever I answer a call from his house."

"I can't imagine," Jacque said shaking his head. "No thanks. I need to get down there to see them this summer. I've been so busy with getting the bakery going that I haven't taken the time."

"Do it, man," Guy encouraged him.

"I need to. Hopefully I'll be better set up this summer and I'll be able to get away. It'll be good to see my sister and her family, too."

"A summer vacation sounds nice. Maybe I'll do that next summer, too," Guy said jokingly.

"You know you probably could, right?" Jacque was serious. "Something. It doesn't have to be a big trip. I'm sure you could get away for at least a couple of days. Everyone needs a break once in a while."

"Sure. I agree. I could afford to do something small for a few days. I'm guessing I could make a plan. I could put down a non-refundable deposit on a cabin up north or something. And then have some kind of crisis with my dad, not go on vacation, and lose my deposit."

"Damn," Jacque said as he marveled at how quickly his vacation suggestions went south.

"At least that's what happened the last time I tried to get away for a few days," Guy shrugged and sighed.

"Damn!" exclaimed Jacque. "You're not kidding, are you? Holy shit!"

"I'm telling you. He has a sixth sense. I stopped over there last night before I went to pick up Michele."

"Oh yeah! You guys went out again last night! How was it?"

Guy smiled. "Oh, man. It was great. She is so hot. It was weird just being the guy who walked in with her. Everybody stares at her. I had no idea."

"That's because you were too busy staring at her, too!" Jacque laughed.

"Yeah, probably," Guy agreed. "The best part was when Dean saw her. I swear his jaw literally dropped when I came in with her. He was so jealous. He was asking me all about her. And Michele was pretty buzzed and was getting a little touchy-feely with me. Right in front of him." Guy laughed. "It was perfect. Dean was absolutely speechless."

"All touchy-feely? Nice!"

"Yeah. Tell me about it. I was talking to Dean and she came up and put her arm around my waist. It was awesome. I saw a bunch of people I hadn't seen in years. And every single one of them asked about Michele and me. It was just so cool to be here with her last night. Nobody asked me about the Gas and Go. I loved it."

"That's great, my friend. I'm happy for you."

Guy's expression abruptly changed. "But see, that's the thing. You know how I said I stopped by my father's before I went out?"

"Yeah?"

"I was trying to take care of shit and make sure everything was good so I didn't have two date nights in a row get all screwed up."

"That was smart. Seems like it worked. I didn't get a call from you," Jacque smiled. "I'm kind of disappointed though, now that I think about it."

"Everything was good. But I found out that his caregiver is quitting."

"Are you serious?"

"Yep. Maybe she's homesick. Maybe it's just the holidays. I don't know. She said her family needs her back in Belize. But that's what they all say." Guy didn't mask his bitterness. "I'm sure the big reason she is leaving is the same for her as it's been for everyone else that has ever tried to live with my father for any length of time."

Jacque looked at him expectantly.

Guy shrugged like the answer was obvious. "He grinds people down. Anyone who can leave, well, does. That's how it's always been."

"Oh man. So when is she leaving?"

"That's the other part of this story," Guy laughed ruefully. "She offered to stay on until we hired a replacement. But my father told her not to worry about it. She'll be gone in a week. Her last day is Saturday. I doubt I'm going to find anyone by Saturday."

"What happens if you don't?"

Guy turned toward him and extended his arms outward, as if presenting himself.

"You?"

"Me," Guy confirmed. "The only one dumb enough to stick around." He turned back to the bar and took a drink of his beer.

"Will you have to stay there?"

Guy shrugged. "There's really no other way to do it. He needs somebody there. Usually we can get somebody before the one who's leaving actually leaves. But a few times I've been stuck having to be there for at least a couple of days. With the holidays though," he sighed with resignation. "I've got four days. I left the placement agency a message last night. But I haven't even heard back from them yet. Tomorrow is Christmas." Guy ran his fingers through his hair and took a deep breath. "I'm going to be fucked again."

Chapter 50

Michele woke up as the muffled sounds of laughter, cabinets, and dishes drifted upstairs from her kitchen. Rolling over toward her nightstand, she reached for her phone to check the time. It was just after ten o'clock in the morning and she was surprised that she'd slept in so late. But she was grateful because she realized she had a bit of a headache. She also saw that there was a missed a call and a text—both from Laura. Michele considered making some coffee before she called her back but was reluctant to get out of bed. Instead, she grabbed the pillows from the other side of the king size mattress to cushion her against the large, ornately carved, wooden headboard and she sat up. After taking a moment to rub the sleep out of her eyes, Michele called her friend. It rang once.

"About damn time!" her friend answered.

"I literally just woke up. I haven't even gotten out of bed yet. I haven't even peed," Michele protested.

"How did it go? No crisis with his dad?"

"No. It was good. We had fun," she reflected. "I had fun. He really seemed like he was happy. Like he was having a good time."

"Alright!" Laura enthused. "That's awesome, honey. That's what I wanted to hear!"

"Yeah," said Michele, starting to feel positive. "I really think it went well. So, besides Dean and his wife, and Bear of course, there were a bunch of other people from high school. People were in a good mood. There were a lot of people there that I haven't seen in years. It was like a little mini-reunion."

"Nice. Now I wish Ron and I were there. That would've been fun."

"I did think about texting you to come out. But then I thought it might be weird, you know? Even though it wasn't like a *date* date, and there were a bunch of other people, it seemed like…it might be bad. Plus, I figured that if you guys did show up, you and I would end up talking a lot. Instead of me and Guy."

"Oh, don't worry about it. I think that was a smart move," Laura agreed. "Definitely good thinking. Even calculating!" She laughed.

"Yeah, I know. It's Christmas. And every time I've gone shopping or bought anything this year, I think about how the heck am I going to be able to celebrate Christmas next year? Even decorating the house this year, I was starting to freak out. Carly doesn't know anything, but I really don't even know if I'll be able to be in this house next year. This could be her last Christmas here," she said. She could feel herself getting emotional.

Laura could hear the stress in her friend's voice. "Hey," she said trying to reassure her, "you're going to be okay. You're making progress. How did the night end?"

"He drove me home. And I kissed him." She said it with so little enthusiasm that she surprised herself. But Laura didn't seem to notice.

"Really? That's great, Michele! Where? Did you invite him in?"

"No. It was in the car. And I couldn't really invite him in because Carly was here with a bunch of friends."

"Well I guess that was bad planning. Next time you'll have to make sure that Carly is at Troy's. Or a friend's house or something."

"Yeah. I'll have to see about that."

"Did you make plans to see each other again?" she pressed.

"No. I mean it's Christmas and everything this week. I probably won't see him until we go out on New Year's Eve." As she talked her headache was worsening and a knot was forming in her stomach. "Hey, listen Michele," she lied, "I've got to get off the phone. The kids are in the kitchen trying to make breakfast and they need my help with something."

"Ok. Call me back later."

"Ok. Bye." Michele dropped the phone on the bed next to her. As she'd been talking to Laura about Carly and Christmas, and the date, and kissing Guy at the end of it, all of the different aspects of what she was trying to do were coming together. And she didn't like the way she felt about any of them.

Her head hurt because she drank too much. She drank too much so that she could loosen up and try and be a fun date. And it was a fun night out. She genuinely had a good time and she thought that Guy did, too. But realistically, she admitted to herself, Guy being there with her last night didn't really add anything to the night. She would have had fun anyway. She was out with a whole fun group of people and old friends and everyone was having fun. It wasn't because she was with Guy. But it wasn't like he made it a worse night either. He was just kind of like one of the group.

That was clear when she kissed him. It was nice. But there was no spark. *And invite him in?* she wondered. *Ugh.* She realized that she was very grateful that Carly and her friends were home and that was a decision she didn't have to make last night. "What am I doing?" she asked aloud. Then she wondered whether or not she would have actually invited him in. And then she didn't want to think about it. Michele slumped back down in bed and lay on her side as she reflected. *So my first possibly real relationship since Troy is with a guy who's not that bad. A guy I don't mind. A good guy. A nice guy. Who will have some money. But don't I want more? Don't I want to be all excited? Don't I want to be in love? Shouldn't I want to invite him in? Shouldn't I be all giddy about my date? And pissed that I didn't make sure Carly would be gone?* Before she could admit to herself that yes was the answer to all of her questions, there was a loud crash in the kitchen, followed by a burst of laughter, and then "Mommmmmmm!" Reluctantly, she got out of bed, found her robe, and headed down the stairs.

Chapter 51

"What was her name?" asked Charles as the door closed and the last available candidate to replace Sharette left the house.

"Rami? Remi?" Guy guessed as he returned to the kitchen table and sat down opposite his father. "Maybe Reemi?"

Charles shook his head. "I couldn't understand her."

"I couldn't either," Guy reluctantly agreed. He was demoralized. If the agency didn't send somebody decent by tomorrow, he was going to be stuck again. He was going to have to come and stay in this house with his father again.

"Well, that was a waste of our time."

Sure, Guy thought, *our time.*

"I don't know what the point is in interviewing women who don't speak English. You need to make sure that they speak English."

"I have told the agency that over and over. I don't have any control over who they send out."

"What was the deal with the Polish gal? I could understand the Polish gal."

"Yes. I could understand her, too. But she doesn't have a driver's license." Two days ago, the interview with Ruta, the Polish woman, had gone very well. Until Guy asked if she had a driver's license. Ruta smiled, gestured to the car in the driveway through the picture window, and said, "I drive myself here." Then Guy asked if he could see her driver's license. He listened patiently to her well-rehearsed explanations about why she didn't have her license with her and how she was a very good driver and never gets pulled over and so on. Then he thanked her for her time. Asking to actually see a driver's license was something he had learned the hard way when Irena from Romania had been pulled over driving his father's Cadillac home from the grocery store in McHenry. Guy had to get Big John to come in and cover for him while he went to pick up Charles and his car full of groceries off the side of Route 31.

"Well, there must be a better way to do it. They keep wasting our time like this," his father repeated. "I don't know why we can't just hire an American gal."

"If you know of anyone, let me know," Guy said. He refused to have this conversation with his father again. It was the same after every bad interview. It was Guy's fault that the agency sent people who could barely speak English. It was Guy's fault that he couldn't find some local woman, with no family attachments, who wanted to come and seclude herself with his father in this house.

"Have you asked around? You can't find anyone?" his father pressed. "There's got to be someone. You need to keep asking around." Charles was convinced that the only thing separating him from the ideal caregiver was the incompetence of his son.

Guy just nodded. "I'm going to head out. I'll call the agency? Tell them to send someone else?"

They sat in silence while Guy watched out the window as Rami, or whatever her name was, got in her car and drove away.

Charles finally relented. "Go ahead and call."

When Guy returned home, he left a message for Stan letting him know that the interview didn't go well because they couldn't understand most of what the woman said. He told him that he and Charles needed to interview someone who both spoke decent English and had a valid driver's license. As soon as possible. That was really the only criteria and Stan already knew it. They'd dealt with this kind of bullshit from him before, but it had never been this bad. It was frustrating and Guy wished he had someone else to call, but he had tried and failed a few times in the past. It was a shady business. McHenry County was Stan's turf and he had it locked up tightly. Anytime Guy had been able to contact another agency, they asked where his father lived. As soon as he'd tell them, they'd tell him to call Stan.

Guy picked up his guitar and tried to put the entire situation out of his head for a while. It worked. His fingertips had finally developed thick enough calluses to allow him to play without tape. And he played a lot. That was a great thing about the guitar, for Guy. As he played and practiced, he could hear and feel actual progress. It was the one area of his life that wasn't stagnant. It was also the one area of his life where he felt like he had some control. The more time he put in, the greater the results. He also was able to choose what he wanted to play. After he'd learned most of the basic chords from *Roy Clark's Big Note Guitar Songbook*, he'd gone to the library to use the internet and find the chords to some songs he'd wanted to play. Anything by Tom Petty was better than "Michael Row Your Boat Ashore."

After a while, his mistakes began to increase and Guy decided he was ready for a break. Setting his guitar on the couch next to him, he turned to check the time on the microwave clock. It confirmed what his stomach had begun to hint at, so he made himself a sandwich and put some water on the stove for mac and cheese. It was Friday night, after all. If he was going to sip beers all evening at The Duke with Jacque, he would need to eat something. While he waited for the water to boil, he grabbed his coat, a cigarette, and his mailbox key.

It was cold out and the late December sun had already disappeared below the horizon. It wasn't particularly windy, but Guy stood on the leeward side of the laundry building anyway. Some of his neighbors had Christmas lights up in their windows and he could see that the lids to the dumpsters wouldn't shut all the way as people had presumably filled them with boxes and hefty bags full of wrapping paper. He liked Christmas, but still felt disconnected from much of it.

Flicking his butt into the parking lot, Guy returned to his building and unlocked his mailbox in the hallway. Along with the usual collection of junk and a bill or two, Guy found a regular white envelope with his name neatly printed on the front. The return address was Mexico Beach, FL and it was from Sophie. His attitude and expression instantly brightened; a smiling Guy went back to his apartment to read it.

Guy dumped the noodles in the now boiling water, set a timer, grabbed a beer from the fridge, and sat down on the couch. Who knew it could be so exciting to get an actual letter in the mail? he mused. He looked at the return address again before opening it. He'd never heard of Mexico Beach. And how the hell did she end up in Florida? Guy carefully opened the envelope and pulled out a sheet of notebook paper full of Sophie's handwriting.

He read it and he felt good. He loved the fact that she was in Florida. Guy looked at the pack of cigarettes on the table in front of him and thought about how cool it would be to go for a run on the beach. He was happy that he wrote her and that she was so happy to get his Christmas card. And that she wanted to request a song. He was happy about everything in the letter. The timer went off and he finished making his mac and cheese, grabbed his sandwich, and returned to the couch. While he ate, he reread her letter and began thinking about what he would write in return.

When he was finished, he cleaned up his dishes and went to get ready to meet Jacque at The Duke. He was excited to tell him about his letter.

Shortly before he left for the night, Stan returned his call. They had their usual conversation where Stan pled ignorance about Rami's lack of English and suggested that Guy and Charles were being overly picky.

"She has accent," he complained in his own heavy Polish accent. "You get used to accents. It takes a few days. You must be patient."

This line of bullshit had been effective with Guy a few years ago. He now knew that there was a very clear difference between a difficult accent and profoundly limited English. It was another lesson learned the hard way. Part of the challenge was that the women with limited English would almost never ask about a word or admit that they didn't understand. They were afraid of getting found out and either not getting hired for a job or getting fired from one. They would nod and smile and say "ya, ya," no matter what. It had taken a little practice to be able to sleuth out the pretenders, but it was necessary. Especially after one of them put Charles into a diabetic coma because she couldn't understand his instructions.

Guy chose not to argue the point and calmly held firm in his request for somebody else to be sent for them to interview. Tomorrow.

"Look, Guy," Stan finally confessed. "I am sorry. That is all I have right now. These women, if they are not working this time of year, they go home for the Christmas holiday. To see their families, yes? You must be patient Guy. It is bad time. They come back very soon. I send you someone good next week. After the New Year's. You have my word. I send you my best girl."

Guy's jaw dropped. "Next week?" He stared at his closet door. On the knob hung the new pants and shirt that he purchased for his New Year's Eve date with Michele.

"Yes. Best girl. Perfect English. Driver's license. Everything for you Guy. I swear it. Right after New Year."

Guy was speechless.

"Guy? Yes?"

"Fine," he finally mumbled and set the phone down.

Chapter 52

"There he is," announced Jacque as Guy entered The Duke. "Where've you been?"

Guy just shook his head as he slowly walked over to sit down next to his friend. "You want the good news? Or the bad news?" he asked.

"Give me the bad first, my friend."

"I just got off the phone with Michele. I had to cancel for New Year's Eve."

"Get the fuck out. You're serious?"

He nodded. "Yep."

"Oh man," Jacque lamented. "That sucks. Why? What happened?"

"Guess."

"Your dad?"

"Yep," Guy replied fatalistically. "I had to call Michele and tell her that I would not be able to go to dinner with her and Laura and her husband because I would need to spend my New Year's Eve with my father. Because he can't be alone. And because he decided that it would be fine if Sharette left tomorrow. Because he declined her offer to stay until we could find somebody else. And, big fucking surprise, we haven't been able to find anybody else."

"Wow. That is brutal." Jacque took a drink. "What's the good news?"

"I got a letter from Sophie today," Guy blurted out as he sat up straighter.

Jacque turned to face him and was happy to see the big grin on his friend's face. "Heyyy! Alright!" he smiled. "That's great! What'd she have to say?"

"She said to tell you hi. She's in Florida."

"Alright. Hi back to Sophie! Florida, huh? How'd she end up in Florida?"

"I don't know," he shrugged. "She didn't say. But she's working at some bar right on the coast. It's in a town called Mexico Beach. I looked it up. It's on the panhandle." The words tumbled out of Guy. "She said she goes running on the beach every morning and it's beautiful there. She's renting a room in a little house from some old guy who lives in Tallahassee. She said she was super happy to get the letter from me. She wants to know if she can request a song for me to learn. And she wants me to write her back."

"That is great news, my friend," Jacque said raising his glass. "Cheers to that."

"Tell me about it," Guy agreed as he clinked his bottle against Jacque's glass and took a drink. "I never thought I could get excited about mail," he said laughing.

"Hey, that was a big thing for a very long time. People wrote love letters."

Guy rolled his eyes. "This wasn't a love letter."

"What would you call it? A like letter? An interested letter? A friendship letter?" Jacque challenged.

"I don't know. It's just a letter."

"Bullshit. You are smitten."

"I'm what?"

"Smitten. That means you like her. You have a crush on her. You are smitten. Look at yourself. You are happy. I haven't seen you like this in some time, my friend. It is nice to see."

"Whatever."

"Ha! Whatever is what people say to me when they know that I am right," Jacque laughed. "It's okay. Embrace it. It is fun to be in love!"

"Holy shit!" Guy exclaimed. "Now I'm in love? You are crazy. I got a letter from a girl in Florida. And yes, I am interested in her but she's in Florida, dude. What difference does it make?"

"I don't know," Jacque shrugged. "Time will tell, I suppose. But for now, you have girlfriends in two states."

"Oh, give me a break. Nothing is ever going to happen with Michele while my father is still alive."

"What about this?" Jacque asked. "How about I go over there for a few hours on New Year's Eve? Just show me what to do?" He shrugged. "You could still go on your date."

Guy smiled and laughed. "You are the best, man. Thank you for offering. But you know I already thought about asking you?"

"So why not? It can't be that hard."

Guy shook his head. "Absolutely not. I'm not willing to risk your life."

"What? I'd be there for a few hours. How the hell does it risk my life?"

"That's not how it works, Jacque," he explained matter-of-factly. "You wouldn't ever make it. It's been ten years of catastrophes that prevent me from doing anything. If you become the solution? If we get it all worked out where you are set up to fill in so I can go out? Well, you'd probably get eaten by a bear or something. And I'd end up not being able to go anyway."

"What? A bear?" Jacque almost spit his drink out. "We don't have any fucking bears around here! I'm not going to get eaten by a bear!"

"Dude," Guy shrugged. "Fine. No bear. Maybe your bakery would start on fire? Or something awful."

"Jesus Christ!" Jacque put his hands up. "Don't even joke about that."

"I'm not joking. I'm telling you. It will be something. It *always* is. You're not going to go over there. My date is canceled. I should have known better. This is what happens when I try to do stuff. He finds a way to fuck everything up. It's just the way it is."

"Alright, alright," said a suddenly spooked Jacque. "I'm definitely out." He sipped his beer and thought for a moment. "What about that agency? Can they get you a temp person? Just for a couple of days?"

"Nobody good."

"What makes somebody good?"

Guy chuckled. "You want the entire list of qualifications?"

"Sure. Let's hear them."

"First, and this is the biggest thing, they've got to be able to speak English. That's the biggest challenge. So many of them just arrived from some Eastern European country and they don't have much of a vocabulary yet.

And they are soooo hard to understand. That's been the best thing about Sharette. She's from Belize. They speak English there."

"Okay. Must speak English. What else?"

"A valid driver's license. My father doesn't drive so they have to chauffeur him around in his big yellow Caddy. And unless they have a valid license, they won't be covered on his insurance."

"Okay. English speaking, valid license. Continue."

Guy shrugged. "That's it."

"That's it?"

"Yeah. It's not rocket science. I show them what to do. My father can tell them when he needs something."

"Why is it so hard to find someone then?"

"Right now it's a timing thing. The agency hardly has anyone because the ones who aren't working went home to see their families for Christmas. And people from the U.S. just don't generally want to go live with someone. They have lives and families and shit. It's pretty much a 24-hour job."

"So that's why you get the foreign women?"

"Yeah. They're over here away from families and friends anyway. They come here for a while to make some decent cash. Sometimes they just send it home to their families. Sometimes they're here for a year and they go back home."

Jacque nodded and took a drink of his beer. "I guess that makes sense."

"So, this week we had one no-show. One woman from Poland who could have worked. But didn't have a driver's license. And then this woman today. Holy shit. Not a fucking clue what she was saying. Just lots and lots of nodding and smiling."

"And the current one leaves tomorrow?"

Guy nodded. "So, I'll be going to stay with him for at least a few days. With work, well, it's happened before," he shrugged. "I'll still open in the morning. I just work a shorter shift. And Big John will be on call in case I need to go deal with something. The guy at the agency promised he would have someone for us by this coming week." He paused. "You see how it works though, don't you? The timing of this was just right to fuck my New

Year's Eve plans. Just enough. I'm telling you, that's what I get for trying to have a life."

Jacque shook his head. "I'm a believer."

"Anyway, I hope they send us somebody good. There's always an adjustment period and I have to listen to my dad bitch about their English. I know it's never going to be perfect. He always complains because I can't find some local 'American gal.'"

"You know," Jacque said slowly. "I know someone who just might be interested in the job."

"Seriously?" Guy was doubtful.

"Yeah. It won't make a difference for New Year's Eve, but she's American. Great English and has a driver's license."

"Don't fuck with me. Are you being serious?"

"Absolutely. She even has experience in this line of work."

"Bullshit. Who?"

"I don't know for sure if she is available though."

"Who is it?"

"I suppose you could ask her."

"Who, goddammit?"

"You really don't know?" said Jacque in disbelief.

"No."

"Your pen pal. Your Florida girlfriend," Jacque grinned. "Sophie!"

Chapter 53

The storms swept in from the Gulf early that evening and chased the remaining beachgoers back to their bungalows and motel rooms. Prior to that, both the sun and the crowds had been abundant and Toucan's was busy right up until the rain began to fall. Sophie had made good tips all day on the deck and was now covering the bar for the dinner shift in the dining room. Other than the small crowd listening to a guy named Mike in a Hawaiian shirt covering Jimmy Buffett and James Taylor in the upstairs bar, the restaurant was dead. Artie had come down for the weekend and he was her only customer. She poured herself a vodka grapefruit and, welcoming the chance to get off her feet, joined him on the other side of the bar. They watched the weather channel and visited.

"It appears our good weather is slated to return tomorrow," Artie observed.

"Yep," Sophie agreed. "At least through the weekend. But it doesn't look good for the rest of the winter break. Damn."

"I'll be leaving Monday regardless. It will be a slow week, but there is work to be done nonetheless. How are you doing? Do you intend to remain with us in Mexico Beach for the foreseeable future?"

Sophie sighed. "That's a great question, Artie." With New Year's just a couple of days away, she'd been thinking it was time to make a decision, to start off the new year with a plan. But she hadn't really come up with anything. Part of her wanted to just hang around and continue to read, run, work, and relax. But she knew she didn't really want to completely fall back into the bar and restaurant routine. And there wasn't much else for her to do in Mexico Beach. "I really don't know what I'm doing. To be honest," she confessed, "I'm kind of lost right now."

Artie considered her response and sipped his gin and tonic. "Certainly not an extraordinary predicament for a woman in her mid-twenties."

"Ohhh! You're the best, Artie," she smiled and patted his leg. "But I am thirty-two."

"A lie!" he said sitting up straighter and turning to look directly at her as if to see if he had overlooked some obvious clues. "I refuse to believe it," he decided.

She rolled her eyes. "Don't oversell it now."

"I am not selling anything, my dear Sophie. You absolutely do not look thirty-two. I actually feel less guilty about lusting after you now," he confessed. "We are a mere thirty-four years apart in age! And all this time I believed the gap to be in excess of forty." He lowered his voice. "You know that's the only reason I never asked you out?"

She laughed. "Sorry Artie. Thirty-three years is my max. That's my rule. You just missed it. Damn," she said shaking her head.

"So close," he said wistfully. "So close."

"I won't go out with you, but I will buy you another drink," she offered. "I don't plan on walking back home while it's still pouring out. You want one?"

"Yes. If you indeed refuse to become my paramour, I suppose I will settle for another cocktail."

Sophie went behind the bar to make their drinks and then returned to her stool next to Artie.

"So, what does a thirty-two-year-old Miss Sophie Ross want to do with her life?" he mused.

"Ha! I'm willing to keep you in gin and tonics all night if you can figure that out," she offered.

His watery eyes grew large. "My dear," he cautioned her. "Do you have any idea how many gin and tonics that could be?"

"I've seen you drink," she assured him. "And I can't imagine that a shrink would be any cheaper."

"Challenge accepted." He cleared his throat and thought for a bit. "Okay. You must answer me honestly and promptly if I am to be able to solve you."

She nodded. "Promise."

"Let us begin. If and when you do decide to leave this establishment, what will you do to support yourself?"

"I don't know. I guess that's part of the reason that I'm still here."

"Do you desire to return to caring for the sick and elderly?"

"No."

"Are you interested in pursuing higher education?"

"Maybe. I don't know what I would study," she shrugged.

"Aha. There is a solution to that! After Christmas break is over, you will come to Tallahassee. We have an excellent community college and they offer career counseling for potential students who themselves face your very familiar uncertainty. And it won't cost you anything..." he paused to drain his glass. "...except an additional gin and tonic at this very moment."

"Okay," she laughed getting up again. "That's good advice. That's worth another drink. I will come up there and meet with a counselor."

"And maybe you will wear something mildly inappropriate and revealing and accompany me to lunch so that my colleagues will be driven mad with jealously."

"Oh my god! Artie! What have you been telling them?"

"I do not lie about our relationship, my dear. Rather our friendship, I should say." Solemnly, he raised his right hand. "I swear."

Her eyes narrowed. "They all think I'm your girlfriend, don't they?"

"I simply cannot be blamed if people make certain assumptions based on incomplete or slightly misleading information."

"Oh Artie! Yes! Yes, you can and should be blamed!" she was laughing as she set his drink in front of him and removed his empty glass. "But you know, that actually might be a lot of fun."

"Oh yes," he nodded vigorously. "It would be magnificent!"

"We'll see. I'm not making any promises."

"I can accept that. Okay. We do not have a career solution, but we have a direction toward a solution. That is something. Now," he continued, "will you be staying in Florida?"

"I don't know. It's only been a couple of months. But I have a feeling I'll miss the changing seasons. I don't love winter, but I am having a hard time with Christmas lights on palm trees."

"Understood. I have heard that can be a challenge. If you do stay for school, you do not need to stay forever. The same ought to be noted for Iowa should you decide to return. But that being said, if school is in your future, you should expect to remain in that area for at least a few years."

"Agreed. I guess that's part of it. I've bounced around my entire life. I feel like I want to maybe try putting some roots down. I've never done that before. It's a scary thought."

"Understood. Your experience is one I can only imagine. I have worn out the road between here and Tallahassee throughout my entire existence."

"Wow," she shook her head. "I can't imagine that."

"Well, if you are to have a family, there are benefits." He paused before continuing, "And, if you truly are thirty-two and not twenty-five, your desire, or lack thereof, for children should be addressed. What are your intentions? Do you wish to have children?"

Sophie's shoulders drooped and she hung her head. "Oh, Artie. The thought of having kids really scares me."

"It should. It is an utterly terrifying experience."

"Gee, thanks for the support," she said sarcastically.

"Do consider that there are around six billion people on this planet. Many, many people possessing much less intelligence and ability than you have successfully managed it."

Sophie shook her head. "Oh no. That's not the part that scares me. I grew up in foster care and most of it was less than ideal." She hesitated. "What if I have kids and something happens to me? I don't have any family, Artie. I'm afraid that my kids will end up growing up like I did."

"Ahh," he nodded, thinking. After a time, he continued. "Two things to consider perhaps. First, although I understand that you faced many challenges, I believe I am qualified to attest to the fact that, despite those challenges, you have turned out to be an exceptionally wonderful person."

"Aww, Artie," she said fighting her emotions. "You're going to make me cry."

"I am quite serious, my dear Sophie." He turned toward her and put his hand on her shoulder. Artie looked her in the eyes and spoke very sincerely and earnestly. "I do not know the circumstances of your parents' lives as we have not spoken of it. But I cannot imagine that they would not be very proud of the woman that you are today."

With that, Sophie hugged him, buried her head into his shoulder, and bawled. Artie held her there quietly and let her.

As the flood of tears and emotions abated, she let him go, sat up, and reached for a cocktail napkin. "I told you, you were going to make me cry," she said blowing her nose. She grabbed a couple more and wiped her eyes. "Jesus," she apologized, "I'm sorry about your shirt."

"No need to apologize," Artie assured her. "My shirt will be fine. I owe you an apology for upsetting you. I am sorry."

"No, don't be. I'm not upset. That really means a lot to me to hear that. Nobody has ever said that to me before," she said as more tears welled up in her eyes. "Thank you, Artie." Sophie hugged him again. Sitting back up, she took a deep breath and worked to collect herself. "Time for another drink," she laughed.

"I will be buying this round," he insisted and he did. "There is another point I would like to address regarding children. If I may." He paused as he waited for permission.

"Okay," she agreed. "Go ahead."

"The probability of both you and your husband being simultaneously rendered incapable of raising your children is rather low. Conversely, the probability of your husband having some extended family is rather high. In all but the most extraordinarily rare circumstances, you should expect that your children will be well cared for by people who know them and love them."

She considered what he said and nodded. "Yeah, I guess that makes sense." Then her head titled to the side and she raised her eyebrows. "Uhh, my husband? Don't I at least need to have a boyfriend first?"

"Well here I sit before you," he offered as he sat up a little straighter and held his arms out, "ready, willing, and...", he cleared his throat and grimaced as he stole a glance toward his lap, "and periodically able!"

"Jesus Christ, Artie," she laughed. "That's too much information."

"Honesty is the foundation of any healthy relationship, my dear."

"I've already told you I have a strict rule about dating men more than thirty-three years older than me. Besides that," she continued, "would you really want to have another baby?"

"No. No I would not." Then he grinned and confessed earnestly and emphatically, "But by god, I'd love to try with you."

"Alright," she patted him on the knee. "Settle down." She sipped her vodka grapefruit and Artie his gin and tonic. Then she sighed. "A husband, huh?"

"Surely you have had boyfriends in the past?"

"Yeah, I have. And some were better than others, but I don't think I've ever really been in love. If I am going to have a husband, I would like to be in love."

"Ahh, love," he said wistfully, "and marriage, ugh," he added.

"You sound a little jaded," she teased.

"Permit me to tell you a tale of two women from my youth gone by."

"Oooh. Young Artie! Please continue."

"While I was in law school, I had a job tending bar in a restaurant. One day at work there was a new waitress. That woman captivated me as no other woman, before or since, ever has."

"What happened?"

"I never got to know her as well as I would have liked because we did not work together as often as I would have preferred. Such was the nature of our different lives and schedules. But when we did work together, I felt such a connection. Such comfort. The fact that she was kind and funny and intelligent, not to mention stunning, was simply icing on the cake. It is difficult to describe. I cannot quantify it. I cannot explain it. It was such extraordinary and unexpected connection that I felt. That I have not felt since."

"Did you ever go out with her?"

"No." Artie shook his head ruefully. "I did not act. I was a student. I was extremely busy with school. And we simply didn't work together for very long before she left. It was all so fleeting. But now, with the benefit of so many years, I understand that I did not act simply because I was incapable of appreciating how special and rare that magical feeling of connection was."

"Well that sucks. What happened to her?"

"I've no idea," he slumped, head down. Then after a moment he sat up again, "Do you know I still think of her and wonder? All these years later." He took a long drink and set down his empty glass. "Now, I must re-fortify myself before I begin the tale of the second woman."

Once again, Sophie ducked behind the bar. "Okay, let's hear about woman number two."

He took a deep breath. "I was out of law school and had begun to practice. I had returned to Tallahassee. I had some friends and colleagues that I did some carousing with. Woman number two was somewhat a part of our group. She was very beautiful and she could be quite a bit of fun when we were out with the gang. But she wasn't very," he paused, searching for the right word, "...nice."

"Was she just a bitch?"

"Absolutely not. At the time, that is. It is difficult to describe. She wasn't horrible. Just a tad selfish, a little fake, slightly shallow, a bit negative in her ways such that most of our group kept her at arm's length. She was never bad enough that anyone hated her. And she was certainly capable of being very nice. But most of the gang could just tell. They had a sense of what kind of person she was. Call it intuition, if you will."

"Okay. Like she gave off bad vibes."

"Yes. But very subtly. Everyone believed they alone were sensing it. They all assumed that the others liked her just fine."

"What about you?"

"My experience with her was quite different. She was a very attractive woman. And she let it be known that she was interested in me romantically."

"You didn't go out with her!? Did you go out with her?"

"She was a beautiful creature. I was very flattered."

"Oh my god! Artie!" she exclaimed laughing. "You did go out with her!"

He took a drink and sighed with resignation as he gently shook his head. "Worse," he said cringing.

Sophie stared trying to imagine what would be worse than dating someone everyone could tell was generally kind of a bitch.

Artie inhaled deeply and exhaled slowly, as if steeling himself for what he was about to say. He looked up, then to the left, and then finally he met Sophie's gaze again. "I married her."

"Ohhh nooooo!!!" she exclaimed. "You didn't. Oh, Artie!"

He nodded. "I did. And they were all absolutely right about her."

"But you didn't know that they thought that!"

"It is true that I did not know how they felt about her when we began dating," he explained, "but before we were married, nearly every single person had taken me aside and cautioned me. A couple friends warned me on multiple occasions. Emphatically."

"Oh Artie," she said sympathetically. "Why didn't you listen to them? Why did you marry her?"

"That is the point of my sharing these tales," he explained. "At one time, I allowed that inexplicable feeling of connection to pass unexamined and unexplored. I did not appreciate how rare or special it was, and I failed to act." He paused and took a deep breath. "Another time, when I decided that I was ready to settle down and have a family, I allowed ego, pride, and my own hubris to delude me into believing that I would have a happy marriage because I would do what was necessary to make it be so. What I failed to realize, however, was that it was not simply up to me. I, alone, could not make it work.

"If you simply want to have children and a husband, well, that is not a particularly difficult feat to accomplish. In fact, it has been my experience that it is what most couples do. They are not all miserable. Many muddle through and make the best of their lots in life. It can be a very tolerable existence.

292

"My counsel, however, is that you do not settle for mere existence. I desire that you choose what I did not. Choose to truly live! Experience that connection, that magic. And act upon it! If you wish for children, a husband, and genuine happiness, be bold! Find your connection. Do not let it pass unexamined from your life. Do not ignore it. Pursue it. See where it can take you."

Finished, Artie turned toward his drink. Sophie had been listening intently and now sat in silence. Her eyes turned away and he could tell she was deep in thought. He permitted her to dwell there for a time before he spoke again. "You appear to recognize what I speak of. Do you not?"

"I think I do," she answered slowly.

Again he waited and allowed her to follow her thoughts. Then he asked, "You have experienced this connection? Yes?"

Sophie was thinking about the morning she left Richmond. And how, for reasons she didn't fully understand, she stopped by the place where Guy worked. And wrote down her name. She thought about their easy conversation at The Duke the night before. And how wonderful it felt to get his letter.

"Maybe?" she answered. "How would I know?"

"Ahh," Artie replied. "You wouldn't know. It does not exist on the plane of knowledge. It cannot be known, only felt. You would feel it and that is your challenge. To recognize and to trust those feelings. To risk the unknown."

As they sat there, listening to the muted sounds of "Margaritaville" drifting down from upstairs, the phone rang. Sliding off her stool, Sophie ducked behind the bar and picked up the handset. "Toucan's," she announced.

"Hi," the man's voice said. "I'm trying to reach Sophie Ross. I'm a friend of hers in Illinois. Is she working tonight?"

Chapter 54

"What do you mean he can't go?!" Laura was stunned.

"It's his dad again."

"Is he in the hospital?"

"No! Jesus. Could you at least try not to sound so excited about the thought of this man dying?" This was exactly why she had put off telling her friend. The closer this plan was to succeeding, the more excited Laura was. She hadn't been able to stop talking about Donavan's and calling with suggestions about what to do or not do and what to say and not say. It was constant strategizing. She'd even forced Michele to go shopping and helped her pick out a new outfit just for New Year's Eve. Though she hadn't said anything to her friend, the more Laura drove everything forward, the more Michele wanted to retreat. More and more doubts were creeping in. "The woman who was working there just quit," she explained.

"You're right," Laura acknowledged. "I'm sorry." Then she quickly forged ahead. "So, she quit. What does that mean? Guy's not allowed to go anywhere?"

"Not really. He's stuck. His dad needs to have somebody there with him."

"Well, shit." She thought about it for a moment. "Isn't there anybody else that can stay with him for the night?"

"I guess not. I'm pretty sure he doesn't have any other family around."

"Yeah. I think you're right. I'm pretty sure he has a sister who's way older than he is, but I don't think she lives anywhere around here. What about like some kind of temp agency? Can't they get like an adult sitter? Isn't that a thing? I think that's a thing!" She started to sound excited again.

"Yeah, I think you're right. In Chicago maybe. Nobody does that out here. Besides, it's New Year's Eve, Laura. And it's tomorrow night. I mean, even if there was a company around here, don't you think it's kind of late? Besides that, who would be paying for it? Guy doesn't have any money."

"I suppose." Laura wasn't giving up though. "What about your mom? What's she doing? Would she be willing to help? I'd offer up my mom, but she's going to have my kids."

"What? My mom? Oh my god no. What would I even say to Guy? And can you imagine how awkward that would be for my mom? And his dad? Jesus Christ Laura!" Michele was exasperated. "I mean I get it. It's disappointing," she lied. "But it is what it is. He can't go to Donavan's."

Laura was quiet for a moment. Then, "What if we just stayed in town? I mean, maybe we could just go to The Duke? Would that work? He'd probably like that better anyway!"

"No," Michele lied again. "He really just needs to be at his dad's." Going to The Duke instead was an idea that she'd already thought of. But she didn't ask Guy because she didn't want to know the answer. "He did say that he'd only be stuck for a few days. They're supposed to get a new person next week," she told Laura, hoping that would convince her to give it up for New Year's Eve.

"That's good, I guess. Did you two make a plan for next weekend then?"

"No. I did mention it, but he said he didn't want to have to cancel on me. Again. He said he'd let me know when they hired someone." That part was mostly true. She did say to him, generically, that they should get together some other time. And he replied with the same kind of vague assurance, "Yeah, sure, I'll let you know when things settle down."

Chapter 55

"This is Sophie," she replied slowly.

"Sophie? Hi Sophie, it's Guy! Your pen pal. From Richmond."

"Guy! Hey Guy! What's going on? Is everything okay?" Her mind searched for a reason for the call.

"Yeah, yeah," he assured her. "Everything's fine. Everyone is good. How about you?"

She looked at Artie, an exaggerated look of shock on her face, and pointed at the receiver. "I'm great. But listen, I am at work. Is there a number where I can call you back?"

"Yeah, sure. You ready?"

Sophie grabbed a pen and a cocktail napkin. "Ok. I'm ready."

"I'm going to give you two numbers, okay?"

"Sure."

Guy read off his own phone number and that of his father's house. "You'll be able to reach me at one of those."

"Okay."

"Hey, I'm sorry to bug you at work. I didn't know how else to reach you."

"You're not bugging me," she smiled. "I'm happy to hear from you. It's been raining for a while now," she explained, "so we're not very busy now anyway."

"Okay. Good. Listen, really quick, before I let you get back to work. My father's caregiver just quit unexpectedly. And I wanted to know if there was any chance you might be interested in the job?"

Sophie was silent.

"Look, I don't need an answer right now or anything. And I mean, I get it if you say no. Don't worry about it. You don't need to explain it. I just, I don't know, my father is always saying he wants an American and..." he hesitated, and then went for it, "... it'd be great to see you again. We never really got to finish our conversation. We were going to help each other figure out what to do with our lives."

"Oh wow, Guy," a hundred different thoughts raced through her mind: being a caregiver again, going back to Illinois, quitting Toucan's, leaving Artie's, and more. Despite all of that, her gut and her heart wanted to immediately tell him yes. But a lifetime of measured, disciplined thinking and decision-making simply would not allow her to blurt it out. Instead, she stammered, "Oh, man...uhh...I mean...I guess I... ummm..."

"Look, just think about it. Give me a call whenever. Okay? Sophie?"

"Okay," she answered finally collecting herself. "Yeah, just give me a little time. Let me sleep on it."

"Okay. Sounds good. Thanks. I'll talk to you soon."

Gently, Sophie set the phone back in the cradle. Then she turned toward Artie wearing a dumbfounded expression.

"Is everything okay?" he asked.

She nodded, thinking. Then, slowly she told him, "Artie, I think I'm going to move back to Illinois."

"Really?" He was taken aback. "Right away?"

She nodded. "I think so."

"May I inquire as to who was on the phone?"

"That was Guy."

"Guy? Who is this Guy?"

"I'm going to go back to Illinois and find out."

Chapter 56

"Good afternoon, my friend," Guy greeted Jacque with a pat on the back as he sat down on the stool next to him. "It's a beautiful day out today, isn't it?"

Jacque leaned back to examine a broadly grinning Guy. "Well, ladies' man," Jacque guessed, "either you found someone to watch your dad for you tonight and your date with Michele is back on, or you heard from Sophie and she is on her way back from Florida. Or even better! Both!"

"Sophie called this morning. She's going to do it. She's going to take the job." He was beaming. "Dude, we talked for a long time, too. She's going to leave tomorrow morning and drive to Nashville. Then from Nashville to here the next day. She'll be here Tuesday night!"

"That is good news, my friend. I am happy for you. Mindy, get this man a beer, please!" he called out. "How's it going with your dad? You're staying there now, right?"

"It's crazy," Guy said shaking his head. "I'm so happy to be in here right now. Just for the heat. Other than his bedroom, that house is freezing. I'm sure it costs a fortune to heat, but come on. If other people are going to be living there, what the fuck? Turn the damn heat up." He hugged himself and rubbed his arms briskly. "I'm still trying to warm up."

Guy continued, "After I packed up some of my shit and was on my way to his house Saturday, I was trying to psych myself up. I was trying to think about it like work. You know how you talked about the difference between hating my job and hating the idea of my job?"

"Yeah," nodded Jacque.

298

"Yeah, well," Guy laughed, "I hate the idea of this job...and I hate the actual job."

Jacque grimaced. "That is a tough spot to be in."

Guy shrugged. "He's just not a pleasant person. But I feel way better knowing that I only have to be there through Tuesday. I can get through a few days. Plus, he's actually happy about the fact that I found an 'American gal.'"

"That's cool."

"Yeah, except of course he had to use it like an 'I told you so.'" Guy imitated his father's condescending speech, "'I knew there would be an American gal who would want this job. You just needed to look around.'" He rolled his eyes and took a drink of his beer. "So, you got big plans tonight? I heard Donavan's had a last-minute cancelation. You could probably get a reservation up there?"

"Ha! I'm happy to see you have a sense of humor about it now. I think I'd still be upset about missing out on that." Jacque closed his eyes for a moment. "Mmmm-mm. That Michele is a fine-looking woman."

"I know," Guy agreed. "But I think I'm actually a little relieved."

"How so?"

"I don't know. I mean, she's just...it just doesn't make sense. Do you know where she lives?"

Jacque shook his head, "Where does she live?"

"She lives in one of those big houses in Sundial Farms."

"So what?"

"It's not just that. It's Donavan's. It's going out dancing afterwards. I don't want to go dancing at a club. She's got a daughter in high school. I don't have kids. I don't know how to relate to that. We're pretty different."

"I can see that," Jacque nodded.

"And that night when we were out? When Dean was in town?"

"Yeah?"

"She was visiting with someone, catching up, you know? She was talking about skiing in Colorado. About going to Hilton Head. All these vacations. You know what I did yesterday before I went to my father's?"

"What?"

"I went to Penney's to return my dress pants and shirt." He laughed. "And I was thrilled to get my $43 back. Which reminds me, I have that tie I borrowed from you in my car."

"I guess I get what you're saying."

"I mean, she's great. She's nice. We just don't have anything in common. And really, what the hell would I do dating her? I can't take her anywhere. I couldn't even afford to go with her if she invited me somewhere. I was freaking out about Donavan's. What would I do if she wanted to go on a trip?"

"Has she asked you to go on a trip?"

"No."

"Well then, what the hell are you worried about? Stop overthinking it. Sometimes just take a ride. Roll with it. It wouldn't hurt you to have a little fun with her. She is fun."

"I suppose."

"Besides," Jacque cautioned him, "I don't want to burst your bubble, but you really don't know what's going to happen with Sophie."

Guy sighed and reluctantly agreed. "I know. You're right. I get ahead of myself."

"It's okay. I'm just saying, you have no reason to completely bail on Michele yet. A bird in the hand, you know what I'm saying?"

"Yeah."

After watching the Bears somehow battle to a halftime tie against a clearly better 49ers team, Guy turned to his friend as he stood, "You have fun tonight, man."

"You leaving?"

"Yeah. I need to stop by Van's to pick up something to eat. My dad gets his food through that tube, so there's never any groceries in the house. Plus, I need to go by my apartment to get another sweatshirt."

"Alright, my friend," Jacque grinned, "See—"

"Don't say it!" Guy interrupted as he stood putting his coat on.

"What?" Jacque laughed.

Bear noticed Guy getting ready to leave. "Hey Guy!" he called out. "You coming back later tonight?"

"No man. I can't. I gotta open tomorrow morning anyway."

"Alright," he paused and grinned at Jacque before calling out, "See you next year!"

Guy turned and walked out with his middle finger extended over his head while Bear and Jacque had their laugh.

Still laughing, Bear walked over by Jacque. "I don't get why he hates that so much."

"I don't either, but I'm glad he does."

"So where's he going?"

"He's stuck taking care of his dad for a few days."

"Wow. Hard to believe that guy is still alive."

"Yeah. That's what I've heard. Guy's told me some of the shit. Must be a tough bastard."

"I don't know him at all. He's always been pretty reclusive. You ever see that house though?"

Jacque shook his head. "Unh-uh."

"The thing is ridiculous. When he does finally kick the bucket, Guy's going to be rolling in it."

"Oh yeah?" said Jacque noncommittally.

"He's supposed to be loaded." Then Bear lowered his voice and leaned in toward Jacque. "I hear a ton of shit walking around this bar all of the time. You know? Bits and pieces of conversations. And between you and me, I'm pretty sure that's why that Michele chick has been after him. She wants to get her hands on all that money."

"Get the fuck out of here."

"I didn't want to say anything, because I don't know anything for sure," Bear continued, "but I'm serious, dude. I guess she's pretty much broke."

Chapter 57

"Happy New Year's Eve!" Laura announced from Michele's doorstep earlier that evening.

"What are you doing here?"

Laura brushed past her carrying a grocery bag and strode toward her friend's kitchen. "You need to go and get ready, honey."

Michele closed the front door and followed her. "What are you talking about? Guy can't go!"

Laura set the bag down on the counter and began unloading it. "You have a date tonight," she said as she held up a bottle of white wine. "We need to keep this chilled for you."

"What are you doing? What is this?"

"You," Laura said triumphantly, "are going to bring your date to him."

"What?!"

"Look," she explained. "It's New Year's Eve. You know he is just going to be sitting there at his dad's house. He can't go anywhere. He's not doing anything tonight. You are going to surprise him with," she reached into the bag, "his favorite beverage," she said, pulling out a six pack of MGD and putting it in the fridge next to the bottle of wine.

"Oh my god, Laura!"

"There's more!" she said excitedly. "There's popcorn for your movie, and I couldn't decide," she said holding up two VHS tapes, "*Groundhog Day*? It's both funny and romantic. Or I have *Boogie Nights*. It's pretty much just sex. Either way," she reached into the bag again, "hopefully you'll be needing these." She tossed Michele a package of condoms.

"Oh my god, Laura!"

"Wait! I have one more thing!" She reached into the bag and pulled out a bottle of champagne and two plastic champagne flutes. "Some bubbly for your toast at midnight!"

"Oh my god," she repeated. "You are crazy! I don't know if I can do this. Can I do this?"

"Honey," Laura advised her, "this is a perfect plan. It's way better than going up to Donavan's and going out to dinner. You said that wasn't his kind of place anyway. You're going to show up with everything. You cuddle up on the couch, you watch a movie together, have a few drinks… It's genius! Plus, Carly's with Troy. You won't have to worry about getting back here tonight. You're going to have a great evening. You've got this!"

Michele took a deep breath, thinking. Earlier that afternoon, she had alternated between relief and panic. She had been ready to quit on Guy. But then she thought about the reality that her maintenance ran out in the summer of 1999. And tomorrow would be the first day of 1999. Guy was definitely the best option they'd found. Staring at Laura's expectant, excited face, she had to admit that it was a great idea. *What the hell*, she decided. *I can give this one last shot.* "Okay. But I need a drink. Will you make me a drink? There's some Captain in the pantry."

"That a girl!" Laura grabbed the rum, two glasses, and some Coke from the fridge.

"Unh-uh. More," commanded Michele as soon as Laura had stopped pouring the rum. "This may be a great plan, but I haven't had any time to psych myself up for this. I'm going to need all the extra help I can get."

They drank and debated the relative merits of *Groundhog Day* versus *Boogie Nights*. Laura argued for *Boogie Nights* as it was less ambiguous. "It's like what Ron said about going inside and buying gum when you went to get gas. If you want something, don't beat around the bush. Be direct. Don't expect him to read your mind."

"True, I get that. But he's also supposed to believe that I want a relationship. Some romance. Not just sex."

"That's true, I suppose."

"And cozying up on a couch for a movie? Well, that's going to lead to something. Don't you think?"

"It better!" Laura exclaimed. "I guess *Groundhog Day* will work. It's pretty romantic. Here," she said topping off Michele's drink, "now go get yourself ready. It's already almost six-thirty."

Fifteen minutes later, Michele stood in the shower letting the hot water run over her, hesitant to turn it off. Once she did, time would begin to move forward again. She would be getting out and getting dressed. And then going to see Guy. Finally collecting herself, she stepped out, grabbed her towel, and hollered downstairs, "Laura! More Captain and Coke please!"

Laura joined her in the enormous master bathroom. "Pace yourself, honey," she said setting a fresh drink on the counter.

"I will." She picked it up and took a couple of big swallows. "I just need to get to a good buzz right now. I'm still kind of freaking out," she confessed.

"What's the matter?"

"I'm nervous. When I made this plan, I guess I thought that I would get some guy to chase *me* and, if I decided he was the one, then I would play along and let myself get caught. You know? Like I'd be doing him a favor."

"Ha!" Laura laughed. "Damn, it must be nice to look like you."

"Well, I'm serious!" she protested. "I don't know what to do. I've never had to do this kind of thing before."

"Look, you are going to have to take charge. Seduce him."

Michele sighed. "I know," she acknowledged. "But it's hard to make the first move."

"You might have to."

"Besides, it's weird that it's Guy. I don't know. He's like a friend."

"Honey," Laura leaned back and gazed at Michele, concerned. "It's pretty late in the game for all of these doubts. And if you like him as a friend, I don't see how that's a problem in this situation. That's a good thing."

"I just don't feel like I'm being honest."

"Oh, honey," Laura hugged her friend. Then she put her hands on her shoulders and looked her in the eyes. "Listen to me. Guy is my friend, too. If I really thought you were screwing him over, I would say something. For real. I like both of you. And I really think you two can be happy together."

"Really?"

"Yes. Absolutely! And I mean, come on," she gestured toward her friend's reflection in the mirror. "Look at you Michele. You're gorgeous! It's Guy. Who never even dates! Jesus Christ, honey! You're going to be the best thing that ever happened to him!"

Ninety minutes and two more Captain and Cokes later, Michele gratefully spotted the overgrown entrance to the home of Charles Bradford. The rum had kicked in by then and she was relieved to be getting off the road. Turning into the driveway for the first time, she cautiously followed her headlights as they illuminated the winding snow-packed driveway. The moon was near the horizon and less than half full, but its reflection off the snow made it bright enough that she involuntarily gasped when she turned the last corner and the entirety of the imposing gray stone manor came into view. Laura wasn't kidding about the size of it, but if it weren't for a faint light leaking out through one window to the left of the front door, she would have guessed it was abandoned. "Holy shit," she whispered.

Michele parked next to Guy's car, took a deep breath, and gave herself a quick check in the visor mirror. Holding her gaze on her reflection, she was stern, "You can give this one more shot." Then she flipped the visor up and got out of her car.

As Guy momentarily halted his strumming to adjust the positioning of his fingers on the frets, he was surprised by his father's seldom-heard door chimes. Setting his guitar on the bed, he walked out of his room and past two other bedrooms toward the great staircase that curved as it cascaded down into the foyer and the main entrance. All the while he tried to imagine who could possibly be standing on his father's porch at almost eight-thirty on New Year's Eve. Guy illuminated the front of the house and peered out through the ornamental glass that bracketed the massive wooden door. He could make out the distorted image of what appeared to be a solitary woman and, before he realized it wasn't possible, found himself very excited at the idea that it might be Sophie already. Instead of Sophie, Guy opened the door to reveal a shivering Michele.

"Happy New Year!" she exclaimed brightly.

"Oh, hey, Michele," he stammered. "Happy New Year. Come on in. What's up?"

"Well, since you weren't able to go out tonight, I decided to bring a little New Year's cheer to you." She handed him the six-pack of MGD and held up the bag in her other hand.

"Oh, wow. That's great. That's really cool. Thank you," he said. "Here, let me take that. Come in."

Michele stepped inside the dimly lit foyer and stomped bits of snow off her shoes while Guy set the beer on a table and took the bag from her. She opened her arms and moved to embrace him, but her timing was off. Guy still held the bag in one hand and she barely managed to peck his cheek as he gave her a brief and awkward one-armed hug.

Guy set the bag down next to the beer and offered to take her coat before stopping himself. "Look," he sighed, "you're probably going to want to wear it. This is as high as my father will allow the thermostat to be set. I mean, I'll take it if you want, but I have two shirts on underneath this," he gestured to his sweatshirt, "and I'm still kind of chilly."

Feeling warmed by the rum, Michele knew that her snug black top with the plunging neckline would be useless to her if it stayed hidden under a bulky winter coat. "Thanks, but I'm pretty warm blooded," she lied as she took it off and handed it to him.

Determined to get a better hug and hopefully a decent kiss, she waited behind him while he hung her coat in the closet. As he turned around, she smiled coyly and said, "Just warm me up for a minute. It's cold outside and I was beginning to wonder if you were really home."

"Oh sure," he obliged. Then Guy wrapped his arms around her and held her close while he vigorously rubbed her back, shoulders, and arms in an attempt to warm her up. "Sorry about the wait. I was upstairs. It's freezing out, isn't it?"

Michele snuggled into him and he put his arms around her. He could feel

306

her entire body pressing into his as she offered her blissful reply, "This is so much better." The smell of alcohol on her breath was unmistakable. Guy held her and wondered how much she'd already had to drink. Based on the weirdly uncomfortable length of the hug he was giving her, he decided it must have been a lot.

"Is that better?" he finally asked.

Definitely better than the first one, she thought. "Yes, thank you."

Guy released her, grabbed the bag and the beer, turned off the outside lights, and said, "Come on, let's get this in the fridge."

Michele followed him out of the foyer, through a darkened, very ornate formal dining room, and into an oversized kitchen where Guy turned on the light. As he put the beer in the almost completely empty refrigerator, a voice, barely audible over the blaring of a television, called out from a stepped-down living room to her left. "Who's here?"

"My friend Michele," Guy answered loudly. "Come on," he said more quietly to her, "let me introduce you."

Friend? she thought as she followed him down the steps, *we'll see about that.* The cavernous living room with its vaulted ceilings was dimly lit with one small table lamp. In a far corner, Michele could make out the disheveled form of a man she assumed to be Charles Bradford. His sat in a recliner with his feet up, wrapped in a blanket that extended up to his chest. He also appeared to be wearing a coat.

"Dad, this is Michele. Michele, this is my father, Charles Bradford."

"Hello, Mr. Bradford. Nice to meet you," she said offering her hand.

Charles tried to shake her hand, but his arm was tucked into the blanket and he struggled to get it out. "Jesus Christ," he mumbled. "You've got this goddamn thing tucked in so tight." His head turned toward Michele to complain, "He's got me trapped like this." Guy moved to his side and helped free his arm. When he was able, Charles extended a shaky hand and clasped hers. "Hi. You too. What did you say your name was?"

"Her name is Michele, Dad," Guy repeated.

"I came to help Guy celebrate New Year's," she explained.

Guy was surprised to notice his father carefully scrutinizing her and was suddenly reminded of walking into The Duke with her for Dean's homecoming. A smile slowly spread across his face and he relished watching his father struggle to comprehend that the stunning, smiling woman with perfect teeth, perfect hair, and an oh-so-perfect figure standing before him, was at his house on New Year's Eve, to see his son. Guy put his arm around Michele's waist before looking directly at his father and asking, "We'll be around. Do you need anything right now?"

Charles Bradford was speechless. There was no thinly-veiled put-down, no criticism, no cutting, snide remark couched in false humor, no complaint, no subtle jab, no sarcastic aside, no belittling joke, no demeaning teasing—not a single comment designed to remind Guy of his place and that he, Charles, was in charge, in control. Only silence. For once, his father had absolutely nothing to say. It was intoxicating. Guy pulled Michele a little closer to him and kept his eyes locked on his father's. Finally, almost dismissively, he told him, "I'll come back and check on you in about an hour or so." Then, as if Charles weren't even there, Guy turned to Michele, smiled, and said, "Come on. I'm going to have a beer. And see what else is in that bag."

Buoyed by the show of affection, Michele smiled, gave Charles a little wave, and followed Guy back into the kitchen. "You grab a beer," she told him, "but I'm going to need a corkscrew." She reached into the bag and held up the bottle of wine. "Also," she added, "we're going to want to keep this chilled for later," and handed him the bottle of champagne.

"Oh wow!" he laughed. "You really came prepared!"

"Yes I did," she replied, thinking about the condoms in her purse. Michele pulled the plastic champagne flutes out of the bag and set them on the counter. Next came the popcorn and she said, "I thought we could have some of this while we," her hand went into the bag one last time, "watch a movie!"

"Hey! *Groundhog Day!* I heard that was great." The enthusiasm in his voice didn't match his expression though. "I wish there was a VCR here so we could watch it. Damn."

"No VCR? Really?" Michele was shocked.

"Nope." Guy said, shaking his head. He lowered his voice "He's convinced that when people get them, then they'll want to rent videos."

Michele hesitated. "Isn't that the point?"

"Uh-huh," Guy nodded his agreement. "But listen," he leaned in and his voice dropped to a whisper, "that man in there?" he said tilting his head toward the living room. "He's crazy."

Michele laughed way too hard at the joke.

"I'm sorry. No movie for us tonight."

"I guess we'll just have to find some other way to entertain ourselves," she smiled.

Guy looked at her for a long moment. Trying to be casual, she reached out for the counter to steady herself. She was drunk. And he couldn't find a way to make sense of it; to explain why she was here, now, drunk, swaying in his father's kitchen. Maybe Jacque was right. Maybe he needed to stop overthinking everything and just roll with it.

"Do you have a bottle opener?" she asked, breaking the silence. "I'd like a little of that wine."

"Yeah, sure," he replied, gathering himself. Guy uncorked the bottle, filled a glass, and handed it to her. "Cheers," he said tapping his beer bottle against it. "Thanks for bringing all of this stuff. I probably wasn't even going to stay up until midnight."

"Cheers," she smiled. Then she leaned in and gave him a kiss.

"Follow me," he said.

Guy grabbed the wine, they took their drinks, and left the kitchen. Not only were there a lot of rooms, Michele noticed as she trailed him, but they all appeared to be enormous. She thought about her home and the others like it in Sundial Farms and suddenly the term McMansion made a lot more sense to her. She also decided that even if Charles did live for several more years, this place would definitely be worth the wait. Houses like Michele's had rec rooms in the basement, but the room Guy ushered her into was not in a basement and it was not simply a rec room.

Sitting on an extraordinary oriental rug, a massive and ornately carved pool table was the centerpiece. Tall windows with long drapes covered either side of the large stone fireplace on the exterior wall. A sitting area with two worn, brown leather armchairs and an equally worn matching sofa was divided by a coffee table and backed by built-in bookshelves. On the far end of the room, where Guy was leading her, was a long, full bar.

"Have a seat." He set the wine bottle down and walked back to the bank of light switches near the door. Different parts of the room were briefly illuminated before he settled on the light over the pool table and one by the bar. "Play me a game?"

"Sure," she agreed. "But don't expect me to compete with someone who has his own pool table at home."

"I don't really play much. And," he corrected her. "This is not my table, and this is definitely not my home."

Not yet, she thought as she went to pick out a cue.

As they shot pool and flirted, they drank the way people attempting to drown their consciences often do. By the time the first game was over, Michele's glass was empty and she held it up to Guy. He poured her another drink and fetched himself another beer from the kitchen. After the second game, she refilled her own glass and decided that they needed some music. "I'm going to want to hear the countdown!"

Guy went upstairs to grab the portable stereo from his bedroom. When he did, the sight of his guitar lying on the bed caught his eye and stopped him. *An hour ago, I was in here practicing and looking forward to showing Sophie what I've learned,* he observed. *I was excited about being able to play a song for her. And now? Now, I'm pounding beers and shooting pool with drunk Michele. Why? Just because she showed up?* That seemed like a pretty shitty reason to Guy.

When he returned with the stereo, Michele was sitting on the couch with the little throw blanket covering her legs and lap. "It's so cold in here and I'm getting a little chilly. I was hoping you would come warm me up," she said demurely. Then she lifted up the blanket and patted the cushion next to her.

In that very unusual moment, Guy realized how grateful he was to be taking care of his father. "You know what? I should make sure my dad is set for the night first," he told her. "I'll be back in a few minutes."

"Okay," she cooed, "don't keep me waiting too long."

Guy knocked on the door to his father's chambers and called out hesitantly, "Dad?"

"In here," came the response from the bathroom.

Guy entered and stood waiting by the foot of his father's bed. "I thought I'd check to see if you needed anything before bed."

Charles exited the bathroom and shuffled toward his chair. "My sugar's too low. I need to eat a little something before I can go to bed."

"Okay," he replied. "No problem. I'll get you set up." Guy was appreciative of the extra time this would take, and he returned to the kitchen to grab a can of Ensure. "Eating a little something" was not a simple task. He took one from the pantry, went back to the bedroom and poured about half of the can into the IV bag. After it was hung from the IV pole, he helped his father with his shirt and connected the tube protruding from his abdomen to the one descending from the bottom of the IV bag. Finally, he opened the valve so that the food, such as it was, could begin slowly making its way into his father's stomach.

He sat on the foot of his father's bed and wondered what to do about Michele. Even if he came up with a reason, he couldn't make her leave. She was hammered. *Why is she so drunk?* he wondered. *That is not attractive. Maybe,* he mused, *I should tell her that I think she's drunk and crazy and although it's really cool to be seen with her, I'm just not that into her.* No, he decided, because then she'd probably just try to drive herself home. *Maybe you should stop thinking about it for once,* he scolded himself, *and go back in there and just fuck her?*

"I think this thing's done," said his father, interrupting his thoughts.

Guy got up and disconnected the bag while his father re-checked his blood sugar. Once he verified it was okay again, Guy helped him get in bed, wished him a happy New Year, and said goodnight. He left the bedroom, closed the door behind him, and paused to gather his thoughts. Then he took a deep breath and went to find Michele.

Chapter 58

Although Sophie's pace was much slower than normal, she was still able to maintain an easy jog out to the end of the pier. She'd had a late night ringing in the New Year at Toucan's but wanted to savor one last morning run before driving into another winter in northern Illinois. Lingering to catch her breath, Sophie closed her eyes and slowly inhaled the humid salty air through her nose. After two months the scent of it remained exotic and she wanted to be able to take it with her, if only in her mind. Turning back toward the beach, she did the same with the little town laid out before her on the other side of the dunes.

Sophie couldn't remember how many different towns, people, and places she'd said goodbye to over the years. It was just something she did; it was a part of her life. This morning was different. Never before had she been so excited about leaving and yet so disappointed to be doing so.

By the time Sophie returned from her run, Artie was awake and had a pot of coffee ready. He sat at the kitchen table sipping a cup, looking every bit of his sixty-six years.

"Good morning, Artie. Happy New Year" she greeted him as she came in through the sliding glass door. "I hope I didn't wake you up when I left."

"Not at all, my dear," he assured her. "My ability to sleep in coincidentally abandoned me the same time I once again began requiring an afternoon nap. Regardless, I would have been greatly disappointed were I not able to see you off this morning."

She poured herself a cup of coffee and joined him at the table. "I'm happy you are up. Thanks for making the coffee."

"I quite need it this morning. Happy New Year indeed," he sighed. "Are you sure I cannot convince you to remain another day and get some proper rest before you begin such a long drive?"

"I'm only planning on driving as far as Nashville tonight. And I promise I'll stop sooner if I am too tired. I'm too anxious to sleep anyway."

"Yes, I imagine so. I find myself with tremendous anticipation for your venture as well."

She took a deep breath. "I'm nervous, Artie."

"Certainly to be expected. There are so few sure things in this life." He sipped his coffee. "One of them, however, is that my door will always be open for you. Should this man prove himself to be a complete and utter fool, it is my sincere desire that you will return and seek refuge once more here in Mexico Beach."

Sophie could feel the tears welling up in her eyes and didn't bother to try and stop them. "I don't know how I can ever thank you."

He smiled broadly, leered, and raised his eyebrows up and down. "You can come have that lunch with me in Tallahassee."

She laughed and wiped the tears from her cheek. "You have my word on it."

Chapter 59

After scraping the ice from his own windows, Guy cleared the ice off Michele's as well. He was happy about getting up and out of the house without waking her and hoped she'd be able to sleep in. Maybe she would have coffee with his dad, he laughed. Before he left, he quietly set up his father's breakfast by hanging a fresh IV bag of Ensure behind his chair. When Charles woke up and was ready to eat, he'd only need to sit down and connect the tubes. Guy also taped a big note to the middle of the television set. He really wanted his father to have everything already hooked up before he noticed it. He liked the idea of him not being able to watch the TV and instead being forced to sit there for twenty minutes looking at the large words written in black marker taped to a sheet of white paper in the middle of his screen.

HAPPY NEW YEAR!
FYI—Michele is still here.
She spent the night.

Michele eased into consciousness, afraid to open her eyes or move. First, she became aware that she was still at Guy's dad's house. Second, she was more relieved than disappointed to determine that she was still wearing her clothes. Third, she was disappointed in herself for being relieved. She opened her eyes to the sight of a sideways pool table and realized that she must be lying on the sofa in the billiards room. Michele sat up, rubbed the sleep out of her eyes, and felt the expected and well-deserved headache beginning to punish her. Feeling like an idiot and a failure, she sighed and said quietly, "Happy New Year Michele."

On the coffee table in front of her was the bag she'd brought with her, a bottle of water, a bottle of Tylenol, and a note. She did not move. She had no desire to read the note. She knew there was nothing in any note that could possibly alleviate her humiliation. Michele glumly sat there and stared at nothing while she tried to piece together the previous night. *The stupid rum*, was her first thought. Then she saw that although her glass still had a little wine in it, the empty bottle sat next to it on the bar. *And all that wine.* She recalled that the night had started out pretty well. They'd played some pool. She remembered being cold and getting under the blanket on the couch. And then Guy had to go do something for his dad. And it felt like he was gone forever. And then she just couldn't keep her eyes open.

Michele did not feel good about herself or her life at the moment. She showed up uninvited. Then passed out by, what, ten? Ten-thirty maybe? Because she was drunk. And she was drunk because that was the only way she could be such a selfish person. It didn't matter what Laura said. This whole thing was wrong and she knew it. And today was the first day of 1999. She was going to have to get some super lame job. She was going to have to sell her house. And Troy would be sure to rub her face in it. Then she thought about having to tell Carly that she would have to sell the house. Michele sat on the expensive leather sofa in the billiard room of the great stone manor house belonging to Charles Bradford, put her head in her hands, and cried.

As the tears slowed, Michele sniffed and wiped her eyes on the blanket. The morning light continued to creep into the room, and for the first time she noticed that she had an actual pillow and blanket, not just the little throw from the night before. When she imagined Guy going to get that stuff so her dumb, drunk ass wouldn't freeze, she felt even worse. And as she reached for the water and Tylenol he'd left for her, she started crying again. The second round of tears didn't last long and she chugged most of the water with a few capsules before sitting, staring, and thinking again.

Michele was grateful that the house was quiet. Her phone showed 7:30am, but fortunately nothing from Laura. She was going to have to tell her friend that she was done with this. She couldn't do it anymore. I'm just going to have to be poor again, she thought and was surprised at how empty she felt about it. Then Michele decided that there wasn't anything left to do but get her stuff and go home. Maybe she could climb back into bed and sleep for the rest of the day. Maybe for the rest of the year, she thought. Then, when she woke up again, everything would be fixed and she wouldn't have to deal with any of it.

Michele leaned forward and looked inside her bag sitting on the coffee table in front of her. The movie and the box of microwave popcorn were tucked in with the unopened bottle of champagne and the two plastic flutes. She allowed herself a half smile. Laura had come up with a pretty damn good plan. Too bad Guy's dad didn't just have a stupid VCR, she thought. Then, she decided that she should probably be grateful that he didn't, because if he did, she probably wouldn't be sitting here alone, crying in her clothes. She probably would have ended up sleeping with him. And then what? It would no longer be awkward with him? No, she sighed. They tried. They liked each other well enough, but there was just no spark. It was pointless. Finally, Michele picked up the note.

Good Morning and Happy New Year!
Thanks for coming to celebrate with me last night.
If you're reading this after 7, it means I'm at work already.
Also, my dad knows you stayed over.
He might be up and around when you get up.
P.S. I thought you might need these
Guy

When Big John showed up at eleven-thirty and Guy walked out of the Gas and Go a few minutes later, he felt like he hadn't worked very much at all. Opening late and leaving early should feel a lot better than this, he thought as he got in his car. But then the only thing he was going to do was return to his father's house and deal with his picky bullshit and mind games for another day. Work would be a much better option. He smiled. *More evidence that Jacque is right; I really don't hate my job after all!*

He considered this as he was passing Not Your Average Bakery!, abruptly hit the brakes, and found a parking spot on the street. He checked the time and decided his father would survive a slight delay while he said hi to his friend. Plus, he was sure Jacque would like to hear about his surprise visitor last night.

Guy nodded to the counter girl and cut around into the back. Jacque had his back to him so he called out, "Hey! Happy New Year!"

Jacque turned and smiled but kept working as he said, "You too, my friend! What's up? You surviving at your dad's?"

"I'm headed there right now. It's going to be weird when Sophie gets here tomorrow. Normally I pretty much flee as soon as I can. But I'm really looking forward to seeing her."

"I hope all that works out," he paused, "for you and for your dad."

"Yeah, me too. Listen, I know you're busy, but guess who showed up last night?"

"Showed up where? At your dad's?"

"Yeah," Guy lowered his voice, "Rang the doorbell at about eight-thirty. Wasted."

Jacque stopped working and stared at him. He immediately recalled what Bear had told him about Michele the previous day. Watching the rest of the game, he had considered the likelihood of those rumors being true. He decided that everything made a lot more sense if they were. Jacque was also glad that it seemed like Guy wasn't that interested. He was much more excited about Sophie coming back. If Michele was just interested in Guy for his dad's money, he hoped that he never had to find out.

"You going to make a guess?"

Jacque shook his head, dreading the answer, "I don't know."

"Michele!" Guy had a huge smile. "Dude, she brought me beer, a movie, a bottle of champagne for a midnight toast! She said she felt bad that I had to cancel our date so she was bringing the date to me."

"Seriously?" Fuck, thought Jacque. That sneaky fucking bitch.

"And I thought about what you said, man."

Jacque could feel a pit in his stomach. He knew exactly what he said. But he asked anyway, "What's that?"

"You told me to stop overthinking everything. You said to 'just roll with it and have a little fun.'"

"Oh, yeah," he pretended to recall. "So," he dreaded getting an answer, but had to ask the question, "did you?"

"I tried, dude. She was drunk and being all lovey and shit. But I couldn't do it. I just wasn't into it." He shrugged and put his arms out, "Go ahead, tell me what an idiot I am."

Jacque wanted to hug him, he was so relieved. He smiled and said, "You are a much wiser man than me, my friend. I think you made a good decision."

"Seriously!?"

"Absolutely. You have to be authentic. You have to be who you are."

"Yeah, I suppose."

"So how did you get rid of her?"

"Oh man, that was the worst. I didn't know what I was going to say. Plus, she was wasted, so I couldn't just make her leave. I wouldn't have let her drive anywhere. It was so fucked up!"

Jacque glared, "Language," he hissed.

"Sorry!" he winced.

"What did you do?"

Guy laughed. "I went to go get my dad set up for bed. And when I came back, she was passed out on the couch. I got her a blanket and a pillow and I went to bed."

"Get the fuck out!" Jacque laughed.

"Language!" Guy scolded. "And it was only like ten-thirty!"

"She must have been wrecked."

"I'm telling you, she was drunk when she showed up. Then she killed almost an entire bottle of wine. She was still passed out when I left this morning."

"Jesus, I hope she's up by now."

"Oh man, she better not still be there!"

"Maybe she's hanging out with your dad?" Jacque laughed.

"That was the best part! I forgot to tell you!"

"What?"

"My father! You should have seen the look on his face when I introduced her. It was beautiful! She's so hot and she comes in all smiling. She looked so good and she's got her arm around me and she's being all touchy-feely with me when I introduced her to my dad. He always has some kind of negative comment, but he just sat there. He didn't know what to say. It was so cool. Plus," he continued even more enthusiastically, "I had to leave him a note this morning letting him know that she spent the night! I didn't want her to end up scaring the shit out of him when she got up. He's not going to know she passed out on the couch. He's gotta think I nailed her last night!"

Chapter 60

After Michele read Guy's note, a desire to avoid any further humiliation motivated her to get off the couch and start moving. She folded her blanket and found a bathroom where she tried to make herself look a little less like a woman who had passed out drunk and slept in her clothes. Deciding it was useless, she pinned her hopes on walking very quietly through the house, finding her coat, and slipping out the door un-noticed. When Michele slowly opened the door and peered into the hall, she realized that the direction of the front door was a mystery to her. "Stupid giant house," she cursed under her breath. Closing her eyes, taking a deep breath, and making her best guess, she stepped out of the bathroom and began tiptoeing very quickly down the hall to her left.

"Good morning," Charles greeted her when she ended up in the kitchen. "Would you like a cup of coffee?"

"Oh, good morning," she replied as she forced her best impression of a cheerful smile onto her face. He was sitting at the table in the corner and she hadn't seen him.

"There should be another mug in the cabinet just above the coffee pot."

She stared for a moment as the meaning of his words wandered through the fog of her hangover in search of comprehension. "No," she finally replied through her plastered-on smile. "Thank you, though." Then, baffling both herself and Charles, she added, "I have an appointment." Michele noticed his head tilt slightly to the side as he recognized the exceptional unlikelihood of a seven-thirty am New Year's Day appointment moments before she did. Holding fast to her smile, she prayed he would let the

320

obvious absurdity go unchallenged.

"Oh," said Charles, kindly playing along, "well, it was nice meeting you."

"Yes, thank you. You too," she replied before fleeing.

Once home, Michele sought sanctuary in her own bed and remained there, dozing off and on until the late afternoon. Finally, hunger and obligation forced her into a sitting position and then she checked her phone. She had a Happy New Year text from Carly and of course Laura had been trying to reach her. The last text from her friend said, "At least lmk you're alive." Reluctantly, she called her.

"Oh my god! The suspense has been killing me all day!" exclaimed Laura.

"I'm sorry."

"Well?"

"It was awful."

"What happened?"

Silence.

"But you're okay."

"Yes..." Michele hesitated, "...but no."

"I'm coming over."

"Will you bring me something to eat? I'm starving."

Thirty minutes later, the sound of Michele's garage door notified her that Laura had arrived and was letting herself in. She put on some sweats and plodded down the stairs.

"Oh, honey," Laura said to her when she shuffled into the kitchen, "come here." She gave her a long hug. "I'm sorry it didn't go well."

Michele sighed with resignation and said, "Don't be. Don't be sorry. You were right. This was a bad idea."

Laura was confused. "I thought we both liked the idea?"

"No, not last night. The whole thing. Trying to find a guy for me to marry. I can't do it," she explained. "I have to sell my house."

Laura could see the tears welling up in her friend's eyes and she hugged her again while Michele cried on her shoulder. "Oh honey, I'm sorry." When she was cried out, they sat down at the kitchen table. "Tell me what happened."

"There's not much to tell," she shrugged. "I basically showed up, pounded a bottle of wine, and passed out on his couch."

"Oh my god," Laura gasped. "You didn't."

Michele nodded. "He has to think I'm the biggest loser in the world."

"You didn't really do that. Did you fall asleep during the movie?"

"We didn't even watch the movie. His dad doesn't own a VCR."

"Really? So when did you fall asleep?"

"He had to go help his dad with something. And I fell asleep while he was gone."

"Did you kiss him at midnight? Did anything happen? How did the champagne go over?"

"The champagne is in my car. With the condoms. Laura," she confessed, "I passed out by like ten-thirty."

Although she was fighting to keep it in, a small giggle escaped from Laura. She bit her lip and tried not to smile.

"It's not funny!" Michele protested.

"I know! I know!" Laura agreed, battling. But more giggles came.

"Stop it!" Michele scolded as her own expression betrayed her with a smile.

Laura tried closing her eyes and clenching her jaw, but when she heard Michele snort trying to control her own self it proved useless and both surrendered to an onslaught of laughter.

When they had mostly recovered, Michele rehashed the details of the night to the best of her ability. She told her friend about the ridiculous house and meeting Charles both last night and again that morning.

"I told him I had an appointment," Michele said and they both burst out laughing again.

"Oh honey," Laura said as they once again recovered, "I'm sorry I pushed you. I really thought you two would be a good fit."

"I know. He's such a nice guy. He even cleaned the frost off my car windows before he left this morning." She sighed. "But I just can't pretend to feel what I don't feel."

Chapter 61

When the alarm clock in Guy's childhood bedroom started buzzing at its usual pre-dawn time on January 2, 1999, he did not hit the snooze button. Instead, he turned it off, sat up, and announced his number, "Three thousand, two hundred and eleven." It was no longer a complaint or a burden. It had become a challenge and he called it out with a grim determination. Another day at Big John's Gas and Go? Fine. Bring it on. He understood that he didn't hate the job. And he knew nobody lived forever.

It was, of course, cold in his room, and Guy dressed quickly before hustling through the rest of his morning routine. Once he was ready, he crept into his father's bedroom to set up his breakfast. It was rare that this woke him and for that, Guy was grateful. By the time he was finished, there were still about ten minutes remaining before he would need to leave for work. Instead of picking up his guitar, Guy walked around the house looking for anything he might have missed in the couple of hours he spent cleaning the previous night. Sophie would be arriving sometime that evening.

With kids still on break from school, work was both busier and steadier than a normal Tuesday. That increase in activity, however, did little to offset time's natural inclination to resist passage in the face of anticipation. Despite his best efforts, Guy was unable to keep his eyes off the clock. He estimated that it was an eight-hour drive from Nashville. If she left at eight and stopped for food and gas, he guessed that she would be getting to Richmond between five and six o'clock. If she left at ten that meant it would be closer to seven or eight. All morning he played with the numbers in his head and imagined where on the road she might be. When Big John finally relieved him, it felt like he was leaving late rather than two hours early. He thanked him and went to confront Charles about the temperature in his house.

Ten minutes later Guy was parking his car in his father's driveway and getting out to light a cigarette. Although there was snow on the ground, it wasn't deep, and he appreciated being able to walk down by the creek before going inside. He wanted to collect his thoughts and review the arguments he intended to make in an effort to convince his father to turn the heat up a couple of degrees. He was expecting a battle. Guy had not sugarcoated anything about his father in his conversation with Sophie. But he also knew that the man had to be experienced to be fully appreciated. It was important to him to do whatever he could so that she would be comfortable.

Guy found his father bundled up in his recliner, watching the financial news network with the stock ticker scrolling across the bottom of the screen. "Hey Dad," he called out.

Charles looked up. "When did you get here?"

"I just walked in." Guy stood at the top of the steps. Charles didn't say anything and Guy caught himself waiting. Typically, there was more. His father would have questions for him about why he did or didn't do something. Or the way in which he did it. There would be some complaint or suggestion or overly specific instructions for a task. The nitpicking, the baiting would commence, Guy would weather it the best he could, and then they would move on. That was the routine. But today there was nothing. He decided not to question it, went to fetch that morning's IV bag from his father's bedroom, and returned to the kitchen to clean it out.

"Are you hungry?" he asked over the sound of the television.

"What time is it?"

"Almost twelve-thirty."

"That's fine. When you're ready."

Once Charles was connected and the bag was beginning to empty, Guy grabbed a chair from the kitchen, brought it down to the living room, and sat down facing him.

"Can I turn this down for a minute?" he asked as he picked up the remote control.

"Yeah, go ahead."

Guy hit the mute button. "I want to talk to you about a couple of things before Sophie gets here tonight."

"Okay."

"First, I think we should order some new IV bags. I'm not sure what Sharette was doing, but she went through a ton of them. There aren't very many left. Plus, I think it would be better for you if Sophie had an appreciation of how they look when they are new. That way she'll know when they are getting old and nasty. You know they can only be cleaned out so many times."

"Okay. You have an order form?"

"It's an 800 number. I'll need your credit card."

"Okay."

Guy took a deep breath before he started. "Also, I really think you need to start keeping it warmer in here. I understand that this place is expensive to heat, but I think it makes it difficult for your caregivers. Before I went to bed last night, I went around and made sure that all the vents are closed in rooms that people don't use. And I shut the doors. I could tell that it made a difference in my bedroom. Sophie is an American, like you've been wanting. And she has a ton of experience doing this work. I think it makes sense to try and do what you can to make her comfortable here. And," he gestured toward his blanketed legs, "I think you'd be more comfortable, too, Dad."

Charles was silent for a moment. "What do you want to set it at?"

"I think seventy during the day is reasonable. And then lower it when you go to bed."

"Okay," he nodded.

"Okay?" a surprised Guy confirmed.

Charles nodded.

"Okay, um," Guy stammered, "okay. Thanks. I think she'll appreciate it."

"Here," instructed Charles as he carefully held the feeding tube out away from his body, "hold this for a second."

Guy took it and watched his father reach into his pocket for his money clip. Charles found his credit card and handed it to Guy. "Order those bags."

Chapter 62

The worst parts of Sophie's long journey were when her progress northward caused her to lose the signal from a good radio station. Good stations were great and necessary distractions. Spending two days alone in her car was affording her far too much time to spend second-guessing her decision. She recognized that much of her doubting was a consequence of the tedium of the drive and she did her best to ignore it. What was it Artie said about connection? "Explore it! Do not let it pass from your life unexamined," she said theatrically and laughed. *That's all I'm doing,* she kept reminding herself.

When, in the fading daylight, she picked up her first Chicago radio station, the challenge of remaining a dispassionate explorer grew. By the time Sophie spotted the lights of the Gas and Go marking the southern edge of Richmond, the butterflies in her stomach were in full flight. I don't even know what I'm supposed to be looking for, she thought before Artie's words again came back to her, "It cannot be known, only felt." His advice, along with the bitter memory of how she "felt" that Abby was her little sister, did nothing to bolster her confidence. Turning off the radio, Sophie cracked her window in hopes that a bit of the cold, fresh air would help clear the cobwebs of the long drive as she slowly made her way through the small town toward the home of Charles Bradford.

Since Guy had calculated that the very earliest Sophie was likely to show up would be about four o'clock, he made sure that he had showered, shaved, brushed his teeth, and put on clean clothes by then. For the first hour or so, he shot pool. Then he took a short walk, careful not to be out of sight of the driveway, and smoked a cigarette. Guy came back inside, brushed his teeth again, and went to sit with his father in front of the television. Then he cooked and ate a pizza, making sure to leave the kitchen just as clean as he'd worked to make it the night before. At six-thirty, when he helped his father with his meal, he'd asked to turn down the volume on the television because he was concerned he might not hear the door chimes. When seven o'clock rolled around, he was sitting at the top of the stairs strumming his guitar and trying not to look at the clock behind him in the hallway. Occasionally, he would think of something he might have overlooked and hop up to check. One time he wasn't sure if there were extra bath towels in the bathroom Sophie would be using. Another time, he verified that the heat vents in her room were all completely open and that nothing was blocking them. Although the house did feel warmer, he was still concerned it was too cold, especially since Sophie had just left Florida.

Finally, Guy saw the high beams of a car glide silently across the windows next to the front door. He took a deep breath and leaned his guitar against the railing before hustling down the stairs, slipping on his shoes, and stepping out onto the front steps. Standing under the light, he smiled and waved as her car slowed to a stop next to his own. Then he walked over to greet her.

Just as Sophie began to question if she was truly on a driveway and not a side road, the house emerged through the trees. Like all first-time visitors, she couldn't help but be impressed. She had worked in some very nice homes over the years, but none of them could compete with the structure before her. Guy was waving from the steps and it struck her how out of place he looked in front of such a house. She'd never seen him outside of The Duke and it was difficult to imagine him growing up here. Sophie parked her car next to his, thankful to be done with her journey. After stealing a quick glance at herself in the rearview mirror and taking a deep breath, she opened her door to the unknown.

"Hey," Guy greeted her as he walked over, "you made it! Welcome!"

The light coming from the house behind him forced his face into shadow preventing Sophie from seeing his expression. But she liked the way the enthusiasm in his voice made her feel. "Yes," she said smiling as she put her arms out, "finally." Guy took her in his arms and held her in the cold, dark Illinois night for a moment while her entire body relaxed and breathed, grateful to be nowhere else.

After Guy helped her carry a few items inside and they set them down in the foyer, he said, "I know you've had a long couple of days. I am not expecting you to do anything tonight. I figured I could introduce you to my father really quick and then show you where your room and bathroom is and then whatever. You can shower. Just crash. Or if you're hungry, I can get you something to eat. Whatever you want. Just let me know."

"Alright. Thanks." She took a deep breath. "I think I'm ready to meet your dad."

"Follow me. He's usually still up, but he was acting weird today. I don't know what his deal is."

"Weird how?"

"I don't know," Guy tried to explain. "Just weird. He didn't argue or complain about anything."

Sophie laughed. "One of those, huh?"

"Hey! I warned you!" Guy protested. "But I don't think you should worry too much. You'll get a decent grace period with him. And as long as I keep coming around, he'll direct most of his garbage at me."

"You better keep coming around!" Sophie fought the urge to tell him right then that he was the only reason she came back to Illinois.

When they got to his door, Guy stopped. "I always knock and call out before I go in. Unless he's in the shower he'll hear me." Then he knocked. "Dad?"

"Come in," came the tired-sounding response.

"Sophie's here with me. Can we come in?"

"Yeah."

She followed Guy into and across the enormous bedroom to the only chair on the far side of the room.

Charles extended his arm toward Guy. "Give me a hand."

Guy helped his father out of the chair and he stood, slightly bent, looking far older than his seventy-one years. The introduction was brief as Guy reminded his father that Sophie had been driving all day. He explained that he would be staying over again tonight and getting breakfast ready for him before he left in the morning. When he was done with work tomorrow, he would come by again and go over everything with Sophie more thoroughly.

"But I will be here," Sophie added, "so if you do need anything, let me know. I'm sure we'll be able to figure it out together."

Charles nodded and again Guy caught himself waiting. But again, there was nothing other than silence from his father. "Alright. Goodnight. I'll see you tomorrow afternoon, I guess."

They closed the door behind them and returned to the foyer to grab her bags. Guy showed Sophie to her room and was pleased that it didn't feel cold inside. "So this is it. Your bathroom is right across the hall. I don't know if you're hungry, but there's not much for food here right now. Some soup and some frozen microwave stuff. And frozen pizzas. But you'll be able to go grocery shopping. He's usually pretty chill about that. As long as you're not planning on eating steaks seven days a week, you shouldn't worry about it. Also, if you take him with you, or go anywhere with him, drive his car. It has giant doors so it is easier for him to get in and out. You'll need to pull it out of the garage and drive it up to the front of the house. And you'll have to close the door for him once he's in." Then he swore, realizing something he overlooked. "Shit. I didn't think about breakfast. There's some cereal, but there isn't any milk. I'm sorry."

"Don't worry about it," she assured him. "I'll be fine. Maybe I can run out and get myself a couple of donuts. I heard there's a cool little bakery downtown."

"Oh yeah! Definitely! Jacque will be excited to see you again. Also, that reminds me," he said, thinking about the call he made to his friend yesterday to verify her drink. "I picked up some vodka and grapefruit juice."

Sophie could tell that he was pleased with himself for remembering her drink and it made her feel good. "Do you have any beer?"

He looked confused. "Uhh, yeah," he said, remembering there were still a few MGDs in the fridge from Michele. "But damn, I was sure you drank vodka grapefruit."

"I do," she smiled, "but I'm pretty sure you don't. If I'm going to have a drink, I'd like you to join me."

They returned to the kitchen, Guy fixed her a drink, grabbed himself a beer, and they sat down at the table.

"I'm sure you've heard this before, but you have a beautiful home," Sophie observed.

Guy laughed as he corrected her, "I actually have a pretty crappy little apartment. Charles, however, does have a beautiful home."

"Yeah, but you know what I mean."

"I do," he acknowledged, "but you have to understand. This was never my home."

"Didn't you grow up here?"

"I did. But from the time I was a little kid, my father made it very clear to me that this was his house, not mine."

"That seems a little weird."

Guy nodded. "I'm serious. When I was in grade school, I can remember coming home after playing at a friend's house. I told my father that I wanted to invite him over to our house next time. He said, 'Our house? We don't have a house young man. I have a house. You want to invite your friend to my house.'"

"Wow," she said flatly. "That's kind of messed up."

"That's Charles."

Sophie thought about it. "I grew up in foster homes. I always felt like I was a guest in somebody else's house. I was jealous of other kids because they got to live in their own homes and they got their own rooms."

Guy laughed. "I'm pretty sure most of them do. I think my father is a little different. It has always been very important for him to be in control. And to have everyone around him understand that. One of the exciting things for me when I first got my own apartment was that I could put posters up on the walls. It seems silly now, but that was a big deal to me."

Sophie laughed. "Jesus. I put posters up in the bedrooms of the foster homes I stayed in."

He took a sip of his drink. "I didn't know you grew up in a foster home."

"Homes," she corrected him.

"Like how many?"

"Too many. Nine."

"Wow. That seems like it would have been pretty tough. Were you and your sister together the whole time?"

The question caught Sophie off-guard. She looked away and bit her lip but was unable to prevent all of the emotions washing over her.

Guy could see tears welling up in her eyes and immediately backpedaled, "Hey, I'm sorry. I didn't mean to get too personal or anything. I didn't mean to upset you."

"No," she said as she sighed and wiped her eyes. "It's okay. She's actually the reason I was in Florida."

Guy stood up, went into the bathroom, and returned with a box of tissues. "Is she okay?"

Sophie shrugged. "She's fine, I guess." Then, after taking a deep breath to steel herself, Sophie said, "Abby was never really my sister." It was the first time she'd said the words out loud and it was awful. Saying it and hearing it made the pain of the betrayal and the grief of her loss all so immediate again. They also carried something of a finality with them and she wept for the little sister that she no longer had.

Confused but sympathetic, Guy waited for her to gather herself and continue.

Sophie blew her nose and then told Guy the story about little Abby and how it was in the beginning. About how they became "sisters." She told him how they always stayed in contact, about all of the letters back and forth. And her decision to make sure Abby would have the opportunities that she didn't. And how good it felt to see her progress and feel like she was making a real difference in Abby's life. Then, finally, she told him about her visit to Morningside College over Thanksgiving and how that led her to Florida.

When she was all done, Guy was in awe. "Jesus Christ, Sophie. You are a badass."

It was not the reaction she was expecting. "What are you talking about?"

"What you did was incredible!" he exclaimed.

"I was a fool. She totally used me."

"Yeah, but you couldn't have known that. You took a kid under your wing. When you were still a kid yourself! And you worked to stay in touch and look out for her? You paid for her to go to school! Nobody does that. Nobody. Sophie, I'm serious, that is so awesome."

She considered what he said. It was not how she'd been thinking about it at all. She decided she liked his perspective a lot better. "I guess I haven't really thought about it like that."

"I really think you should. Look, what you did was great." He hedged a bit before continuing. "I mean, I guess it looks like you maybe did it for the wrong person?"

"Yeah, maybe. There's a lot of well-meaning people, but also a lot of ugliness when you are an unwanted child. And you know it. For whatever reason, I was able to get through it okay. I'm grateful for that." She took a drink before continuing. "Abby got exposed to a lot of the ugliness. Her mother is such a rotten person. She would get custody back of Abby once in a while when she was out of jail. She worked every angle, every scam, took advantage of every single person who ever trusted her. She believed that anyone who ever helped her was a sucker and she mocked them for believing her. I knew that, and I guess I thought Abby did, too. I was always very careful about saying too much about her mom though. I knew she loved her. I guess I thought Abby could see through her like I did." Sophie paused, thinking. "You know, that's exactly who I was dealing with that night when I surprised her. Once she knew she was busted, she was exactly like her mom. I was just another sucker that she had no respect for."

They were both silent for a while before Guy said, "Well, I guess we're a couple of geniuses."

She laughed. "How so?"

"We've both spent our adult lives helping people who think we are idiots. You busted your butt for Abby. And the only reason I'm still here in this town going to work at the Gas and Go every morning is because I know he'd be screwed if I left. He can't drive. He can't deal with everything in this house. He'd have to go to some kind of assisted living place. And I know that would kill him."

Sophie tilted her head slightly, considered the man across the table from her, and smiled. She felt good. Raising her glass, she offered a toast, "The things we do for love."

Guy smiled back at her and raised his bottle. "Cheers. Welcome back to Illinois."

Sitting at his father's kitchen table, Guy and Sophie continued in easy conversation for another hour. He asked about her drive and living in Florida and she told him about eating too many Corn Nuts and described her newly adopted little town. Sophie asked about his guitar playing and wanted to know if his fingers had healed. He told her they did.

"I'm excited to hear you play something."

He laughed. "I wish I was excited for anyone to hear me play."

"Oh, come on," she insisted, "I'd really like to hear you."

Guy didn't say anything. He smiled at the amazing woman across the table from him as she held his gaze and smiled back. "I honestly haven't played a single note in front of anybody," he confessed, "but I would be honored to attempt to play a song for you."

"And I would be honored to be your first audience," she smiled.

"Just give me a day or so. I'd like to pick something and practice it enough so that maybe someday you'll ask me to play a second song."

"That seems fair."

They talked a little longer and neither of them wanted to call it a night, but once they'd begun trading the same yawn with an increasingly shortened interval, Sophie finally surrendered. "It's been a long couple of days," she said.

"Yeah, I need to be up early for work tomorrow. I should get to bed, too."

He stood up. "When I stay here, I usually make a quick check in on Charles before I head upstairs. I guess it's easier on me if I know he's asleep." Then he added, "Plus, he wasn't himself today."

"I'll go with you."

As they turned off the lights in the kitchen and walked toward Charles's bedroom, he told her, "It'll be different for you. With your room across the hall, you should be able to hear him if he's up or if he needs something."

Stopping outside the bedroom, Guy listened carefully before he quietly opened the door and peered in. "All's well," he whispered to Sophie as he shut it. "I should be back here around one. But please do call me if you have any questions or if you need something."

"Okay, I will." Then she suggested, "Maybe tomorrow, we can start helping each other figure out what to do with our lives? If you're going to be around," she added.

Guy smiled. "I will make sure that I am. Goodnight, Sophie."

"Goodnight, Guy."

As he turned to head toward the stairs up to his bedroom, Sophie whispered after him, "Guy?"

"Yeah?"

"Thanks for calling me."

Chapter 63

When Guy closed the front door quietly behind him as he left for work, all he could think about was getting through the day and returning as soon as he was done. Sitting around the kitchen table with Sophie had been just like the night he met her at The Duke. He never knew it could be so easy to be himself. And the more he learned about her the more impressed he was. Guy knew that when he came back that afternoon, he had a bunch of stuff to go over with her about the house, doctors, medicines, his father's quirks, etc., but it really seemed like Sophie wanted him to be there otherwise. She'd brought up the plan to help each other figure out the rest of their lives. And he'd promised her a song.

Guy was also relieved that he didn't have to be leaving his father home alone again. Even though he hadn't shared many details with Sophie about Charles's health, she was more experienced than anyone they'd had before. Like she told his father the night before, if something came up, she'd be able to figure it out with him. Guy was sure she would.

When the morning rush dissipated, Guy found opportunities to check the coolers and restock the milk and the energy drinks. He cleaned up by the coffee pot and refilled the cups, lids, and other supplies. Then, while he was putting more cigarettes into their appropriate slots, a regular customer came in to pay for a tank of gas and buy some cigarettes. As she wrote out her check, she asked him, "What's today?"

Guy stopped what he was doing and stared at her as he realized that he didn't know what day it was. *How do I not know what day it is?* he wondered. *Why don't I know what day it is? I always know. Is it three thousand, two hundred and eight? No. I'm pretty sure I said that. Am I in the teens? Is it three thousand, two hundred and fifteen?* He recognized that he was guessing and he didn't know what to think.

"Hello? Guy? Is it the third or the fourth?" She could tell that he was somewhere else and she waved her hand a little to try and draw him back into the present moment. It worked. His mouth closed and he blinked as he refocused his attention.

"Uhh," he stammered, "I'm sorry. What did you need?"

"The date. What's the date today?" she repeated.

"Oh, it's um, the third. Sorry."

"Thanks," she replied and finished writing the check.

Guy took it from her as she put the cigarettes in her purse. Once she left, he started trying again to figure out the day's actual number. Then he decided that it didn't matter.

Chapter 64

Sophie did not wake up with any part of her body dangling off the side of a twin bed. Nor did she open her eyes and see the underside of the top bunk. She didn't hear any neighbors' car doors slamming or even the faintest sounds of distant traffic. Instead, she woke up sprawled across the clean white sheets of a very comfortable queen size bed and stared up at the decorative crown molding of a large bedroom in a wonderfully quiet house. Stretching out, she tried to reach the edges of the mattress and smiled when she could not. Then she grabbed the other pillow, propped herself up into a sitting position against the headboard, and thought, so far, so good.

Guy had been the same person she remembered and had felt so comfortable with that night at The Duke. He had an easy smile that lit up his entire face. When she pulled up in front of the house, he'd come right outside and given her a warm hug and helped carry her bags inside. Sophie decided that he must have been waiting for her to arrive, and she liked that. She liked the way he talked to his dad. She knew he was frustrated with him and that Charles could be difficult, but when she heard Guy speak to him, there was still kindness and patience in his voice. She knew how unusual that was—especially after so many years. Sophie smiled thinking about how he'd remembered her drink and that he had made a point of having it in the house. And talking to him at the kitchen table, he was supportive and funny and seemed to be so genuine. So far, every single thing was exceeding her expectations.

Sophie got out of bed, opened her door slightly, and listened for Charles to see if he was up and about. Although she couldn't hear anything, she was pretty sure she could smell coffee. It didn't take her long to find some sweats in her bag and she threw them on to go investigate.

She found the coffee in the kitchen with Charles. He was sitting at the table with a cup in front of him while he looked at a newspaper through oversized reading glasses.

"Good morning," she said, announcing her presence.

Charles looked up from his paper and stared at her for a moment as if he were trying to figure out who she was. When he finally replied with his own, "Good morning," it wasn't clear to Sophie that he knew. It was sometimes hard to tell with a new client. Maybe that's just how he is, she thought.

The coffee pot was nearly empty and she decided that he must have made just enough for himself. "Would you like the rest of this?" she offered holding up the pot. "I think I'm going to make some more."

"Sure," he replied as he took off his glasses for a moment to rub his eyes. "I'm having a hard time waking up this morning."

Sophie topped off his cup. "Did you sleep okay?" she asked as she readied another pot.

"Eh," he said fatalistically, "I haven't slept okay for many years."

"I'm sure that is frustrating." Sophie sat down across from him at the table while she waited for her coffee. "Guy said he's going to come back here after work this afternoon to go through everything with me. In the meantime, I'm going to bring the rest of my stuff in from the car and get settled a little bit. Also, I'd like to be able to run out to the grocery store. Is there anywhere you would like to go today?"

He thought about it for a moment. "I'll guess I'll go to the grocery store with you. I'd like to stop by the post office on the way back. Will you be able to go before lunch? I want to be able to be done running around before I have to eat again."

It was almost nine. "Sure. How about eleven? I won't be long at the store." Sophie had been thinking that it would be nice to cook a real dinner and she hoped that Guy would be able to stay and eat with her.

"Okay."

"Well then," said Sophie as she stood up to pour herself a cup of coffee, "I guess I should go get busy so I'm ready to go at eleven."

Charles looked up at her again as if he were trying to focus. "I might go lay down again." He hesitated. "But come and get me before you go."

Sophie assured him that she would, took her coffee, and left the kitchen.

After a quality night's sleep, some coffee, and a leisurely shower, Sophie was feeling great. She got dressed and went out to her car to fetch the rest of her belongings. There was more than enough closet space in her bedroom and two large windows that let in a healthy amount of natural light. Additionally, they offered her a beautiful view across the lawn to the creek and the woods beyond it. When she had everything put away, Sophie stowed her suitcases under the bed, and sat down for a few minutes in order to soak it all in. Guy was great, the house was beautiful and out in the country, which was an added bonus. Her room was big and with a great bed. Her bathroom was private. And there was nothing about Charles to suggest that he was going to be any kind of extraordinary challenge. Again she thought, so far, so good.

Sophie went to the kitchen to check the pantry for basic cooking staples like butter, olive oil, salt, pepper, sugar, etc. Experience taught her to make sure a house contained a set of measuring cups and spoons and to check the dates in the spice cabinet. It was amazing how long ago some of them had expired. She found Charles's kitchen to be in pretty good shape, and after digging around for a pen and paper, sat down to write her grocery list.

When she was done, she still had some time to kill and decided to explore the rest of the house. The lower level included the oversized kitchen with a dining area, the step down living room where Charles spent much of his time watching television, a formal dining room with an enormous and ornately carved dining room set, a large formal living room with a wall of picture windows, her bedroom and bath, Charles's bedchamber, a large laundry room, the front foyer with the grand staircase, and finally a room that seemed like a cigar lounge with a pool table, bar, and sofa. Walking around, the house felt like a museum to her. Outdated fabrics and patterns adorned furniture and window coverings from another time. But it wasn't just that, she noticed. There was no clutter, almost as if no one were living there. In fact, in the entire downstairs, the only evidence she found of any inhabitants was by the pool table. There was an empty bottle of white wine on the counter behind the bar. She threw it away in the kitchen before heading upstairs.

There was a large, open area at the top of the steps with two chairs and a small table. Down the wide hallway were bedrooms and an oversized bathroom with multiple sinks. When she opened the door to the first two bedrooms she was greeted by cold air. Their drapes drawn, they appeared to have been sitting dark and empty for years. The third bedroom was different.

Sophie could tell that it was Guy's, not just because the bed wasn't made, but also because the drapes were open, and it had heat. She looked down the hallway behind her and listened for a moment before turning on the light and stepping inside. It felt very personal, almost intimate, to be going into his room. But once she entered and looked around, that feeling went away. His bedroom was nearly as sterile as any other room in the house. Aside from the unmade bed, a duffle bag with some clothes hanging out of it, and his guitar, there was not a single item that would suggest it could have been his childhood bedroom. Sophie looked at the bare walls and smiled thinking about him hanging posters up in his apartment. Wow, she thought as she closed the door, he really wasn't overstating it when he said this wasn't his house.

It was almost eleven when Sophie went downstairs to get her purse and her grocery list. Not seeing Charles, she went to his bedroom door. It was slightly open and she could see that he was dressed and lying down on top of his covers. He looked small on the side of the king-sized bed. "Charles?" she said, hoping to get his attention. Sophie waited a moment, but there was no response. Then she knocked gently on the door and repeated his name a little louder. The second time he stirred. "Hi Charles, may I come in?" she asked.

Charles sat up slowly and hung his feet over the side of the bed with his back to Sophie. He was slouched and gave no indication that he'd heard her. She tried again. "Hi Charles. Would you still like to come to the grocery store with me?" She waited. "Charles?"

By the time he looked around and saw her, Sophie was feeling increasingly uneasy. She wished that she had a better idea of what he was normally like and she was looking forward to having Guy get back from work.

"If you're still tired, we could go after lunch," she offered.

Charles studied her face for a moment. Then he said, "Come here and give me a hand."

Sophie walked across the room and helped him to a standing position. She wasn't sure how stable he was, but he said, "That's good." He fished in his pocket for a moment and found his keys. "Here," he said handing them to her, "you'll need to pull my car up front." Then he let go of her hand and said, "Just give me a minute to clean up," before shuffling into his bathroom and closing the door.

This was clearly not the man Guy had described to her. And he had told her he was concerned about the way his father was acting before they went to bed last night. Seeing the phone on the table next to the television, Sophie considered giving Guy a quick call at work. She could hear the sink running in the bathroom. Maybe he'll be able to give me a sense of how normal this is, she thought as she stood up and moved toward the phone. As Sophie reached for the handset, she froze. Lying on the table, next to the phone was a sheet of paper with a handwritten note on it.

HAPPY NEW YEAR!
FYI-Michele is still here.
She spent the night.

Sophie stared at it. She didn't know who Michele was, but the handwriting was familiar. It was the same handwriting that was in the Christmas card she was so happy to receive two weeks ago in Mexico Beach. It was Guy's.

She thought about the empty wine bottle she'd found earlier.

Charles opened the bathroom door, shuffled to the edge of the bed, and sat down.

"Charles?" Sophie rasped, suddenly having no voice. She cleared her throat, breathed, and forced out the question, "Who is Michele?"

He lifted his head to meet her gaze, but gave no indication he understood.

The slight quiver of the note as she handed it to him belied her efforts to quell the adrenaline surging through her. Sophie willed herself to calmly repeat, "Who is Michele?"

Charles took the note, adjusted his glasses, and studied it for a moment before setting it on the bed next to him. "Michele is Guy's girlfriend."

Chapter 65

In the bathroom across the hall from what would be her bedroom, Sophie sat on the floor, face in her hands, forcing herself to breathe, and wondering how she could be so stupid. Again. When Charles responded to her with the only answer that would make any sense, she had waited a moment for him to elaborate. But there apparently wasn't anything for him to add. Michele was Guy's girlfriend and she had spent the night, here, just a couple of days ago. Guy had a girlfriend. Sophie had mumbled to Charles that she would be back in a moment, turned, and somehow walked out of the room.

How? How did I do this to myself? she wondered. *What did I miss?* Sophie replayed their conversations, their correspondence, searching for clues. She was positive Guy hadn't mentioned anything about seeing anyone, let alone a girlfriend. But then, she decided, he never suggested that he was single either. Was he just nice? Did she just misread every simple kindness? Yes, he sent her a Christmas card, but wasn't that just because she left her address for him? Yes, they had stuff in common, but so what? Did that have to mean anything? He reached out to her to offer her the job. She sighed, feeling hollow as the realization hit her. "It's just a job," she whispered. *I speak English and I'm the "American gal" that he said his dad was always looking for.* "It's just a fucking job," she repeated with resignation.

Sophie hugged her knees to her chest, put her head down, and bawled. She felt broken and exhausted and alone. Again. After a time, a numbness replaced her anguish and she blew her nose in some toilet paper and tried to take some deep recovery breaths while she reluctantly steeped herself in this new understanding of her situation—one she appeared to have completely misread. She couldn't help feeling like it was Sioux City all over again. She wanted so badly for Abby and Guy to be people they weren't, and it blinded her. The past several weeks had afforded her the opportunity to reflect on the little inconsistencies in Abby's letters and other clues that she had so easily dismissed or simply ignored. Recalling the empty wine bottle again, Sophie sighed and wondered how she could ever trust her own judgment again.

Eventually, an image of Charles sitting and waiting slipped through to her consciousness. Sophie didn't know how long she'd been in the bathroom, but figured it was probably long enough that her new employer was wondering what had happened to her. She tried to care, to get up, to do what was expected of her, but could not. Instead, hollow and motionless, she remained on the floor. It was one thing to accept a new reality, but quite another to get up and act in it. All she wanted to do was to go back to bed and wake up a thousand miles away in Artie's cottage, staring at the bottom of the upper bunk, inhaling the humid ocean air. Sophie thought about her confrontation with Abby in Sioux City and was grateful that she'd at least been able to leave the moment she realized what a fool she'd been. Quietly packing her belongings back into her just-emptied suitcases, loading her car, and vanishing was tempting, but she knew that she couldn't do it. Besides, neither Charles nor Guy had done anything wrong. This was on her. This had been her own delusion.

Finally, Sophie forced herself to her feet and considered her options. The only thing certain was that she would be returning to the only place she ever really cared about leaving: Mexico Beach. The question was when. It seemed pointless to stay even one more night. She could start driving, stop for a hotel when she got tired, and then push through to Florida tomorrow. That part made sense to her, but she still needed to figure out what to say to Guy. She rubbed her temples and ran through all sorts of phony explanations in her head before deciding that they all sounded terrible.

As Sophie wondered how much time she had until Guy returned, she was reminded again that Charles was waiting for her. "Shit," she swore to herself, realizing that although she didn't need groceries anymore, she would at least need to take him to the post office. She felt for the keys in her pocket and went to find her shoes and coat.

The garage wasn't far from the house, but the path was uneven and made of stones. Inside she hit the button to open the overhead door, hurriedly climbed into the big, pale yellow Cadillac, and adjusted the seat and mirrors before backing it out and pulling in front of the house. *Hopefully, I'll be able to come up with something before Guy gets off work*, she thought as she turned off the car and went back inside to apologize to Charles for disappearing.

When Sophie returned to his bedroom he was dressed and ready but lying down on the bed. She felt bad about keeping him waiting, walked over to the side of the bed, and spoke softly trying not to startle him, "Charles? I'm back. I'm sorry I kept you waiting." He didn't stir and she waited a moment before repeating his name in her normal voice, "Charles?" The third time she put her hand on his shoulder and said it sharply and loudly, "Charles!" Sophie could feel her adrenaline start to surge as she put her hands on either shoulder and shook him, yelling, "Charles! Wake up, Charles!" Then she called 911.

Chapter 66

Maybe this is what I should have been counting all these years, Guy thought as he steered his car into the entrance of the hospital and wondered how many times he'd been through this same situation over the course of the past twelve years. His father's caregiver would call, voice always loaded with stress, sometimes frantic, to tell him that an ambulance was on the way or that she was leaving to take Chàrles to the emergency room. Then Guy would call Big John and let him know he needed to leave. Within twenty minutes, his boss would be hustling inside saying the only thing he ever said when Guy called because of his father, "Go."

It was impressive to Guy how consistently Big John reacted. Even after all these years and all the different calls, he dropped what he was doing, drove to the station, and sent Guy on his way. In the early days, Guy felt guilty and was apologetic, but Big John cut him off, pointed to the door, and said, "Go. We'll talk later. Just go."

After parking near the emergency room entrance, Guy stepped out of his car and into the cold. Zipping his coat, he leaned against the passenger door, took a drag from his cigarette, and speculated about his father's current crisis. When Sophie called him at work, she was clearly stressed, but didn't sound panicked. She'd told Guy that Charles had been lying down for a bit and when she tried to wake him up, she couldn't. She said that he seemed to be breathing normally and had a pulse, but wouldn't respond or even open his eyes. To Guy, it sounded like a diabetic coma. At the hospital they would either lower or raise his blood sugar, depending on the type of coma,

347

and he'd probably be sent home in a couple of hours.

The coma itself, if that's what it was, didn't particularly concern Guy. The cause, however, did. Charles managed his diabetes very well and the only time this kind of thing occurred was when something else was happening with his health that put his body under stress. After flicking his cigarette into the dirty pile of snow at the edge of the parking lot, Guy walked inside to find out.

The woman behind the counter in the nearly empty reception area greeted him right away and he was grateful that midday during the week was not a busy time. She directed him through the doors and into the back to the only occupied bed. The paramedics had been able to lower his father's blood sugar on the way to the hospital and Guy found a frail, tired-looking Charles awake and sitting up at a forty-five-degree angle. He was connected to various monitoring devices and had an IV in his arm.

"Hey, Dad," Guy greeted his father as he pulled the curtain closed behind him. "How are you feeling?"

Charles looked up. "Better than a coma," he replied sardonically. After struggling to clear his throat, he added, "I'm still so goddamn tired, though. I don't know what the hell happened."

"Well you seemed pretty out of it last night," Guy observed. "Do you think you're getting sick?"

He shrugged. "Maybe? I don't know. I'm just wiped out."

"Do you feel okay otherwise?"

Charles nodded.

"Well, they said your sugar was too high. That usually means there's something else your body is dealing with, right?"

"They said it was too high?"

"Yeah."

"Well, maybe I am coming down with something." Charles lay back, closed his eyes, and attempted a deep breath only to have it be interrupted by coughing. When he recovered, he looked at Guy for a moment before asking, "What time is it?"

"Almost one."

"Did you bring me here?"

"No. Sophie found you and called the ambulance. Do you know if she's here? I didn't see her when I came in."

Charles shrugged. "I don't know."

"I'm going to go and check. If she's not here, I should probably give her a call and let her know you're okay."

"Yeah, go ahead."

Guy pulled the curtain aside and went to look for Sophie. When the woman at the intake desk told him no one had accompanied his father to the hospital, Guy stepped outside to have a cigarette and tried to reach her on the phone. He wanted to thank her and let her know that they would probably be back in a couple of hours. While the phone rang unanswered, Guy worried about her. He knew she had a ton of experience, but he figured that having to call 911 for an ambulance on her first day had to be stressful. When she didn't pick up, he decided that she must have gone for lunch or groceries or something, so he hung up and headed back inside.

A nurse was changing his father's IV when Guy returned and she asked, "You're his son?"

Guy nodded. "Yeah. What's up?"

"The doctor has decided to admit him. As soon as they have a room ready, we'll be moving him out of the ER."

"Really?" Guy was surprised. "Why? What's the deal?"

"Your father has some pneumonia. I'm getting him started on some antibiotics right now," she explained as she gestured to the new IV bag. "We want to be able to keep an eye on him until we know they are working."

"Okay. Dad?" Guy looked to Charles, "You have any questions?"

Charles shook his head. "I can't think of any right now."

"Alright," said the nurse as she finished up. "I'll be back to help get you moved upstairs. In the meantime, if you need anything, just use your buzzer."

They thanked her and she left.

Guy turned to his father. "Pneumonia, huh?"

Charles shrugged. "I guess so."

Guy waited around until his father had been moved and was settled into a regular hospital room. He spoke briefly with the admitting doctor, met the nurse on duty, and helped Charles figure out the television. By then it was nearly three in the afternoon and his father was starting to doze off. Guy decided it was a good time to leave. He still hadn't been able to reach Sophie and he hadn't eaten anything since breakfast.

"Hey," he said quietly, "Dad."

Charles's eyes blinked open and found Guy standing next to his bed.

"If you're good, I think I'm going to head out." He put his hand on his own stomach. "I never ate lunch and I'm starving."

His father nodded and said tiredly, "Yeah, sure. Go ahead."

"Alright. I'll talk to you tomorrow. Rest up."

Charles nodded again and then uncharacteristically added, "Thanks for sticking around with me this afternoon."

Because he was hoping to ask Sophie to get something to eat with him, Guy resisted the urge to hit a drive-through before leaving McHenry and heading back to Richmond. When he pulled up to his father's house though, he was disappointed not to see anything other than his father's yellow Cadillac parked out front.

He went inside to wait for her to return, but after practicing the guitar for most of an hour, Guy gave in to hunger and put a frozen pizza in the oven. Dinner with Sophie would have to wait for another day. Sitting in front of the television next to his father's empty recliner, Guy ate his pizza and wondered about pneumonia. By the time he put the leftover slices in the refrigerator, it was after six o'clock and he found his coat, stepped outside, and lit a cigarette. The air was cold and still, the first stars were dotting the night sky, and he felt very alone.

Back inside, Guy wandered, unsure of what to do with himself as he waited for Sophie. It had been over six hours since she called him at work, and he wondered if she'd gone to eat at The Duke. He thought about calling over there and asking for her but decided to look around first to see if she'd left him a note. Not finding one in the kitchen, his room, his father's room or anywhere else, Guy eased open the door to Sophie's bedroom and turned on the light.

The only evidence of Sophie that remained in the room was a note left on the center of the neatly made bed. Stunned, Guy's eyes searched the room for any sign of her as he walked over to the bed and picked up the sheet of paper.

Dear Guy,

I'm very sorry, but I had to leave.

I hope your dad will be okay.

I think you're a great guy and I wish you lots of happiness.

Sophie

Chapter 67

By the time she left Indiana and crossed the Ohio River into Kentucky, the sun was long gone and Sophie could barely keep her eyes open. She probably should have stopped earlier, but there was something symbolic about getting out of Indiana. Indiana was part of the Midwest and Kentucky was not. When she found a hotel outside of Louisville, checked in, and immediately climbed into the bed, exhausted, Sophie felt good about leaving that part of the country behind. Her existence there had been accidental, unrewarding, and now it had come to an end.

Because she planned on drinking her morning coffee with her cruise control set at seventy while she made her way straight south down I-65, Sophie requested an early wakeup call from the front desk. She hoped to arrive back in Mexico Beach by late tomorrow evening. It would be Thursday and she imagined the scene in Toucan's. When she left there on Monday, clouds and rain were expected to linger for the remainder of the week so she was guessing it would be slow. There would probably be only a few families in the dining room and, of course, Artie perched on one of his usual barstools. She knew that he would be surprised to see her back so quickly and disappointed that things didn't work out the way they'd both hoped. She also knew that he would be sympathetic and do and say whatever he could to help her feel better about everything. She was looking forward to seeing him again.

With nothing to do all afternoon in the car except think, she'd done a lot of it. Sophie valued the past couple of months she'd spent working at

Toucan's and living at Artie's. It had been helpful for her to have a safe place to rest and recover and she was grateful that she hadn't been forced into making any big decisions right away. But she felt like it was time to pick a direction. She thought about taking Artie's advice and driving up to Tallahassee for a day to check out the community college and take advantage of the career counseling. She considered the idea of just staying put in Mexico Beach. But she also knew that there was a whole wide world still out there and all she'd seen of it was some rural areas in Iowa and Illinois and her tiny little part of Florida. When she was with Guy and thinking about all of the endless directions she could take her life, it felt exciting. But now it was just overwhelming. And it felt lonely. She wanted to go explore the world, but with Guy. She was tired of being alone.

When Sophie thought about Guy, she was mostly just disappointed and sad to miss out on what might have been. She'd been so excited to get a letter from him, then to have the opportunity to see him again. And that one night sitting at the kitchen table with him at his father's house could not have been any better. It felt so good and it felt so right. They were kindred spirits in a lot of ways. She'd been becoming convinced that they shared that magical connection Artie talked about. But instead, she'd done it again. It didn't matter how badly she wanted something to be real or true; if it wasn't, it just wasn't. And this wasn't love, it was only a job.

She also thought about Charles and wondered whether or not he was okay. The paramedics had arrived quickly and before she could start explaining, it was clear they knew much more about his health than she did. They immediately checked his blood sugar and began the work to bring it back in line. Sophie guessed he would probably recover and go on making Guy miserable for years to come. She did feel bad about not going to the hospital. Families always appreciated her being with their loved one and it gave her the opportunity to elaborate about what happened and answer their questions. But Sophie found it hard enough to have to call Guy and tell him what was going on. The idea of waiting around at the hospital until he showed up with his girlfriend, well, that wasn't something she was willing to put herself through.

When she'd ended the call with Guy, Sophie had packed up her belongings, turned off the lights, and closed the door to Charles's house behind her. Then she started her car and sat there with the engine running. Everything about that morning felt so abrupt. Sophie replayed her arrival, the note, the explanation from Charles and tried to decide whether or not she should be mad at Guy, and if so, how much? Then she decided that it didn't matter. If she wanted to blame him, it would only serve to make her bitter. Blaming herself wouldn't help either. She had taken her chance and it hadn't worked out. Maybe it was just bad timing, she wondered. After all, she was dating Bear and leaving town when they met. That wasn't her fault, was it? No, it was just life, she sighed.

The idea of starting a drive straight back to Florida, right then, seemed extreme, but when she tried to weigh it against other options, she wasn't able to find any. There was not a single reason for her to remain in Illinois. Just before she put her car in drive though, Sophie's conscience stopped her and demanded that she inform Guy. Another phone call was out of the question and he was sure to have left for the hospital anyway. She had no way to reach him. Leaving him a note would be fair, quick, and easy. When Sophie turned off her engine, got out of her car, and headed back inside, she wasn't sure what to write, but she did know exactly what to write it on.

Chapter 68

Guy sipped his whiskey on the rocks, set the glass down, and observed the intermingling of its elements. Sitting alone at a table in the corner of The Duke, he watched the ice, overwhelmed by its surroundings, slowly dissolve into nothing. A brief rush of cold air ushered Jacque into the bar and Guy waved him over.

"Uh-oh," Jacque commented as he joined him, "that looks like big medicine, my friend."

Guy nodded solemnly.

"And I see that we are at a table instead of the bar," he continued, "so this is not advice. This is a counseling session?"

"I need both. She's gone."

"Who's gone? Sophie's gone?"

Guy nodded morosely.

"Gone how? Like she quit?"

"Yep."

"Bullshit. What the hell happened?"

The note was in his pocket and Guy took it out, unfolded it, and pushed it across the table toward his friend.

Jacque picked it up and read it before looking back at him, confused. "That's it? She just got here last night, right? She didn't say why she left?"

"Turn it over," Guy instructed forlornly.

Jacque did and saw the note Guy had left for his father:

HAPPY NEW YEAR!
FYI-Michele is still here.
She spent the night.

He groaned and said, almost in a whisper, "Oh Michele, you fucking bitch."

"I don't know," Guy shrugged. "It's not really Michele's fault."

Jacque looked at Guy, thinking, reluctant to speak. Finally, resigned to spilling the truth, he sighed, "Here's the deal, my friend. I don't know for sure if this is true or not, but based on what you've told me, it seems to make sense. Michele is broke. And the reason she has been chasing you is because she thinks you're going to get a bunch of money when your dad dies."

As Guy considered the information, his face slowly broke into a smile, followed by a chuckle, which cascaded into full-on laughter.

Jacque stared, confused. "I don't get it. What's so funny?"

"When my dad dies?" Guy asked. "Oh man. I wonder how long she would have lasted dating my broke ass before she figured out that Charles is immortal." He started laughing again. "That would have been funny."

"That is actually pretty funny. I'm sorry I didn't say anything, but I didn't hear about it until after your whole New Year's Eve date was canceled. And you sounded like you were pretty much done with her. I had no idea she was going to show up at your dad's."

Guy shrugged, "Don't worry about it. I knew it didn't make sense."

"So, what happened with Sophie? When did she leave?"

"I don't know. This afternoon, I guess. She called me at work late this morning to let me know that she had to call an ambulance for my father. I didn't find the note until about an hour ago."

"Wait! What happened to your dad?!"

"He went into a coma. He's actually still in the hospital."

"What!? He's in a coma? Jesus Christ!"

"Not anymore. And it was just a diabetic coma. I mean, it's not like that's not a big deal, but it's not like a *coma* coma. It happens when his blood sugar is out of whack. And his blood sugar goes out of whack when he's sick. So, it's really the pneumonia that's the issue."

"Pneumonia? What the fuck, my friend. You have had a busy day."

"Yeah," Guy smiled bitterly as he gave a thumbs up. "It's been fucking fantastic. Anyway, I tried to call Sophie from the hospital to let her know what was going on. No answer. When I was done, I drove over there and was hanging around waiting to talk to her before I went home. I figured she was out running errands or getting some food or something. But she wasn't showing up. Finally, I checked her room and everything was gone. She's gone. That note was the only thing."

Jacque thought for a while. "How was last night?"

"Last night was amazing. She got there around seven. I introduced her to my father. Then we sat and had a drink and just talked for a couple of hours. She's incredible, dude."

"Really? It went that well?"

Guy sighed. "I sure thought so. I thought it was great. I was really looking forward to being over there tonight. Just hanging out with her or something. I don't know."

They sat in silence for a little while before Jacque spoke. "I don't think this is terrible," he said, holding up the note. "This actually might be pretty good."

"Really?" Guy was skeptical.

"Really. Think about it. There's one reason she left."

"Why?"

"She left because she thinks you've got a thing with Michele. Why else would she write her note to you on the other side of that piece of paper? She wanted you to know that she knows."

"Okay. I get that. But how is that good?"

"Because it means that she cares whether or not you have a girlfriend! She's into you, my friend!" He looked at Guy expectantly as his friend considered the idea.

"Yeah," he said slowly. "I guess that makes sense." He allowed himself a brief smile. "How do I explain this though?" he said gesturing to the note about Michele spending the night.

"Easy. Just be honest with her. Tell her what happened. Tell her everything. Tell her you had plans, but you canceled them. Tell her why. If she doesn't believe you, I will tell her, too. She is a smart woman, my friend. I think you're going to be okay."

Feeling only slightly better, Guy nodded. "I suppose I could do that. If I knew where she was."

Chapter 69

When he woke up on Friday morning, Guy was hungover, depressed, and part of him wanted nothing more than to go back to sleep. Since he had stayed at The Duke longer than he should have, he spent more money and drank more than he should have, too. Part of the reason was that he could. With Charles safe in the hospital for the night, it was liberating to not be on call for a crisis. But the main reason he stayed and drank was because, despite what Jacque said, Sophie was still gone and he was afraid that he would never see her again.

After trying and failing to fall back to sleep for most of an hour, Guy surrendered to the day and went into the kitchen to start some coffee before taking a shower. Once he was cleaned up, dressed, and on his second cup, the caffeine was kicking in and he began to feel a little better. Sitting on his couch, he tried to figure out where Sophie would be. His best guess was that she would be on her way back to Florida. It sounded like she had a cool setup and that she really loved it there. The glowing way she talked about the little town she'd been living in made him surprised that she was willing to come back to Illinois. He allowed himself a little smile as he recognized how it supported Jacque's contention that she was actually into him. The sweetness of that realization quickly turned sour when he considered the thousand miles that separated them. It wasn't like he could afford to hop on a plane to Florida and go find her.

Sophie's note sat on the table in front of him and he looked at it again. Then he turned it over to see his own stupid note to his father, sighed, and shook his head. Part of him wanted to be angry at Michele. It would be easy to blame everything on her, but Guy knew he was complicit. He thought about how he'd asked her out only to show her off to Dean and he knew that was a shitty, selfish thing to do. He thought about how content he was to have his father see her and believe they were together. And how happy he was to tape that fucking note to the front of his father's television, knowing full well the impression it would give. He had been in love with the idea that people thought he was sleeping with Michele and now it had all come back to bite him in the ass.

Guy stood up and got his guitar out of the bedroom. When Sophie had asked him about playing her a song, he immediately knew what he would play for her if he ever got the chance. It had been on the radio a lot the past few months and he'd already been working on it. There was one chord progression that was still pretty rough, and he ran through it several times while he thought about what might've been. He wanted to ask her to come back. He wanted to tell her that he was sorry and that he was a fool for ever agreeing to go out with Michele and that he wasn't interested in her. He wanted her to know that he thought she was an incredible person—that she was the only woman he'd ever met who made him feel the way he felt when he was with her. He wanted her to know that he hadn't been using her or playing her. He wanted her to know how badly he wanted to see her again.

Guy thought about writing Sophie another letter. He could try to explain himself and tell her what the deal was with Michele, but he doubted there was anything he could put in a letter that wouldn't just sound like an excuse. He wanted to see her in person and be able to talk to her. It was always so easy when he was with her. He tried to figure out a way he could get to Florida. Driving would take too much time and Guy doubted his car would make it. He'd probably get stuck somewhere along the way and create an even bigger mess for himself. Plus, he didn't see how he could leave his father for that long. The best thing to do would be to hop on a plane and beat her down there. He could go hang out in that place she'd been working and surprise her. With his father in the hospital for at least the next couple of days, it could actually work. But Guy knew that buying a plane ticket on short notice was something way beyond what he could afford. *If only I hadn't been working at a gas station and living paycheck to paycheck my whole life*, he thought, *I might have some extra money laying around.*

Suddenly, Guy jumped up, hurried into his bedroom, and yanked open the top drawer to his dresser. He had plenty of money. Staring up at him were over a dozen uncashed checks written to him by his father for either his birthday or for Christmas.

"Holy shit," he whispered, "I think I'm going to Florida."

In the moment that followed, Guy wavered. As he scooped up the checks, the first of what could become an endless series of paralyzing second-guesses, doubts, and questions tried to storm his consciousness. He looked around his crappy little apartment and understood that if they breached it, this was where he would continue to be stuck. And he'd probably never see Sophie again. Guy took a deep breath and steeled himself before restating his intentions in a firm voice, "I'm going to Florida. Now."

He found his duffel bag and hurriedly shoved a couple changes of clothes inside. On top of the clothes he added his toothbrush and some deodorant. Then he tossed the bag by the door and called Big John to let him know he wouldn't be able to come into work on Sunday. The clock on the microwave showed 8:50am. He could get to the bank just as it was opening and then be on his way to the airport. The rest he could figure out when he got there. Shoes and jacket on, he paused for a moment in a last effort to make sure he had everything he needed. And then the phone rang.

"Hello," he answered.

"Hi, this is Diane at Northern Illinois Medical Center. I'm trying to reach Mr. Guy Bradford."

"This is Guy."

"Mr. Bradford," she spoke calmly and professionally, "I'm one of the nurses taking care of your father. I'm calling you because his pneumonia hasn't been responding to the antibiotics we've been giving him. This morning the doctor determined that he needed to be put on a respirator. Your father has been moved to the Intensive Care Unit."

"Okay." Guy's mouth was suddenly very dry. "What does that mean?"

"The respirator is helping your father breathe right now. His breathing wasn't strong enough on its own to supply his body with the oxygen it needs. With the respirator helping him, he will be able to rest more effectively, and his body can use the energy it has to work on fighting the illness."

"Okay," he repeated slowly. "Is he awake? Does he know what's going on?"

"He is resting. But Mr. Bradford," she hesitated, "your father's body is in a very weakened state right now. In a healthier patient we would have expected the antibiotics to have been effective already. Your father isn't responding to them. That's not typical."

"Okay. So what does that mean?"

"It means that if you have other family, now is the time to contact them."

Chapter 70

The third quarter of the final Bears game of the season was nearly over by the time Guy showed up at The Duke. He hadn't slept well for days, it showed, and he didn't care.

"My friend," Jacque welcomed him earnestly, "I am glad you are here." He caught Mindy's eye and ordered an MGD for him.

Guy climbed onto the stool, put his elbows on the bar, and rubbed his face. "Jesus Christ, I needed to get out of that fucking hospital." When Mindy set the beer down in front of him, he picked it up and raised it toward Jacque, "To your health. May you never get old and sick."

"Cheers. May we all be so lucky," Jacque said clinking his glass against the side of Guy's bottle before taking a drink. "Did you get hold of your sisters?"

Guy nodded. "Yeah. They were nice about it. But nobody's coming." Guy shrugged. "Whatever. I didn't expect them to. He's been dead to them for a long time already."

"That's too bad. How is he doing?"

Guy shook his head. "It's bad. He hasn't been responsive since Friday afternoon. He did come around for a little while after I got there." Guy rolled his eyes. "Guess what he wanted to talk about?

"I don't know. What?"

"He wanted his mail. And then he lectured me about making sure to turn down the heat at his house since nobody is there." He paused. "Those might end up being his dying wishes: Bring me my mail and stop wasting my money heating an empty house."

"Wow," Jacque winced. "Dying wishes though? Is it really that bad?"

Guy nodded. "It looks like it. They said he's cascading. His other systems are failing. His kidneys shut down. I think he might actually be dying this time."

"I'm so sorry, my friend," Jacque put his hand on Guy's back. "That's tough."

"I don't know. It's strange. The idea of him dying isn't what is upsetting to me, I don't think. I've lived with that thought for a long time." He paused and took another sip of his beer. "What's been upsetting is that I'm being forced to give up on my own crazy delusion that he might ever change."

"Change how?"

"I don't even know. I guess I never realized how much I was holding out hope for some kind of fucking miracle, that he would somehow figure out that people were more important than money. That somehow, one day, he would wake up and decide to be a real person, instead of just, well, whatever he was. But," Guy sighed, "he never broke, never gave an inch, never did anything that showed he might have given a shit about anybody other than himself. I'm not going to mourn the loss of the man my father was, but I'm having a tough time accepting the finality of it all—that who he was, well, now that's all he'll ever be. I guess I am mourning the loss of what might have been."

They sat in silence for a while before Guy volunteered, "I called Toucan's this morning."

"And?" Jacque asked hopefully.

"They said Sophie doesn't work there anymore."

"That was it?"

Guy nodded. "They couldn't tell me anything."

Chapter 71

As she navigated her car through the bustling midday of downtown Tallahassee, Sophie was grateful she heeded Artie's advice and took the scenic route up from Mexico Beach. Instead of heading north out of town, he suggested she continue south and east on 98. It took longer, but the highway separated the beautiful Gulf Coast to her right from vast expanses of state and national forests to her left. There hadn't been much traffic on a late Wednesday morning in January and it felt good to be out in the country.

Now, however, she was bumper to bumper looking for Duval Street and the entrance to a parking garage. Sophie was on her way to meet Artie for lunch. When he gave her the address, he told her it would be easy to find since it was across the street from the Capitol, which also happened to be the tallest building in the city. They were going to be eating at Andrew's Downtown Grill. It was only a couple of blocks from his office and a routine dining choice for Florida's political establishment. There was no better place for Artie to show her off and help perpetuate whatever misconceptions his peers may have about the nature of their relationship.

When she'd finally made it back to Toucan's from Illinois just before nine the previous Thursday night, she found him right where she expected. His initial surprise was quickly replaced by sympathy and he stood to give her a welcomed hug. Then he ordered her a drink and informed her that his cottage was unlocked and at her disposal. Her presence on the stool next to him sadly and sufficiently illuminated the outcome of her venture north.

"Well, Artie," she'd said with more resignation than excitement, "I believe

I'm ready to head up to Tallahassee and check out that community college." He replied that he thought she was making an excellent decision.

Sophie then spent the weekend lolling about Mexico Beach and regretting giving up her bartending shifts. On Monday morning she contacted the advising department of Tallahassee Community College and was able to make an appointment to meet with someone on Wednesday afternoon. When she called Artie to let him know that she would be coming, he nonchalantly suggested that they meet somewhere for lunch.

"Oh Artie," she laughed, "You are so casual. I haven't forgotten our conversation. Of course I will meet you for lunch. And I will play my part," she assured him, "so that you can continue to have everyone believing whatever it is they believe."

"Wonderful, my dear!" he'd answered. "It will bring me such joy." Then he added, "Since we are dispensing with all pretense regarding the nature of our lunch date, will you be so kind as to wear a sundress?"

Sophie was surprised. "That's pretty specific."

"Red preferably," he continued even more specifically. "I loathe the notion that I may somehow deprive my colleagues their greatest opportunity to detect your presence on my arm."

"Wow," she laughed again, "you are very invested in this! I'm starting to feel like one of those animals at the county fair that a kid cleans up and walks in front of the judges. You know I'm more than just a piece of meat, Artie," she protested with false sincerity.

"My dear Sophie," he replied earnestly, "of course you are. To me, that is. I know your heart and I know your mind and have the utmost respect for both. My colleagues, however, maintain a deep and abiding commitment toward the superficial regarding your perpetually maligned gender and it will be their world in which we are to dine."

"So, you're saying that they are a bunch of old, lecherous, sexist men?"

"Yes, my dear. Absolutely. Imagine the daily trials a man such as myself must confront mired in such a base and unenlightened environment!" he said dramatically.

"Oh my god," she responded slowly, her voice dripping with sarcasm. "It must be so difficult for you."

"My dear Sophie," he observed, "were it possible to hear you rolling your eyes, I believe I should be deafened."

She'd laughed again. "Yes, Artie. Yes you should." Then she sighed. "But I will wear a red sundress and meet you for lunch so that you can parade me before your leering colleagues."

"You shall have my eternal gratitude," he replied. Then he added, "Lest the company of my colleagues make you uncomfortable, please consider the nature of the journey upon which we have all embarked. You understand well that not everyone has the privilege of traveling down the road of life as long or as far as we have. We pay the price of our good fortune by suffering the degradations of time. We are stooped and wrinkled, what hair remains on our heads has turned thin and gray. We awoke long ago to find ourselves weary and withered mimics of the vibrant young men we once were. I assure you, my dear, that a day will come when you spy a beautiful young man or woman who, like you are now, is in the prime of their life, their figure, their features, utterly sublime. He or she will be impeccably dressed in the fashion of the day. And you will see them, and you will fondly recall what it was like to look and feel that good—to be the envy of all who gazed upon you. My colleagues may be leering, my dear, but consider that they will also be experiencing a wistful nostalgia for a time when they would have reveled in their pursuit of a creature as extraordinary as you are today."

Sophie found Duval Street and turned out of the sunshine into the underground parking structure. She looped lower and lower until, finally locating a spot, she pulled in and turned on the interior light in order to check herself in the mirror. Carefully, Sophie re-applied the bright red lipstick purchased to match the dress she'd found Monday in Panama City. Then she got out and assessed what she could see of her reflection in the windows of her car. The neckline of the dress plunged lower and the hemline rose higher than anything she'd worn in a long time. But she was in the best shape she'd been in for a long time as well. Smiling, she recalled Artie's words about being in her prime and decided that she wouldn't argue the point.

After putting her lipstick in her clutch and grabbing her sunglasses, Sophie found the stairs and climbed out of the garage into the Florida sunshine. The temperature had reached the mid-seventies and she appreciated the large trees shading her walk to the restaurant. There were quite a few tables set up on the sidewalk and it looked busy, but Artie had instructed her to wait for him inside. While the outside seating had been a lively cacophony of couples and families eating in the dappled sunlight, the interior by the bar was dim and subdued. Sophie hesitated as she removed her sunglasses and allowed her eyes to adjust to the lower light. She wasn't expecting to see Artie and did not. He had previously confessed to her his intention to be late. He explained how her stunning and unescorted presence at the bar for even a mere ten to fifteen minutes would in and of itself provide a measure of intrigue. "We're simply building the suspense, my dear," he told her. "Think of it as theatre."

Sophie took a deep breath and appraised her audience. Clusters of older men with white hair and dark suits huddled in twos and threes while they murmured their conspiratorial intentions to one another and sipped their lunches. Committed to playing her part in this absurd tableau, she stood up a little straighter, smiled confidently, and boldly made her entrance.

The appearance of a bright red sundress, breezily flowing over her tanned and toned figure as it crossed the room had precisely the effect Artie suggested it would. She had laughed, certain he was exaggerating, but now marveled at the comically abrupt hush that accompanied her arrival. Sophie found a vacant seat at the bar and occupied it as the muted droning of conversation resumed behind her. More self-conscious than she had anticipated, she ordered a drink and hoped that he wouldn't keep her waiting long. He did not.

Behind the bar was a mirror, and a few minutes after receiving her drink she was stunned to see a barely recognizable Artie walking toward her. This was not the gin-soaked Artie of Toucan's that she was so used to. This was Arthur Bergsman, attorney and politically connected lobbyist, clean-shaven with his hair slicked back and wearing a custom-tailored suit. He moved confidently through the room, nodding acknowledgement to some, and stopping briefly to glad hand and chat with others. It was clear that he was in his element. Showtime, she thought as he came up behind her and put his hand on her lower back.

Feigning surprise at his arrival, Sophie turned, smiling to embrace him. He apologized and said he hoped he hadn't kept her waiting long. Not at all, she replied and gave him a kiss. As they left the bar area, arm in arm, to be seated in the dining room, she could feel every eye following them out.

Relieved to finally be tucked away in a booth away from the barroom, she leaned in and laughingly exclaimed, "Oh my god, Artie! You look great. I've never seen you in a suit. And that whole thing was exactly how you said it would be."

He grinned. "You are a marvelous co-conspirator, my dear Sophie," he said as he took her hand and kissed it. "And you look magnificent. Thank you. I shall enjoy this for weeks."

"I believe it. Your friends appeared to be very impressed."

"Colleagues, my dear," he corrected her. "I am playing at politics. Friendships require a measure of trust and loyalty, and in a town such as this, both of those honorable traits are too often subjugated to self-interested expediency."

"Which is why you come to Mexico Beach?"

"Whenever I can, my dear. It is an ugly game we play in this place," he admitted before smiling mischievously, "I'm almost embarrassed by how well I play it."

As they lunched, Artie identified selected men as they entered and exited. He would then describe the various factions to which they belonged and the intrigues currently playing out among them. Sophie marveled at how far the actual functioning of government was removed from the simplistic and sterile version she remembered learning in high school civics.

Toward the end of their meal, Artie cleared his throat and changed the subject. "I fear I may owe you an apology, my dear Sophie," he began earnestly. "Since your return, I have been plagued by guilt. While you haven't offered any details, and," he held up his hands, "I am not asking for any, I can only surmise that your return to Illinois was a disappointment. I have reflected on how I waxed so poetically about the magic of connection that I fear I nudged you in a direction more compelling to me than perhaps to you. If that was the case, please accept my most sincere apology."

Sophie sighed. "No, Artie. You don't need to apologize. I guess I haven't talked about it because I can't decide how I feel about it." She paused. "There is a part of me that is certain I had that connection. It was there when I met him, and I really believed it was there when I went back." That was the undeniable feeling that had been growing within her and it felt strange to say it out loud. "But there was other stuff going on…" her voice trailed off. "I don't know," she shrugged as she reflected on the past few months of her life, "I guess I just couldn't bring myself to stick around and see what happened."

Chapter 72

On the afternoon of Thursday, January 14, 1999, when Guy left the menial monotony of his low-wage job and said "So long, John. Have a good weekend," he genuinely meant it. He wasn't feeling any secret giddiness regarding the idea that it could possibly have been his last day behind the counter of Big John's Gas and Go. He was just tired. Lighting a cigarette and climbing into his car, Guy did what he had done every other day after work that entire week; he drove to the hospital in McHenry to sit with his father.

When he arrived, he got out but stood close to his car and pulled his jacket tight against the cold winter wind while he smoked one more cigarette in an effort to delay the rest of his evening. After taking a last drag, Guy stepped on the butt and headed inside. Then he took the elevator up to the ICU and checked in at the nurses' station. They recognized him by now and provided him with an update on Charles's condition. It had not changed. He thanked them and walked over to his father's room.

The quiet mechanical hiss and click of the respirator as it methodically switched from inhaling to exhaling lent the room a feeling of calm. On Monday, when it had become clear that Charles was not going to be able to resume breathing on his own anytime soon, he had been given a tracheotomy. One of the doctors had explained to Guy that patients could only be intubated for a few days without it causing secondary problems. Although the breathing tube connected to the opening in his father's neck was disconcerting, he did appear more comfortable without the oxygen mask strapped over his mouth and nose.

It was strange, sitting in a room next to someone arguably more dead than alive. Awkwardly, Guy said hello to his father and told him that it was Thursday afternoon. He hesitated, wanting to say more, but then sat down in the chair beside the bed. Putting his hand on top of his father's, he gave it a gentle squeeze and although he wasn't expecting a response, Guy still felt the disappointment of not receiving one. Then he turned on the television.

After a time, one of the nurses came in and asked him how long he was planning on staying. She told him that the hospital's outpatient coordinator would be coming by because she needed to speak with him about the next step. Guy told her that he intended to be there most of the evening. When the woman showed up an hour later, she informed him that his father needed to be discharged soon. In the hospital, she explained, patients were either getting worse or they were getting better. Since it had become clear that Charles was no longer doing either one, a different type of facility would be more appropriate. Then she gave him a couple of brochures and talked to him about the options available in the area. When she was done, Guy thanked her and asked when he would need to make a decision. She said that tomorrow would be fine.

Taking the information she'd given him, Guy went downstairs to the cafeteria. While he ate, he read about the different places he could choose to have care for his father. Then he went outside, walked well past the sign that read, "No Smoking on Hospital Grounds," and had a cigarette. Back upstairs, Guy sat down beside the bed but left the television off. He thought about his father being consigned to a facility and considered what the profoundly degraded quality of his life might be like. It was no longer realistic to believe that Charles would ever be healthy enough to return home. A body, even one as stubborn and resilient as his father's had proven to be, could only take so much. Guy wasn't sure that anyone believed he would ever regain consciousness. If he did, adjusting to his health being further compromised was going to be a challenge, but not an unfamiliar one. The greater issue was going to be his inability to return to his home. For a man who had been unequivocally in charge for nearly his entire adult life, being forced to live in a nursing home and exist according to the schedules of others, well, Guy could only imagine what kind of misery that would bring his father.

As he pondered such imagined futures, a gentle knocking intruded on his thoughts and he looked up to see an unfamiliar woman in scrubs standing at the door.

"Hi," she said, "I'm the dialysis tech. I'm here for Charles."

"Okay," Guy replied. "Do you need me to move?"

She smiled sympathetically as she explained, "The hospital actually requests visitors to step out while we get patients set up. Once I have it started you are welcome to come back and sit with him though. Do you know where the lounge is on this floor? It should only take me about fifteen minutes and I'd be happy to send someone to get you."

"How long does the whole process take?" Guy asked.

"Dialysis typically takes about four hours."

"And how often does he need to have it done?"

"It needs to be done three days a week."

Looking at the clock, he stood up and sighed. "Can you give me a couple of minutes? I think I'm just going to say goodbye now and then head home for the night."

"Sure, I'll come back in a few minutes."

Guy watched the gentle rising and falling of his father's chest in time with the click, hiss, click, hiss of the respirator. Charles's eyes were closed and his brow was gently furrowed. He appeared as calm and as peaceful as he ever was. Guy put his hand on his father's shoulder, leaned down toward his ear, and said, "I know you're fighting." He stopped and took a deep breath before continuing, "But you don't have to fight any more. It's okay to let go. I'm going to go home now, but I'll be back tomorrow." He paused once more before saying quietly, "I love you, Dad."

On the way home, Guy wept. But it wasn't because he loved his father. He wept because he didn't, and he wept because he was exhausted. When he got back to his apartment, he took a beer out of the fridge and sat down on the couch with his guitar. After an ineffective and distracted few minutes of strumming he set the instrument down next to him and let out a long sigh. He was utterly and completely mentally and emotionally drained. It had been more than a week since Sophie left. And with each day that passed, he couldn't help but feel that the chances of ever finding her again were slipping away. Like he'd done so many times before, he sat staring at the wall of his little apartment, trying and failing to figure a way out.

Then the phone rang. "Hello," he said, answering it.

"Hello. This is Elaine at the Northern Illinois Medical Center. I'm trying to reach Mr. Guy Bradford."

"This is Guy."

"Mr. Bradford, I'm very sorry to inform you that your father passed away about fifteen minutes ago."

Chapter 73

"We should go," Laura had argued when she called her that morning.

"I know. I know we should," Michele agreed, "but I don't want to. I'm going to feel like an idiot."

"I get it," Laura countered, "but that's why this is perfect. It's a wake. There'll be a bunch of other people there. We go through the line, give our condolences, and it's done. You're going to have to see him again eventually. This is really a perfect, minimally awkward time to get it over with. Plus, his dad just died! You should probably be going to the wake anyway!"

Michele let out a long sigh. "You're right. But I still don't want to go."

"Too bad," Laura insisted. "You're coming with me. It goes from one to three. I'm picking you up at quarter-to-two. We'll be in and out and you'll be done. And you will have done the right thing."

"Fine."

When they pulled into the parking lot of the Ehorn-Adams Funeral Home that afternoon, both women wondered whether or not they had been mistaken about the time.

"There's nobody here," observed Laura quietly. "I swore it was one to three. Today."

"It is," groaned Michele pointing at the marquee. It read *Visitation Charles Bradford 1-3pm Sunday*. "And that's Guy's car," she added pointing to the only other car in the parking lot.

Laura's jaw dropped. "Wow," she said slowly. "How is this even a thing? I mean I've never been to a wake that didn't have a bunch of people coming and going. Have you? Have you ever seen anything like this? This can't be right."

"No. I don't know," Michele offered. "Maybe he just has a really small family?"

Laura looked at the time. "It's two o'clock now," she said, still trying to make sense of how empty it was.

"Well I don't want to go in there if we're going to be the only ones!" Michele complained. "That was the whole point. You said it would be easy!"

"Hey," Laura scolded, "that was not the whole point. The main point is to offer condolences. I thought this would be a nice way to kill two birds with one stone though. Shit."

Though the car was parked, neither woman made any kind of move to get out. Then Laura suggested, "What if we wait a bit until someone else shows up? Then we can just kind of casually go in with them. How does that sound?"

Michele made a face. "I suppose."

"If you have a better idea, I'm all ears."

"Let's leave?"

"No," Laura was emphatic. "Look, I'm not going to make you go in with me. But the fact that there is literally nobody here makes me feel like we should go in. He's sitting in there all by himself."

"You're right," she sighed. "But can we still wait for someone else to show up?"

"Fine."

When Guy checked the time and saw that it was just after two, he was grateful to have finally reached the halfway point of his father's wake. There'd been very few people and time was reluctant to pass in their absence. Bear stopped by with Mindy, but only briefly as they were on their way to work. Big John and his wife Amy were next. They stayed a bit longer and Amy asked him if he knew what his plans were. Nobody said it directly, but they all seemed to understand that his days at the Gas and Go were probably numbered. Guy really didn't know what he was going to do, and he told her that.

The only other visitors had been a former neighbor and two people who used to work for his father. When they left, Mr. Adams, the funeral director, politely lingered with him making small talk before he needed to excuse himself to answer the phone in his office. And now it had been over ten minutes since anybody else had entered the funeral home. Guy took a slow deep breath, looked around the empty room, and observed how well it reflected the time and energy his father had invested in relationships with friends and family. He was sitting in the front row of far too many chairs, all empty. There was one floral arrangement next to the casket and it had been sent by the accounting firm that his father had used. *Well,* he mused darkly, *if I have to be stuck in a room alone with my father for an hour, I guess this is the way to do it.*

"Here comes somebody," Laura said abruptly, "let's go."

Michele saw the car pulling in behind them. "Don't you want to wait and kind of go in with them? At the same time?" she asked.

"Absolutely not," she explained, "we have to be in there first. That way we see him, say our condolences, and then we can pass him off to the next person. If we go in together and those other people go talk to him first, then we might get stuck with no one to pass him off to. If you want to get in and get out, well then, come on."

The two women exited their car quickly and easily beat the other couple to the entrance. Inside, they could see Guy sitting alone with his back to them. "Oh my god," whispered Michele, "that may be the saddest thing I've ever seen."

"Yeah," replied Laura. "Wow. Now I feel bad for waiting out in the car."

As they entered the room, Guy turned and they could see his face brighten when he saw them.

"Hey," he said, standing up and walking over to greet them.

Michele and Laura hugged him in turn and they both told him they were sorry to hear about his father.

Guy thanked them for coming and then he shrugged. "You know, he had a ton of health problems for many years. It's actually pretty impressive that he made it as long as he did."

"Oh really?" they said, feigning ignorance and feeling guilty for doing so.

"Yeah," Guy nodded. "He was in and out of hospitals pretty much my whole life."

Laura could see that the other couple from the parking lot had entered the room and were approaching the casket. The timing was perfect. "That had to have been tough," she said sympathetically. Then she nodded toward the other couple so Guy could see them. "It looks like you have some more people. We're going to get going. Hang in there, Guy," she said as she gave him another hug. Michele followed suit. Guy thanked them again for coming and they started walking toward the exit.

"Perfectly timed," Laura said a bit smugly.

"Yeah," agreed Michele, "that was pretty good."

Then they walked out the front door and saw Jacque walking toward them. He stopped when he saw them and his initial expression of surprise quickly turned into a withering stare as he cocked his head slightly.

"Oh," he deadpanned. "What a surprise to see you here."

"Hi Jacque," Laura said nonchalantly, "It's too bad, isn't it? I guess he was sick for a while."

"Yes. He was in poor health for some time. You weren't aware of that?" Jacque looked Laura in the eye, debating whether or not she knew about Michele's plan or even if the rumors were true.

"No," she replied unconvincingly as she stared right back, daring him to call her out.

Uncertain, Jacque shifted his gaze to Michele and immediately had his answer. She stared at the ground uncomfortably. "You just met his dad, didn't you?" he asked her. "On New Year's Eve?"

Michele could feel her face flush. "Yeah," she nodded. When she said it, her eyes briefly met Jacque's and then she quickly looked down again.

The standoff continued for a moment with Laura determined to protect her friend and Jacque determined to do the same for his. Then Jacque sighed and said, "Well, I'm sure Guy appreciated that you stopped by."

"Yeah," Laura agreed. "We're glad we did, too." Then she gestured toward the almost empty parking lot. "Not much of a turnout."

Jacque nodded, "Yeah. Well, I should get in there, I guess. It was good to see you."

"You, too," Laura said answering for both of them as they started heading toward their car. "Take care, Jacque."

Instead of going right inside, Jacque remained on the steps watching them cross the parking lot. Then he turned to walk after them. "Hey," he called out, "hang on a second."

Michele and Laura looked up and stopped just as they were about to get into the car. "What's up?" asked Laura as she stood by the open driver's side door. Michele stood on the side opposite her and Jacque.

"Listen," he began. "I'm looking for someone to help out a few mornings a week at my bakery. It's not a lot of hours, but it's something. No experience necessary." He focused on Michele before adding, "If you know of anyone looking to make a little money, have them give me a call."

"Okay," Laura replied as Michele nodded. "Thanks. If we think of anyone, we'll send them your way."

"Thanks," Jacque said and then as Michele opened her door and got in on the far side of the vehicle, he leaned in and said quietly to Laura. "Not a lot of secrets in a town this small."

Guy was talking to an elderly couple when Jacque went inside to pay his respects. Not wanting to interrupt, he arced around them and approached the casket. He'd never met Guy's father and was curious to lay eyes on the man he'd heard so much about. Stern and gaunt, Charles was dressed in a dark blue suit with a white shirt and a tan tie and Jacque decided that he looked like a man who was used to being in charge.

"Hey," Guy said walking up behind him, "thanks for coming."

Jacque turned and gave him a hug. "Of course, my friend." Jacque looked back at Charles. "I can definitely see a resemblance."

"Yeah," Guy shrugged, "I guess that's how I'll look when I get old."

They were quiet for a moment as each of them considered both their own mortality and the journey toward it that lay ahead of them.

Guy broke the silence. "Hey, there's nobody in here right now. Keep me company while I have a smoke?"

Jacque nodded without protest and followed his friend outside. "How are you holding up?" he asked as Guy fished out a cigarette and lit it. "You good?"

"Yeah." He took a drag and exhaled slowly. "I guess. I don't know. I've known this was coming for so goddamn long...I think I thought that it would make everything easier when it finally did happen." He shrugged. "I don't know that it makes a difference."

"It's your dad. It's got to be tough."

"Yeah," he laughed a little. "And we didn't even really get along. I can't imagine what this has to be like for people who are close to their parents. Jesus Christ, it's got to be brutal."

Jacque took a deep breath thinking about his own and nodded his head in agreement. "Do you need help with anything? Like at the house?" he shrugged, "or whatever?"

"No, I don't think so. Thanks for offering though. It's just strange. To go from being so completely tied down to the total opposite. So fast. I mean, I've been basically trapped, for I don't know," he shrugged, "I guess forever. And now...it's just weird."

"Do you know what you're going to do?"

Guy shook his head. "No. I told Big John I'm not coming in this week. I know I need to meet with my father's attorney at some point and I suppose I need to get his house ready to sell, but I don't really know how any of this shit is supposed to work."

Jacque stayed and kept Guy company until the wake was over.

"Come on," Jacque suggested when it was over, "let's go get a drink."

Guy didn't argue and they headed to The Duke. On the television, the Dolphins were battling the Seahawks in the wild-card game. The Seahawks were heavy favorites and Bear was confident they'd win but Jacque swore he'd never bet against the Dolphins as long as they still had Marino for their quarterback.

Bear laughed. "This isn't 1985, Jacque! He's got no knees anymore! He can barely move."

"I don't care," Jacque insisted.

"Look at him try to drop back! He's a gimp!"

Guy smiled and watched the two of them argue and talk shit back and forth. He liked coming here to hang out on Sundays during the football season. He thought about his father and how many games he must have watched sitting alone in a corner of his enormous house and felt sad for him. Guy was grateful for the friends that he had.

Both Bear and Jacque made sure that Mindy kept him supplied with MGDs and, for the first time since Charles was admitted to the hospital ten days earlier, Guy could feel himself starting to relax. There was no longer another shoe to drop. He wasn't going to get a text and have to leave to go and fix anything or meet his father at the emergency room. It was over. By the time Marino led the Dolphins on a 99-yard, fourth quarter touchdown drive to give them the lead, Guy was exhausted.

When the game ended and the Dolphins had their upset, Jacque laughed, "See? See that?" he slapped his hand down on the top of the bar, "Fucking Marino!"

Guy started to chime in and agree but his words were interrupted by a prolonged yawn. "Jesus," he said shaking his head, "I can't keep my eyes open."

"You've got to be tired, my friend."

"Yeah," Bear agreed. "Get out of here. Go home and get some sleep, dude."

Guy stood up and stretched before putting on his coat. He thanked his friends and they both told him to be sure to call if he needed anything. Walking through the parking lot, he felt revived by the cold air and after starting his car to let it warm up, leaned against the door and lit a cigarette. The Gas and Go was across the street, and while he smoked, Guy stared at the island of bright lights on the edge of his little town in an otherwise dark night and wondered if he would ever go back to work there. He was surprised to realize that the thought of it didn't bother him. *I guess Jacque was right,* he smiled. *I guess it really was only the idea of being stuck that I hated. Or maybe I'm just too tired to care right now.*

Instead of going home, Guy drove past his apartment and continued north through town to his father's house. He'd been inside the day before to get a suit for Charles to wear for the wake, but otherwise it had been empty. His headlights illuminated the front, and when he parked he left them on for a moment and sat in his car looking at it. There was no point in avoiding it any longer. It had now become his house to maintain; it was his responsibility.

Inside, it was dark and quiet and Guy was immediately aware of how different it felt without the looming presence of his father. It was as if somebody had pulled the plug or somehow switched it off. The house no longer had power; none of the rooms were charged with the anticipation of confrontation. They were empty rooms in a lifeless structure and it was oddly calming, almost like walking through a cemetery. The dead were there, but they couldn't hurt him.

After turning the heat up to a more comfortable seventy-two degrees, Guy took the last MGD out of the fridge and meandered through the different rooms of the house as if he were on a tour. When he got to the room next to his father's, the one used by his caregivers, he sat down on the bed and thought about Sophie. *One night,* he thought, *she was here for one fucking night.* It felt like forever ago. He sighed and wondered if she really went back to Florida. Or if he would ever see her again.

Chapter 74

Sophie opened her eyes and was happy to see the ceiling high above her instead of the underside of the top bunk. Since she'd signed an actual lease, she felt comfortable taking the bunks apart and leaning the top one up against a wall in the garage. Artie said he didn't care about a lease, but she explained that it would be necessary to prove that she lived in Florida. When she met with the counselor at the Tallahassee Community College, he showed her how much cheaper tuition would be if she waited a year and became a resident of the state. Artie agreed to accept a token amount of money and even though Sophie was only renting the room and not the whole cottage, it felt good to have her own space. It felt like she was moving forward and in a positive direction. Even then, when she hung up a painting she found at a garage sale on one of the bare walls, she couldn't prevent her thoughts from returning to Guy and what might have been.

This morning though, Sophie was only thinking about getting her run in before heading over to the Buena Vista to see Dorothy. The motel wasn't very busy in January, so she'd been helping her with some maintenance projects. Dorothy paid her in cash and let her use the washer and dryer for free. Sophie was determined not to dip into her savings before she started school. After getting dressed and putting her hair up in a ponytail, she grabbed her new Tallahassee Eagles sweatshirt. She liked the way it looked on her and enjoyed thinking of herself as a college student—even if she was already in her thirties and her first class was at least a year away.

When she jogged away from the place she was comfortable referring to as her home, it was a little after seven o'clock and the sun had only just cleared the horizon. It was noticeably cooler than it was when she arrived a couple of months ago, but she could still feel the humidity and relished the smell of the ocean air. Sophie was adjusting to the novelty of putting down some roots. She didn't know if Mexico Beach or even Florida was the right place for her, but she did know that she liked the town and the people she'd met. Sophie was starting to feel like she was a part of it and that felt good. And maybe that was good enough for right now.

Jogging down the shoreline toward the long Mexico Beach Public Pier, she noticed a single car sitting under the tree near the restrooms. When she reached the pilings, she turned to run parallel with them and up toward the parking lot so that she could finish her run with the usual sprint out over the water on the long pier. As she did though, her pace involuntarily slowed. It wasn't because of the deep, soft sand; rather, it was because of the car. It was a type of car that she almost never saw. It was a big, long, older Cadillac, the kind that had two huge doors and was all front end. And it was the same washed-out yellow as the one that Charles Bradford owned. Sophie's pace slowed to a walk and although she was winded from her run, her breath became shallow. When she reached the parking lot, the car was about thirty yards to her right and on an angle so she couldn't see either the front or the back. She paused for a moment and then instead of turning to run down the pier, she began to walk across the parking lot so she could approach it from behind. She told herself that it would have Florida plates and that she was being crazy, that it was just a painful coincidence. But as she got closer, she didn't see the telltale orange silhouette of the state. Instead, it was a plain white background with dark letters and numbers. Across the top and to the left of the words "Land of Lincoln," it read Illinois.

Sophie froze, heart in her throat. She looked up and down the beach for somebody, anybody other than Guy or his father who might own the car, but she was alone. Keeping a distance, she crept forward on the passenger side trying to see in the window. The neck of a guitar was sticking up from the seat and leaning against the headrest. As she stepped closer, she realized that the car wasn't empty. The driver's seat had been reclined and there appeared to be somebody sleeping in it. He had a coat pulled over himself like a blanket and a hat covering his eyes, but Sophie could tell that it was Guy.

"He's here," she whispered to herself. *He drove his dad's car down here. Guy is in Mexico Beach.* She bit her lip and fought to keep her emotions in check. Sophie knew the only logical reason that he would be sleeping in a car on this particular beach was that he came for her. And even though there was absolutely nothing else that made any bit of sense as an explanation, she was still terrified of being wrong. She didn't want to know what it would feel like to be wrong again and be that hurt again.

Sophie walked around to the driver's side and watched as his chest slowly rose and fell with his breathing. Stepping back, she crossed her arms and looked out to the gulf and the rest of the beach. Then she took a deep breath and loudly cleared her throat.

Guy started at the sound and used the steering wheel to pull himself into a sitting position. Groggy and disoriented, the hat fell into his lap and his eyes blinked and squinted at the brightness of the morning sun. In front of him was an empty beach sloping gradually down to the gentle waters of the gulf. To his left, out his window, he saw Sophie watching him. She wasn't smiling. His heart racing, he tried to get out but the car was locked. He reached back to manually unlock it and swung the long door open to get out.

"Hey," he said nervously. "Hi. Good morning."

"What are you doing here, Guy?" she asked guardedly.

"You said in your letter that you liked to run on the beach. By a pier," he said. He rubbed sleep out of his eyes. "And I thought this was maybe the pier you wrote about." Guy looked up and down the beach. "It was the only big pier like this I could find around here last night."

A faint smile momentarily betrayed itself in her expression. "That's not what I meant. What are you doing here, in Florida?"

Guy took a deep breath. "Sophie," he confessed, "I didn't offer you that job with my father just because I was trying to find someone to work for him."

"Well," she replied, "I didn't take the job with your father because I needed a place to work either."

Guy could feel his heart beating in his chest. "I called you because I wanted to see you again."

She smiled again, sympathetically. "And I took the job because I wanted to see you again, too. But Guy," the smile went away and he could see the hurt in her expression, "you never said anything about having a girlfriend."

His head dropped and he sighed. "Michele was not my girlfriend."

Sophie looked skeptical. "She spent the night with you on New Year's Eve," She shrugged and then added, "and why would your dad tell me that she was your girlfriend?"

Guy looked up and winced before allowing a small smile. "He told you she was my girlfriend?"

Sophie nodded.

"She wasn't," he said shaking his head. "I ran into Michele just before Christmas," he began slowly, "and she asked me, or her friend asked me really, if I would be her date for New Year's Eve. She said she had a dinner reservation for four and Michele needed a date. I said yes. Mainly because she's nice and I'm friends with her friend Laura. And I didn't really have a reason to say no. But the whole thing was just kind of weird. When my father's caregiver quit, I was glad to have a reason to get out of it. I cancelled that New Year's Eve thing before I even called you about coming back to Illinois. I thought it was done. But then she just showed up at my father's house on New Year's Eve. She was hammered when she got there and it was weird and it was awkward. She brought wine with her and drank the entire bottle in like an hour. And then she passed out on the couch by the pool table. It was barely after ten o'clock." Knowing it sounded like a stupid story, Guy tried to read Sophie's face.

"Okay," she offered noncommittally as she waited to hear more.

He sighed again. "My father thought she was my girlfriend because I let him think it." Embarrassed, Guy continued, "I haven't exactly brought a lot of women around my father. So, when she showed up on New Year's Eve, and he met her, well, I could tell that he was impressed." He shrugged. "I don't think my father was ever impressed with me. And I really liked how that felt. So I let him think it. When I wrote that note about her spending the night, I wanted him to believe she was my girlfriend."

"Well, it worked," she said. Then she asked, "How is he anyway?"

He grimaced and looked out toward the water and she had her answer.

"Oh no, Guy," she said stepping forward to give him a hug, "I'm so sorry."

Raw and tired, he let her hold him and neither of them spoke. After a minute, he sniffed, took a deep breath, wiped at his eyes, and let her go. Gesturing to the car with the still-open door, he joked, "He wasn't exactly the kind of father who would have let me borrow his car to drive to Florida."

Sophie smiled, "I suppose not. So when did you get here?"

"Late last night." He looked out to the gulf again. "I've never been to the ocean before."

Her face lit up. "Really?"

Guy nodded, "Yeah."

"Come on," she said and took his hand. "Let's take a walk."

Guy pushed the big door on the Cadillac closed and walked with Sophie across the parking lot toward the entrance to the pier. The heavy air and flat horizon of the gulf glinting in the morning sun, the calling of the gulls starting their day, and the gentle way her hand held his as they strolled out over the water felt like a dream.

As they walked, Sophie told him about the town. She pointed up and down the beach in the direction of Artie's, and Toucan's, and the Buena Vista. When some pelicans floated by, just inches above the water, she excitedly pointed them out, too. Mostly, she enjoyed being able to share her world with him. When they got to the end of the pier, Sophie let go of his hand and rested her elbows on the railing as they looked out over the gulf.

"I can see why you love it here," Guy observed. "It is beautiful."

They were quiet for a while as they appreciated the solitude in the company of one another. Then Sophie asked, "So what now? Do you know what you're going to do?"

Guy turned to face her and laughed a little. "Well, I'm on a leave of absence from the Gas and Go right now."

"Oh really?" she smiled.

"Yeah," he nodded. "Since you left and my father went into the hospital…
it just seems like it's been a whirlwind. He ended up in the ICU for a week.
I was going from work straight to the hospital every night. Then, last
Thursday, his heart finally gave out on him." He paused to take a breath and
gather himself. "Anyway, the wake was on Sunday and that night I went
to his house, which I guess is my house now, and I was exhausted and I
just kind of sat there. For the first time since you left, everything stopped
moving and it all started to sink in, that it was over. He was really gone and
it was finally over. I wasn't stuck anymore. I wasn't going to have to go
back to work at the Gas and Go and always be broke anymore. I thought
about how I was free to do whatever I wanted." He paused and took a deep
breath before continuing. "And I realized that the only thing that I really
wanted to do was to find you."

Sophie turned to face him and took his hands in hers. She smiled and
said, "Here I am."

Guy let go of her hands, put his arm around her waist, and pulled her
close. "And that makes me very happy," he said as he leaned in and kissed
her.

Sophie kissed him back and then she put her arms around him and leaned
her head against his chest. She took a deep breath and let it out slowly. Her
head was turned so that she looked out over the waves with the sunlight
dancing on them. Guy held her close and she could feel his chest expanding
and contracting as he breathed with her. *This*, she thought, *this is where I
belong. This is the place for me.*

About the Author

Paul Costoff lives in McHenry County, Illinois and enjoys teaching high school social science. He has three great kids and a cool girl-friend. Every year he gets a little bit older.

Paul likes to do lots of different stuff.

"Welcome to Your Life" is his first novel.

You can connect with me on:

🌐 https://www.paulcostoff.com

📘 https://www.facebook.com/Paul.Costoff.Author